Lore

A Pirate's Charm

Chad T. Douglas

Chad T. Douglas

9. 3. 2016

LORE: A PIRATE'S CHARM
by
Chad T. Douglas
Copyright © Chad T. Douglas 2015
Cover Copyright © Andraya Avery 2015
Published by Chimera
(An Imprint of Ravenswood Publishing)

 CHIMERA

Ravenswood Publishing
6296 Philippi Church Rd.
Raeford, NC 28376
Http://www.ravenswoodpublishing.com

Printed in the U.S.A.

ISBN-13: 978-1511739979
ISBN-10: 1511739975

I
Roll the Bones

Storm and Sea danced a slow and foreboding dance, waves and clouds crashing inland with secret speed. Some of the more superstitious folk in Bridgetown that night would have said it was an ill Mama Dlo who was tossing Sea about, making her restless and wild. Some would say they heard Papa Bois blowing on his horn, but they could not say why. Was a man lurking about in the dark streets who had thoughts of killing? No, the folk would have said, but the circumstances and the sounds of the night were speaking to the island and whispering to those who knew how to interpret the signs. Most people did not pay Molly Bishop any mind as she walked swiftly past their homes, vaulted their fences, crept through their yards, slipped between the alleys and skirted past the dense and scrubby shore trees. Some people noticed but not a soul cared too much about the attractive, young foreigner, where she was headed, or why. But Mama Dlo and Papa Bois had their eyes on Molly Bishop that night—at least, some folks would say.

Sea sighed and blew her humid breath inland, cooling the tropical air, hushing the insects and forcing most of the locals indoors. In a small shack near the woods, a young woman was covering her fruits and moving them further inside her house, where the rain and rodents would not touch them. No one had come to buy anything during the day, and it had been that way for a long time. Still, the young woman remained hopeful, thinking that soon people would forget their qualms and at least come and inspect her goods, purchase some of her sewing, maybe take a fruit or two. The folk in the nearest port were afraid of her aging father—a man who did not speak to anyone but the spirits, such as Mama Dlo and Papa Bois. People called him a crazy old wizard. They accused him of making deals with the devil. The young woman knew it was not true; her father hadn't spoken or gone outside in years, let alone conjured devils or raised his hand to do any more than call a dragonfly close so that it might land on his bony fingers.

Sea breathed another long sigh and sent an especially chilly breeze flying through the door of the shack, just as Molly Bishop came along. The young woman listened to the way the breeze upset her wind chimes—reeds and pebbles on strings—and stood as her father began to stir. He said nothing but pointed out the door. The young woman interpreted it in the only way she could: *Look there, daughter, see if that stranger is tired or needs something to eat.*

The young woman hurried outside, shivering and squinting through the dark. She held out a candle, guarding it from the wind with a cupped hand. "Hello? You there, girl! You need shelter? The storm is on its way!" she called out to Molly.

Her body protesting the bitter air, Molly decided she had no other choice in the matter. Guarded and wary, she approached the woman quietly.

The young woman was surprised at how little effort it took to persuade the stranger to come anywhere near her home. A part of her was happy; maybe the people had forgotten about the old gossip and rumors and she could expect visitors more often now. At the same time, a part of her reasoned that the stranger was not from town. Perhaps she was lost and knew no better. Regardless, the young woman was determined to try to prove her hospitality and repair her father's reputation. Maybe the stranger would tell all the people in the port about her generosity, and the threats and shame would end.

She led Molly inside and scavenged through her house for a sturdy box. Bringing it to Molly and offering it as a chair, the young woman smiled and placed it on the floor for her guest. She offered Molly a fruit from her baskets and realized she had nothing to say, having long forgotten how to properly converse. Instead, she held out the fruit and smiled with every bit of sincerity she could bring to bear.

Hesitant, Molly politely took what was offered to her, trying to hide her discomfort, not sure what to make of her current situation. Without removing the bag she had looped around her neck and under her arm, she fidgeted nervously on her makeshift seat and fiddled with the fruit in her hands. "Thank you," she mumbled softly.

Another gust filled the house, blowing a stack of woven baskets over and upsetting the wind chimes. The young woman heard her father moving about. Looking into the next room, she saw he had set himself up against the wall and was beckoning to her. *Come in, come in, bring the guest, I must speak to her.*

Sensing her father's mute urgency, the young woman stood, motioning for Molly to come with her and sit in the next room. She knew the stranger had no reason to trust her, but if her father was making such a fuss, he was concerned, and the ancestors were telling him something important.

"Is something wrong?" Molly asked, startled by the woman's abrupt change in composure. Without waiting for a reply, she stood and followed the woman, full of curiosity. *This woman was kind enough to allow me into her home—perhaps there is no reason for concern,* Molly thought. She shivered, knowing she would much rather be hidden in a small keeping such as this than be wandering the streets exposed and alone.

The old man in the room waited until his daughter and Molly were seated and the breeze had settled before gathering up small items around him on the floor. He was truly a man who had seen more than his years. The skin on his arms and face clung weakly but stubbornly to the old bones beneath. The wrinkles around his eyes were as numerous and intricate as any of the patterns his young daughter could sew into a rug. His expression was distant, and yet it felt as though his thoughts filled the room, floating about like dandelion fluff. The old man scooped up a small pile of animal bones and a few pebbles, took a breath, and cast the handful to the dirt floor before him.

The young woman gasped upon hearing words come from her father's mouth for the first time in many years.

Slowly he spoke in a hoarse, heavy accent that creaked and cracked like driftwood baking in the Caribbean sun.

"There is a wolf," he said. "You chase 'im, an' he chases you, but you have never met before." The old man scooped up the items delicately, smoothing the dirt on the floor, then cast his handful to the ground again, studying them with tired eyes. "The wolf, he took something that belongs to you, and you want it back," the old man continued, squinting. He picked up the bones and pebbles and cast them again.

Molly studied the old man carefully. How did he know she was looking for anyone? She listened intently.

"Your mother will lead the wolf to you, and your sister waits for you in a garden of stone." The old man blinked slowly, looking up and listening to the breeze, then cast the bones again. "You will fall in love. The Octopus will steal it away, but a black bird will bring it back to you."

Molly frowned and turned her gaze to the floor. The old man knew nothing. Yes, she was looking for someone, but that had been a lucky guess—a fortune teller's intuition. Molly's mother, however, was long gone. The cruel and ultimately fatal tribulations of childbirth made sure they'd never meet, and as for her sister—well, Molly had no siblings. The rest, the Octopus and the black bird, those simply meant nothing at all, and nothing, especially a bird, was going to raise the dead, be it her true love or anyone else.

Again the man scooped the bones and cast them down. Molly sat quietly and let him finish. As much as she'd have liked to stop him there, she couldn't bring herself to be rude to her hosts.

"You will…" the man stopped, as his attention shifted. He reached into his shirt at the collar and fingered a small, violet gem hanging from a string about his neck. It shone in the candlelight like nothing Molly had ever seen. "Fly away, child, they are coming," the old man said, his hands shaking like twigs in a squall.

Startled and confused, Molly saw something change in the old man's eyes, putting her on edge; there was urgency in his face that she knew would not be wise to ignore. His warning was not part of her fortune. Struggling to collect her thoughts and her nerves, Molly stood on rubbery legs. Breathless, she fled from the house and was gone.

Molly sped through the soggy streets of Bridgetown, rain pelting down in torrents upon her heaving form. She grasped her cloak tightly around her shoulders and dared not look back. Though she couldn't see them, she knew her pursuers were close. Skirting around a corner and into a crowded tavern, Molly squinted as orange light spilled upon her from the windows and through the rain. The inn was rollicking. Townsfolk drank and sang and cackled happily as they waited out the heavy downpour. Molly used the atmosphere to her advantage, pulling her hood over her head, blending in with the figures around her. Drunken calls and laughs disoriented Molly. Had someone called her name? Was a greasy looking woman in the corner just glancing her way, or pointing her out to the dark man clutching her fair shoulder? Molly caught sight of black jackets and gloves. They had followed her, one coming from the back and one from the front.

"Excuse me sir, may I trouble you for some company?" Molly asked a stranger, grabbing the inebriated young man's hand, taking his drink and batting her eyelashes. He grinned dumbly at her.

"Of course." The man seized her forcefully around the waist and led her to the door, squeezing past the crowd.

8

Molly cringed, but she was close to safety. She could escape.

Her escort walked her out the door and into the pouring rain. "Now, where are we headed, lass?" The man leaned against Molly, though she wrinkled her nose in disgust. His breath was sour and burned her eyes. She quickly stepped away, leaving the drunken man to fall flat on his face with a surprised yelp. By the time Molly was nearly out of sight, the darkness had caught up with her again. Black figures spotted her from the inn doorway and were conspiring to cut her off. Molly had to escape, but her legs were barely strong enough now to carry her through the mud-laden streets. Her hair stuck to her face, and her clothes weighed her down. She followed what little light the lamp posts provided down to the docks where a ship, the *Nymphe Colère* sat achored in Deep Water Harbour. Her face brightened with hope.

"That's the last of it, Cap'n!" A sailor called out as he boarded the ship, rolling a barrel up the gangway and humming to himself.

"Good! Prepare to weigh anchor!" cried someone else.

Molly's heart raced, and her eyes widened in fear. She let herself up the gangway without a second thought. "Wait! Please!"

"And who are you?" The bearded sailor handling the barrel turned to her, blocking her path onto the ship and eyeballing her vexedly but interestedly.

"Please, sir! I need to get off the island. It's of utmost importance that I board this vessel." Molly glanced back nervously. It wouldn't be for too long …

"What's the matter?" The captain of the *Nymphe Colère*—a young, handsome man with a short, normally-golden, now-rain-soaked beard and long hair tied up under a tricorn hat—approached the pair with a handful of rope. "Mr. White, I asked for this ship to sail an hour ago, and yet here you stand in idle conversation with a strange girl!" The captain shoved the coil of rope into White's arms and scowled at him. "If you owe her money, settle it now," he growled.

"What?" Molly squeaked, "I never!"

"And pray that I am in a better mood when we review your pay tomorrow evening!" he barked at the sailor and ignored Molly, who was offended by being taken for a prostitute.

The captain hopped up onto the railing of the ship, untied another rope from its cleat and looped it around his elbow. "You, girl!" he addressed Molly for the first time, "What business do you have here? Not hoping to steal away in my stores, I'm sure." His dark blue eyes bore down on her.

Molly turned her face down, hiding her eyes behind her thick, dark hair. "N-no, sir! I am indeed in urgent need of transportation. I have little money, but I can offer my help and labor as payment. I'm afraid that's all I have. I'll do whatever you will have me do…" she trailed off, wincing and immediately scolding herself for her poor choice of words, "…B-but I must leave this island as quickly as possible! Please!"

"Sir, she can't be much trouble, can she?" White asked, looking up at the captain hopefully.

"Mr. White, I did not ask your opinion. Besides, I have all I need to sail with. That's precisely the reason I am anxious to leave port, so if you please, sir, stop wasting time. And you, girl," he turned to Molly, "get off my gangway."

"Please, sir!" Molly begged the captain, pouting and employing her charm again. Perhaps it would save her neck twice that night.

"You ..." The captain began to speak. His eyes narrowed and a gleam of curiosity flashed across them. His lips parted as he studied Molly's face. Behind his dark blue eyes, she knew, his mind was at work.

Molly glanced over her shoulder once more, peering through the softening rain for signs of movement. Her face hardened when she turned to the captain again, determination lending her some gall. She had either to make her way on deck or face the dangers that awaited her on the island. She picked the former, running up the gangway past Mr. White and onto the main deck.

"Do I...know you?" The captain mumbled to himself as he watched the girl shove White out of her way and scurry past. He made no effort to stop her. A group of men in black were approaching quickly from the dock. One of them stopped and pointed up at Molly, signaling the others to come. They headed up the ramp.

The captain snapped out of his trance and sneered, running to the top of the gangway. Booting White down the ramp, he forced the men in black backward. White's tumbling body bowled them over, toppling them into the waves beneath the docks. White stood and staggered forward as the captain pulled the gangway up and out of reach.

"Wait, Captain! Wait!" shouted White as he tried to reach the ship.

"You've squandered enough of my valuable time, Mr. White, and your place on my crew manifest has just been forfeited. So kind of you to help that poor young lady. Goodbye." The crew turned the capstan with great heaves, and as soon as the anchor was up, the *Nymphe Colère* drifted away from the dock as more of the men in coats arrived. Several of them drew pistols, firing stray shots at anyone who didn't take cover. The captain turned away from the railing and moved back to the quarterdeck. "Mr. Hobbs, full sail, please. Get us away from port, now," he commanded the helmsman.

Hair and clothes sticking to her body, Molly shivered and patted herself with some old, dry rags she had found. Mud was beginning to set in her clothes and kept her from moving much. She stared off into the distance where the island she once called a refuge slowly disappeared from view. Bridgetown and all of Barbados was gone in no time at all. The crew tended to the sails and rigging, positioning them to catch optimal gusts of stormy breeze. The captain paced about the deck, barking stern orders, relaxing only when the ship was safely hidden in the dark of the night. He gave Hobbs a few instructions before searching for his new stowaway.

"Thank you," Molly said gratefully to a man in the galley as he handed her a pewter cup filled with boiled water. The burly man grunted in response before turning to the next person waiting. Molly kept her eyes down as she headed back topside. She didn't want to make eye contact with any of the other crew members. She was only an extra on board. She was also a woman, and for that reason she preferred remaining invisible. On the main deck again, Molly's eyes searched the night for the ship's captain. The bright moon shone on the planks and made them white as spilled milk, revealing a path for her as she made her way over to a quartet of salt barrels. Taking a seat atop one of them, Molly sipped her water as she looked out to sea. What she wouldn't have given for wine, or brandy. Oh, to have been able to have a glass of brandy after the evening she'd had!

A bewitching breeze had followed the ship—that, or some magical presence had been there to begin with and Molly had only sensed it after the storm breeze had subsided. A pair of boots clip-clopped against the deck and their owner appeared before her. The captain, dressed in a clean, loose cotton shirt and baggy tanned pants, tamed by a thick leather belt with a large brass buckle, folded his arms and stood akimbo, haunting the half-shadows gathered about the foremast. Tucked into his belt, two long-barreled pistols winked at her, and at his side hung an even longer and grimmer saber, nicked and jagged like the grin of a crocodile. He examined her in a curious manner and said nothing, but acted as though he were debating with himself.

Molly looked up at him from under her eyelashes, keeping her head low. She felt awkward under his penetrating stare, unsure of what to say or do. What could she, after so rudely stowing herself onboard? She cleared her throat, trying to dispel the silence that hogged the air between her and the captain. It was a moment before she could find the simple words: "Thank you."

"Orange?" he asked, presenting her with a small fruit. His tone was friendly but didn't exactly acknowledge her thanks.

Molly's eyebrows rose in question and she stared at the orange, trying to decide whether the captain was being serious. She managed a small smile and accepted the odd token.

"Um ... thank you, once again," she said.

"Who were your friends back there?" he asked. Long strands of dark blond hair fell against his sun-bronzed face as the deck teetered.

Molly fiddled with the orange in her hand for a moment before replying. "I would tell you if I knew exactly."

"Hmm." The captain turned and walked up to the bow. "They seemed interested in you."

"That's the reason I needed to get off the island."

"If that's the case, you chose the right ship. I'm in a hurry myself."

"Where are you ..." Molly stopped herself. "Pardon me, I suppose that's not my business. I would just like to know where I could get off next."

"Oh, by all means, ask. It isn't as though I'll tell you the truth." He grinned.

Molly's smile became crooked. "Well then, my shouldn't be a nuisance."

"Not at all. For formality's sake, my name is Thomas Crowe. I sail under my own flag, go where I please and do as I please when I get there. Sympathizers, well-wishers and friends—few in number—call me an adventurer, while the narrow-minded and antagonistic set refer to me as a pirate. Can you believe that? Personally, I prefer the term 'tradesman.' Traveling and buying and selling is my business. And you, miss?"

"Oh. I am Molly Bishop." She decided to make her introduction not quite as detailed. "May I ask what you trade, Mr. Crowe?"

"It varies with my mood and current interests," he answered plainly.

"I see." She glanced down and clawed away the rind from her orange.

"You know, miss, you don't look like the type of woman one would find out at sea or this far into contested waters."

"Well, I guess I'm not, not until recently, anyway."

"I see. The one thing that surprises me most is your reaction to my name. You see, when I meet new people, I can usually expect them to turn a pistol on me ... or a sword or a knife or, well, I think you get the point. It is refreshing to have met a nice young lady who doesn't shy away. Thank you for that."

"I can't see why I would. You seem pleasant enough, for a pirate, or ..." Molly stopped short, choking on her words. "Oh! I didn't mean to say it like that!" She blushed crimson, unable to finish her sentence and wondering whether the man would shoot her or cut off her head. *Pirates...*she thought, kicking herself...*I'm out of the pan and into the fire!*

"No, it's all right." Thomas smiled.

A man approached him from the left and waited until Tom saw him before speaking. "Captain, sir, the cannons on second deck need cleaning and we're out of rags. Permission to go to the stores?"

"Yes, and check on the condition of the hull on the third deck if you're going down below." Tom handed him a ring of keys.

"Yes sir." The man turned to leave.

"Mr. Bardow?"

"Yes, sir?"

"I'll want a full inventory count by morning. We'll be docking again soon. And this time, have one of the men accompany you." Tom's look suggested that he did not completely trust the man's integrity.

"Aye, sir," said Bardow as humbly as possible. He turned to leave again, glancing quickly from the captain to the strange girl standing by him. Tom didn't like the way Bardow studied Molly, but he excused the man and turned his attention back to the young stowaway who was busily eating her orange.

"Miss … Bishop, was it? I'll have a cabin prepared for you before the crew cleans up for the night." He pointed to a door on deck. "That cabin there happens to be unoccupied at present. It's adjacent to my own. It will be yours."

"I appreciate it, Captain. Thank you again," Molly said, wondering what had just transpired between Tom and Bardow. She knew there was something, but she didn't understand it.

"While I'm on the subject of your living arrangements," Tom continued, pausing to think for a moment, "you'll need to serve some purpose. On a ship it is crucial that each and every man—or lady—contribute in some way.

That is the way of life out here," he explained. "But more than anything, I cannot afford to show any one person any favor, you understand. I can't think of anything specific for you to do, unless you're anything of a cook or seamstress. We're shorthanded in both."

"I have the basic skills, yes," Molly replied. "I would be happy to help in some way. I did offer my services, after all."

"Very well. Oh, and you'll need one of these," Tom added, taking a pistol from his belt and tossing it her way. "I can't promise you'll never need it. It's better to be armed than to allow your fellow man the benefit of doubt, wouldn't you agree?"

"That's awfully cold, but yes, I suppose that's also the 'way of life' here, as you put it, Captain. That's why I keep two pistols of my own." Molly revealed twin pistols concealed within her cloak. By their appearance, it was obvious they were crafted by a specialist, but not a gunsmith. The pearl setting in the grips was an instant giveaway.

"Ah, so I take it the lady does have some experience behind a trigger?" Tom was admittedly impressed.

"Not much experience, but I have the necessary knowledge and skill."

"Well, I can't say you look much like a pirate, but still, we may be able to make something indecent of you yet," Tom joked.

"I'm not what one could ever consider to be a pirate."

The captain released a mock gasp. "No?" His eyes widened as though in disbelief.

"What?" Molly pressed.

He paid her no mind. "Not a pirate?" He made a show of mumbling to himself and shaking his head.

"I don't believe my upbringing prepared me for the lifestyle, no," Molly repeated firmly. "That, and I rather dislike sailing," she admitted. The sea breeze wafted between the pair, the edges of Molly's muddy skirt folding in the wind. There was silence for a moment as Molly watched the clouds thin from the dark sky, her wavy dark brown hair flying about her face in the occasional gust. The captain kept his eyes on her for a long while.

"So what does that make you then?" he asked. "On this ship you'll find nothing but others like me, you know. You'll have to blend in with thieves and killers somehow."

"Are you suggesting I exchange the position of a sophisticated young lady to that of a sailor, Captain?"

"Well there are always other options, miss," he said curtly. He was standing against the railing, enjoying her with his eyes.

The captain's remark piqued Molly's interest. He seemed fond of wit and conversation. She could play those games. "And what would that be?" she asked. "I'm always open to other options if they are more reasonable than conversion to piracy. Unless of course you had something like a personal mistress in mind, in which case I'm afraid I'd have to throw myself overboard and trust my luck to the brine."

Tom hesitated before explaining his meaning. "Well it's a bit riskier than being a pirate. I don't know if you could imagine yourself in the role," he said quietly, gazing up at the moon, his eyes unreadable.

Molly wouldn't be swayed by the gravity of his tone. "I may be capable," she replied, her eyes intent on the man before her. "That's why I left my old life, anyway—to seek, among other things, a purpose. A profession or forte, if you will."

Tom tossed his head in laughter. "A forte, yes. If that's what you want to call it." He looked at Molly out of the corner of his dark eyes. They gleamed yellow, though Molly could have sworn they had been a deep blue a moment earlier.

"You think me incapable?" Molly huffed in aggravation.

"No, no, it's just your curiosity." The captain grinned, his white teeth shining at her. "That's an awfully dangerous quality to have in my *profession*." He shook his head. "I'm a little reluctant to elaborate now, is all." He paused, chancing a peek at Molly's chemise when the wind pressed it to her skin and it took on the contour of her figure. Molly was too busy wrangling her fluttering hair to notice. "Put it out of mind," he said finally and with a dismissive wave of his hand, "We'll put you ashore somewhere as soon as the wind favors it, and you can part without carrying my secrets with you."

Molly turned her back to him. "You never really told me anything to begin with," she complained. "There's a reason I shouldn't trust you, isn't there? You said yourself that people—" Molly frowned and sighed as she heard the captain's retreating footsteps. When she looked for him again, he was gone.

Molly wasn't certain why she was suddenly so interested in the stranger Thomas Crowe. Perhaps it was his unexpected friendliness, the aggravatingly obscure and evasive way he spoke ... or his deep blue eyes. Though she didn't know exactly why, Molly felt as if she could place her trust in Captain Thomas Crowe for the time being. He offered an inexplicable comfort to the young lady—someone who was lost in the world and in desperate need of finding, or being found.

Tom paused as he opened his cabin door, looking back at Molly with unease. His eyes turned to his boots as he contemplated sharing his secret. There was something about Molly Bishop that made him want her to know everything about him, but he had no reason to share anything with a stranger. Maybe he'd just been alone for too long. Smacking a palm against his head, Tom reprimanded himself for wanting to be too honest.

He let the door slam behind him without going in. A sudden chilling gust blew across the main deck and clouds billowed across the face of the moon. Tom turned and saw Molly's cloak fly from her arms, exposing her soft shoulders.

Trembling in the cold and cursing the gales, Molly folded her arms for warmth and headed to her meager cabin to shield herself from the chill. It would give her shelter even though it had not yet been prepared for her. She would get no answers from Thomas, and maybe it was best not to go asking. She took one last look at the captain's quarters before continuing on her way.

Molly awoke as first sunlight made its way through her window. She had changed from her muddy clothing, which lay in a heap on the floor. She would inquire of the captain where she could wash the soiled dress and cloak.

The sky had cleared considerably since the day before, and Molly was relieved to have awakened in one piece. She stretched as she got out of the cramped confinement of her bed, which in truth was a hammock, and walked out of her cabin. Most of the crew were already awake and working, not paying Molly much mind as she made her way down to the galley. She was sure the captain wouldn't mind if she began her duties, so she set out to find something to prepare for breakfast.

Shouts coming from deck disturbed Tom but woke him only gradually. Once fully awake, without bothering to dress completely, he left his cabin to survey the progress of the crew and to figure out how long he'd been asleep. On the main deck the sun warmed his body. The hot, solar shower was inviting. Tom stretched and shook back his hair. Looking about, he rubbed his tired face and massaged the purple bags beneath his eyes. His fingers scratched the stubble on his cheeks and chin that shone like tiny sprigs of gold foil in the light. A man in his mid-twenties, Thomas could best be described as a fine woodcarving that had been misappropriated as an axe rest—his tight and muscular arms, legs and torso were marked by old scars that gave his otherwise strong and lean body a weathered appearance for someone so young. Tanned by tropical summers and tattooed by violence, his skin told tales as if it were a red oak etching of El Dorado or Shambhala.

Bardow met him outside the door and reported that the inventory, at least food stock, was high. He fidgeted when he handed Tom the ring of keys. His fingers showed streaks of grease—the kind meant for maintaining firearms. Tom nodded and excused Bardow, who headed below deck quietly. Tom made certain the helmsman had kept a steady course, and then gave him new orders before going below to the galley. Bardow hadn't mentioned taking inventory in the armory and gun deck. Not expecting to see Molly, Tom found some plates and an old, dented pewter mug to collect a bit to eat.

The galley aides moved about with tireless speed, wiping their brows and picking up their tired feet like agitated pack animals. Tom's presence encouraged them to work faster. The captain inspected their work, stirring a pot of stew, turning over a slab of pork and giving it a jab with his finger.

"I admit I'm impressed," Tom said to Molly. "Usually I come down here expecting the worst." Tom's eyes swept over the meal with delight.

Molly grinned. "I'm glad it's satisfactory."

"So am I. I may have to consider assigning the duty of galley chef to you if you maintain this kind of productivity." Tom turned to the kitchen aides. "Let the lady's direction be your muse from now on, gentlemen. I'd like to see more meals like this."

"Thank you, Captain," Molly said gratefully, pleased with herself. Thomas's blue eyes commended her in a way that his words couldn't. She noticed this and felt giddy.

Tom plucked a potato from the chopping table and took a bite out of it. "Do let me know when everything's ready. I'd like to be the first to try that pork." He smiled again and returned to the deck to deliver strings of orders through mouthfuls of potato.

Molly watched the captain as he climbed the stairs and vanished from sight, wishing she were finished cooking so she might talk with him again.

Bardow had just left the powder store as he met Tom at the top of the main deck stairway. Nodding to the captain, he quickly headed down to the galley for his own breakfast before Tom could get a word out concerning the armory. Bardow spied Molly from the end of the corridor and walked into the room slowly.

"Oh, good day, Miss Bishop," he called, a sly demeanor about him. His dirty blond hair shaded his eyes in a way that forced them back into his head, like two ferrets spying on her from inside their burrow.

Molly nodded to him politely, remaining silent as she collected dishes.

"Cap'n usually don't see it fit to pick up strange travellers." He continued to speak to her. "But I s'pose I can see why he let you onboard last night," he added coolly, loitering near her with hungry eyes.

Molly swallowed a knot in her throat, keeping her head low. Trying to maintain an easy composure, she walked quickly past him to place the dishes into the immense wash basin.

"Quite fortunate, if you ask me. But if I was you, I wouldn't get too close to Cap'n. For your own good." Bardow collected his breakfast and left.

The dishes ceased their clatter as he left the room. Molly stared down into the basin, contemplating Bardow's words with a mix of concern and fear. Suddenly aware her hands were gripping the lip of the basin uncomfortably hard, she relaxed. What reason did she have to be cautious? The captain had been hospitable, allowing her safe passage on the ship. Yet something about Bardow's words and the captain's own unwillingness to speak with her at length was unsettling. She tried her best to brush off the feeling, and set her mind to the dishes.

By late afternoon Tom had left the crew to their work and headed to the quarterdeck to enjoy the coming sunset. That wish was thwarted by a cluster of large, dark clouds blocking his view. A storm would be upon them some time after nightfall. Displeased and disappointed, Tom walked to the railing overlooking the main deck.

"All hands, secure rigging and sails! Let's not be caught off-guard!"

The helmsman looked at the captain. "Sir, what bearing do we keep?"

"Keep this course, Mr. Hobbs. This ship's been through much worse."

"Aye, sir."

Tom walked about the deck impatiently as the crew prepared for the approaching storm. For the second day in a row, Bardow was missing from his post. Tom searched the lower decks for him. Bardow and several other men were sitting in the galley, chatting quietly amongst themselves. The captain stepped into the room and leaned across the table. The men looked up uneasily.

"Gentlemen, we are but a few hours away from some nasty weather. If it's no burden, do you think you could lend your fellows a hand?" Tom shouted, slamming a fist onto the table and spilling three full mugs. "All of you! On deck, now!" he raged. As the men jumped from their seats to leave, Tom turned to Bardow.

"Mr. Bardow, you have the first watch tonight. Do try to be punctual."

Bardow sneered as he followed the other men out.

"Mr. Bardow," Tom added, returning the scowl with one of his own, "If you leave your post for any reason tonight and you do not announce the decision, expect to go another month without pay." Bardow paused, almost speaking, but decided against it and stormed away. Tom went to the ship's bow and rested against the railing, suspicion growing in his mind like algae.

"You have yet to relieve my curiosity," Molly said quietly. She'd come upon him without letting him know. "Perhaps it's gauche, and I shouldn't pry, but what were you about to tell me the other night? Mr. Bardow told me I ought not to get too close to you, Mr. Crowe. What's that mean, exactly? I'd like to know, whether we part ways next we see a shore and never meet again."

"Henry Bardow's secret is the same as mine, and between us he's the devil you ought not to be close to," said Tom, cutting his eyes at her. "Here, this is silver." He held out his hand and dropped a small, round ball in hers. "You still have those pistols, yes?"

"Of course, in my cabin," she answered, furrowing her brow, "But why do I need this?" More conclusions cluttered her mind than she let on.

"If you ever need to turn those pistols on Henry Bardow, use that silver ball, understand?" The captain turned away again. "It's a nice evening, isn't it?" he said, just as before. "It won't last."

"Is something going to happen?" Molly tried to stop him as he turned away.

"You should go to bed early. Just try to sleep. Stay inside during the storm, and don't open the door for anyone unless it's my voice that asks you, yes?"

"What's going to happen?" Molly took the warning to heart, but demanded an explanation. "Captain!" she raised her voice as he left her.

"If all goes well, by tomorrow you'll have no need for that bullet. Trust me."

"I *will* see you in the morning, then?" she persisted. She began to realize how much, in her current predicament, she depended upon the young man. If anything happened to him, she wouldn't have a friend on the ship. She'd be adrift and in the midst of several dozen miscreants whose lecherous gazes she drew like flies to honey, and if her suspicions were correct, some of them were not human.

Going below the main deck to her little cabin, she watched Thomas pass by and head to the deck below. Molly wondered what Henry Bardow was up to, and why Thomas wouldn't say what it was. Drawing one of her pearl pistols from her cloak, she loaded the silver bullet into it and blew out the candles before going to bed.

Midnight, and no noise broke the silence that settled in the innards of the *Nymphe Colère*, although the storm quickly approached. Thomas had been absent for three hours, and Molly lay asleep. A fourth hour passed, marking the beginning of thunder and rain. Molly stirred in her sleep. Rain pattered softly against the window. There were footsteps below deck. Voices could be heard ascending the galley stairs. Another distant clap of thunder rang out. As the sky flashed dull white, Molly's eyes slowly fluttered open. Muffled shouts from the main deck could be heard, and there were barks and snarls amid the commotion. The crew did not keep hounds aboard. Molly sat up in a start and lit a candle. The ship rocked, and the candle flew from Molly's hand, tumbling across the floor and snuffing out.

Lightning flashed. Molly tripped twice as she crept up the galley stairs to the main deck. Lifting the trap door at the top of the stairs, she struggled to make sense of what was happening on deck. Many silhouettes were standing together, fists in the air. The two figures in the middle of the group were moving quickly, obscured by the heavy rainfall. Hearing voices approaching from behind, Molly gasped, fled the stairway and ran across the main deck and into Tom's cabin, shutting the door behind her. Pressing herself up against the cabin door, she peered through its small porthole window. The two large figures on the main deck squared off with one another, and the onlookers backed up a few steps. From the window Molly watched, horrified. Lightning illuminated the lupine faces of two, muscular, bipedal beasts. The bright light gleamed on their white fangs and cast jagged shadows across their drenched, furry, clawed limbs. They stood heads higher than men, but their ankles were jointed like a dog's. Their posture was hunched and burly, and their arms were humanlike, except for the large clawed hands attached. Their ears stood tall on their heads, and their lips curled up on their snouts when they growled at one another. The onlookers began to panic and dodged the animals for their lives as the beasts set upon each other, locked together in a game of death.

Lightning flashed again. One of the monsters appeared to grow larger, its yellow eyes shining through the blackness. Molly recognized those eyes. There were confused shouts from the spectators. The beasts collided, sprinting about and leaping from the rigging with supernatural agility, claws tearing at each other. An inhuman howl of agony split the air and made the hair on Molly's neck stand. The first beast pummeled the second, lifting it and hurling it across the deck. The second beast was forced toward Molly's door by a flurry of strikes to the body that followed the first beating. Molly shrieked and backed away in fear of what was happening just outside her door. The first beast seized the throat of the second and swung a fistful of razor claws. There was another howl of pain, a sound like a cleaver splitting a heft of meat, and something dark splashed against the small window, obscuring Molly's view entirely.

Trembling anxiously, Molly drew her pistol and waited, prepared to kill either of the beasts if the door did not withstand their struggle. The first beast dragged the second toward the bow of the ship. A dark stain was left on the deck by the body of the second beast, but it faded quickly under the relentless rainfall. Faceless shadows dashed about, stumbling and tripping on one another. The two beasts passed in and out of view between the silhouettes. They had changed shape and were smaller, more human. The first stood in place, looming over the one lying motionless on the deck. It raised a hand, appearing to aim an accusing finger at the second. There came a sound like thunder, followed by a blue plume of gun smoke that crept through the rain like a fog.

Molly knew that sound. Discovering the doorknob to have jammed shut, she began to kick and pound the door, desperate to know what had happened. The door gave way and she fell onto the deck, dropping her pistol. The shouts of the mob were muted by the furious rain. A foot kicked the pistol across the deck. Molly tried to run past to retrieve it but was knocked to the deck, landing painfully on her elbows.

Scrambling to maintain the sails and fasten themselves to sturdy supports, the crew tumbled and tossed about with every heave of the ship. The waves rocking the boat were monstrous. Lightning revealed large shore rocks peeking up over the ship's railing like mountainous heads. The storm had driven the *Nymphe Colère* into a deathtrap. The ship jarred violently. As Molly struggled to stand, she spotted the pistol just an arm and a half away.

The figure looming over its dead opponent looked directly at her, standing eerily still amid the rush of crewmen struggling with ropes. He was unrecognizable in the darkness, except for a pair of luminous yellow eyes.

The sound of one of the wooden masts cracking and splitting alarmed Molly. The dark, yellow-eyed figure rushed toward her as lightning broke the sky, dividing the clouds with bright, spidery bolts. The mast creaked and lurched over like a massive, felled tree. The dark figure suddenly collided with Molly. There was a tremendous crash and a loud shout, and Molly's vision blurred as an immense pain filled her head. Her consciousness faded rapidly, then blackness. A single white flower floated aimlessly in a rain puddle next to her, heedless of the catastrophe.

A flower and flotsam; beauty and disarray; order and chaos—I suppose that describes Molly Bishop and

Thomas Crowe quite well. At least, in such a way as I always knew them, though, I am no poet. My name is Geoffrey Mylus. Dr. Mylus, if you prefer. If you asked a common man, he would tell you I am a scientist, though often I don't find that to be perfectly true. My methods are that of the mystic sort—the forbidden sort, to some. The truth, whatever that word implies, is that I am a lorist, a collector of knowledge and artifacts, and an amateur magesmith.

If you, the reader, are of the common sort—I beg your pardon—I mean a mortal man or woman, you might be amazed that I knew the infamous Thomas Crowe. Pirate! Monster! Murderer! I've heard him called many things. But please, delve on before you shut these pages in repulsion, disinterest or horror! I did know Thomas Crowe, yes. I sailed with the captain and his lot for a time. A surviving witness to the life of a man of legend! Does that not make you curious?

The story that follows is not the one you have been told, but I swear on my honor that every word of it is the truth, not hearsay, not speculation, and not fanciful fairy tales. I ask you: do you dare wish to know the truth? You have not heard the story in full, say I. What you've heard until now is a lie; a fantasy, say I! I have applied logic, reason, and modern understanding to everything I've touched with my hands or seen with my two eyes, and yet ... what happened in the age I am about to describe—this age between ages—is history lost, is often reason unwound, is something of wonder. I ask myself and my readers, where do the thresholds of factual and fanciful meet, and what should we find there? What is the difference between fantasy and lore? Please, dear reader, let me tell you a story.

Geoffrey Mylus,
April 9, 1833

ﻌﻌ

Molly woke to an ensemble of pleasing sensations, among which were the warmth of a featherbed, the aroma of fresh food and the crackling and popping of a fireplace. Through three generously large windows sunshine softly filtered into the room. Her memory was cloudy, but she certainly had no memory of such a place. How had she gotten there? Rising slowly, struggling to ignore the throbbing in her head, she listened to what she realized were the sounds of an inn, and there was some kind of business occurring downstairs. Numerous voices were talking and laughing. Dishes clanked and chairs and tables groaned. Outside the window and below her room was a busy cobblestone street that wound around and between various buildings and markets.

Scrutinizing her filthy clothing with abjection, Molly pilfered through her bag for a skirt and blouse, stepped into a wardrobe nearby and, every now and then as she disrobed, poked her head out and clapped an arm across her breasts to make certain she was still alone. Too late she realized her new skirt was stretched; the blouse, oversized—items she had been given when she left the

American colonies. Thinking she would change into something more suitable, she backed out of the wardrobe.

"Good morning," Tom said cheerfully.

Molly spun around, and clutched at her blouse like a squirrel falling from a tree. Her untamed hair flew and her unrestrained breasts swung at Thomas like a pair of medieval flails beneath her blouse and she poised to strike.

"Oh...I..." Molly blushed. "I thought you were...I'm sorry." She swept her hair from her face and straightened her blouse. "Where are we? What happened?" Molly folded her arms tightly as Tom looked her over. She wished she'd found a bodice already.

A grin and equally warm blush lit Tom's face. Dressed in a baggy white shore shirt, new pants, a leather sash and a modest tricorn hat, he'd clearly been awake longer than she. He pocketed some throwing knives he'd been fiddling with in his hands, tugged at his belt and shook one leg as he adjusted his pants.

"How did you sleep, Miss Bishop?" he asked, averting his gaze while she combed the room for a bodice.

"Very well, thank you."

"See?" he said with a smile. "You had no reason to doubt me now, did you?"

"I …" Molly began to recollect the frightening events that had led to the present.

"Are you hungry?"

"Yes, very mu—" Molly's eyes flashed with worry. "You're hurt!" She started toward him, extending a hand. She placed it delicately on his shoulder where the collar of his shirt met his skin. A deep cut crossed his collarbone. It had only recently stopped bleeding and had dried black and crimson.

Moving away, Thomas discouraged any further inspection. "Come on then, let's get you some breakfast, Miss," he said with a smile.

Molly drew back her hand, embarrassed by his rejection. "I suppose I am a bit hungry…No, wait!" She exclaimed, finding a sash and tying it around her waist. Next, she plucked a dingy hand mirror from her bag and scowled at her reflection. "My hair is ghastly!" she cried. "Where is my brush?" She rummaged about through her bag in a frenzy.

"You're perfectly decent," Tom said as he took her hand firmly and hurried her out of the room and down the stairs.

"But I can't!" she protested, combing her free fingers through the salty mess on her head as Tom tugged her on. "Let me finish! I'll pluck your eyes if you see me like this a moment longer!" she wailed, fighting him like a cat about to be thrown in a river. Molly was morbid and began to dread someone mistaking her for a common prostitute. Once had been quite enough! She shrieked at the thought and tried to pull away. Tom released her in surprise.

All varieties of stranger passed them as the captain led the way through the bustling corridors of the inn. Some appeared to be of noble lineage, others were of questionable social standing, and some were beyond description. On the streets outside the dining hall were gypsies, pirates, mercenaries, businessmen, clergy, foreign tribesmen and shamans, farmers, sailors, shopkeepers and the town blacksmith. Horses and mules were tugged along by merchants, and the noises of life were abundant. The crowd was strange and unusual. Turning her head this way and that, Molly felt as though she were being led through a fairy tale. The girlish half of her was rapt, while the outward, womanly half of her kept becoming engrossed in pulling the knots from her hair.

"This place is the largest, busiest, most crowded, and best-kept secret in the Caribbean, miss."

"But there are so many people here!"

"And yet *you've* never heard of it!" he retorted with a witty grin. With a perfect Spanish accent, he continued, "La Isla del Sol is what we call it. Always sunny here, always hot."

"Just as the name implies?"

"It's the only name I've ever heard, of course, but then again, why give an official name to an unofficial secret?"

"I suppose."

Tom procured a basket of biscuits and a platter of boiled eggs, leaving a few pieces of gold in their place for the innkeeper.

"Looks wonderful," Molly said with a smile as she sat down at a table.

"Tastes like it looks." Tom sat down across from her, watching with a content smile as she ate. "Eat all you want, but after breakfast we must hurry and be off."

Molly stopped in mid-bite, becoming much more self-conscious as the captain watched her eat. "Off? Where to,

Captain?" she asked, hiding her face behind her thick brown hair.

"I've scheduled us to meet a friend of mine. He lives here on the island. Great fellow. He has a few things for me ... er, *us*, rather. How are the eggs?"

"Oh, delectable, thank you." Molly answered after carefully chewing and swallowing discreetly, putting a napkin to her lips and then resting it in her lap.

"Very good, very good," he said, standing and pushing his chair up underneath the table. "Well then, enjoy your breakfast, miss. When you finish, meet me upstairs again, yes? We're going to meet a friend of mine!"

"But I—" Molly began, covering her mouth and quickly swallowing her next bite of eggs, "I won't be going with you, I'm afraid. Now that we're ashore, I'm sure I can—"

The captain smiled and hurried away before Molly could manage to get out another word.

Left to herself, Molly took the opportunity to study the people around her, looking for crew members from the ship. She felt awkward sitting there alone, looking like a worn-out pirate's plaything. She could not recall anyone's swimming to shore or even surviving the incidents of the previous night. *What had happened again?* The thought concerned her greatly. No crew were to be found in the immediate area, but she met the gaze of a man standing by the stairs smoking a pipe. His hair was matted, destroyed by years of salty wind, as were his garments. She averted her gaze, not wanting to attract any attention to herself, as she continued with her breakfast. Thinking about all that had happened over the course of the past days, she now had many questions for the captain, the most disturbing of which concerned the terrible events on the ship. She shuddered at the thought and lost her appetite, remembering the dark stain against the cabin door window. Molly froze. *The stain! The fight!*

The stranger with the pipe approached the table and distracted her. Molly looked away, but she smelled his tobacco as he came near. The stranger leaned forward on the table with both hands. Unable to ignore the man's presence, Molly bit her lip and looked up hesitantly. The stranger had a disturbing smile on his face. By his appearance, Molly had no doubt he was a criminal of some kind. Puffing away at his pipe, the man eyed Molly's possessions. Realizing this, Molly withdrew, trying to obscure the pistols in her belt. The stranger laughed in a gruff voice.

"Where did you find those, lady?"

"It's not proper to ask a lady personal questions, especially upon first meeting her," she came back sourly, trying to hide her creeping fear.

"A lady shouldn't be carry'n' arms around. That's a good way to find trouble."

"So is intending to steal from kind ladies." Thomas reappeared, slipping up from behind and pinning the thief's left hand to the table with a straight dagger. With one hand he seized the handle, and with the other he took the tip of the blade that poked through the underside of the table, bending the dagger in two places, thus affixing the thief to the heavy piece of furniture. The criminal yelled and struggled with the dagger. People in the inn turned and glowered at the captain.

"Miss, if you're finished with your breakfast?" Tom calmly motioned for her to get going, leaving behind the wailing thief.

Molly's expression was one of shock. She was still too confounded by Thomas's feat of strength to focus on his words, but she nodded and followed the captain back upstairs.

"How was your breakfast, then?" Tom asked casually as he locked the bedroom door behind them.

"I don't want to talk about food!" Molly burst. "There was no need to rouse such commotion! I was more than ready to use my pistols if the need arose!"

"No need to waste shots on common robbers, miss."

"We have more to talk about, too!" she continued, tossing her bag aside. "I know what you are! I know why you didn't want to tell me before!"

"Are you ready to leave?" he asked, pretending to ignore her and pulling up a floorboard to fetch a hidden stash of coins.

"Don't deny it!" she said, storming over to him and giving him a push, "You're one of *them*. You're...*cursed*." Molly lowered her voice to a whisper and glanced at the bedroom door.

"I'm surprised you believe in such things at all," Tom replied, holding up his hands in surrender.

"I may be of higher birth, and come from a much more civilized place than you, Thomas Crowe, but I've been on my own for a long time now, and I've seen a few things in the New World that my governess told me were children's stories." Molly shook a finger and smirked, finally having got one over on the clever pirate.

"You've found me out. It was a pleasure meeting you, Molly Bishop. You'd best be on your way now," Tom started with an attractive smile. All his teeth lined up like square-cut pearls.

"I…" Molly backed off and brought her hand to her hip. For a moment she'd have liked to have left; she'd have liked to have reveled in her discovery, packed her bag and set off on her way as she'd planned since having gotten on the *Nymphe Colère* in Barbados, but she deliberated. Thomas had helped her once in Barbados and again just moments before. Molly really had no plan, no particular place to go—she hadn't given it much thought. She'd just been happy enough to have fled from a danger that had been after her since long before Thomas Crowe came along…

"What is it? Have you changed your mind?" Tom asked, reading her mind.

"I think I'd like to accompany you a little longer, yes. You've done right by me and the least I can do is stand by you until you…find a new ship or somewhere to be, or…"

"I'd be happy to have you," he interrupted, putting her at ease.

Glued to her hand mirror and having only begun to repair her features, Molly sighed and followed Thomas out the door when he could wait on her no longer. The captain stood politely aside for her and let her out before him, then looked over the room quickly before following her out.

The village streets were as busy as ever. Traders haunted small alleyways in the company of wealthy individuals, no doubt making dishonest bargains. Other shady and exotic characters wandered to and fro, and a woman played a fiddle on a street corner. Her hair was heavy with beads made of precious stones, she wore a great big golden hoop in her nose, and she chanted in an Eastern European dialect. Someone bumped into Molly's shoulder as he hurried to pass.

"Is it always so busy?" complained Molly, picking up the dawdling ends of the red, tiered skirt she'd thrown on back at the inn.

"Busiest little port town I ever saw, Miss." Tom brushed up against her each time they met an oncoming cart. It was obvious to Molly that his presence offended a few vendors. She saw, too, that Tom tried to avoid eye contact with anyone who watched him too closely. A few people flashed silver charms at him as he and Molly passed by—a clear warning from anyone who practiced scant tolerance toward Tom's kind.

"Who exactly is this friend of yours?" Molly asked, looking ahead curiously.

"A long-time business partner," Tom answered, crafting the sentence carefully as they came upon a shipyard. Opening a rusty old iron gate, Tom held his breath, praying his old friend was still alive. "His name's Bart Drake," Tom clarified. "Shipbuilder. The *best* shipbuilder. Well, least the best I know of."

They began their trek through the yard, stepping over planks, chains, and large lumber intended for masts and old piles of nails. The captain caught Molly's arm as she stumbled over a bit of scrap wood and simultaneously swatted away a small swarm of flies, all the while trying to keep the neck of her hand-me-down blouse from falling off her shoulders.

"Careful."

The littered path led to a large, old wooden structure sitting at least ten metres above the sea below and leaning shy of perpendicular to the ground. The building was built with its inhabitant's life's purpose in mind and was big enough to house two complete ships. The building itself looked like an ocean-going vessel. A collage of scrapped hulls comprised the structure, and a few of the exterior supports were made from unused masts.

Molly gaped at the sight. "This must be bigger than—"

"Colossal mess of a thing, I know, and yet he keeps it so tidy on the inside. Right here's the door I'm looking for." Thomas led the way to a weathered iron door on the backside of the ship house, cautiously pushing it ajar. The inside of the ship house was dusty and cavernous. Two incomplete ships were set in rigid scaffolding frames, and two more small boats beyond the first appeared to be near or at completion. Workbenches bowed under blueprints, maps, designs and other odds and ends. Large, old naval cannons sat collecting dust, and humongous anchors leaned against the support beams of the ship house.

"Bart!" Tom called. He listened carefully for a moment, waiting for an answer. "Hey, Barty, my old friend!"

Standing on her toes, Molly placed her hands on his shoulders, peering curiously around his body and across the room. The ship house appeared empty. "I thought he was expecting us?"

The captain called out again. "I've got enough for the ship this time, Bart!" Then he turned to Molly. "Oh, he's been expecting me for years, Miss."

Suddenly, from a dark corner of the house, Bart approached. A boxy, wheezy fellow, he had the gait of a tired old horse. In a raspy voice he called back. "Ah, well hello, Cap'n! Eleven years now, yes? Has it been more since—"

"Bart, I did come for the ship today, yes, and I have more than you've been asking for it!" Tom interrupted him. "I didn't expect to need it so soon, but the weather last night was not gentle when it came courting, and prised a few irreplaceables loose when it fondled the *Nymphe Colère*'s fair figure."

The old man grinned. "Cap'n, someone as unlucky as you is not always good for business and never good for his own coins." The old man came closer. His face was enveloped in a white beard, and the head above it had not much hair to speak of at all. He wore a vest more typical of a London businessman than a sailor. One hand palmed a broken compass and a pair of tweezers. The other hand was not there at all. In its place was a simple gold cap, crowning the end of the wrist. A small, wiry dog followed closely and bashfully behind him.

"Got all you could ever want right here, Barty." Thomas displayed the small pouch he'd retrieved from the floorboards at the inn. "I planned to come by and ask for another extension, but circumstances changed and well, I came across the funds I needed just a day ago," Tom explained vaguely. He brushed the maps, documents, and other items off a nearby desk and placed the pouch in the center. Bart took a seat at the desk.

"So, we got a deal, Bart? Eh?" The captain watched Bart as he opened the pouch.

Bart picked up and examined the small leather pouch, then eyed the captain curiously. "How many did you get?"

Tom, sitting in a chair opposite Bart, leaned his forearms on the table and spoke clearly. "A full set—more than you'll ever see again in your lifetime. You know what a complete set is worth, don't you, Bart?" he asked, posturing proudly.

Molly left the two men to their negotiation, examining the large, unfinished ships with awe. They were quite beautiful. Their hulls were decorated with hand-carvings, and their figureheads were nothing short of works of art—wooden maidens with flowing dresses and faces of angels. *It's a shame they'll be ruined by the same kind of hands that wrought them*, thought Molly.

"Cap'n, I wish I could believe you," Bart sighed, his tone doubtful. "But what you're good at is deceit, not bargaining."

Tom's expression revealed irritation. "Open the pouch, Bart."

Bart laughed at Tom as he became even more annoyed.

"Open it, Bart. You want to sell a ship or not?"

Lingering close enough to listen, Molly overheard bits of the conversation, ignoring the dull jargon and sifting for the important details—anything concerning Tom and Bart's history or what either of the men were doing in La Isla del Sol other than business.

Opening the pouch, Bart stopped laughing. The bony dog approached and rested at his feet. The ship house creaked, and the lanterns flickered due to a sudden gust of wind bursting through the open doorway.

"It's teeth!" Bart said in surprise as he spilled the pouch's contents out on the table.

Startled by the comment, Molly moved her gaze toward the table and squinted, seeing an arrangement of inches-long objects around the mouth of the pouch.

"It's *teeth*, Cap'n."

"What kind, Bart?" Tom persisted with a grin.

"I know very well what kind of teeth they are!" Bart snapped. "How did you get them?"

"I found them. We got a trade, Barty?"

"You don't just *find* these kinds of things, so don't be tellin' stories, Cap'n!"

"No story, I promise, Bart."

"Now I may be an old man, but I know better'n to believe you *found* these."

The dog's ears perked up. It stood and walked away timidly.

"Who was it, Cap'n? You better tell me if I should expect someone to come looking for these teeth and the man who collected 'em. I don't want no trouble, especially not with *your* kind."

Realization dawned on Molly, and she suppressed a gasp, resisting an accumulating sickness in the pit of her stomach. Rushing to the open door for air, all she could think of were the teeth on the table—the teeth she had seen in the mouth of a living, breathing, quite real werewolf only a day earlier.

"Don't matter who it was, Bart, I didn't have a choice. Fellow didn't show much favor toward following my orders. He got a good number of men thirsty for higher wages and my blood. Came for me last night, so I put him down."

Molly stood in the door frame, looking back over her shoulder. She was nauseous, imagining Henry Bardow having his teeth yanked out. It was upsetting, even if she hadn't any sympathy for him.

The captain continued in a whisper. "Bart, if he ever got his hands on her ... Do you understand what that does to a person? Do you know what would happen to me if anybody were to come looking for her?" he asked, looking intently at the teeth. "You know me, Bart, think about what's happened before. When one of my kind gets killed, the world couldn't care less. But, when someone like her gets killed by someone like Bardow or myself ... If I make a mistake I'll have every English soldier's shooting eye trained on my chest."

"Cap'n, you never said anything about *her*. If you need the ship, all you had to say ..." Bart trailed off. He looked toward the door and forced a weak smile. Molly looked away, feeling ill. Tom stood and walked to her.

"Stop," Molly commanded him, thrusting a hand forward and looking at him from the corners of her eyes.

Stopping in his tracks, Tom's expression was a guilty one.

Molly closed her eyes. Taking a deep breath, she tried to form a proper sentence. Realizing the captain had saved her in more ways than one, her words seemed to stick in her throat as quickly as they formed. On the night of the shipwreck he had risked his life for a woman he hardly knew. But those *teeth...* Did Thomas Crowe truly regret having killed Henry Bardow, or was it just a day's work for a "tradesman"?

"Miss? We have a new ship, miss," Tom was saying, unsure how to speak to her. You can come with me if you do not wish to stay here, or we can part ways. Morgan Shaw, a former first mate of mine, is collecting a new crew right now to be ready early before dawn tomorrow. Some of my other men made it ashore as well. We're not stranded here."

"I don't know a Mr. Shaw," she said, unable to think of anything else to say.

"Chestnut brown hair, hazel eyes, ugly as sin…" Tom laughed but Molly didn't, "…I'm joking, he's a handsome man. He cleans the deck."

"That sounds fine." Molly nodded, stood up straight and took a deep breath.

"I mean to sail to London," Tom continued.

"Why London?"

"Another trade. If you wish, you may stay there when I sail again. It's your choice."

"Very well. Perhaps I will see my uncle." All Molly could think was how badly she wished to see someone familiar for once. Maybe that's what she needed—to go home for a while.

Tom turned around. "Bart? Tomorrow?"

Bart nodded from his desk. "Cap'n, if you owe the lady money, I can loan it to you so you don't have to drag her all the way 'cross the Atlantic to…"

"I am not a comfort woman!" Molly barked, shooting the old man a look.

"We have a ship," Tom said enthusiastically, trying to disarm the tension. As Molly turned and walked away, he hurried out the door after her. "It won't be long now. Shouldn't be."

Molly forced a smile for the captain. He was a rogue, no doubt, but if Molly knew anything, it was that eyes didn't lie, and Thomas's weren't threatening. Those deep, dark blue eyes settled her nerves like warm bathwater.

"Should I expect your company at noon tomorrow? The ship will be ready to sail by then."

"Yes," she chimed with a strained cheer in her voice, like an out-of-tune choir bell. It didn't carry the softness of her former gratitude, but it was firm.

Content with her response, Tom grinned. "I believe we'll need to find another inn for the night. Before dark would be best. We'll take a different path into town."

The moon was already rising—no clouds yet. A safe inn lay past the northernmost docks in town. All of the usual market patrons and businesspeople were gone. Stranger individuals began to fill the streets. Bart's ship house gradually disappeared from sight, its few windows glowing yellow. Veiled shadows and anonymous figures slunk through the alleys. Their eyes watched Tom and Molly. Some were piercing white; others, a strange, golden yellow, and still others, hollow black. Molly grasped Tom by one arm and squeezed his hand. Tom kept the free hand on a pistol. Coming from a tavern close by, strange music spilled out into the streets and hung in the air. Odd, animalistic noises were uttered by shadows in the streets. Something about the darkness distorted the shape of the once-friendly shops and markets into abstract and ominous monsters. Eventually a fog settled in the town. Once past the main streets of the city, Tom changed course and took a sudden turn into the smaller alleyways.

Molly, struggling to catch her breath, managed a whisper. "Captain, how much farther?"

When Tom simply gestured for her not to speak, Molly kept quiet. The alleyways inspired claustrophobia. Growing ever darker, the path felt constrictive. Little was visible, yet pairs of eyes floated past in the dark as if not attached to a physical body at all. Something below the docks bellowed a screech. A cry of fear escaped Molly's lips, and she tucked her free arm into her chest. The captain moved faster, turning left into a new, wider street. Stopping in front of a small shack, he read a sign posted outside: "Isla del Sol Trade Post." Not a single living thing appeared to be inside. The front door was nailed shut, but the captain opened a small, hidden window next to the base of old brick steps that led to a false doorway. Molly became fearfully critical of her judgment. Why hadn't she run from him? Why hadn't she waited for the right moment and fled, she wondered. *Because he isn't going to harm you*, her heart told her. Climbing down, the captain called quietly for her to follow. For reassurance, one hand appeared from the dark to offer a safe climb down. Molly took his hand without hesitation.

The window fell shut immediately. The cellar of the trade post was abysmally black, yet the captain tugged Molly forward, feeling by memory his way through the darkness. The cellar slowly became a narrow corridor, lit by fading candles every twenty or so paces. Terrified of the blackness, Molly moved closer toward the captain, clinging to his shirt as he walked forward. A brick staircase was visible at the end of the passage. Upon seeing it, Tom hurried forward and up the staircase, throwing open the heavy wooden door at the top. It led not to a trading post; in fact, it was an inn in which Thomas Crowe and Molly Bishop found themselves upon exiting the dark underworld. The inn was comfortably illuminated by lantern light and fireplaces, its silent owner gazing curiously from across the room at his visitors. Molly, comforted by the inn, still refused to release Tom's hand. The owner beckoned to Thomas, directing him without a word toward a vacant bedroom.

Tom nodded and turned to Molly. "Now, Miss, you'll sleep comfortably once more without worry." He dressed his face in his best smile. Molly threw her arms around him. Her voice was muffled in his shoulder. How pleasant it felt to be close to him, as if being hidden in a thicket of trees, or buried in sun-warmed sand.

"Thank you," she said.

Thomas, unsure of how to react, returned her embrace, and then guided her to the carefully hidden bedroom. Molly walked into the room and Tom stood in the doorway, taking the brief opportunity to study her features as she poked about the furnishings. Her hair was thick, wavy and dark—a deep mahogany, like her eyes. Her skin was not bronzed by the sun as was his, but she was not fair, either; rather, olive. Her eyelashes, he noticed, were long, making her irises look darker than they were. She had lips that reminded him of large rose petals. She couldn't be any older than he, if not a year or two younger, he concluded as his eyes wandered down to her red skirt, which spilled over her backside like melted candle wax over a ripe, round peach.

Thomas wondered about her past. Who had her family been? Tom had had a family once. Surely she must have had one, too. She had an English name, but her appearance was not entirely English. He suspected she was, at least in part, of Spanish descent. "Goodnight Miss Bishop," he muttered bashfully, tugging his belt and stepping away with a subtle wobble.

Molly paused before climbing into bed. "Thank you for everything."

Tom nodded without a word, put out the candle in the sconce by the door and quietly shut the door behind him.

Molly awoke with a start in the early morning, disturbed by a vivid dream. Thomas was in it. His eyes had been a strong golden yellow. She'd been standing on the beach with him. The moon in the sky behind him was incredibly large, swallowing the rest of the night sky.

The sun had not yet shown itself, and Molly sat on the edge of her bed for a moment, trying her best to settle her nerves. Soft, orange light flickered and peeked into the room, outlining the door through the otherwise pitch darkness. There were occasional sounds of movement, muted somewhat by the walls. There were also loud voices. A table overturned and feet scuffled. Chains clinked together.

Standing, Molly locked her eyes on the door. She grabbed her bag and pistols and slowly made her way toward the door, listening intently. She hadn't changed out of her clothing, just so she'd be ready for anything. There was one audible voice, but she heard only broken sentences: "Under arrest ... piracy, smuggling ... the murder of Henry J. Bardow ... are to be executed ..."

Slowly she cracked the door open and peeked through. English armed guards were forcing a man outside in iron cuffs. Molly grabbed her only bag and hurried to the scene as the loud voice continued.

"Enough with you! Come along peacefully, sir!"

The innkeeper looked on, unaffected. Molly turned to him in distrust. He glanced back at her then quickly away, guiltily. Chains clanged against the door.

"Quit your struggling!"

Molly's eyes widened in realization as the guards wrestled with their captive. The door of Tom's room was open wide, and various items were strewn on the floor. One guard batted the captive over the head with a club. The blow caused him to stumble. Seizing the opportunity, the soldiers dragged the captive out and down the staircase into the basement corridor.

"What luck it'll be if they don't hang *you*, you bloody animal!" a different voice spouted from down the stairs. The sound of another clubbing punctuated the outburst.

Molly ran after the soldiers. "Stop!" she yelled in a panic.

One of the officials wheeled around abruptly as the soldiers continued on. "Take him on out, you two," he commanded them. He faced Molly, looking upon her with an authoritative posture. "What's your business, ma'am?"

"Why is that man being arrested?"

"*That* man?" The official scoffed. "Bloody *pirate*, he is. Not any ol' pirate, mind you. Damn *good* one if ya were to ask me, ma'am, and those are the worst." He shook his head. "We're sorry to wake you."

"You don't understand. I have every reason to believe that man is innocent!"

"Innocent?" he repeated in a mocking tone. "I have reason to believe you are mad, madam." He turned about and hurried downstairs into the corridor.

"Wait! You could at least hear a lady out."

The official's voice echoed from the dark, rudely. "Good *evening*, madam!"

She followed, refusing to give up. "Wait! Please just hear me out!"

No response. Molly hastened toward the dark corridor she had so recently traversed with Thomas, this time without him to guide her. Bumping against the cold stone and brick, she let her senses guide her until she was certain the basement window could not be much farther. In the blackness she stumbled, falling to the ground. Looking up, she saw the small window in clear view, opened wide. The street outside was visible. Hopeful, Molly raced toward the exit, using light from the streets above as a guide. A full moon sat in the sky like a witch's eye—wide, round and pale. The street was empty except for three English soldiers lying sprawled on the ground, weapons still in hand.

Molly looked upon the scene in terror. There were links of chain lying bent, twisted and broken on the ground, the cuffs split in two. The soldiers lay motionless. Molly walked up to the men on the ground, her pistols ready, not sure if they were still alive. Large teeth and claw marks crossed the bodies of the men. Fresh blood oozed from the wounds and pooled at the men's sides. Molly turned away, trembling and sickened by the gruesome sight. On the ground lay crushed white petals, similar to the flowers Thomas had aboard his ship. Deliberate marks had been made in the cobblestones beneath. Molly examined the marks more closely. They were scratched in, barely legible, but she deciphered them: "Ship house." Molly dashed away. Again she let her senses guide her, for she had depended totally on Thomas to lead her through the narrow streets and alleys the previous night. Shortly after dawn, breathless and weary, she caught sight of the ship house and prayed that Thomas would be inside.

The windows of the house glowed dimly. Bart's candlelit lanterns were burned down to waxy, cypress-tree stumps. Sitting atop the old roof, the moon watched Molly like a spectre through the morning mist. Large prints—like a dog's, but larger—dotted the path ahead. The sight was ominous, but Molly ventured on, following the prints. The shipyard was quiet, but a strong wind blew, breaking the hush and tumbling the sea beyond. As Molly pressed on, the prints grew smaller in size and more humanlike in shape. Reaching the old iron door of the ship house, Molly felt to make sure her pistols were on her person. Bright light seeped through the doorway and into the scrap yard from within. Cautiously, Molly stepped inside.

Brief shouts and immediate responses came from somewhere nearby, including some Molly recognized as Tom's.

"Need a few more, Bart! Mr. Shaw! Help Bart, there."

Hearing the captain's voice, Molly rushed toward the source.

"Allow me a moment, please! You there! Be of some good use, eh? Take the rest o' them boxes onboard!"

Tom's voice rang out again. "If that's the last, Bart, then we're prepared to leave. Only need one more thing."

"Which is, Cap'n?"

The captain grinned and gestured toward the ship house door where Molly stood, catching her breath.

Bart turned to look. "Ah! Good evening, miss. I've arranged you a cabin fit for the King himself."

Flustered and confused, Molly called out to Tom. "What's happening? Are you leaving now?"

"Soon!"

"But the soldiers at the inn …" She trailed off.

Tom nodded. "Precisely, you have the idea. We can't wait for morning, Miss. I'm sorry to have left you behind, but you're clever and I knew you'd receive my message. My crew is here, supplies are loaded and we're about ready to sail. Now, please do hurry and come aboard!"

Molly felt dizzy, frightened and confused. "I'm not sure." The grown woman inside Molly's head wrung her hands and told Molly she'd be a fool to conspire with an outlaw, and the girl on the inside tightened her bodice, strapped her boots and told Molly she'd be a coward not to finish what she set out to accomplish. Molly, the hapless heroine wedged between the two warring voices, decided she'd rather be a fool than a coward.

The new ship, the *Scotch Bonnet*, sat in the seawater below, ready to sail. From outside, encroaching English guardsmen could be heard. Through the windows over the ship house doors everyone could see the glow of rows and rows of torches lighting the shipyard. Dozens of soldiers surrounded the front of the house. The voice of their commanding officer thundered out.

"Captain Thomas Crowe! You are under arrest by order of His Majesty's Royal Navy and the Caribbean Royal Guard! Surrender your ship and arms, reveal yourself and come along humbly!"

Thomas looked down intently, his eyes fixed on Molly. "You can come with me, or you can go with them. You have the blessing of choice. I, less than human, do not." He pointed toward the ship house door. "You have nothing to fear. They want only me. They'll probably take you back to wherever it is you came from."

Molly looked back over her shoulder and then again at Tom. Wherever she'd come from was far away now, both geographically as well as in her heart, but the young captain did not know that. Still, she allowed herself a moment to settle into her decision. Was she really considering fleeing the authorities with a wanted man? Was she really in need of a purpose so much that she would allow Captain Thomas Crowe to be her doorway to a new life? Why did she even stop to think about whether or not she wanted to sail with a convicted criminal? Perhaps, she thought, because Tom was something more than a crook with a curse.

"Miss Bishop, please decide."

One last look into the captain's eyes made her decision for her. After all, where else had she to go? "All right," she agreed, following him to quickly board the ship.

"Hurry, now." He quickly showed her to her cabin, a special one, constructed at the last minute as an extension of his own, with not much more than a dividing wall between the two.

From outside came more angry shouts. "Surrender your ship, Crowe!" There was a pause and then the voice became even more strident. "Very well! Then be executed *here*! Fire!"

Shots rang out and Molly screamed. Bullet holes riddled the ship house as splinters of wood fell to the ground and showered the deck of the ship. The crew called out to one another. Ropes were uncoiled and sails raised. The captain barked out his orders.

"Bart!" Tom cried.

Bart ducked and hurried toward a large, iron winch, cranking the sea gates open. Numerous counterweights shifted across the ceiling and rafters of the ship house. The ship crept forward into the tossing ocean. Bullets grazed the hull. Thomas shouted triumphantly, waving fists at his attackers. Bart, followed by his old mutt Jezebel, scurried up the ramp onto the ship an instant before the gates crashed together. As the vessel escaped, the ship house began to burn, set afire by the soldiers' torches.

Cautiously Molly walked out onto the deck, and Tom placed an arm around her, throwing the other in the air. "To London!" he ordered the crew with victorious gusto.

"Crowe!" A voice bellowed.

The captain turned toward the source. Standing at the edge of the ship house, the commanding English officer huffed and puffed, and raised a blunderbuss loaded full of scrap silver. Molly gasped. Thomas quickly swiveled around again, wrapping himself around her with his back to the shooter.

Molly screamed in horror. "No!"

The gun thundered. A hail of shrapnel cut up the Scotch Bonnet's newly-painted railings and hull, and a single chunk bit Tom's left shoulder as it whizzed past his neck. He grimaced, suppressing muffled epithets as the ship sailed out of range. Molly gazed up at Tom, her eyes filling with tears. Scoffing at the soldiers, Thomas's eyes were fiery.

"Didn't touch you, did it?" he asked Molly, examining her closely. "Miss?"

Molly's trembling voice was barely audible. "I don't think so."

A relieved smile crossed his lips, but his eyes became yellow as the smile gave way to solemnity.

"You had better rest," he advised Molly, "You didn't get the full night's sleep I promised you."

"What? But, no! You're injured! You need to mend it! I can help!" she refused to go as she looked over his bullet wound. "What's happening to you?" Gingerly, she brushed her small fingers over the fresh cut in his shoulder. Where the shrapnel had struck him, the flesh sizzled and melted like a burn. It did not bleed like a bullet wound, and crusted over an ashy black and gray, not dark red or brown. Wisps of smoke rose from the grisly canyon in his skin.

"I will mend it myself. It is not as severe as you think," he argued, opening her cabin door and shielding his wound from view, "It would have been much, much worse if the shot had stuck inside."

"That's nonsense! Why won't you allow me? You could bleed to death!" Molly stared into his strange yellow eyes, confounded by his obstinence and hesitant to allow his soothing gaze to sway her again.

"Look," Thomas said, displaying his wound to her. "It has already stopped bleeding."

"But, how?" Molly saw that he was not lying. The great damage the shot had done moments earlier had already become less severe.

"Now please, rest, please." Thomas waited for her to step inside her cabin before shutting the door.

"What a terribly powerful curse it must be," she said to herself, unable to do more than obey his wishes as she pondered the curious behavior of his injury. Once Tom shut her door she went to her bed, but she couldn't rest. Thomas was so quick to push her away when she approached him. Molly became terribly self-conscious, wondering if she'd unintentionally communicated something to him she'd rather have kept secret. There was a basin and a pitcher filled with water in her new cabin. Taking a kerchief from her pocket she dipped it in the water and washed her face and arms. How long since she had used a brush? She took one out of her bag and proceeded to untangle her hair. As the knots grew fewer, so did her thoughts grow more tangled. What had she really been after when she left Bridgetown? A purpose? A second chance? When she first left home for the New

World she'd had only one goal. That mission had become another when ill fate intervened, and since then, her problems had multiplied and become much more complicated in nature. She'd known Thomas for no time at all, and she wondered whether he was any of the things she was looking for. How could she tell? Her eyes downcast, Molly quietly shed a few tears for her own sake.

The ship continued as though in a slow sleepwalk, wallowing out into open sea. Tom shut his cabin door and sat wide awake at a charting desk. After an hour or so passed and the stars shifted position, Tom stood and walked to the cabin windows, fastening them open so he could feel Sea's loving whispers against his cheeks. His cabin was just like the one on his last ship, but still unfamiliar to him. He'd given Molly the adjacent half, the only other room now situated at the rear of the main deck. Tom stood facing the stern-side windows. The view was of the ship's wake—a view of the past. Funny, how it swirled and whirled rather than make a straight line—how it changed shape in ways that were never predictable, and became indistinguishable from the ocean waves before shrinking into the dark.

A spray of salt sent a fiery pain racing down his arm, beginning from his shoulder, which had long since stopped bleeding. He flinched and wandered back to his bed, where he collapsed, exhausted, and fell asleep. His last conscious thought took his mind back to the strange and beautiful Molly Bishop, lying asleep in her cabin. He wondered if she had dreams. Not ordinary dreams, but dreams like those he had, exceedingly vivid and too real not to be true.

A few hours later Tom sat up straight in a frenzy, waking from a particularly alarming dream. He looked at his open hands, expecting them to be drenched in blood; they were clean. Then he looked all around him. Still unaware he was fully awake, he stood and swung wildly at the blackness, shouting his brother's name, afraid someone was lurking somewhere in the cabin. "Harlan!" Confused, he yelled out the name again, clenching a dagger in his right hand. Throwing open the cabin door, he found nothing but moonlight loitering on the deck of the *Scotch Bonnet*.

Werewolf's teeth are a valuable commodity, especially in certain dark corners of the Caribbean isles. The folk who live on the islands, both rich and destitute, are greatly superstitious and will pay large sums for even the smallest amounts of traditional remedies for all variety of "curses." Those who are not afraid of what they believe to be fairy tales find a different kind of value in the teeth, and prize them above ivory and even gold.

Werewolves' teeth, when ground to a powder and burned in the home, are thought to protect the residents and provide them a spiritual immunity to a condition called "lupomorphosis," as I have named it. You may be more familiar with the term "lycanthropy," which, I will explain, is not a condition but rather a practice. You see, a werewolf does not choose to transform by means of magic or ritual. A lycanthrope does. Yet, I have never met a lycanthrope, and I do not expect to.

I would suppose that Bart Drake, though well acquainted with things of myth, was not a lupomorph, and was simply, as Thomas was convinced, a normal man. A normal man, perhaps, but an extraordinary shipbuilder, from what I have heard told by a number of sources, excluding Captain Crowe. Mr. Drake, or Sir Bartholomew Drake as he was known before his dismissal from the Royal Navy and the graces of the Crown, was the source of many revolutionary ship designs that, I regret, never received proper laudation. He sailed with Thomas after the destruction of his ship house, and afterward he vanished with time. He was already far too aged when Thomas Crowe approached him after so many years, but he managed to act as quartermaster for both the London trip and a subsequent trip to Barcelona. After that his story ends abruptly.

In London, Thomas Crowe was pursuing what I shall call a matter of familial interest. He was an unusual werewolf. Often he described to me things that had happened to him that do not normally occur because of one's contracting a form of lupomorphosis. Thomas Crowe had dreams, and not in such a way that you or I would dream. He would often envision things to come. He claimed to have met certain individuals in his sleep whom he would not meet for many years after experiencing the dream. Often, he would dream of his brother, Harlan. These, he told me, were particularly unpleasant dreams.

Geoffrey Mylus,
April 10, 1833

❧

Tom sat comfortably on the very tip of the ship's bow, arms supporting and balancing himself as he surveyed the endless blue, sparkling with a crisp solar lustre before him. It was noon, the sun high overhead, and the crew was hard at work, systematically maintaining the sails and course of the ship. Bart had been below deck since early that morning, scouring over blueprints and charts and inspecting the functionality of his masterpiece vessel. The weather was balmy, although shade was still welcome. Tom waited patiently.

He turned around on his perch as Molly suddenly appeared wearing a dress of soft peach, the neckline dipping in a demure curve. She had carried it in her bag since her flight from Bridgetown. In her hand was a bottle of brandy and a rag. She had not forgotten his wound. "Good day, Captain."

Tom peered up, squinting through the sunlight, and smiled, his blue eyes striking Molly and making her shy. "Good day, miss. Thirsty for a drink, eh?" he asked with a playful smirk, pointing at the bottle.

Her eyes narrowed teasingly. "Hardly." She stepped up to him, her gaze coming to rest on his shoulder. "You had best let me look at that."

"Oh, yes of course, *look* all you want, but don't touch." He waved a finger, grinning.

Molly rolled her eyes.

"Stings, you know," he complained dramatically. "Unbearable! Unbearable!"

"Well, Captain, if you don't think you can withstand the pain ..." She shrugged and feigned to turn back around.

"I only mean to joke, Miss. Thank you." He gestured at the rag and brandy, then unlaced his cotton shirt and pulled it up and over his head, cramming his lion's-mane of blond hair through the collar and shaking it into shape again.

Molly, waiting and watching, lingered on his bare chest and arms. The muscles beneath his bronzed skin moved and flexed smoothly like thick bubbles rising on the surface of a pot of simmering caramel. Molly pinched a corner of her bottom lip between her teeth, caught herself, and looked away before Thomas freed his head from the clutches of his tangled, fluttering shirt.

"Do your worst." He said at last, shrinking back with a mock grimace.

"*Honestly*, Captain ..." Molly tore the rag into two strips, soaking one piece in the brandy. She fought a smirk, which revealed two dimples in her cheeks, and flashed her eyes at him. Without warning she pressed the rag hard to his wound and smirked. "Might sting," she teased.

His eyes widened in surprise and he squirmed. "Easy, now!"

More gently this time, she continued dabbing the wet rag, cleansing the wound. Discarding the brandy cloth and replacing it with the dry one, she tied it securely around his shoulder. The wound was much less visible than it had been the previous night, but she did not comment on it. "That should do well for now. At the least, it won't become infected."

Inspecting the bandage, Tom agreed. "This should do fine." He patted the bandage. "Thank you," he added.

"You know, I was never much good with medicine. Being out in the world on my own changed that in no time."

"What? You've treated gun wounds before?" Tom inquired.

Molly abruptly changed the subject, taking her hands away from his body. "Did you sleep well?"

"I slept as I always do," he answered vaguely. "You know, Miss, you remind me that you've yet to disclose what you were doing before you came aboard my ship, er … *ships*. I'm eager, I admit, to know much more about you." He paced lightheartedly about the deck. "You fascinate me, Molly Bishop. I must know all you have to tell me."

"I can offer nothing interesting, I fear." Molly felt the tickle of cold nerves.

"Oh, but I'm easily captivated by a story, my lady, easily," he insisted. "Go on, then."

Contemplating how to begin or what to say, Molly looked down at her hands, folded in front of her.

"Where does the lady hail from, eh?" Tom asked, stopping in front of her.

"What is my story *worth* to you, Captain?"

He quickly responded and widened his eyes emphatically. "*Everything.* What would you like in

---

83

exchange for your story?" Tom greatly enjoyed the company of his new, conversational sparring partner.

"Well that depends on how valuable *you* think my story is." She smiled, shaking her head and touching a finger to his chest.

"Well if I put a price on it I'd never be able to afford the bargain," Tom replied. "I surmise you would like to know about me as well, eh? How about a trade?"

"No tricks?"

"Tricks?"

"I trust your story will be a truthful one?"

"Tricks are for petty thieves, Miss Bishop."

"Then I have nothing to worry about, except for the cunning of a pirate."

"*Pirate* ..." Tom murmured, wagging a finger. "You know I don't care for that description."

"I meant no offense," she apologized. "Where to begin? My father was of mixed heritage, Spanish and Taíno. His mother's family were natives of Culebra and his father was from Madrid. My mother, however, was Scottish. Her ancestors were from Wigtownshire and her parents came from wealth. I'm not sure when or how my own parents met, but after they married they moved to my father's home in Spain."

Pacing about again, Tom nodded. "Yes, go on."

"My father took my mother to her familial home in London for my birth, which is where she passed away when I was but moments old. My uncle—my mother's unmarried brother, Samuel Bishop—took me in and gave me his surname, raising me as his daughter in his home outside of London. He and his maids and my governess watched after me as I grew. According to him, my father was a soldier, but I have no proof. I've neither seen nor heard from him once in my life. I really don't know much about him, only that he sailed often before I was born, and he was involved in trading before he became a soldier and disappeared. My uncle always assured me that my father loved my mother very much and that she was very happy with him. I haven't seen my uncle in years either, but I remember his being so good to me. He was a frail man with a strong spirit."

Tom tilted his head knowingly. "I've seen the like. Please, continue."

"He raised me on a small farm just outside the city, and I helped him with its upkeep. He taught me everything I know. He taught me how to read, write, cook even. His head maid, I don't recall her given name, was my governess, and like a mother to me, teaching me refinement and modest pride. I always called her Aunt. Samuel almost married her. I suppose he saw her as the closest thing to a mother I'd ever had, and probably wanted to signify it by taking her as his wife, but he was always torn between her and a woman named Charlotte, who lived nearby."

"Your aunt's teachings are evident in you."

Molly's face softened in remembrance, and she blushed at the compliment. "Perhaps I will see her again. I think I would like that. Well, the time came when I decided I needed to find myself, to seek what I was destined for. I was just a girl whose head was filled with the idea of adventure—you know, as in stories. It was silly. I thought perhaps I could find some answers about my past. My uncle gave me the twin pistols for protection before I left. They were my father's, he told me. I've always kept them close. I received a few lessons while living with a companion." She paused for a moment, hiding her discomfort. "I lived in the American colonies for a short while before an unfortunate tragedy changed my life.

Somehow I came to live in Barbados after and here I am now. I suppose I'm a wanderer, just looking for something to live for. I think Uncle Samuel was sorry to watch me go so eagerly." Molly hoped he wouldn't notice an absence of important details.

"And when you hurriedly boarded my ship in Bridgetown, is that what you sought at the time? A life? A purpose?" Tom questioned.

Molly hesitated, thinking carefully. "I suppose. That, among other reasons. I was more frightened at the time, just needing to get away from the island. Once aboard the *Nymphe Colère*, another life was all I could think about."

A thoughtful expression crossed Tom's face. "You're lucky, Miss. If not for my intuition and remarkable curiosity, you might still be somewhere in Barbados."

"I can't begin to tell you how grateful I am of that now."

"Perhaps I may be of some aid in finding for you what you seek. It would be no burden. Besides, I am familiar with the wanderlust you describe, ma'am."

"I would appreciate that."

He smiled. "Thank you for your personal account, Molly. My curiosity has been satisfied." It was the first time he'd used her first name.

Molly nodded, looking away.

"You don't find your life fascinating as I do, then? Odd ..." he commented with a grin.

"Oh, it's not ..." she began hastily, then was unable to find words to go further.

"Well, you have at least kept your end of the bargain, and on my honor I swore to keep my own, didn't I?" Tom sat casually on the railing, swinging his legs.

Molly looked up at him. "That you did." She was bursting at the seams for even a few details of Tom's past, but she held back her enthusiasm to avoid embarrassing herself again.

"Ah, well it isn't as interesting as your story I assure you, but in any case ... I was born en route to Eastern Europe, one night in a caravan camp. My father, an Englishman, was also a trader, but he fancied himself an adventurer as well. He headed a caravan that travelled through the long trade routes from Austria and into the easternmost regions of Europe, where he met my mother. My mother—Moldavian—was the daughter of a woodsman. She met my father in the late summer of a year of unknown date, when his caravan stopped to rest for a night. My mother agreed to travel with him when he promised to take her back through Austria at the end of his seasonal trek and back to his familial home in Greenwich, England, to make her his wife." Tom paused and caught his breath. "After living for several years in Greenwich, my father decided to earn more money with the caravan, and my mother wouldn't let him go alone. They brought my younger brother, Harlan, and me along. In the winter of the return trip, the caravan stopped in the mountains to camp for the night. One night it had snowed, and we were forced to huddle around a weak fire that sustained us in spite of the bitter weather. Long after the fire had gone out we remained lingering over the embers to take in the last bit of warmth. We stayed out much too long, and this unwise decision turned to disaster."

Molly frowned at the sudden turn of events in Tom's story.

"In our hunger and chills we were unknowingly being watched by others in the same desperate state as we. Later I would count twelve of them. With but one startling bark as our warning, they descended on our camp, surrounding and pouncing on the easiest—my mother and younger brother. My brother was bitten several times before escaping into a tent. My mother was dragged away instantly. I ran after Harlan, finding him shivering in the corner of the tent. His eyes were different. I called his name, but all he did was stare up at the full moon, which had pierced the snow clouds, through a tear in the tent. He started to pant. His body convulsed." Thomas shuddered as he remembered, then continued. "He grew pointed teeth. When I called out his name again, I choked. As I backed away quietly, his eyes locked on me and he pounced. I screamed and seized his shoulders, throwing him over me and collapsing the tent on both of us. Growling and barking, Harlan's snout jabbed at me through the canvas, trying to snap closed around my arms and legs. I kicked and fought, narrowly avoiding his attacks. There was a sudden brightness, and I shut my eyes in pain, for it had been so dark before. A heavy, clawed hand pinned my chest, and I felt two rows of teeth clamp down on my shoulder. I shouted in agony. There was a rush of heat, and the hiss of fire. The jaws released me, and the weight was lifted. My father dug me out of the tangled canvas, picked me off the ground and rounded up our horses, the two of us fleeing in our wagon. He tied a blindfold over my eyes and forbade me to look up at the full moon. Our attackers gave chase. They barked and growled furiously, realizing we'd escaped. However, one of them was able to keep pace with us—one I had not counted moments before, a thirteenth—which leapt at me before falling and losing the chase altogether. My father and I made it to Austria, and later we moved back to Greenwich. There he became a gunsmith. Just before I turned sixteen I left to sail to the New World on a merchant ship that carried sugar from the colonies in the Caribbean."

"But why?" Molly asked.

"One day some unexpected visitors entered our house in Greenwich. They were Black Coats—vampires—and they had heard that my father crafted ingenious magical weapons. My father refused to do business with them, and they threatened to return. When they did, my father armed himself with his five best rings and told me to flee as we heard the front door being clawed to pieces. I looked back at him only once before climbing through a high window in the back of the room he'd locked us up in. He was smiling at me, as if nothing in the world was wrong." Tom shook his head and his voice caught in his throat. He took a moment to compose himself. "For a time I sailed with merchants from many parts of the world—Europe,

91

Asia, Africa—and learned the ocean quickly. I can't remember how many ships I set foot on, or how many captains—both noble and despicable—I served. I never stayed with one ship for more than three months. I eventually earned enough wages to purchase my own ship, and I simply traveled port to port from that day on. One morning, two years ago, I docked the *Nymphe Colère* in Cape Hatteras, and while on shore I caught a glimpse of a familiar face in a local tavern. He was leaving as I entered, looking at me only out of the corner of an eye. It was Harlan."

"Harlan?" Molly interjected.

Tom looked up and nodded. "My brother, alive," he continued. "I turned to reach out and stop him but Harlan was nowhere to be found the next moment. I dismissed the thought and spent the night in the town inn, trying to convince myself that seeing him was a lie of my imagination because my brother had disappeared many years before. The next morning one of my crew was speaking excitedly over breakfast of the terrible murders that had taken place overnight in Hatteras. He exclaimed wildly, recounting the tale as it had appeared in the town papers. A group of thirty men, well-known pirates at that, were killed by what appeared to have been a pack of wolves as was deduced by the numerous bite wounds on their bodies. However, only one wolf had been spotted by a witness, who claimed it was the one and only assailant. He also said there were other men at the scene, all wearing black, and he couldn't identify them. The man in the tavern continued his story, raving about wild beasts and the absurdity of the circumstances, but only one person came to my mind. Harlan. I know you must wonder why I immediately thought of my brother, and I can say only that I knew for reasons based on my own experience that ... for ... well, it ... was strange, you see, that Harlan ... not that *he* was the culprit ... I ... It was intuition again, you see? I can't really say *why* I thought ... well, no matter. I've been interested in finding Harlan since Hatteras. No, obsessed, would be more honest. That is my story, I suppose." He maintained an uncertain expression and feigned a smile.

"You arouse my curiosity only further," said Molly. "This brother of yours ... what is it about him that makes you so uneasy? Why do you want to find him?"

"I just have dreams, is all. I see him and can't sleep. That, and he and I have a very significant connection.

There's something between us that must be resolved. Don't put too much thought into it, Miss. No need to concern yourself. It's silly, really."

Gazing at him intently, Molly pressed on. "What kind of dreams?"

"Unpleasant dreams. Dreams that are too real to be just dreams," Tom replied, looking up, squinting into the sun and spying a gull. Was there land near?

Regretting her prying, Molly looked away, suddenly uncomfortable. "I'm sorry. I didn't mean to overstep . . ."

Tom shook his head. "I'm concerned only about getting you safely back to London. It will be a month or two at the least, and until then I will keep you safe." It was unclear if Tom was speaking to her or himself at that point.

"How long do you intend to stay in London after your business is concluded?"

"The trade will dictate how long I stay. When the trade is complete I will have no business in London. I'll sail again as soon as I have it."

"What do you mean to obtain?"

"Just a personal item," he replied, avoiding the whole truth. "Well, my lady, I recall that you can cook, and very well at that. Have you had anything to eat since yesterday?"

"Now that you ask, no, I suppose I haven't."

Tom led her to the galley insistently. "We have any and all spices, meats, fruits and vegetables you could ever need, I assume, although I am no cook. I just had Morgan Shaw procure a bit of everything." He directed her to the stock. "I would accept a few more meals for the crew as payment for your passage to London."

"Of course." Molly picked through the stock.

An idea suddenly struck Tom and he clapped his hands together. "Another bargain, perhaps? Teach me your trade and I'll teach you mine, yes? We have *months* yet to occupy us."

"What would you teach me, Captain?

"The sea—maps, sails, winds, stars, trading, exploring, exotic peoples and, as my father would agree, adventure."

Molly's dark eyes glowed with excitement.

"You'll have to teach me all your culinary techniques in exchange."

"Agreed."

"Well then, I won't keep you from your duties," he finished.

"Nor I from yours." Molly gathered up some ingredients and began chopping. As Tom excused himself, Molly began to prepare the stove, collecting wood and lighting a fire. Stars and maps and exploring and travel—it all sounded so romantic.

Tom shouted for all sails to be raised. Haste was paramount if he hoped to reach London on schedule. He consulted Bart on the ship's condition. Bart led Thomas around the ship, listing inventory and various components that had been prepared for use during the early morning watch. "Forty cannons ... thirty boarding hooks ... reinforced hull ..." The captain nodded happily as Bart continued. "The helm has been adjusted for maneuverability. Basically, Cap'n, I built the ship of your dreams." His laugh was characteristically raspy.

"I think it'll be enough to surprise him when I find him."

"Where is he then, Cap'n?" Bart asked quietly.

"I don't know. Been two years since I saw him in Hatteras. I've had a map to him for a long time, only I could never read it, and that's going to change soon."

Finished with mixing the dough for loaves of honey bread, Molly wiped her brow, cleaning her hands on a spare rag. Cutting up a bit of pork and adding it to her pies, she finished her preparations. She grinned broadly at her work before a pain in her stomach erupted, gone as quickly as it came. She shook her head, figuring it was from lack of food and sleep from the previous day, in combination with a need to adapt to the behavior of the ship on the waves beneath her feet. She grabbed an apple and made her way up on deck and to her cabin. The captain noticed her and offered her a friendly nod from up on the stern, standing with Bart. She smiled politely in return before entering her cabin.

There was a long pause before Bart spoke. "Cap'n? Is she …"

Tom simply nodded, looking out beyond the bow.

"But does she know anything 'bout it?"

Tom shook his head. "No, she wasn't raised by her parents. Doubt her father said anything about it."

"Then the ring you were given was made in—"

"Spain. Yes."

"I thought you'd given up looking for the other years ago when I last saw you."

"I had, but then I went to Hatteras. That changed everything. Then I had a dream about the man who made my father's rings. Then I dreamed of Molly Bishop."

Molly sat quietly on her bed, looking out the window at the crew. Noticing Tom and Bart talking quietly amongst themselves, Molly briefly found herself wondering about their conversation. The two spoke frequently, always keeping their voices down. Molly, knowing no better, assumed it was just the nature of a captain to keep much of his business private, but she wished he'd share his plans with her, considering he'd warmed up to her enough to share his personal history. The matter of the captain's past life led only to more questions. Was he aware that the Black Coats, the devilish lot that came after him and his father, were the same rogues she'd fled from in Bridgetown? She also wondered where the captain planned to travel after London, and at some port, somewhere else across oceans, was a woman waiting for him?

"How do you know it's her?" Bart questioned.

With two fingers, Tom turned to Bart and pointed to his eyes.

Bart nodded. "Really? That's all you needed to be able to tell?"

Tom suddenly shouted out. "Helmsman, full sail! Northwest, five degrees!"

"Bermuda?" Bart asked curiously.

"Temporarily. We need to collect something."

"How many ashore?"

"Ten. The rest will stay and watch under your command."

Bart's tone lowered. "What about your condition, Cap'n?"

"The moon won't be strong in the coming weeks. I'm learning about how to control it as well."

"Aye, Cap'n."

Thomas never dropped an anchor in places any navy would have expected. Tortuga, Port Royal, San Juan— those ports were for pirates, and Thomas Crowe would have preferred having tea with a witch over being caught associating himself with criminals and other accursed... In those days, werewolves, vampires, and magesmiths—mortal or otherwise—were essentially considered members of the broad family of sinners and ne'er-do-wells that any civilized government, colonial or not, happily and indiscriminately listed as "criminal." Yes, there was an era in which such was not the case, but after significant violent events during the early 1500s involving the first truly ambitious werewolf clan—the Children of the Blood Moon—the English and soon the French, Spanish and so-forth began to look upon their resident lupomorphs with contempt, and thus began the Age of Sorrow in the long tale of the werewolves.

Vampire cults long lived closely beside mortal man as well, yet with much more social intimacy. Werewolves have long preferred agrarian life to that of an aristocratic nature, for which vampires are more commonly known. Werewolves, after all, have long claimed a close relationship to the natural. I believe werewolves came into existence many ages before the time of Rome, which is when vampires first attempted to mesh their tribes with the lands designated as Emperor Augustus's territory, mostly in Italy and the rest of the Mediterranean, extending toward Eastern Europe. Ancient vampires feared the consequences of resisting imperial rule, and willingly became Romans. After Augustus, vampire history is rather quiet, until the time of the Christian emperor Constantine. But that is not important to consider at this time.

During the time Thomas Crowe was sailing to Bermuda, a modern vampire cult—The Black Coat Society—was beginning to colonize the Caribbean, right along with the European powers. The original Black Coat Society had originated in Europe, supposedly in France, and had since been reorganized by new leaders—and influential ones at that.

Geoffrey Mylus,
April 11, 1833

❧❧

The *Scotch Bonnet* cut through the waves for several days when the captain ordered the crew to anchor in the port of Bermuda. He and ten others rowed into port with a small shore boat while the rest remained aboard the ship, waiting nervously by the cannons and occasionally peeking out through the armory bay windows for any sign of trouble. Molly awoke suddenly due to the activity outside. She stretched and rose to her feet. Reaching the main deck, she saw the shore boat bobbing up and down like a child's toy in a bath, quite a distance from the ship. Stained by the sunrise, the red waters carried it toward the nearby docks. Unable to find Thomas, Molly realized he had gone ashore. Each time the crew grew anxious or lingered by the cannons, she would pace.

The shore boat returned in the late evening—no more than a small shadow on the still sea. The ten crewmen carried large barrels and crates aboard. The captain himself was lugging a lockbox, held tightly shut by a weighty iron lock and thick chains. It clanked loudly against the deck as he shuffled toward his cabin.

"Sails up!" Bart sang.

The crew hurriedly raised the sails, towed up the anchor and manned their positions next to the cannons below deck. The captain calmly strode into his cabin with the chest, letting it drop with a loud bang to the floor. Having paced laps around the deck all day and eager to learn what Tom had been doing ashore, Molly contemplated going after him to inquire about the visit to Bermuda.

"Full speed! Sixteen degrees northeast!" Bart shouted again.

Molly suddenly remembered that a kitchen crew had not been assigned and there were pies in the oven in the galley. She headed toward the stairs to finish dinner for the crew, vowing to question Thomas later. The crew raised black sails, blending quickly into the darkness of the night sky. Reflecting brightly in the seawater, the port of Bermuda came alive with the percussion of cannon fire. Molly paused at the galley stair, startled by the raucous noise. The port shrank in the distance.

"Too late now, fellows!" Bart cackled.

Molly's brow furrowed. "Too late?"

The captain soon returned to the main deck from his cabin and looked toward the port. "Now what would they want with *me*? I guess the officials in Bermuda haven't forgotten us, eh?" He grinned at Molly. "Shame, I guess those lads just missed us." He placed his hands on his hips and called to the crew.

As Molly hurried down to the galley she heard Tom say, "All right then, pull those guns back inside! We won't need them tonight! From here, straight to London!"

Removing his tricorn hat wearily, he untied his hair, shook it out of his face and followed Molly into the galley. "Evening."

She ignored him, moving about and placing the pies carefully in the oven. Tom pretended not to notice. "Good seas tonight. I caught a bit of spray, though."

"Warm yourself by the oven if you wish." Molly was still vexed by the fact that she had no warning of his side journey—one that surely involved the Royal Navy again and likely risked his life. She didn't approve of his habits and decisions, regardless of his hospitality.

Tom waved off the offer and instead sat across the room. "I'll live."

"Very well," Molly muttered, her expression hard.

"Ooh, this one might take a while to clear up." Tom looked down at his right leg, annoyed, and began wrapping it.

Molly's eyes flashed suddenly in concern, but she kept her distance. "What happened?"

"Our friends in red came out for a hunt," he said, flinching.

"Let me help," she suggested, with scorn buried in her voice like a bear trap under a few unsuspecting leaves.

Noticing her tone, Tom stopped, holding the bandage. "No, thank you." He went back to tending the bandage, mumbling to himself. "It's *my* bloody box. Should have left us alone!" He flinched again. "Shoot a man for taking what's *his*. What a world this is!"

Molly mimicked his flinches subconsciously and sighed. "What were you doing in Bermuda?"

Tom, still mumbling, failed to hear her at first. "What I'm willing to do for a bloody *ring*, I ... what?" he asked, looking up at her.

"What were you doing in Bermuda?" Molly repeated, forgetting to hide her temper.

Tom stood quickly, despite his injured leg, his expression pale and furious. His eyes gleamed yellow.

"What was I doing in Bermuda? I'm the captain of this ship. If I go to Bermuda, I go to Bermuda. What concern of yours is it?"

Molly remained firm, eyes fixed on his. "*Temper,* Captain. It was only a question."

A twinge of dark amusement crept into Tom's expression, yellow eyes glowing. Molly failed to hide the shivers that tickled her arms. Tom's tone was soft and eerie. "Don't challenge me, Miss Bishop. This is my ship and my crew. What is it you suppose I was doing, eh?" he asked, moving toward her with a domineering gaze. Molly took a step back as he moved forward. "Perhaps I was collecting the necessary food to sustain an extra passenger aboard my ship? And getting a bloody bullet in the leg for it? Does that sound like a reasonable thing for me to have been doing all day?" His eyes, now dark blue again, communicated hurt.

Tears stung the corners of Molly's eyes. "Not at the expense of your life!"

"Call the rest down to dinner. Goodnight," he bade her, staggering up the stairs to the deck without another word. Molly remained rooted to the spot, unable to move. Tom stumbled against the stairs, swearing at the pain in his leg, and Molly flinched at the sound as he forced the door open. She leaned against the wall, breathing raggedly and trying to compose herself, hearing Thomas cough and shout out above deck. "Dinner! Anyone who cares to make it to London!"

Calmly filing one-by-one into the galley, the men helped themselves to dinner, chatting and moving the eating tables around noisily. The tables filled quickly, and latecomers began to sit on barrels, crates and counters. Bart was slowly moving down the stairs when Molly slipped potatoes and a piece of meat pie onto a plate and covered it with a cloth. Making her way toward the stairs, she met Bart.

"Oh look at you, you barbarians," she heard him scold the crew, shaking his head. "Evening, Miss," he greeted Molly.

Molly offered a pleasant hello before continuing up to the main deck, searching for the captain. The deck was void of any straggling crew, and behind her the galley livened up with loud conversation, chairs scraping the floor, plates moving about and bottles knocking against one another. The moon was not out that night. In its place the stars shimmered and crowded the heavens like sugar spilled across a black table. The only source of light peeked out faintly from Thomas's cabin. It touched the tips of her toes as she stood outside his door. Pausing, Molly knocked softly, almost hoping the captain would ignore her and wishing to make amends for being cross with him at the same time. The door opened before she touched the knob.

"Oh," he said quietly, noticing the meal she had brought with her. He smiled weakly. Molly looked down awkwardly and presented him with the plate. Tom opened the door wider and stepped aside, his tone soft. "Come in." Molly did so, keeping quiet until she felt it was safe to speak to him again. Closing the door carefully behind them, Thomas limped to fetch Molly a seat. Unable to find something comfortable, he searched for a cushion. "Here you are." Then, hobbling over to his bed, he propped his leg up onto a pillow.

"Would you prefer my absence?" asked Molly.

"No, please stay." He stood to offer the cushion again.

"So obstinate. Captain, don't mind me, really," Molly implored.

Still reaching for the cushion, Tom's blue eyes revealed a desperate determination, disheveled light strands of hair hanging in his face.

"All right. Look, I'm sitting," said Molly, taking a seat on the floor. "You would do well to do the same."

Embarrassed, Tom climbed back to the bed, his eyes fixed on the floor. "You have managed well to make decent meals out of the few scraps I've had to offer you. I'm pleased." His good humor returned as he ate the wrapped portions she brought.

Molly kept her eyes on her feet, forcing down the feeling rising in her throat. Guilt, she thought to herself, does not help seasickness.

"Made a miracle out of potatoes. *Potatoes!*" Tom went on, grimacing between bites.

"Someone should look at that. It could be a lot worse if it's not tended to," Molly reminded him quietly. His tendency to neglect his wounds concerned her greatly.

Tom shook his head, unconcerned. "It'll be gone by morning." Finishing his food, he looked up, smiling. "Never takes long to heal. I'm just unusually fit."

"If you're finished, I'll be on my way," Molly said, taking the bare plate and walking to the door.

Surprised, Tom raised a hand. "Miss?"

Molly paused at the door, not wishing to look back at him in his condition. Tom shakily walked to the door, supporting himself against the cabin wall. Molly turned to him, slightly frustrated. "You shouldn't be walking with your leg so damaged," she warned. Her eyes glanced back toward the door. Tom placed his hands against her shoulders, and Molly attempted to support him. "Captain, please," she protested softly.

"Miss, you—"

"Yes, Captain?"

Tom's eyes studied hers. "Will you sleep all right tonight?"

"Don't worry yourself with me, Captain."

His eyes darted across her features. "Truthfully now?"

"I'll sleep peacefully when you're well again."

"Goodnight. I'm sorry." He struggled to communicate something to her.

Suddenly compelled, Molly reached out to touch his cheek, smiling and staring deeply into his eyes. "You have no reason to apologize. This is the second time you've taken a bullet because of me."

"But it'll heal."

"It's still enough to make me fear for you." She stepped closer to him, her longing to be close to him overpowering any of her insecurities. Fighting her nerves, Molly steadied the hand resting on his cheek and rested her face against his neck.

For the first time, Thomas did not speak or retreat. He stood in place quietly, paralyzed by the affection of the young woman. He couldn't remember the last time he'd felt a total disregard for pain or discomfort. He also couldn't remember the last time he'd blushed or been short for words. When Molly's fingers brushed his face they reached places far below the skin. For a brief moment, Tom's body was at rest, and the dark things inside him ceased their stirring. The tendrils of sorrow and anger released his soul, like a savage monster subdued by song. For a moment, as Molly's breath met his neck, Thomas Crowe was human, and for just a moment, Molly Bishop felt immortal.

Troubled by the untrustworthy silence of the night, Molly could not will herself to sleep. Darkness made her restless. She did not fear it, but it pestered her—made her think too much—kept her from resting peacefully. She'd always had an inner darkness, an uncertainty toward herself and her life. Now that she'd met Tom and begun to witness strange things, the darkness came to her each night with new questions and fears.

Molly opened her eyes in defeat as she sat up in bed. Leaving her cabin, she made her way below deck and into the galley. The night was black with the exception of the dim glow from the embers left from the dinner fire. Sighing at the disastrous mess left in the wake of the crew, she decided she would clean everything in the early morning. And she would mention that the new crew had not been given galley assignments. As she poured herself some boiled water from a barrel in the corner, she fully realized that the reason for her sleeplessness was, most assuredly, a combination of guilt, seasickness, *and* being a pirate—at least by association. Nothing in the mix agreed with her stomach.

Grabbing her pewter cup again and preparing herself another drink of water, Molly sat back down. She'd have killed for even a crude cup of hot tea. Obviously, the men onboard preferred rum or ale, so no one would think to lay in a supply of tea. Perhaps she would ask the captain to get some at their next stop.

"Thomas Crowe." She barely breathed the name, placing the cup to her lips as she did so. She hated not being able to help the man. She felt as if she were of no great use to the ship or its crew. A shame, she thought, because the new life she'd found was indeed an exciting one.

The captain tossed about vexedly in his own bed, his leg rapidly mending itself with the aid of the wickedly efficient powers of his body's curse. Overheated, he cast his covers to the floor, staring up at the mesmeric swaying of his unlit ceiling lantern and muffling oaths of pain through gritted teeth.

Tom held his leg in a fierce grip. It didn't help the degree of pain at all. The wound slowly shrank and sealed with a hiss, the lead ball tumbling out of his torn muscles and flesh cleanly and striking the floor with an anticlimactic, metallic *tink*. Tom, in agony, let out not a shout of pain but a piercing, deep howl. Surprised, he covered his mouth with both hands, muffling the noise and mistakenly cutting a finger on elongated teeth.

Molly's head rose in surprise. She had heard something—a ghastly howl. She stood quickly, knowing immediately the source of the noise. The sound and its implications were enough to convince her to remain in the galley for another hour. It was a terrible sound, and a terrible, long hour.

Frustrated, Tom lay unmoving in his bed, which he'd nearly ruined in his thrashings. The curse evoked wonder and fear in him. He'd been captivated by his wounds for years. Watching a miniscule bead of his own blood roll down the bitten finger, he asked himself how much blood he could lose without being empty. The small lead ball on the floor rolled underneath his bed with the rhythmic rock of the ship. How much blood could he lose and not be empty?

It is a curious thing, what happens to a werewolf when wounded. It is something of magic, and it is something of science. I've had many colleagues who practice the medical arts, and it is an exciting age indeed. We know little, but the exciting thing is we recognize that we know little. What possibilities are upon us?

I've spoken with some of the forerunners of medicine, and I've recently ventured into a realm of science in which I am a novice—biochemistry. The colleagues I speak of will remain anonymous because I have earned their trust and am aware that they have yet to reveal all the discoveries they have made. But I have learned much, and I now truly comprehend the anatomy of the werewolf curse. What is most puzzling is that I know not whether the magical werewolf or the scientific one frightens me most!

For centuries, folklore has provided simple, universal conditions under which a person contracts the werewolf curse. The reader surely knows that one must be bitten and undergoes a slow maturing process before becoming a true lupomorph. The reader is also surely familiar with the various "cures" associated with alleviating the symptoms. Of course no cure provided by folklore promises life after recovery. The silver bullet is perhaps the most widely known, and most ... effective.

Would it surprise you to learn that folklore was not wrong? Ah, yes, I tell the truth! However, folklore does not give us the details behind the magic. It so happens that during maturation of the curse within the body, the afflicted begins to produce a chemical that is not natural to the known human anatomy. It is a "growth hormone," according to the knowledge I have collected, and a natural anesthetic during the morphing process. Unlike vampires, whose physical traits, such as retractable fangs, are part of the anatomy and ever-present, werewolves experience mutation of their human components each and every time they transform, due to the hormone. When a werewolf transforms again back to human shape, the excess fur is shed quickly. The overgrown teeth fall out and are replaced rapidly with new, human teeth. This hormone induces rapid and efficient blood-clotting when the body is wounded, and thus no strike of an ordinary blade or pierce of lead shot will scathe a werewolf. How sympathetic nature can be.

As the curse giveth, it taketh away. Only weeks ago, while steeped in study with a colleague, I discovered something groundbreaking and so incredibly obvious that I wonder why I did not realize it sooner! The hormone that grants the werewolf a hyper-recovery period and transformative qualities is also a compound which reacts quite violently to metals containing any amount of pure silver! I watch the substances interacting in this controlled environment of mine, and I can only wonder what agony it must be to be dissolved from the heart outward! Yet, how just it is that a gift of natural magic is balanced with a *punishment. I ask myself, is physical immortality more a curse, or more a blessing?*

Geoffrey Mylus,

April 19, 1833

❦

Two weeks passed, and Molly was eating breakfast when Tom burst into her room.

"I've brought all the charts I have," said Tom, entering with an armful of parchment. "I expect you'll learn them quickly with my help." He looked at Molly, who moved to her small desk, awaiting instruction.

Intrigued, Molly began to examine the charts. The various old papers were richly decorated and yet still marked as one would expect of an instrument of navigation. They depicted constellations, the cardinal directions, seasonal changes (and resulting astrological events), while others showed plotted courses of merchant convoys and numerous ports of the Caribbean, Mediterranean, the British Isles and the Indian and African coasts. All along the margins were notes Tom had scribbled. They were written together thickly, wrapping carefully around sketches of strange creatures and symbols. Molly looked up at him, grinning.

"Not difficult, by any means," Tom commented. "And you, being the daughter of ... Well, you shouldn't take long in proving to be an excellent navigator."

Her grin disappeared. "Wait, what did you say?"

The captain paced about the cabin and continued. "Yes they aren't the *best* maps, but nevertheless. Oh … I apologize. I haven't left you any time to eat your breakfast. Will an hour suit you?" He quickly retreated to the cabin door.

Molly interjected. "Captain!"

Tom stopped, winced and turned. "Yes?"

Molly feared jumping to the wrong conclusion but asked anyway. "My father? I know it's he whom you were going to name. Do you know him, or merely know *of* him? Answer me truthfully."

"*My* father knew *yours*. I am not sure, but I believe I may have seen him once as a much younger boy, yes." He sounded sincere.

"It's just that I know nothing about him. You didn't mention this before."

"My father held yours in very high regard, as do I. His talent was what impressed me. I'm sorry, I should have said something." He shrugged. "I just didn't want to assume anything and be wrong."

Molly's eyes widened, suddenly anxious. "My curiosity outweighs my ire, I assure you. Magic? I thought he was gone! Can you tell me anything else?"

"Admirable fellow, your father. His was a very rare trade and a very difficult one to master. Not many have the innate skill for it. However, you, as I said, would, in theory, master it in no time. You *are* his daughter."

Her smile was bittersweet.

Tom continued talking, attempting to cover his chagrin over keeping the secret from her for so long. "Haven't seen him in ages. I can only assume he is still where my father last went to visit him. I've had a favor to ask of him for a few years now. I hope he's up to aiding us along our way. Have you ever been to Barcelona?"

Molly thought for a moment. "No, not to my knowledge."

Tom's smile widened, and he nodded. "No matter, it will be a new experience, then. London isn't far off, now. I must teach you these charts quickly if we are to keep our schedule, yeah?"

"Of course." In truth, Molly was too surprised and lost in thought to think of anything but her father now. To think she was fortunate enough to run into a man who knew more than she did about her own father. She was thrilled, yet at the same time, saddened and embarrassingly suspicious of Thomas. More and more, his life seemed enveloped in a lattice web of secrets.

"I didn't even know he still lived. Do you suppose I'll ever see him?" she asked Tom.

An amused expression crossed his face. "Unless you intend to stay onboard while we stop in Spain, why shouldn't you? That is, assuming you won't be parting with me in London."

Gasping in excitement, Molly threw her arms around Tom. "This is so wonderful! I can't thank you enough! It's been so long! I'll finally get to see him!"

Tom grinned, trying to maintain balance while holding onto her and reveling in the relief of escaping a lashing-out of anger. The girl was pleasant, he thought, but pleasant in a way that one would attribute to a housecat, whose moods were as serene or volatile as the weather at sea.

"Wonder if he's still working his trade?" Tom said, half to himself.

Molly pulled back slightly. "Yes, about that..."

"Well, you've most likely never heard of such a trade. That is, my father and his fellow tradesmen always called him a ... Oh, what was the term? ... Magesmith! That's it.

My father and the like were the travelers who sought out valuable gems and minerals in Eastern Europe. Rather than selling them, they'd extract magic essences from stones and imbue them in something else. That was their business, and it was a hushed one for numerous reasons. Your father, like mine, was the kind of man who had the tools and skill to make them of use, you see." Tom could see that the term held no meaning for Molly. "A magesmith determines the magical capacity of a precious or semi-precious stone, mineral or metal," he explained, "evaluating its strength and yield and then crafting it into a tool or weapon. Take heart—gems are not just little, pretty, trivial trinkets, Molly. Beautiful, yes, but not *only* that, you see. My father owned twin rings, both fitted with identical sister gems. Each would seek out the other in case they should become separated. My father wore one, and my mother wore the other one. They were wedding gifts from your father, and when my family ..." Tom frowned and looked away, not wishing to speak of the tragedy again. "Well, my father gave me his ring before I ran away to sea, and the other was meant for Harlan, but it never made it into Harlan's hands. I think my father sold it after I left," he explained, dipping a hand into his pocket and bringing out the ring for Molly to see. "This was inside the lockbox I took from Bermuda."

As Molly took the ring, her eyes shone at the sight. Exposed to the morning light cast on the bed, the ring—gold-banded with a pale pink gem set into it—sparkled more brilliantly than an entire chest of treasures. The band was shaped to look like a natural vine, marked by grooves and ruts. Where both ends of the vine met was a detailed, oval frame that encompassed the nearly colorless gem. The gem itself was something of wonder. It was cut into the likeness of a woman's face—her eyes closed and a faint smile on her lips. A white point of light appeared to swim within the stone, moving this way and that like a little fish in a bowl. It was not perfect or new. A slight patina marred the gold here and there, and the band had suffered some nicks, as if the fingers that had worn it previously hadn't been all too kind to it. It was lovely and tried by time, traveled and worn—a befitting look for a pirate's charm.

"The stone contains a map. But I can't read it," Tom said in disappointment.

"My father made this?" Molly asked, touching each detail with her fingertips.

"His name should be engraved into the underside of the band, there."

Molly looked carefully, discovering the initials G.V.

"Gabriel Vasquez," Tom explained.

By chance the ring caught the sunlight at the perfect angle and, in a bright flash, across the entire length of her bed, projected a luminous, expansive pattern of constellations that tilted and rotated with the slightest shift of Molly's hand.

Molly gasped quietly in amazement. "These are the constellations."

"What is it?" Tom asked anxiously, leaning over her and staring into the ring.

"You're correct, it's a map. An astrolabe, or sextant, maybe?" She looked to Tom in a questioning manner. "Can't you see it?"

"I've never seen anything with it," he admitted, still searching the ring, oblivious to the bright display stretching across the bed, visible only to Molly's eyes.

"I don't understand why you don't see it. It's shining on the bed." She pointed where the stars shimmered most vividly. "As clear as day, er...night."

"Seems you have the gift of magesight," Tom said, happy for her. "Gabriel will be glad to see his daughter once more, I should think."

Molly paused suddenly, her smile fading. "*Once more*? But I have no memory of ever seeing him. Why didn't he come to find me in London or in the colonies?"

"I'm sorry, I forgot about that detail. Well, it's merely a guess, mind you, but … Do you, perhaps, have in your possession any jewelry your adopted family bestowed on you long ago? Specifically, anything crafted of pearl?" Tom asked, knowing she'd mention the pistols.

Molly thought for a moment, her brow furrowing. "Wait." She drew one of her two pistols, showing Tom the curling arrangements of small pearls embedded in the handle.

Tom examined it carefully. "Clever man. It's no surprise you can't remember him. A magesmith can do many things with his materials, such as keeping my father and mother always within sight of one another. Your father can craft a star chart without parchment, manipulate the elements, conjure spirits and even shroud himself from someone's memory." He handed the pistol back to Molly. "Very clever. He must have been quite concerned for your well-being, Miss, to have given you those items."

Molly examined the pistol again, her gaze downcast. "I don't understand."

"Pearls are mysterious little rocks. They are most affiliated with the magical manipulation of memory and time. Do not think your father wished you away. You must understand that such a tradesman, a crafter of magical artifacts, attracts undesirables. You were likely only a little girl, and he knew if he even existed in your deepest memory, you would try to find him as an adult. Hence, the pearls. They would always be with you and, therefore, always being subject to their spell, you would have no recollection of him whatsoever. Despite his concern, your father kept himself out of harm's way, and I expect he no longer risks trading such dangerous wares. I doubt he would object to helping an old friend, though, and of all things a visit from his daughter."

"I see. I'm eager to meet him. I suppose I'll be staying aboard after London."

"I'll leave you to your breakfast, Miss, and return in an hour. There is much to teach you yet." His eyes widened with emphasis. "Much!"

"Oh, wait. Here," called Molly before he left, handing him back his ring.

"Keep it on hand if you don't mind, eh?" he said. "Doesn't fit me that well." He tossed it back.

"Thank you, Captain," she replied with a soft look in her eyes.

The ring, upon being returned, shrank to fit her left index finger comfortably, still shining in its brilliant glory.

Leaving Bart temporarily in command of the crew's operations, Tom gave the helmsman a final instruction— approximately fourteen degrees northeast, nonstop to the Thames, and London harbor. As Molly waited, she attempted to angle the ring in the sunlight to make the constellations appear again. The powers it held fascinated her. If magic was not just something of tales, as Thomas made it seem, what else was possible? How much of the world had Thomas seen that she knew of only from stories, legends and a handful of her own personal escapades? A light knock on the door interrupted her thoughts.

Molly stood up quickly, eager to begin. "Come in!"

"Good news! One month till London! I intend to collect all my useful possessions there before we leave for Spain. I've changed my plans only a bit. Rest for about a week, perhaps, and find new clothes, for you *and* myself. I wouldn't keep a civilized lady far from civilization for long, that's just inconsiderate." He stopped. "Well I have only a month to teach you these charts, and for time's sake, would you agree to begin now?"

"Of course."

"Excellent." Thomas arranged the various papers and pulled another chair up to the desk. "Here you are, then."

Molly sat with him, examining the charts before her. Tom began to explain the numerous constellations of the night sky, how each will appear to the eye in different seas in different latitudes at various times of the year, and how each will always indicate a certain direction.

"You have Draco, Scorpio, Orion, Ursa Major, Ursa Minor, the Big and Little Dippers, Leo, Crux, Canis Major, Sirius ..." Not only did he elaborately describe the shape of each of the major constellations, he also took time to recount the mythological tales concerning each's origin. "Not important, but I find it fascinating," he explained, finishing the story of Orion.

Molly nodded quietly with great interest, watching the captivating spark in Tom's eyes as he related the stories. "Quite exciting, actually."

"These stars were even more symbolic to ancient cultures—Greek, Chinese, Roman. Your father must have held quite an interest in the heavens, if he crafted the star chart you claim to have seen through the ring."

Molly looked down at her hand, the stars dancing along her wrist. "So you really can't see it?"

Tom frowned. "I remember my father showing me once, but since then I haven't been able to see it again."

"I wonder why."

"So do I," admitted Tom with a sigh.

"When I was just a little girl," Molly shared, " I imagined the stars were giant, glowing diamonds and that my mother was up there with them, keeping them shining brightly." She smiled sadly, looking back down at the ring.

Thomas watched her shifting gaze, his voice quiet. "Which star is she?"

"The one star I can always look to—the North Star. I always believed my mother was in charge of keeping that one particularly bright, a task I knew she could never fail to do."

"Coincidentally, that's the star you need to be most familiar with on these seas."

"I think it may be much more than coincidence," she replied. "Those we love find ways of staying close to us after passing away. They're always watching us from places we wouldn't expect."

"Then we think alike," Tom said.

"Everything falls into place, it seems." Toying with the ring on her finger, Molly turned to Thomas. "Why didn't you tell me any of this before?"

"You answered your own question, Miss Bishop. It fell into place. All of your questions will be answered in time. Until then, trust what you have found already."

Molly looked away in distrust. "But you knew this whole time."

"There are many things I know. Some things haven't come to pass yet, others are long gone. Some I can tell you, others I cannot. It would only cause you to wonder and try to change the way things are and change the things to come," he reasoned as he reached for the maps, folding them. "Shall we continue tomorrow?"

"You know so much, and I've been looking my whole life for answers," she continued, not willing to let him slip away yet. "I feel as though my entire life and past have been withheld from me. I thank you for telling me everything you have already, I truly do. It makes me wonder what else you're keeping to yourself. For these past months you're the only source of a past or future I've had to look to." Molly turned the ring around and around.

"I'll always tell you what you need to know, and the truths, not the myths. But Molly, a life in the past is a life spent as a ghost. I don't mind carrying you along with me into tomorrow. I can't promise all the answers you seek, but I have a knack for finding out." Tom smirked. "Maybe if destiny favors me, I'll be given the duty of delivering you to your place of purpose. I admit it would please me greater than anything else. If what you say is true—that you believe things fall into place—I hope you'll stay on my ship. It would be good luck."

"Good luck?"

"Well, yes. Believe it or not, I've been injured less frequently since you've been aboard. I can always look forward to meals, too."

Molly laughed.

To my knowledge, England, the British Isles and Scandinavia have been home to modern werewolves for longer than any other region of the world. I believe their ancestors migrated south from the Siberian Arctic and into Europe. I once thought that their country of origin lay somewhere in Eastern Europe. Dissimilarly, vampires first came to greater Europe by moving north and east from the Mediterranean and west from the oldest Christian holy lands. The oldest clans of werewolves exist in the northernmost expanses of the British Isles today, but a multitude of werewolves have always called London home. Perhaps, being the large city it is and the heart of an empire, it attracted werewolves just as it has drawn cultures from the most distant locations known to modern maps. Like a small spore, the clans were swept up by the buzzing drones of English exploration and brought back to the hive, to speak, to London—by force or fate.

Traditionally, werewolf clans and vampire cults have been rivals. Both depended upon mutual relationships with mortal man for survival ever since coming into existence thousands of years ago. Their conflicts are almost always incited by territorial offenses, which always become more violent when the world experiences broad-

ranging hardship. Simple differences sometimes complicate when a particular clan or cult will promote "superior species" attitudes among werewolf or vampire youths. This kind of irresponsible teaching has led only to the formation of radical clans and cults over time. As mortal man's empires grow, clan and cult territories shrink, and tensions rise.

In recent years the clans of London have become sparse, far outnumbered by vampire cults. The clans were not as easily assimilated to urban, civilized society, and many simply chose to live in the north, where their rurally adept traditions and methods were best suited. Before long, the cult population flourished, and the clan population shrank to a handful of individuals. English citizens were not disturbed, for the vampires were a quiet addition to London's culture, and, unlike their monstrous ancestors, politely abstained from slaughtering and feeding upon the citizenry. They were out of sight and far from mind. They attracted livestock merchants to the city in droves. The demand for a reliable and consistent supply of warm blood was so great, it became easier to sell to vampires than to sell to meat markets.

The reader may take issue with this telling of history, and argue, "But vampires feed on the blood of man!" There is undeniable truth in this, and there is some truth yet to be explained. Ancient tribes of vampires fed on human blood exclusively, yes. But that was in a time when subsistence farming kept man from growing thin and impoverishing his body and his pockets. When man was still an animal, in the sense that he was strong and wild, his blood was rich and full of vitality. Time, however, changed man and his body. These times are times of poverty and thinning, and thus man has become thin, his blood no longer savory and as nutritious as it had been in his ancestors. He is still healthy, yes, but his body is far displaced from the original design. He has a city body. A business body. His blood is ink and oil, no longer pure virility and vitality, ferocity and fire.

Still, as I have suggested, not all modern vampire societies have taken this course, and the more ancient cults, who hold themselves in higher regard than mortal kind, frequently and viciously prey upon small villages all across Europe. Some even quietly settle into larger cities and employ cleverly disguised hunting grounds. With that in mind, I discourage the reader from venturing into any brothels in Old Orleans or any bordellos in Venice...

I refer to vampires as experiencing a rather mysterious state of existence—a condition referred to as "anecrosis." The body is self-sufficient and without age, but the blood beneath is ephemeral and requires replacement. Blood is not taken for sustenance in such a way that you or I would eat bread. Rather, the vampire must obtain new blood using a specially adapted, hollow and pointed set of teeth that lie hidden over top of their human teeth, in order to maintain the body. The teeth are similar to the retractable fangs of a poisonous viper, in that they appear only when forced to extend by muscle contraction.

The vampire's body differs from the werewolf's in other ways as well. The vampire's skin is exceedingly elastic upon transformation. They can will their skin to stretch and form working wings in order to take flight. People say the wings look like rigid black curtains when spread open. Their skin is also adapted to blend in against very dark colors, making them formidable creatures of the night. Like werewolves, the vampire "curse" is an infectious entity. It is spread to a human body through a bite, causing the infected to develop vampire qualities and abilities if they are not killed by the rapid infection, as nearly two of every three are.

Vampires, like the werewolves, experience a physical immortality, and exactly like the werewolves, they experience it at a cost. It is my belief that their appetite is far greater than that of humans because their bodies so frequently demand the resource with which to maintain the body, and that resource—blood—is their one and only resource. Their bodies are volatile in the direct light of the day when they are transformed. Perhaps the supernatural upkeep of the inner body sacrifices the invulnerability of the bare external flesh. This is a matter of great debate among my colleagues and me.

Vampires are often described as "the damned" in traditional folklore and religious texts. Damned because they, in truth, own no blood of their own? Because they cannot claim permanent ownership of life in its precious flowing form? Or damned because, like the werewolf, their greatest strength is an open aperture into their subtopic mortality? One of my colleagues once asked me, "Are these that we call monsters not eerie reflections of our own selves?"

Geoffrey Mylus,

April 20, 1833

∾৩৽

Without any trouble, Tom's ship sailed north through the Atlantic and into the British Isles, where it cruised into the Thames. The crew made good time, and the ship had landed on a cold, snowy night in December. Tom arrived at Molly's cabin as the ship slowed to a stop in port. Molly was diligently reviewing the charts she had learned over the past month onboard. Working sleepily by lantern light, she yawned and wrapped her shawl tighter around her shoulders as she looked over the charts and wrote some final notes.

"A long month, but we've arrived," announced Tom cheerfully as he entered her cabin. "You'll enjoy London, even if it's a bit frozen over. No small, uncomfortable inns here. Only the finest. I've arranged us accommodations in a more suitable residence. All you'll need are the clothes you've brought and anything you'd like to hold your interest during our stay."

Molly smiled, familiar with the comforts of London. "It'll be strange being close to home again. It's been so long, though. I'm sure much has changed in England since I left."

"Shall we?" Tom opened the door for her. "I'll fetch a lantern," he said, taking one off the desk as she grabbed her bag.

"One moment," she said, taking a caraco from her bag and putting it on over her bodice. The short jacket would give her a bit more warmth. She exchanged her slippers for a small pair of boots Tom had found for her weeks earlier. Trying not to waste time, she tugged her skirt low enough to conceal the awkward masculine boots beneath.

The bitter cold air nipped at Molly's cheeks as the two made their way down the gangway. The snow flew hard in the streets, and deep drifts collected around every corner lamppost. Tom, dressed in a heavy grey coat and wool-lined cap, led Molly by one hand through the streets of London. Buildings were awake with bright light, and carriages slogged silently through the white powdered streets. The city was pleasant yet bitterly chilled by the winter weather. Tall buildings lined every street. The city was far more grandiose than anything Molly had become accustomed to in the Caribbean. Here it felt like civilization was being perfected and maintained like a fine working clock. It was certainly one of man's proudest dwelling places, by sheer size and character alone.

Tom stopped on the stoop of a large house in one of the wealthier districts of the city. It was a large brick home, well-kept, showing no sign of life or residence.

Molly gazed up at the house curiously. "Thomas? There's no one here."

"Well no, not until recently," he remarked, taking a ring of keys from his pocket. "I sent a letter home a few months before I met you, so the house would be ready upon my return." He unlocked three large iron locks on the door, each different and very elaborate, then spoke something inaudible as he rested his hand to the right of the door knocker. A latch on the inside of the door shifted, and a collection of bright snaking lights scattered away from the place where Tom's hand rested, vanishing into the seams of the doorway. "Ah, very nice, very nice to be back," he commented, lighting various lamps in the rooms of the first floor and beckoning Molly in. She walked behind him, looking around with much curiosity. The furniture was large and new, the floors were clean, paintings hung from the walls, and a fireplace begged to be lit.

"This is a lovely home, Mr. Crowe."

"Thank you," Tom replied, preparing a fire. "Just needs to be warmed a bit. Oh, pardon my manners! This way."

He beckoned her to follow and climbed the main stairs by lantern light. The iron staircase spiraled tightly upward and deposited them in a hallway leading to three doors on the right and another on the left. "The master suite is on the left," Tom said, gesturing, "and all the doors on the right also lead to bedrooms. Choose whichever suits you most comfortably. Each has its own bath and wardrobe, as well as trunks for whatever items you have to store. One has large library bookshelves, another, a balcony and patio above a small garden and the third, a staircase to the roof and modest observatory."

Molly beamed in astonishment. "They all sound lovely. I suppose the room leading to the observatory will do just fine."

A smile appeared on Tom's face. "My favorite." He led her to the end of the hallway, unlocking all doors along the way. "Here you are, then." Opening the bedroom door, he allowed her to enter first as he lit the room. Silently he checked the contents of the wardrobe. "This room has its own fireplace."

"This is perfect. Thank you, Captain. Or, is it 'Mr. Crowe' on solid land?" she asked with a coy grin.

"Charles Walsh, actually," he corrected her, "In London, anyway. How else could I buy such a house? No one would sell this building to a man like Thomas Crowe."

"You have other aliases?"

"You didn't notice we weren't questioned upon anchoring in the harbor?"

Molly chewed her lip and thought to herself. "That *was* a bit odd."

"London is one of the few havens I have left, Miss," he said with a laugh. "Here you may rest easy."

"Thank you then, Mr. Walsh," she said, playing along.

"Well, for the night I suppose I will let you sleep. Tomorrow I have arranged a full day for you while I do my errands. I will elaborate more in the morning after breakfast. I set a fire in the hearth downstairs so the house should be cozy in a matter of minutes, and if you get too cold, call for me and I will light the one in your room as well. I believe you will find the bed very agreeable, for it's been scarcely used at all. I have only tea in the kitchen now, but before you retire for the night you may have as much as you please. I brought it here myself a year ago after visiting India. Very rare here in the Isles, very flavorful, though. The kitchen is adequate. I'm sure finding cups and other things will be no trouble. Do you need anything else?"

Molly was flattered by his generosity but shook her head with a polite smile. "No, thank you. You've done so much already."

"If you do need anything, please wake me without hesitation, yeah?" he offered kindly. "I'll be in the bedroom at the top of the staircase on the left. I'll leave you a lantern so you don't have to wander through the dark." Tom set it on the large oak trunk in front of Molly's bed. "Well then, tea?"

"I suppose."

Thomas led Molly back downstairs to the kitchen. Once lit, the kitchen appeared much larger. As Molly expected, there was ample space for cooking, many pots and kettles, utensils and cups. Under normal circumstances, it was the kind of home she'd have dreamed of living in when she had arrived in the colonies years before. Molly felt as though she were beginning to relive the life that had been denied her so long ago.

There were also two iron ovens and many cabinets. Tom retrieved tea from a chest-high cabinet at the far end of the kitchen and a small tea cup with elaborate Ming Dynasty decorations around the edges.

"I've set some water in a kettle over the stove. It will be ready in a moment, I believe. Well, miss, I shall return to my room. Wake me if you need anything at any time. I shall see you not long after sunrise."

"Goodnight. I thank you again."

"It is no burden at all."

Molly's eyes followed him for a moment before she returned to the kettle on the stove. She prepared herself a cup of tea and walked over to a nearby window, peering outside at the frosted grounds. She felt at ease within the warm home, especially in Thomas's company.

Soon after finishing her tea, Molly went upstairs to her own room. She closed her pistols in the drawer by her bed, examining their pearls before shutting them away. Midnight passed, and snow continued to sweep over London.

Tom had set his only luggage—the locked chest—next to his bed, falling asleep easily. Outside, the city was quiet, sleeping like a sedated giant beneath a blanket of ice.

Tom slept continually through the night and awakened only when he heard a knock at the front door. Sleepily he walked downstairs to answer it. Standing outside the door was a thin, dignified old gentleman with a greyed mustache and beard to match his equally grey features and hair. He smiled cordially at Tom from behind small, circular bifocals. Brushing off snow from his large black overcoat, the man tipped his hat in a businesslike manner and extended a hand to shake Tom's.

"Hello, Mr. Walsh."

"Ah, good morning, Ozias."

"Not too late to begin breakfast, I hope?" Ozias said as he picked up a large leather bag in each hand and walked inside.

"Just in time, actually. How are you? Come in."

Ozias's voice was aged but strong and clear. "I have no complaints. My eyesight's a spot off, though. No longer good for the hunt! You've been away for two years, Mr. Walsh. Did you have any difficulty trying to return? I should think the terrible weather may have kept you away. It's been bitterly cold these last two winters."

"Oh, no trouble, just travelled here and there," Tom replied, sounding very convincing.

Upstairs, Molly listened intently at the sound of the two voices. Rays of morning light trickled onto her face as she sat by the window.

"The house has been very well kept since I last left," Tom said, complimenting his old friend.

Ozias's eyes shone. "Oh, well I visited once a month to tidy up. I wasn't sure when you intended to return, so I came as often as the house needed. Except for the locks on the front door, I have put new locks on the doors and windows. We've had a terrible crime spree in your absence, Mr. Walsh. In fact, there have been many incidents just recently. Valuables have been stolen—rings, mostly. A few were from the building that was your father's old shop, as a matter of fact. Only two nights ago some poor chap was attacked by a wild animal, too, just there in front of the house. Curious, isn't it? To think, here in London! Wolves! The city watch must be growing idle, Mr. Walsh. I tell you, the authorities had a tighter grip on this old city a long time ago. No riffraff got away with anything. Life was predictable and civilized. Why, when I was still a young soldier, I—"

"You don't say?" Tom interrupted before the man could rattle on any further. He was greatly intrigued by the information concerning the robberies. "When were the shops broken into, Ozias?"

"Oh I believe it was Tuesday, sir."

"Who was the fellow who died?"

"Can't say I remember the name, sir. Heard it from a man I met on the street."

"I see. What became of the man who was attacked?"

Ozias replied quite frankly. "Dead."

"Shame."

Molly appeared quietly at the top of the stairs, looking below curiously at the newcomer as she made her way down, already dressed in her day clothes. Tom didn't notice her presence.

"By the way, I thank you for gathering the items I requested and putting them in the armoire upstairs. I predicted correctly the room my guest would choose. I'll soon introduce you to the person who will be in need of those garments. She'll be staying here with me. She's asleep at the moment, though."

"I'd better cook extra for breakfast then, I suppose, yes?" Ozias seemed not at all disappointed to hear he'd have more work on his hands.

Tom laughed. "I'd advise it. And I warn you, she eats quite a breakfast. I've seen it firsthand."

As Ozias disappeared into the kitchen carrying the bags of edibles, Tom grinned up at Molly playfully. "Good morning."

She saw that his face was clean and shaved, his hair was tied away behind his ears and he wore a tidy vest and jacket.

Molly chuckled quietly. "Good morning, Mr. Walsh." She couldn't help but stare at him. She'd hardly recognized the gentleman in the foyer below her—the neat and handsome man who had been a ragged, devilish vagrant only days before. His cleaner, sharper appearance enhanced his already compelling lupine eyes and brow, made his face smooth and statuesque. She felt almost under-dressed; though, unknown to Thomas she'd been up for hours already in order to allow herself to put on a special green blouse and white skirt she'd kept safe in her bag, and to undo the weeks of damage to her hair. She'd polished herself to the bone in order to allow herself to make a new impression on the captain—to show him a lady he was not accustomed to.

Ozias could be heard rummaging through pots and pans in the kitchen nearby.

"Sleep well?" Tom asked, walking to the base of the stair.

"Very much so, thank you. I'm quite sure I haven't slept that comfortably in a long while. Who was with you just now?"

"Oh, you must meet Ozias. He is the groundskeeper here in my absence and resident cook while I'm here in London.What is it?" He noticed she was beaming and staring.

Molly turned away, her cheeks slightly reddened. What a generally lovely situation she'd found herself in: a lavish home, a new adventure, and an intriguing young man whose secrets she desired like desserts. "You spoke of some errands you had to attend to today?"

"Yes, I have to visit a silversmith today and inquire about an item I purchased last year and never had the chance to retrieve from him. I also need new clothes, and I have some questions for the keeper of London port records. You, Miss, I have considered thoroughly. The clothing Ozias gathered will not be adequate for everything. Earlier this morning I sent my maid to purchase something more suitable for this evening. You will be attending the opera at seven o'clock. My maid will return by four to dress you. She will also arrange a coach to and from the performance."

Molly accepted the letter of invitation from him gratefully.

"Ozias will see that you have dinner before you leave."

"How did you prepare all this?"

"How? Why, I am Charles Walsh, one of the wealthiest colonial businessmen in London," he replied tongue-in-cheek.

Molly was surprised at herself when she giggled like a child. "But of course."

"I have my ways, Miss." He discovered in his mind's absence his hands had found her waist and embarrassedly withdrew them with a concealing smile.

Molly blushed crimson as Tom left for the kitchen. *He isn't avoiding me*, she thought happily, *he's just being shy*. Molly bit her lip and smiled as she walked about the room, her hands clasped together behind her back, toying with the magic ring still on her finger. An incredible fragrance drifted through the first floor of the house from the kitchen, filling the dining room. The scent was mouthwatering, and Molly realized she felt an animalistic hunger, having been nearly starved while out at sea. She was certain her nose detected bacon, fried eggs and toast, ham and muffins.

Tom finished his breakfast first and excused himself to get ready to leave for the day. Molly's gaze lingered on the window by the dining table. Light snow was falling, and the sun was just barely scratching its way through the clouds. About half an hour later, Tom returned, dressed in a heavy grey cape, its collar turned up to protect his ears from the weather. Molly gawked once more at his new appearance.

With his left arm he held the large chest with the heavy chain and lock under the cape, and with his right hand he placed a wool hat on his head. Tom told Molly goodbye for the day. "I expect we'll see each other again this evening after the performance. I hope you enjoy it."

"Have a good day, Mr. Walsh," she said, her voice cracking.

"And you, Miss Bishop." He tipped his hat and stepped out into the snowy street, making his way up town to the silversmith's. Ozias, waving, shut the door behind Thomas and gathered the empty plates on the table.

Outside it continued to snow. Tom trudged through the biting cold, his locked chest of valuables tucked beneath his large winter coat. Huffing a plume of steam, he wrenched open the large door into the silversmith's forge up the street.

After taking a winter coat from a hook on the back of her door and putting it on, Molly followed the observatory staircase toward the roof of Tom's house. Something in one of the candles on a wall caught her eye. Inspecting it, she noticed that where a wick should have been there was a red gem—a ruby—sunken into the tip of the candle. In fact, the candle itself was not made of wax but, rather, some kind of glass. Deciding it best not to fool with anything valuable in Thomas's house, she continued to climb the stairs. As her hand passed the candle, mounted close to a railing, a little flame burst to life from the ruby in the glass candle. Molly tried to blow it out to no avail. Licking her fingertips, she then reached to snuff it by hand, but the flame died before she ever touched it. *How odd*, she thought. *Is this a type of magical artifact my father would make?* Waving her hand over the candle, she played with the device for several minutes, then, letting the other candles alone and keeping her hands close to her, Molly continued up the stairs.

The city rooftops spouted identical columns of chimney smoke. Looking down from the canopy of the observatory, Molly thought the brick structures formed a dark grey jungle. Below were rivers of white, and above were tree trunks of black. Molly's hair collected snow as it fell steadily downward through an open skylight in the glass dome surrounding her. Shivering, she noticed how many people walked the city streets below her—schools of coats in a wintry stream. After a bit, the snow fell harder still, and Molly retreated downstairs, but not before shutting the skylight and wiping the collecting snow from the lens of a large telescope positioned in the center of the room. She hung up her coat to dry and started a fire in the fireplace—it worked just as the candles in the observatory stair—and her room became comfortably warm in a matter of minutes. She caught sight of the wardrobe in the corner and decided to see exactly what Thomas had purchased for her.

The wardrobe was lined with beautiful silk gowns, dress coats, cotton dresses and various other garments. She closed the wardrobe shut, her spirits high. Deciding she was in need of a way to pass the time, she went into the bedroom that featured a library, started its fireplace with a flourish of her wrist (thoroughly amused with herself and searched for a book that might capture her interest. Eyeing the shelves slowly, her attention was suddenly drawn to a particular book, *Magical Practices of Southwest Asia*. She took the book to her room, set herself comfortably in front of the fire and allowed her imagination to carry her away. As Molly continued to read, the warm glow of the room set a soft, dreamy atmosphere. *Nothing like something magic to pass time during an adventure*, she thought, laughing to herself. Tom seemed to have plenty of books on the subject, after all. *London, and all this magic business, might just grow on me*, she thought.

Tom shut the large door of the silversmith's behind him, denying the bitter cold entry into the hot forge. He removed his coat quickly, having already broken out into a sweat. Tom approached a tall, weighty, ox of a man, Fenn, who leaned over a massive anvil, pounding tirelessly away at a carriage wheel. By the look of it, it was for someone important.

"Afternoon, Fenn."

Fenn shuffled around slowly, laying down his hammer (larger than Tom's head) and responded loudly. "Ah! Hello, Mr. Walsh!"

"It's been quite some time, yeah?" Tom chuckled as he shook Fenn's gorilla hand, or rather, Fenn's hand shook *him*.

"True, it has, Walsh! Travel abroad much, did you?"

"Extensively. Fenn, I meant to ask you today, would you happen to have the item I ordered two years ago after I returned from Hatteras?"

Fenn paused in thought. "Ah, if I remember correctly … Oh yes! You wanted that—"

Thomas nodded quickly, hushing Fenn.

"It's fortunate that I expected you to return. I stored it in the back of the shop till I'd see you again." He led Tom to the storage rooms. "What a feat it was, Walsh, making such an item. I'd never thought to attempt it before. I remember warnin' you how expensive it would be, but," he laughed loudly "I could tell you meant to have it nonetheless!"

"And I do," Tom replied with a friendly gesture. "I've brought the full sum you asked for." Tom took the locked chest from under his cape and placed it on a table with a heavy crash. "Worth every pound," said Tom enthusiastically, seeing Fenn glance at the chest.

"Well, one would expect it. I had to have this item sent off to a specialist." He looked around as though there might be others lurking in the corners of his shop. "I'm no scholar of magic you know, Walsh," he whispered.

"It's quite all right, as long as it serves its purpose."

"Yes, but do you realize how difficult it was to hide it? I lost my nerve every time the authorities strolled by the shop, even if they didn't seem interested in my shop at all."

"And I apologize for placing that burden upon you," Tom replied sincerely.

"Nah, don't make no fuss about it, Walsh." Fenn handed Tom the inconspicuously wrapped item.

"Oof! It's quite heavier than I expected." Tom unwrapped the package, smiling contently at the prize. It shone as cleanly as the day it was forged. He unlocked the chest on the table, revealing a small fortune in gems and golden Spanish coins. He never paid for anything in silver, a lesson he had learned a long time ago. His palms were scarred for every time he'd forgotten the lesson. "A pleasure to do business with you, sir."

"As always, Walsh! As always!" Fenn replied with much volume.

"Good day, Fenn." With the exchange complete, Tom departed.

Tom's maid returned just as the large grandfather clock in the dining room rang out four o'clock. She entered the house and searched the downstairs rooms for the female guest Tom had told her about. "Miss Bishop?" she called from the foot of the stairs.

Molly looked up from the pages of her book. She spied the clock on top of the fireplace mantle reading four o'clock and stood quickly. When she arrived at the top of the main staircase, Molly leaned to look down at the maid in the foyer below. The older woman, startled, hurried to Molly, carrying a large package in both arms.

"How do you do, Miss?" she asked with a curtsy. "We must get you dressed!" She turned to call downstairs. "Ozias! Dinner, please!"

"Forgive me. I must have forgotten the time," Molly explained timidly.

"Yes, of course," she replied. "No worries, dear. Would you like to see what Mr. Walsh has purchased you?"

Molly eyed the woman curiously, finding something familiar in her appearance. She shook the thought away. "Yes, of course."

The maid led her to her room without asking which one she had chosen. "Oh, I'm anxious to see your reaction, dear." Once inside, the maid pulled an extravagant dress from its package and laid it neatly across Molly's bed. "It was quite an ordeal to carry such a delicate thing safely in such horrid weather. Let's get you dressed, then."

Molly's face brightened. "It's beautiful." The dress was long and flowing, golden in color. It came low around the neck, where many fluffed layers of silver fabric swept down from the collarbone and across the neckline. Silver stitching created a weave of graceful vines that cascaded down the front of the dress all the way to the ankles. The neckline started below the shoulders, meant to show off the skin and delicate figure beneath.

The maid was smiling, revealing her small pearly teeth. Perhaps two or three decades Molly's senior, the woman spoke with a slight French accent that occasionally interrupted her otherwise clear English. She was a pretty woman despite her age. Her fair skin was disrupted by wrinkles only around her eyes. Her straight, light brown hair was tied and obscured under her maid's cap. Friendliness and a tendency to overinteract with things—including Molly and her dress—marked her nature. "I'm pleased you like it," she said.

"Thank you. I don't believe I got your name?"

"Oh! Excuse my manners. I am Charlotte."

Molly knew she'd sensed *déjà vu*. "I wonder, Charlotte, if you happen to know a man by the name of Samuel Bishop?" she asked.

"Oh! Why, I almost married him many years ago, before things between us went sour. How do you know Mr. Bishop?"

Molly closed her eyes suddenly, her memories flooding back to her. "You don't remember me, do you Charlotte?

You were often a guest in the home of my uncle when I was a girl."

Charlotte looked puzzled. "You don't mean … What is your name, dear?"

"My name is Molly. Samuel Bishop was my uncle."

"Molly? Oh, my! Where have you been, dear?" She suddenly sat on the bed by the dress. "Please forgive me for sitting—"

"It's been too long, Charlotte."

"Considerably long! You're all grown! And so beautiful a woman! I did not recognize you at all!" Charlotte's expression was one of shock. "You know, though, that your uncle is … well, after his head maid, the one you called Aunt, passed away, he decided to live here in the city. He sold his country home to a wealthy horse breeder. I assumed you were aware of all this, wherever you might be."

"My uncle is living in London? Will you take me to him?" Molly asked.

Charlotte wrung her hands, and her eyes told Molly there was trouble. "Something happened to him just recently."

"What happened?" Molly asked impatiently.

"Only recently, your uncle moved here permanently, and he quickly went into business with a merchant who owned several shops here in London, including a jeweler and a gunsmith, both of which were robbed."

"Robbed?" she repeated. Tom and Ozias's earlier conversation came to mind. "Oh, no!"

"Dear?"

Panic-stricken, Molly grabbed the maid's hand. "Charlotte, what of my uncle? Is he all right?"

"Dear, he ..." She hesitated. "Your uncle was pronounced dead and missing as of Tuesday night."

Molly stood suddenly, shaking her head back and forth in denial, her breathing shallow. "Both dead and missing? How can that be?"

"Signs were that he could not have lived through the ordeal, but his body was missing," Charlotte replied.

Molly's eyes filled with tears. Returning to London had meant a great deal to her, but with her uncle now gone her memories of the city seemed to die with him. He was the only real family she had ever known.

"Oh, dear, I'm sorry, I didn't mean to upset you," Charlotte apologized, trying to comfort Molly. Only when

Charlotte tried to hold her still did Molly realize she was trembling.

"Please, dear," Charlotte said, "let's just get you some dinner and then into your dress. You'll feel better." She took Molly by the arm and walked with her downstairs to the dining room, calling for Ozias.

Ozias immediately put dinner on the dining table. Molly sat silently, sipping Pinot Noir and eating some roast beef. As soon as she had eaten all she could manage in her present mood, the two women went back upstairs so that Charlotte could help Molly into her dress. The older woman had managed to settle some of Molly's tears, though the girl still expressed a downcast, forlorn disposition. An opera didn't appeal to Molly's current mood. Not much of anything did. Silently, she blamed herself for what had happened to Samuel. If she hadn't run off, would he have still sold his home and come to London?

Charlotte began with Molly's hair, starting with one long braid and wrapping it into a tidy French twist that rested centered on the back of her head. Molly forced a smile for Charlotte's sake, but her attention wandered off to the window, the condition of the weather matching perfectly the way she felt—cold and dismal.

Tom waded sluggishly through the driving snow, making his way toward the harbor. Dusk was darker than it should have been, the sky still obscured and seemingly saddened by thick winter clouds. The streetlights cast hazy, spherical glows on every corner, the crowd thinning as quickly as daylight. Tom was forced to squint through the biting chill, fighting the relentless cold more and more. *Blasted weather,* he thought to himself with a scowl. The package grew heavy and burdensome in his arms.

The docks were dark, so Tom paused to rest. There were no lights glowing in the customs office's high windows. *Odd,* thought Tom. Exhausted, he crouched in the snow, slowly being blinded by the furious weather.

"You look beautiful, dear!" exclaimed Charlotte.

Molly looked into the mirror, hardly recognizing herself. Her red lips contrasted with her complexion, its usual olive tone now pale. The blush in her cheeks hid the puffiness her watery eyes had created. The gown had been chosen well, for it brought out her glowing eyes and bright features, however dim they were now.

"Thank you, Charlotte."

Ozias was off in the kitchen again while Charlotte prepared for Molly's departure. Molly sat on a sofa in the sitting room.

"Dear? Your coach has arrived."

"Hm?" Looking up to see Charlotte smiling at her, Molly stood and walked to the door, where Charlotte placed a heavy fur coat over the girl's shoulders.

"The weather's not very agreeable tonight, so mind your surroundings," Charlotte offered kindly. Molly nodded as she walked out to the coach waiting at the street, then turned to look through the window to see Charlotte waving to her. Molly began to shiver as she entered the empty carriage, the warmth of her coat just barely enough to sustain her through the freezing wind. She wrapped the coat tightly around her as the carriage took off with a jerk.

Shadows gathered beyond the last lamp post leading to the docks. The wind ceased to blow, and long, inky shadows ran down the nearby edifices and pooled in the drifts. A flutter of wings stopped Thomas in his tracks, and heavy, black coats appeared all around him swaying menacingly in the dark. One shadow chuckled. Tom's expression quickly devolved to one of instinctive hatred. A voice shouted at him.

"Thomas Crowe? Oh yes, it is, I see! We were informed you would be here, but you're earlier than we expected. I have to ask you, Thomas, are you anxious to meet your end? Do you grow tired of living, or did you not believe he would know you were following him?"

"Who?" Tom demanded to know. The shadows stirred, laughing and mumbling. Tom tucked a hand into his cape, feeling for the wrapped package, untying the string silently. He kept still, squinting intently at his aggressors, waiting.

"Why, your brother Harlan, of course! Thomas, you don't know how eager we were to find you. I assure you we can do much worse than the Royal Navy." The shadow scoffed as he spoke the name. "After all, His Majesty's officers are still too human to hope to catch a man like you." An evil, white smile spread across the spectre's face, his cheeks glowing pale white, eyes stained pink, veiny and engorged. Tom began to fidget.

"I wholeheartedly despise your kind, Thomas. Uncivilized pests! It's no mystery why Parliament is conspiring against the northern clans. Harlan was wise to join our cause. We're the only reason left in a confused and troubled mortal world."

The shadows raised their arms to chest level. Tom heard hammerlocks clicking and the laughter of the shades. London harbor erupted with thunder, the port office buildings reflecting the bright muzzle flash of guns. Deep snowdrifts and the walls of the offices could not adequately muffle the cacophony of the assault. While most of the city remained oblivious to the commotion, everyone in the district around wondered at the noise. Yet there near the docks, people were loathe to investigate such noises. When the street was silent once more, Tom's cape lay riddled with holes in the snow.

Molly closed her eyes as the carriage rolled on, fiddling with her ring in an attempt to distract herself from her thoughts. Just two days earlier, Uncle Samuel had died, and she had been too late to see him. If she had arrived sooner, might she have saved him?

The carriage came to a sudden halt, and the driver came around to assist her, taking her hand as she exited. She stared up at the opera house, debating whether to enter. Like the hands of an ill-behaved child the wind batted at her dress. The opera house was colossal and radiated a celebratory aura, as the sounds of the orchestra warming up spilled out into the snow. The crowd flocked inside, fleeing the bitter chill. Shivering from the cold, Molly hurried in with the crowd. Once inside she wandered aimlessly. There was a seat for her on the first balcony between a well-dressed gentleman and an extraordinarily round woman in grand attire. The gentleman looked curiously at Molly from the corner of his eye before returning to the program in his hands. Molly waited impatiently, keeping her eyes forward on the stage.

The spectre lowered his pistol. The barrel exhaled its last breath of smoke, and he hid it once more within his coat, smiling wickedly. He approached the destroyed heap of clothes lying in the snow, strewn about and twisted from the hail of bullets. "It's a shame, Mr. Crowe," he said with a sneer, eyeing the heap. Turning around, the spectre stopped immediately, his deathly pale countenance expressing a confused terror.

All seven of his accomplices lay motionless in the snow, guns in hand. The viscous moonlight that dripped through the clouds illuminated their forms. They were marked by deep sword strikes that sizzled and hissed, burning them continuously until their remains vanished in dark clouds of smoke. "It truly is a shame, Mikael," Tom's voice spat through the flurries.

The startled vampire spun around, staring into his own reflection six inches away, cast by the blade of a shining silver sword. A blood stone, set in the hilt, stared him straight in the face. Behind the blade hovered a pair of yellow eyes. Mikael screamed as his heart was pierced and Thomas's blade drank his life away like a hungry leech on the pulse of his soul.

Molly applauded as the curtain for the first act closed, beginning the intermission. She stood suddenly, making her way to the bottom floor. For some reason she felt uneasy, her stomach twisting. She headed outside, hoping her coach would still be there. The sleeping driver sat in Molly's coach, which was parked only a few paces from the opera house doors. The horses reacted to her sudden appearance, shaking off the snow collecting in their manes.

The driver awoke with a snort. "Miss? Over already?"

"No, but there is somewhere else I need to be. Do you know the whereabouts of Samuel Bishop's shop?" she asked quickly.

The man squinted through the storm. "I believe so. What business do you have there, Miss? Don't you know that place has been robbed?"

"I'm quite aware. I just need you to take me there for a moment. I won't be long."

He shrugged. "If you say so. I've been hired for the whole night."

Royal soldiers arrived in London harbor, puzzled about what had startled half the district moments earlier. A man's winter cape, a shattered lamp post and several dark patches in the snow were all there was to be found. There were no footprints. The stains in the snow appeared to be soot or ash, but nothing had been damaged by fire.

Tom sighed heavily, collapsing into a large armchair by the fireplace in his suite. He tossed his books and other purchased items on the freshly cleaned sheets of his bed, and Ozias silently picked them up and put them in their place. Seeing Tom's clothes hanging in tatters on his nearly nude body, Ozias covered him with a light blanket and walked out of the room as though nothing extraordinary had happened. It wasn't unusual for the master of the house to come home late after what he always told Ozias had been a "fight". Ozias, of course, was no fool, and werewolf or not, Charles Walsh paid his help well. Charlotte, knowing Molly was in good hands with the driver she had arranged to transport the young woman, went home shortly after Ozias had left for the night, confident that Molly would soon be home from the opera.

Molly stood outside her Uncle's old shop as the carriage driver waited patiently on the other side of the road. The door swung loose on its hinges as she gingerly made her way in. A lamp post outside offered a bit of illumination within the deserted building. Molly stifled her tears as she entered the mess left in the shop. Crying would do her no good now, and she knew it, but it was difficult to hold back the tears. Various tools and jewels were strewn across the floors, tables were upturned, and papers were littered everywhere. Unmistakable markings caught her eye in the walls and tables—claw marks set in the wood. She knew those markings. What could they have been looking for so desperately to take the life of an innocent old man?

Before Thomas killed him, Mikael McGreary was the patriarch of the Black Coat Society of London. He and several other men had come to capture, not kill, Thomas at the request of Thomas's brother, Harlan, who coveted a seat with the Black Coat Society. Mikael did not quite follow Harlan's instructions because he hated werewolves, pure and simple. A prideful vampire, Mikael had planned to return to Harlan with a clever story about how Thomas had struggled and had to be put down. His plan was perfect, except for the fact that he hadn't counted on the most important factor: Thomas.

The Black Coats had put Harlan through hellish rites of passage when he came to them as a young boy, wishing to be inducted as a vampire. He'd rejected his werewolf curse and his brother, but especially his father, John, for abandoning Harlan when he was bitten and turned into one of the creatures he so hated for tearing his family apart. Harlan believed to truly rid himself of the werewolf curse, he must find Thomas, an object of his hatred ...and he meant to do just that. Unlike Thomas, Harlan was ambitious in the dangerous sense of the word. However, he did share Thomas's keen interest in magic. He, too, obsessively sought after his father's old rings. Two days previously the pleas of old, frail Samuel Bishop were not enough to dissuade the young Black Coat from his selfish wrath when he came storming into the little gem shop looking for the ring Thomas had yet to find.

Samuel Bishop never dealt in the magical trade directly, and to my knowledge he was hiding nothing when the robbers attacked him that night so long ago. Many jewelers closed their businesses during those times. They were afraid either ill-meaning werewolves or greedy vampires would raid them, take their gems (and possibly their blood) or that the authorities would have them tried as suspected magesmiths—many of them wrongly convicted. Magic was a risky enterprise, and only those who knew the trade best stayed the course and crafted *magical artifacts. It was a dangerous business, but a profitable one. Who wouldn't pay a fortune for magic?*

Geoffrey Mylus,

April 25, 1833

❦

Tom awoke in the wee hours of the morning aching all over, his skin sensitive as if it had been stretched and put through a wringer and wrapped around his flesh once more. Looking for decent clothes—any at all—in a frantic rush, he was grateful Ozias and Charlotte had left for the night. Grabbing the first garments that met his touch when he reached into his wardrobe, he threw them on and staggered downstairs, weak and dizzy, rubbing at his aches and pains and searching for any spirit or medicine strong enough to put him to sleep again quickly.

Molly sat silently in the coach outside Thomas's home, her gaze searching through the blackness outside the window. She wasn't sure how long she had stayed at her uncle's shop. Now all she wanted was to fall into bed, go to sleep and try to forget what she had seen in the shop.

Tom, in his clumsy state, hadn't taken two sips from a newly purchased whiskey bottle when his legs gave out and—knocking his head against the wall—he fell onto the kitchen floor, doused in the remainder of the bottle's contents. He heard the sound of the front door being unlatched and then closed again carefully. There was a sharp pain in his forehead at the site of a sizeable cut. As he heard soft footsteps quickly climbing the stairs, he limped into the living room. *Molly*, was what his disoriented mind figured. He considered trying to get her attention, soaked in whiskey and bleeding from the forehead, but he decided against it, turning back to the kitchen. He had sat in a chair and put his head on the table.

Molly sat up in bed, unable to sleep. She sighed hopelessly, deciding that perhaps a bit of tea would help her relax. She wrapped a robe around her shoulders and headed downstairs. As she arrived in the kitchen, Tom was stirring. His neck hurt from lying on the hard kitchen table, and he rubbed his aching head. "Well, at least it won't be there in the morning," he muttered. "Never does last."

"What never lasts?"

He turned lazily toward the sound of Molly's voice. "A good drink," he replied, thinking quickly. "Good ... evening? Morning? Er, how are you, Miss Bishop?"

Gazing at Tom, who appeared quite drunk, Molly stood with arms crossed and lips pursed. Her nose crinkled slightly from the overpowering smell of alcohol.

Tom managed a smile. "Did you enjoy the opera?" he asked, standing shakily.

She shook her head in disdain and crossed the kitchen to place a kettle on the stove before returning to the table. "It was lovely."

"Wonderful!" He raised a hand to his gashed head "Agh! Did Ozias make dinner before you left?"

"Yes. What have you done to yourself now?"

"Just played a little too rough with some friends."

She examined his cut closely. "Old friends?"

"Oh, yes. However, I don't believe you'll ever get a chance to meet them now. It's a shame." He laughed to himself at his private joke.

Molly was not quite as amused. "Meaning?"

"Oh, never mind them."

"Would it have anything to do with why you're drenched in whiskey?" She crinkled her nose again.

"*That*," he began intently, "was an accident. But I suppose it does explain everything."

Molly took a cloth off the counter and dabbed gently at his cut. Tom smiled contritely at her again, speaking softly. "Thank you."

"You certainly have a knack for collecting injuries," she replied, beginning to feel lighthearted.

He held up a small cup. "Drink? I've already had my share," he joked.

"I have tea," Molly replied, eyes narrowing.

"I see."

"Vile drink! Look what it's caused you!" she muttered darkly, retrieving the tea.

"Yes, it's terrible. Before tonight I had no sense of humor," Tom rebutted.

"Poor man."

Tom shook his head. "You missed my joke, I see."

"I've other things on my mind, I'm afraid." She sighed and sat down beside him.

"Yes, do tell me where your mind led you tonight … unless I'm mistaken, and the opera lasted until two o'clock this morning."

Molly hesitated, looking away guiltily.

"Just as I guessed," he said, and then added quickly, "But it's all right. However, now that I know the Black Coat Society is still in operation, I must ask that you stay close to this house until we leave again."

"Black Coat Society?" she asked, her brow furrowing. There was that name again.

"Afraid so." A frown indicated his displeasure. "One of London's local nocturnal organizations. You don't want to draw their attention. I already have. Of course I doubt they will confront me again for a while, so I don't intend to sail just yet. Well, I mean I *didn't*, until I heard Harlan's name spoken again tonight."

Molly's tone lowered. "What of him?"

Tom's voice turned sour. "Harlan? He was here in London, and not two days before we arrived. Tuesday. He knew I was coming somehow." He pointed down at Molly's finger. "He has the other ring. It was here in London, and he beat me to it. Harlan must have gone through every gem shop in the city. The papers are filled with recent robbery incidents—the crime spree you must've heard of by now, yeah? Harlan left his ship in port long enough to find the ring my father sold, and then he departed, after leaving some of his fellows to deal with me."

Molly was appalled by the eerie similarities between the crimes and her uncle's death. She stood suddenly, tea cup smashing to pieces on the floor. Angry tears filled her eyes, but her voice quieted as she put together the obvious. "It was he?"

Tom watched her curiously.

"He killed him? Harlan killed my uncle!"

"Where? Here? When?" Tom didn't know what she meant.

"The shop he robbed and the man he killed just two days ago … it was Samuel." She glowered darkly. "I know it was him! I know it! All the signs were in that shop!"

"Oh, *that* shop. No, miss." Tom shook his head.

Distressed and confused, she turned on him. "What are you saying?"

"The Black Coats are who you speak of. Harlan sent them out to that particular shop. He was involved, yes, but your uncle did not *die* on Tuesday night." Tom looked away and swallowed. He felt a very uncomfortable explanation mounting.

Molly's voice emerged through gritted teeth. "Either way, he is responsible."

"That isn't my point."

"Then what is?" she demanded, wiping away her tears.

"Your uncle died early this morning. I witnessed it in person."

Molly stared at him, shocked.

"He was not killed by a 'wild animals.' The Black Coats coerced him into their brotherhood. They're vampires, Molly. Samuel was bitten." Tom placed two fingers on the side of his neck. "Between that and death, I do not know which is the worst fate."

"Vampires? I'd ask if you were joking, but I know better by now." Molly felt her world spinning around her. "And what do you mean you saw him? I was told he died Tuesday." Molly struggled hopelessly to sort out the situation.

"His human life ended Tuesday. His immortal life was ended tonight. He was already past recovery. The bite acts quickly, sometimes within one night if the afflicted lives, I've been told. There was no help for him, and I wish I'd arrived in London sooner." Tom took another drink of the whiskey. His hand trembled and he almost dropped the bottle.

A strong pang filled her chest, and Molly eyed Tom intensely. "Y-y-you ... you ..." she stuttered, unable to finish her sentence.

"What is it?"

"You said you were there! What did you do?"

"I saved him. I'm sorry."

Molly shook her head in confusion at Tom's choice of words. "He was a good man! I never got to say goodbye!"

"I saw in his eyes the remnants of an honest man, but that man was not the one standing in the street tonight with that unnaturally young face and eyes estranged from the light," Tom tried to explain. "I salvaged the good in him. I was at least able to do that. I stripped him of the curse, but I could not save his life, Molly."

Molly backed away from Tom, stumbling into a chair behind her. "You killed him?"

Tom shook his head in frustration. "No, *Harlan* and the Black Coats killed him—at least, the part that mattered. Does it upset you that I brought your uncle back from the forced servitude of those *monsters*? Well, pardon my behavior!"

"Were you even planning on telling me this?" Molly cried.

She flinched as Tom left the kitchen, spilling bags of flour and bottles of liquor on the floor and slamming the door behind him. He stormed upstairs to his room. Left alone, Molly sank to the floor, burying her face in her hands. She could find no will to move, and she cried herself to sleep on the kitchen floor, her tears making sticky clumps in the fine layer of flour beneath her.

Before its end, the Black Coat Society of London underwent a violent and rapid change in attitude and purpose. The original Black Coats, as I have said, first came to England from France because of the good relations the Beaumonte family established between Parisian cults and the Red Legion and Sons of Nyx (both English). After the death of Arnaud Beaumonte, the noble house of vampires fell to pieces, for there was no son beneath Arnaud to inherit the title of patriarch of the Black Coat Society. Leon Beaumonte, the inheritor, was missing. Arnaud's brother, Rene, died under mysterious circumstances shortly after his brother's passing, and the title of patriarch was quickly swept up by young members of the London house—many of whom succumbed to their prideful natures and encouraged fierce loyalty to the house among their peers. It did not take long for the new Black Coat Society to make enemies with several European powers. Their numbers and their influence grew, nearly to the point of diminishing the power of already long-established cults such as the Red Legion in

London and the House of Roses in Paris. The Black Coats exercised their will over their territory often by seizing control of the magic trade in major European cities and settlements, but often by illegal, bloody means. At the height of their power, some of the Coats, including the serpentine Simon Deschamps, advocated feeding on human blood instead of animals. The Black Coat Society would be the first great cult to do so in centuries.

Geoffrey Mylus,

April 26, 1833

❦

Spring came before Molly knew it was upon her. Tom had changed his plans after his encounter with the Black Coats, deciding to stay the winter in London. Molly had spent most of the cold months indoors, passing the hours making herself new clothes with Charlotte's help or venturing into the upstairs library and reading through one of Tom's myriad unusual books. Her mind clung to things she learned in magic books, though the knowledge was still useless to her, and was often written in a language comprised of nonsense and symbols. Ever since learning of her father's trade, Molly was eager to learn much more, and though Thomas tried on many occasions to explain the books to her, Molly couldn't make sense of the magical arts.

Tom spent most of his time in London out in the city, trading, as far as anyone knew. He would never say much about the places he went. He always returned with something for Molly; sometimes flowers, sometimes new fabrics for her and Charlotte, and very often candies and rare teas, for which Molly was most appreciative.

One day near the end of their stay, Molly and Thomas went out into the city together. Thomas talked about the many places he had been, pointing them out all along the way. Molly had never known there was such an extensive world of magic and monsters, existing right under her nose in London's back streets and basements. But Thomas made it sound as though if one did so much as pull up a loose stone in the street, a vampire or two would spring out.

Listening to Thomas was one of Molly's favorite ways to pass the time on land. He had never been so talkative while out at sea. In fact, he was a generally more amiable person on solid ground, and this made Molly wish never to leave London. *Life*, she thought, walking next to Thomas, *is so simple and comfortable here.*

Tom was nowhere to be found the following day. When Molly had come downstairs, Ozias was busily cooking breakfast. Charlotte had gone to fetch some flour and sugar in the market; it was always best to buy it as soon as ships arrived in port. Molly, not wanting to bother anyone (or be bothered), stepped out the back door, the chill from outside making her shiver and wrap her arms tightly across her chest. She closed the door behind her and, crossing her arms again, walked around to the small garden, taking a seat on one of its stone benches.

A swift shadow passed overhead, and then landed heavily on the roof. It seemed to have leapt from the neighboring building. Molly looked up suddenly, startled by the movement.

"Hello?" she called out.

Muffled groans and complaints could be heard above. "Leg. I can't keep this ... bandage ... agh!"

"W-who's up there?" Molly demanded of the presence.

The voice was broken by canine snarls. "Need breakfast ... Ozias had better ... ow!" The roof door opened and shut loudly.

Molly shook her head, exasperated. She muttered to herself, slightly amused. "Stubborn man." She'd figured out that it must be Thomas.

Small scraps of clothing drifted down into the garden. A shirt collar, one pant leg (and belt), shoe strings. Molly turned pink upon realizing Tom was running about mostly nude. Ozias's voice called from within. "Breakfast, Miss Bishop!"

"I'll be right there!" She called back, avoiding a ragged bit of shirt, which caught the branch of a tree just out of range of her hair.

Charlotte arrived soon after, large sacks of flour in her arms. She knocked on the door, almost toppling the big bags. Molly came to her rescue, opening the door for her. "Let me help you with that, Charlotte."

"Thank you, Miss Bishop."

Molly lifted one sack and followed Charlotte toward the kitchen just as Tom wandered carelessly, and quite nakedly, downstairs.

"Ozias, honestly, at this rate my wardrobe will be ..." Thomas came striding down the stairs without having looked up.

Molly dropped her sack on her foot. She stared at Thomas, then the bag on the floor, then Thomas again, her eyes pinned open as they panned left, right, left, right—following the rhythmic swing of his rather prominently displayed indiscretion like a pendulum on a grandfather clock.

Thomas, looking up and spying Molly in the doorway, turned his bare tail and ran back up the steps like a cat over hot coals.

Molly's cheeks alight and burning the color of rose gold, blinked, cut her eyes down to the floor and scrambled to stop the flour rupturing from the burst sack. Ozias entered the room a bit too late and was altogether oblivious. "Breakfast!" he announced, smiling and crinkling the skin around his jovial old eyes, "Today's special addition is kielbasa!"

Molly flushed again, swallowed, handed Ozias the bag of flour and fled upstairs to her bedroom.

Tom soon returned downstairs wearing a *whole* pair of pants, confident of his quick escape. He bade a good morning to everyone and finished his breakfast hastily.

Molly reappeared some time after him, quietly arriving at the table and pardoning herself for being late.

"Ah, there you are! We're leaving this afternoon," he announced happily.

Molly stirred honey into her tea and nodded, trying to catch up on breakfast before Ozias began to clear plates.

"Charlotte is packing your things right now," he said, avoiding eye contact and looking at his plate. Clearing his throat, he turned to his groundskeeper. "Ozias, I realize I told you it would be a week longer, but I've left you and

Charlotte each more than an extra week's pay to compensate."

Ozias nodded. "No trouble, sir. How were the sausages?"

"Delicious," piped Molly.

"Where do you plan to go, Mr. Walsh?" Charlotte interrupted, entering the dining room. She'd overhead the announcement.

"Barcelona," Tom answered, smiling as though he'd woken from the best night of sleep he'd ever had.

"Barcelona, sir? Whatever for?" asked Ozias.

Carefully, Tom looked up from his breakfast, not at Ozias, but momentarily toward Molly, expecting some sort of reaction. "A trade," he said plainly.

Ozias laughed, picking up his tea. "As usual, I see."

"You must be quite the busy man, Mr. Walsh. Only a four months' rest and you're off again!" Charlotte exclaimed.

"Quite."

"Well it was a pleasure meeting you, Miss Bishop." Ozias nodded politely to her. "I'm sorry you two must be off so soon."

"As am I," Molly replied softly. "Thank you both so much."

Tom rose from his seat and excused himself. Frowning into her tea cup, Molly felt hesitant about leaving London, although she longed to see her father in Spain.

"Thomas?" she called after him.

"Yes?" he called back.

"May I bring a few books from your library along?"

"Certainly! May I collect them for you?"

"That would be wonderful, thank you. You know which ones I've been reading, right? They'll be marked," she added as an afterthought.

"Should be no trouble!" His energetic footsteps vanished up the main stair.

In the library bedroom, Tom found a hefty stack of Molly's recent reading already neatly arranged and brimming with little decorative page markers Charlotte had found for her in town. The fireplace had been left alight and so before he gathered up he went to the hearth and dispelled the enchantment keeping it aglow. One of his glass and ruby candles was missing from the desk by the fireplace. Momentarily perplexed, he let it be; Ozias would likely recover it while cleaning. Thomas didn't take time to carefully check, but all Molly's books were accounted for. She had exhausted many of his books on magic and had recently taken a great interest in philosophers, writers he hadn't read much of, himself— Plato, Homer, Sun Tzu, Kant, Herder, Descartes, Vatsyayana...

Across the hall, in her bedroom, Molly tidied up. Charlotte had already packed most of her things for her, but Molly had returned to her room to gather a few extra personal effects she'd gradually taken ownership of over the winter and early spring months, such as a handy glass and ruby candle that helped her keep warm.

Within the half hour Tom had reappeared downstairs with two large pieces of luggage in addition to all the belongings with which he and Molly had arrived. Pausing in front of the door, he waited for Molly to speak with Charlotte for one last time before their departure.

"I plan to return within the year. I won't be away as long as I was last time if the sea carries me favorably," Tom told both Ozias and Charlotte.

"Good to hear, sir," Ozias responded.

Charlotte opened the door for the pair. "Godspeed, Mr. Walsh, Miss Bishop."

Smiling at them both, Molly went to meet Tom at the front door. About her shoulder was her small bag full of light clothes and accessories, and in her arms, her favorite tomes.

Thomas led her to an awaiting coach and placed the luggage in the back compartment. "Driver!"

The driver spurred the horses at Tom's order, and the coach made its way to the port of London. A cold April rain was falling.

Molly's expression was unreadable during the entire ride. This stirred something in Tom. He touched a finger to his forehead, feeling a small pain, unable to recall the night before and wondering if he'd injured himself. Looking out the window, he dropped his hand again. He didn't completely recall having transformed the previous night and wondered where his curse had taken him in his sleep, that is, until the carriage passed a butcher's shop where, outside, the owner was complaining loudly to two authorities who, shrugging their shoulders, looked upon his wrecked shop. Tom sank low into his seat and turned up his collar. The markets outside were mostly empty, for not many braved the rain that day. The coach came to a slow stop in the port. Tom got out and gathered the luggage, Molly exiting the coach behind him and walking on ahead. Solemnly, she looked at the *Scotch Bonnet*, waiting by the docks.

Catching up to her, Tom hauled the bags onboard, placing them in their respective cabins. The crew had been preparing the sails and rigging since early morning, their beards and eyebrows collecting rain. Bart scrutinized every detail of the operation. He wanted to make sure his last voyage across the sea was one the young Captain Crowe would talk about when Bart was long gone.

"I prepared a fire in your cabins, so if you'll wait a minute or two they should be fit for sleeping again," Bart explained to Tom and Molly.

"Ozias wrapped the rest of the breakfast in a cloth, and I placed it on your desk," Tom told Molly, "Your bags have been stowed under your bed, and I placed the books on top of it. I told Charlotte to keep the opera dress safe with her until you return. No sense in risking it on the sea. I found a safe chest to keep your pistols locked in." He whispered its location to her and added: "The key is in a boot next to your bed, behind the door."

"Thank you." she replied quietly.

He opened her cabin door for her. "Best stay in here, Miss, the weather is only going to get worse."

The crew raised the sails within the hour. The anchor creaked as it was hauled up with slow, persistent force. Bart unfastened all the dock tethers from their cleats and took the helm as Tom arrived on deck.

"Barcelona!" Tom shouted to Bart and the crew.

"Barcelonaaaa!" Bart repeated.

Molly closed her cabin door, the excited cries of the crew ringing in her ears. Feeling weak, she lay down beneath the covers on her bed. Though the fire burned hot, she continued to shiver, but it was not because of the cold. Molly wrapped the covers tightly around herself.

The crew scampered about the main deck, climbing the rigging and unfastening the sail and yard locks. The precipitation did not discourage the men as they scurried about high in the sails with simian agility.

"Full speed! The weather's biting at our backsides, boys!" Tom called out to the men.

"Barcelona, eh Tom?" Bart inquired of him.

Tom looked on, unresponsive.

"A long detour, yeah?"

Tom still provided no answer.

"They found you, didn't they?"

The rain continued until late that evening. The spring chill, however, lingered until the following morning and would continue into the next week, even out at sea. Tom performed his daily routine, and the crew bustled about tirelessly, keeping up with their captain's persistent orders. Around midday Tom entered Molly's cabin.

"Barcelona will take us a month." He sat by the bed and, after a while, spoke again. "How are you, Miss Bishop?"

Molly was turned away from him, still wrapped in the covers, and replied hoarsley. "I could be better."

"Sick? Bart gathered medicines before launch."

"It's not just that," Molly said, sighing.

"Too cold in your cabin? I can bring wood."

"No, no." She turned around, sitting up slowly with a soft groan, and looked down at her hands. "I want to apologize."

Tom's head snapped to attention. "Apologize?"

"Yes. There was nothing you could have done for my uncle. And I don't blame you for his death. I want you to know that. I was just scared and confused. It was wrong of me to accuse you, and I'm sorry for it. So much that's happened is new and frightening to me. I feel that the world I've lived in for so long is now a stranger. All these people and things that existed in stories and out of sight ..." Molly looked away from Tom's uneasy expression.

"I don't mean to place you in harm's way."

"There's just so much I still don't know," Molly said forlornly.

"I know."

Molly covered her mouth as a sudden spurt of coughs erupted from her lungs.

"I knew you were ill. I'll get you some medicine." Tom moved to stand, but Molly grabbed his hand before he managed to get up, and gazed up into his eyes.

"Miss, I really ought to find you something." he protested softly.

"Thank you, Thomas." She took his hand in hers.

"I won't put you in danger again," he promised. "I'll take you to your father, and then you'll be out of harm's way. Please rest."

Molly slept lightly, her dreams strange and scrambled. Her coughing had finally settled as the medicine Tom returned with took its effect, but she shivered as the fire in her cabin slowly dimmed. She stirred, waking suddenly. She wasn't sure if it was night or day due to the dark clouds that covered the sky. She shivered as she went to place more logs on the fire in her cabin. She walked over to the desk and took a seat, her blanket still around her shoulders, and gazed out the window. Windows were comforting things, she realized—portals to an alternative world, when one's environment became stale and dark.

Defiantly Tom squinted into the fierce gusts outside. Atop the quarterdeck it was difficult to see, and the helmsman looked uncertain, becoming uneasy with the captain watching over his shoulder. It would be impossible to determine when and if the ship should ever stray off course because, as far as human eyes could see, the evening sky was nonexistent—covered by clouds—and the ocean, by nightfall, would bring pitch-black oblivion. Bart, standing nearby, cast the sextant aside and threw his arms in the air in surrender. "Impossible! Can't see a thing! Devilish weather!"

Tom was too deep in thought to hear or respond to him. A decision lingered heavily on his shoulders, and he'd have to come to some sort of conclusive judgment within two months, before the ship reached Barcelona. He was glad he'd decided to take a slow route to Spain because he'd need some time to think about Molly, himself, and their respective fates.

He moved suddenly, walking slowly toward the helm and putting a spyglass to his eye. A dark shape sat on the horizon. "Five degrees eastward." He folded the spyglass and set it down.

Twenty minutes passed and Tom returned from the main deck to the helm once more, scanning the dark sea for any unfamiliar forms. He focused on a single one. "Merchant," he said with great relief, as he collapsed the spyglass. "Remain in this course and then seven degrees southward once you can't see that ship anymore."

The helmsman nodded with a stern expression, the cold rain on his chin making his jaw quiver.

After the last light faded, the crew spread extra salt across the deck so it wouldn't freeze and retreated below to warm themselves by fires and eat dinner, which Bart had haphazardly prepared during his last routine duties of the day. Tom sat awake in deep thought in his cabin, staring into the blazing fire.

The star charts Molly had been looking over shifted slightly with a movement of the ship. Startled, she peered out her window once more. She could not see much at all—only the eerie blackness of the sea. Noticing the emptiness of the deck, Molly took the opportunity to wander outside, knowing she wouldn't have to worry about being in anyone's way. She wrapped her blanket tighter around her shoulders and walked out toward the helm. The icy slush on deck stung the soles of her feet. The air was bitter cold, but Molly felt the need to momentarily escape the confines of her cabin. She could almost hear the witty chatter among the crew at dinner, and she smiled softly, staring out into the ocean.

Tom, alone, picked up his silver sword, moving it from hand to hand, examining the deadly edges of the painstakingly crafted blade. As the blade turned, it reflected the firelight onto his face. On its surface he could see a reflection: a solemn, golden-eyed, sandy-furred wolf stared back, white teeth protruding from closed jaws. Tom stared back angrily. The wolf snarled silently, baring its white fangs. As Tom turned the blade, its face vanished.

The blade Thomas had ordered forged by the smith, Fenn, was unique. I had never seen one like it. Tom told me he had known he would need it upon facing his brother, Harlan, and he knew this only because of a dream he'd had sometime before he'd found Molly Bishop in the Caribbean. In that dream he held a silver sword—crafted in the style of French cavalry sabers of the day—that held in its hilt a bloodstone.

Bloodstones are gems that have always been connected to vitality and immortality. Bloodstones may lend great strength to a person who carries one without coming into direct contact with it, but they can also sap the life from a man in mere moments, should their alluring surface so much as brush the skin. They are discreet, immensely dense sources of life- force; they tug at vitality much like a massive body generates gravity. Things coming too close experience a stronger tug, while things keeping just enough distance can pull back. In this way, life can actually be taken from a bloodstone for the owner's benefit.

Not as popular as holy magic (light-producing spells), bloodstones are often used as defence against vampires. The bloodstone has a particularly deadly thirst for the near-limitless life force that exists in anecrotic tissue. The rate at which it drinks the life of a vampire is enough to turn one of them to ash in the blink of an eye.

Thomas took to calling the weapon "Brother". The blade was also special because it held powers beyond what was lent to it by the bloodstone. Brother was what magesmiths and sorcerers call a "soul well."

A soul well is any inanimate artifact that has the capacity to steal any number of lives from any number of living beings and house them within the artifact for the user's purposes. Needless to say, such artifacts are rare. Soul wells are historically most sought after by necromancers for the purpose of implanting stolen lives into the bodies of the dead, whom they use as personal slaves or guardians. It has been discovered that a soul well also strips any and all curses from its target as well, because curses affix themselves to a life, not a body.

The reader will recall that, according to folklore, those who are bitten and infected with the werewolf curse must kill their infectors in order to remove the curse from their body. Folklore is correct, yet it spares us the most important details. The infected must have a soul well in his possession upon killing the infector. Because any two lives are very different but curses are not, a soul well will almost always sap a werewolf curse from both a slain werewolf and his or her killer. At the same time it drains the life force from the slain. It is important to keep in mind that curses are not the same as sicknesses. The werewolf curse, for example, is passed like a sickness, but is not one. A curse can be stripped of a body with a soul well, nullifying the effects of a curse, but the effects themselves cannot be stripped in this way. They will disappear in time, yes, but recovery is needed.

A carrier of the werewolf curse cannot kill just any other carrier and hope to be cured. Since a werewolf's curse is most similar to their infector's, one hoping to relieve themself of the curse must find the lupomorph who infected them.

It is perhaps relevant to note that the vampire curse cannot be removed by any known means. If it is taken from the body, the body experiences instant and fatal atrophy. This is one crucial difference between the curses because while both vampires and werewolves' children are born with their parents' curses, a werewolf may remove the curse, while a vampire's condition is permanent.

Thomas was wise to heed his vision and craft Brother as a weapon and a soul well. The more intimate a relationship a soul well and a victim share, the more effective the process, and the more likely any curses will be completely absorbed. Still, a soul well need not be created with a weapon. It may be as simple as an old shoe, a piece of magic cloth, or even something as small as a ring.

Geoffrey Mylus
April 28, 1833

II
Lucia

Nine weeks, and the worst of the spring storms were long behind and in the North Atlantic, but they had slowed the ship's progress considerably. As the *Scotch Bonnet* approached the Mediterranean at the Strait of Gibraltar, Tom once more stood authoritatively behind the helm of a ship full of outlaws, transformed back into the maritime miscreant. Once the Strait was within sight, the ship was in unfamiliar seas.

"Quartermaster on deck, man your posts," the helmsman warned the crew.

"Resume your duties," Bart ordered the men, wandering over to Thomas, who gazed out over the sea. "Captain, we're now in Spanish waters. I'm not familiar with them. Should I alert the watch to be wary of anything?"

"Spanish galleys and any peculiar English ships—man-o'-war, to be specific," Tom replied. "I'd rather not become acquainted with a man I've been told now patrols these seas. Captain Roger William Locke."

Bart's brow furrowed. "Locke? I'll tell the watch—"

Tom cut him off. "Don't alarm anyone. They'll know very well whether or not such a ship should be avoided. I expect Captain Locke will be sailing quite an impressive ship—one of the Royal Navy's trophies, no doubt. Monsters, those ships are—easy to spot from a long way off. We should be able to make a fairly quick excursion into Barcelona and be on our way to familiar seas once again."

"Yes, Cap'n."

Thomas handed Bart the spyglass. "I'll be in my cabin."

"Yes, Cap'n."

Tom made his way to the main deck. Molly, coming up on deck from the galley, watched as he lurked about, marinating his brain in private thoughts. She felt compelled to follow him about, but something held her back. Tom opened the door to his cabin and, in no hurry, entered and shut the door. Molly sighed, unable to comprehend what stopped her. She couldn't be sure if it was the nature of things at that moment, her uncertainty, or her fear. Above all, Thomas wasn't as approachable when he wore his tricorn hat. To Molly, it was a standout feature that signaled her that the wolf, not the man, was in charge. She headed back to the galley, deciding to save

Bart the trouble of preparing dinner that night. She needed to keep herself occupied.

Later that afternoon shouts could be heard above deck. Tom's voice rang out above all the rest, issuing quick orders. Molly, just finishing her dinner preparations, snapped to attention and turned to the galley stairs, startled by the sudden commotion. Twenty or so crewmen cascaded down the deck stairs and further below onto the gun deck. Powder barrels were rolled to the deck below, cannons were heaved into place, and the gun bay portholes unlatched and opened wide. There were more shouts, most of them Tom's. Quick responses called back in the distance, in loud Spanish. Molly's eyes widened and she ran upstairs, swinging around the corner in haste.

"You will let us pass!" Tom was yelling angrily. A hostile reply came from the adjacent ship, less than seventy yards away. "My ship is carrying only scarce amounts of sugar and some arms!" shouted Tom. More hostile remarks followed. Molly gazed out over the water at the opposing ship and anxiously clutched her blouse.

Thomas called out again. "I am a supply ship for English war vessels! You do not wish to draw that kind of attention to yourselves!" The adjacent ship's deck was lined with Spanish and Moroccan pirates. It was now fifty yards away. The ship's captain began negotiating a nonaggressive "trade."

Bart translated for the crew. "He will board the ship and receive two hundred pounds of sugar in return for no casualties."

"Is that so? All right, invite him aboard." Tom remarked, trying to hide a smirk.

Bart gazed at Tom questionably. "Captain?"

"Tell him."

Bart relayed the message. The gap between the ships closed slowly. The Spaniards smiled with dark delight. Molly, concerned, moved her gaze back and forth from Thomas to the Spanish ship.

"Captain?" Bart said, fidgeting and tugging at his vest.

"Not yet," Tom replied, folding his arms.

The Spanish captain stood high up on the railing of the port side of the main deck of his ship, prepared to board Tom's. His men twirled boarding hooks and axes. Molly sucked in her breath. Thomas whispered something to a crewmate, who immediately dashed below deck, pushing past Molly. The Spanish Captain noticed, and his crew broke into a panic.

Thomas burst into crazed laughter as thirty cannons erupted and beat the Spanish ship's port side hull into mulch. The sudden recoil of the broadside assault startled Molly, inducing a scream as she dropped low to the deck, covering her ears. The Spanish crew, most of whom were thrown skyward, rained down onto the decks of both ships and littered the sea. The Spanish captain got to his feet again after having involuntarily flown the distance between the vessels and landed at Tom's feet. The remaining fifteen or so Spaniards boarded the ship, blades whirling. Tom's crew—double the Spaniard's in number—retaliated instantly. Molly ducked quickly onto the galley stairs. Unarmed, and having left her pistols in her cabin, she could do nothing but listen to the battle above.

The cannons sounded again, delivering a death blow to the Spanish ship. The noise died down gradually as the crew finished off the last of the assailants, and the Spanish vessel began sinking.

"Take whatever you like and return quickly!" Tom ordered the men. "Clear the deck, and prepare to raise sail on my mark!

The deck hatch above Molly groaned loudly as it was thrown open. Captured cargo was being lugged through the hatch, down into the store rooms.

"All crew on deck! Tally up any missing or dead!" Tom shouted. Molly slowly made her way upstairs, following the crew's lead.

"All accounted for, Cap'n!" Bart called, counting the heads on deck.

"And the lady?"

Scanning the scene, Bart could not immediately spot Molly. Smoke from the Spanish ship drifted through the air. Molly lingered timidly among the crew, mostly hidden from view.

"Present, Cap'n," Bart reported, seeing her and pointing.

Tom approached her quickly. "Are you all right?" he asked, looking Molly over for injury.

Molly offered him a weak but reassuring smile.

"Don't be afraid. There was never any real danger," he whispered.

"Of course not." A small smile crossed her lips.

Tom smiled back. "You may stay in your cabin for now if you like. Your duties will be taken care of." He turned, facing the crew. "If all are accounted for, raise sail and resume our bearing! Any injured, report below deck! Plenty to eat tonight!"

After a loud victory cheer, the crew dispersed.

"Got more pork than I can cook, Cap'n. And they were carryin' some heavy coins," Bart said, laughing, as he reported the new inventory taken from the Spanish.

"Any arms?" asked Tom, nodding as Bart listed the prizes.

"Seventeen pistols, only one good blade, Cap'n."

"Keep them on hand anyway."

"Yes, Cap'n." With that, Bart descended to the galley.

Crossing the deck, Thomas discovered the Spanish captain alive and clinging to a taut line. He was mumbling angrily and aiming a loaded pistol at Tom. The Spaniard, with one eye shut, was bleeding heavily, but his finger had the strength to pull a trigger. His one open eye glared a hole in Tom. His last wish: to put a shot in the body of the man who had ruined his ship and killed his crew. A stream of blood rolled down the Spaniard's forehead and fell into the open eye, dyeing the cornea a pale pink and forcing him to blink, but the pistol never wavered.

Thunder shattered the calm on the main deck. Molly stood at the door of her cabin, her pistol still smoking. The Spanish Captain looked at the place where his right hand had been. Tom flinched, clutching at the pain in his hip. Molly's eyes widened as she dropped her pistol in shock, rushing toward Tom. She hadn't been quite fast enough.

The Spanish captain chuckled, his emptied pistol lying on the deck covered in his blood, smoke rising from the barrel like a dark soul from a spent body. He sneered victoriously despite his fatal, throbbing stump. Trying to help Tom, Molly fought the tears stinging her eyes. She cried out across the deck and hurried to him.

"Oh, thank goodness!" she panted, "It's not silver." Delicately treating the spot with a scrap torn from her sleeve, she hugged him.

Tom stepped forward, approaching the laughing Spaniard. Molly gently tugged his arm. "Thomas, please … you're alright … he's as good as dead already." She hesitated to coax him further when she noticed the yellow flooding his irises. She released her grip.

Thomas stopped to stand before the Spaniard, who grew silent. Suddenly the man yelled furiously and drew a sword with his left hand. Tom continued forward, the

Spaniard backing away, swinging the sword in a vicious panic. The crew stopped to watch what was happening. They knew what to expect. Everything and everyone grew silent. The Spanish captain screamed again and thrust the blade forward, cleanly through Tom's torso.

Molly put her hands to her mouth. Some of the crew grew uneasy at the sound of her terrified whimpers. Tears streamed down her face.

Tom continued forward a few steps. The Spaniard unsheathed another, smaller blade, burying it in Tom's shoulder. Tom caught the knife hand, cracking the man's wrist and finger bones in his grip. Lifting the Spaniard off his feet like a doll, eyes flashing, Tom hurled the captain across the entire length of the deck. The battered man crashed violently into the opposite railing. He tried to stand, fell immediately, and stood again. Tom was in front of him again by the time he recovered, and, swinging one arm into the Spaniard, Tom lifted him off his feet again, sending him spinning into the deck. The man's bouncing body stained the planking red. He stood one last time, dizzily, and stumbled backward over the railing. A splash punctuated his fall.

Thomas spoke calmly. "Helmsman, what is your bearing?" Receiving no reply, he continued, "Calculate your bearing and report to me. Full speed, all sails! Barcelona!" Internally, Tom tried not to panic, or look at the blood that had drained from his stab wounds. *It's getting out! Have to get it back in! Need to make it stop!*

Fumbling, the crew returned hastily to work, not wishing to upset the man who just survived two deadly strikes to the body in addition to a bullet. Tom swiftly removed the blades from his body, casting them aside and wincing. With a painful intake of breath he limped toward his cabin as his flesh began to stitch itself. Molly again rushed to his side. Thomas clung to her arm for support. "I need only something for the pain. Please bring it. The amber bottle in the cargo deck next to the other medicines …"

Molly led him to his bed in the cabin before heading out again. She returned shortly with the amber bottle and a few rags. "H-here," she stammered, standing aside and waiting to see what he was going to do about his injuries.

Taking the bottle, Tom placed a kettle of fresh water over the fire in his cabin. "Just needs to boil. It tastes awful, but the effect is lasting."

Molly fumbled with a rag, dropping it to the ground. She looked at him and then quickly away, shuddering at his wounds.

"Here, I'll take it," Tom offered, taking the rag.

"A-are you sure?" Molly stuttered.

Tom nodded, wrapping the wounds. "I'm sorry. I didn't mean to frighten you."

"Well you did! Scared the life out of me!" She snapped at him, trying to quell angry tears. "I was so worried. How many times should you have died, Thomas?"

"I don't keep count." Tom replied with nonchalance, "And I suppose I owe Harlan."

"What do you mean?"

"Harlan...He's saved my life a *hundred* times, if you want to think of it that way." Tom continued. "Today was no exception. And that's why I'll find him and make him stop." He wrapped the bandages angrily. "That's what I'm doing out here. That's my only real purpose in carrying on this wretched existence."

Molly gazed down at the floor. She pitied him.

"I'll wait for my medicine to boil, and after dinner when the pain subsides, you can return to my cabin. Come then and inquire of me everything you will. I'll tell you no lies,"

Tom offered. "This could have been much worse." He touched his bullet scar. "Who taught you to shoot?"

"An old friend," she replied, shaking her head dismissively. "If I had just acted sooner this never would have happened at all."

"Nonsense." Tom argued.

"I'll be back when your medicine is through and we'll talk more," she said softly, turning to leave.

"All right," Tom said as he continued to bandage his wounds.

As she exited, the tears began to flow freely from Molly's eyes. The sight of Thomas, injured and in pain again, did nothing to improve her feelings. So what if he'd be like new tomorrow? She felt like a bad luck charm to Thomas, to Samuel, to all those she cared for.

Molly shoved her pistols back into their hiding spot and tossed a few logs on the fire before going to the galley for dinner. Bart had put food for her in a cloth, and she took it gratefully before heading back to her cabin. She forced herself to eat a little but finally put the remnants away and left it. She could wait no longer. Sneaking to Tom's room, she opened the door stealthily, trying not to disturb him. When she saw him sleeping peacefully she felt better. His wounds had already been healed. It was like magic.

"How was dinner?" Tom asked, yawning and propping himself up on his elbows, "I was told we gathered a few rare delicacies from our Spanish friends. Chocolate, perhaps? Now *that* would be good fortune. Doesn't happen often though, I'm afraid."

Molly grinned. "No chocolate, but *plenty* to drink, I assure you."

"Well that's good." Tom got up, moved about, and placed various papers into desk drawers, slid a sheathed sword quickly underneath the bed and took a seat near his stove.

"What need do you have for that?" she asked, looking under the bed at the silver saber.

Thomas smirked. "What would *any* self-respecting *pirate* need one for?" He immediately tried to change the subject. "You'll be pleased to know a few of the men found a unique item on the Spanish ship just before it sank. I had them take it below deck so I could give it to you later. It was odd to find one on a ship, but nonetheless I believe it will make your life onboard a bit more civilized. I hope you like it."

"What is it exactly?" Molly asked curiously.

"Would you like to see?"

"Of course."

Tom stood. "Follow me, then."

Tom led Molly to a large store room below the galley. "This is just for storing trinkets we find." The lantern in his hand cast its light on piles of chests, loose heaps of coins, Spanish armor, jeweled weaponry, African royal headdresses and various silver and gold forks, knives, and daggers—things salvaged from the Spanish pirates' ship.

Molly gazed around in awe. "Quite a collection, Captain."

"I'm only saddened that I've had to begin again, ever since the *Nymphe Colère*. Here we are." Thomas held the lantern above the large object in front of him.

The light revealed a large ivory bath tub with solid gold metalwork around the feet and rim of the basin. A royal crest was set in gold in the outside of the basin. Molly gasped, a broad grin growing on her face.

"From what I've concluded, it was fit for royalty, so I supposed you wouldn't have any objections to using it," Tom joked.

"The *Scotch Bonnet* just became a lady of class," sang Molly. "I'm taking this to my cabin," she insisted. "I will not have those filthy ruffians peeping at me in it down here or anywhere else!" She crossed her arms and dared him to object.

Thomas sneezed through the dust. "I have no objections. It's a bloody *heavy* thing, though. I'll have it moved into your cabin by tomorrow morning."

"It can't be done by later this evening?" she complained with a pout.

"Well, that doesn't give me much time to cut a hole in my cabin wall…"

Molly gasped. Her mouth fell open in a large "o", and then she laughed and smacked him good.

"Is Harlan like you?" It was Molly's first question when they retired once more to Tom's cabin.

"We have some physical similarities, yes. The most striking being a mark we both carry," Tom explained, unbuttoning his shirt and tossing his gun belt on the bed.

Laying the shirt aside he turned his back to the firelight. On his right shoulder blade Molly saw a scar comprised of three claw marks; in the center was a black, tattoo-like symbol, which looked like a natural birthmark, as much a part of the skin as the scar. The mark resembled a moon in its crescent stage. It had been where Tom was first bitten. Molly was compelled to reach out, tracing the mark softly with her fingers.

"Strange … and beautiful in a dark and terrible way. You both have this?"

"I have it on my back; he, on his left forearm. I could as easily have had one on my neck. Thankfully, Harlan missed."

"Why would Harlan do that?" Molly shook her head in confusion.

"Harlan is more like them than I am. The curse took hold of him instantly. His adoptive family raised and nurtured that monster. I, inversely, raised a monster within myself. Harlan became his own demon. I and mine are still at least separate entities. Harlan gave in to it. If I ever wish to be free of the curse, I need Harlan. To find Harlan, I needed a ring. To use the ring, I needed to be able to read the map within, but I can't. Harlan can't either. If he could, he'd have found me by now."

Molly hesitated before speaking. "I don't have any answers, but since *I can* see the map I'll do whatever I can to interpret it for you. I have only to study it more." She paused. "How will finding Harlan help lift the curse?" When Tom didn't respond, Molly became concerned. "Captain?"

Avoiding her initial question, Tom continued, "I'm hoping I'll find some answers concerning the rings in Barcelona. I need to learn why I can't read the map. We should be arriving tomorrow or the next day." His eyes became distant.

Molly looked away, irked by his avoidance, but decided not to press the matter. Trying to lighten the dark mood, she placed her hand in his, squeezing it gently and reassuringly. Tom looked at her in response, searching for some reason or motive in her concerned eyes. *Why does she care so much for me,* he wondered.

"Everything will fall into place," Molly said, trying to settle him.

Thomas smiled suddenly and didn't know how she'd soothed him so easily.

"It's good to see you smile," she said. "You don't seem to do it very often. Not like that." Her eyes softened. "Thank you for your honesty."

Still smiling, Tom turned away to walk to the bed long enough to let one tear escape. The silver sword flashed back into his mind. The crescent scar seemed to grow hot. He remembered the night Harlan and his mother were taken, and the day the Black Coats came for his father. Then he remembered the night Molly came aboard the *Nymphe Colère*, the ship house burning and the gunshot, London and Samuel Bishop. "You'll like it in Barcelona," he said, and that was all.

When a person is bitten or scratched by a werewolf, enough to draw blood, a topical symbolic mark is formed over the area where the damage was done. Particular bacteria will produce the crescent moon-shaped scar.

I believe Thomas was also correct about one thing: Harlan transformed immediately because, by chance, his infection occurred under a full moon, and, being a younger, more easily corruptible child, the infection was met with no resistance. The curse did not require his body to wait until the next lunar cycle.

My own study is not yet conclusive, but some of my fellow scholars believe that werewolves who are first infected under a full moon must still wait until at least the next lunar cycle before they can successfully infect a person with the curse. Unlike the anecrosis that creates a vampire, lupomorphosis is a much more gradual in its maturation, and often the process of conversion to a werewolf is marked with terrible fevers, aching bones and episodes of insatiable hunger.

Geoffrey Mylus
April 29, 1833

అుఈ

The waves in the port of Barcelona rolled easily in the early morning light. Its visiting ships sat silently, fixed in place. The trip from Gibraltar had taken a few more days than expected, making their arrival the first week of July.

"Drop anchor!" There was a quick rattling of chain links, a large splash and spray of salt water. "Secure lines! Drop a gangway!" The men busily moved about the deck of Tom's ship. "All crew ashore. The watch will stay."

Molly sat quietly on her bed, a packed case by her side. She fiddled with her ring distractedly. This was it. After so many years, she would come face to face with her father. She couldn't tell if she was scared or if the anxiety was causing her to shake.

Tom dressed quickly in his cabin, tightening his boots, selecting a light shirt appropriate for the dry, warm weather, retrieving a gun belt, two pistols and his preferred knives, and searching in vain for his tricorn hat.

Molly took a deep breath and stood. She grabbed a blue ribbon off the desk in her cabin and tied up her hair neatly, then picked up her trunk and her magic books and headed toward her cabin door. She paused to look back at the dresser. She thought for a moment before setting her small trunk on the bed and grabbing her pistols from the drawer, packing them with her few sets of clothing before finally heading out on deck.

Tom emerged from his cabin—hat and all—and scanned the deck. "Barcelona! Ha!"

Molly quietly stood outside her cabin, staring out at the coast of Barcelona and wringing her hands. She spotted the captain and managed a small smile for him.

"Enjoy the solid ground, gentlemen!" Tom called out. Most of the men departed down the gangway and into Barcelona. The watchmen ventured down to the galley and lower quarters to rest. Tom followed the shore-bound men down the gangway. "Will you be coming, Miss Bishop?"

"Oh. Yes!" Molly shook off her nerves, picking up her blue skirt and following Tom quickly down the ramp.

Barcelona's streets were far busier and more crowded than London's in the early morning. Dust blew around every corner and forced Molly to rub her eyes and clear them of grit. Merchants bargained and traded with great enthusiasm and showmanship. Molly browsed a bit as Tom strode ahead, unconcerned about his surroundings. The crowd was thick, and he darted around and between the strangers with ease. Molly just barely managed to keep up with him.

Thomas shouted over his shoulder to her. "We have quite a way to go, Miss, don't get lost!" He extended a hand backward for her to hold.

"Where are we going exactly?" Molly asked him, grabbing his hand.

"Home!" he shouted over the commotion. Quickly pulling her forward, Tom skirted around a large cart of oranges. "Pardon!" Tom apologized and continued on quickly. They escaped the crowd and reached a small cluster of large villas. The roofs were red clay shingle, the inner courtyards comprised of white stone block encircled by iron gates.

"This one," Tom stated plainly, pointing at one of the houses to his right, taking a ring of keys from his belt and unlocking the gate. "This way," he said, stepping up to the large front door and knocking. A housemaid answered the door and looked them over.

"Ah! *Señor* Garcia!" She motioned for them to enter. Tom smiled widely, thanking her and tugging Molly along.

The house was capacious. It was easy to see all the way through to the inner courtyard and the large garden and pools. Tom hurried with Molly into the main house and toward a large staircase. At the top he invited her to settle into a bedroom of her choosing. The housemaid called to Tom again, and he excused himself to go downstairs. Molly entered the nearest bedroom and stood awkwardly for a moment before setting her trunk and books on the bed and sitting down next to them. The atmosphere was strangely familiar to her, but she wasn't sure why. After a moment she stood and headed back to the stairs.

Tom had just reached the top again. "The kitchen is preparing a meal. It will be ready very soon." The smell from the kitchen reinforced this news. "Rest and enjoy the day. Tomorrow we will resume business as usual. I will be in the room at the end of the downstairs hallway." He grinned, kissing her hand before descending the stairs.

Molly stood in place for a moment, blushing, then with the tips of her fingers touched the spot he had kissed. When Tom was out of sight she went downstairs. Despite the wonderful smell radiating from the kitchen, she decided to explore the back garden and wandered outside. The sky was overwhelmingly bright compared to London's. The nearby sea reflected a great deal of warm light through the numerous apertures of the multistory villa. The garden, beautiful and green, and patio linked the four main halls of the large home. She strolled quietly across the patio, discovering a large brass fountain. Looking down into the water, she ran the tips of her fingers over the surface. Her ring caught the bright sun. As before, the constellations appeared, dotting the water in a dazzling display.

A housemaid appeared in the window of the kitchen and called to Molly. "*Señorita! Tienes hambre?*" Tom's footsteps thudded down the hall and into the dining room.

It took Molly only a moment to register what exactly the maid had said. "Oh … yes!" she replied enthusiastically, "Yo *prefiero una cerveza, pero comida es buena también!*"

The maid laughed and beckoned her inside to the dining room. Standing up and leaving the fountain, Molly walked back inside the house, watching the constellations disappear from sight. Tom was well into his second plate of *paella*. He showed no sign of slowing when Molly arrived in the dining room.

Molly barely managed to hold back a chuckle as she sat across from him and prepared a plate. "You seem in such a hurry today."

The maids struggled to keep up with his pace. "*Gracias! Gracias!* No hurry, but more than two months of pork and potatoes is enough for me. Taste it." He pointed to her plate. "You'll understand."

Smiling at his enthusiasm, Molly took a bite, nodding her approval. "*Riquísima.*"

The maids grew tired quickly. "*Él come como un cerdo, no?*"

Tom ignored the comment that he ate like a pig. He made sure his gratitude was known.

"*De nada, Señor Garcia,*" one of the maids replied with a wary huff, "*Pero por favor, come más despacio!*"

Molly shook her head in amusement. A few glasses of wine and a quarter of what Tom had shoveled into his mouth was more than enough to satiate her.

"Well, I think now would be a good time to rest. We should have at least four hours until our transportation arrives," Thomas commented, finally finished with his meal. "Oh ... I'm sorry, I changed our plans slightly. We'll be staying a bit longer. It will soon be July thirteenth!"

Molly raised her eyebrows. "July thirteenth?" she shrugged and smiled at him. The date meant nothing to her.

"*El encierro?* In Pamplona? You have never heard of the festival, I see. The Running of the Bulls, Miss Bishop."

"Sounds like great fun or great danger."

"It's a spot of both. I learned your father will not be in town until the fifteenth. We'll be arriving back on the sixteenth. Does that suit you?"

"Of course," she said, nodding.

Cradling his full belly like a pregnant mother, Tom stood suddenly and tossed his hands in the air. "*Excelente!* Well, Miss, rest as long as you see fit, and we will depart this evening. You may leave any unnecessary items here with my maids. Your things will be safe. Oh, and have them purchase for you a suitable dress for the festival, yes? White and red would look beautiful on you." He pondered that image for a moment. "Yes, white and red. Let them know."

"I will do just that." *Thomas would never admit to it*, she thought, *but he enjoys seeing me in fine clothes.*

"Very good. I'll leave you the remainder of the afternoon. I must make preparations." Thomas exited to the kitchen. "Sofia!"

After asking Sofia to get the dress the captain requested, Molly ascended the stairs to her bedroom and lay down on her bed, contemplating the night to come. She found comfort in the joy and ease of the day, happy that things had taken a turn for the better.

After finishing off one more plate of rice from the kitchen, Tom spent the afternoon sleeping. He lay, completely gorged, on his bed in full dress, pistols and all. The housemaids went about their cleaning, but otherwise the house was quiet for the duration of the dry, lazy afternoon. A knock on the door woke Tom about an hour before dusk, and he climbed the stairs to the higher bedrooms in search of Molly.

"Miss Bishop?" He called, waiting by the railing.

She soon appeared at the door. "Sorry, I fell asleep."

"Understandable. Dinner has that effect on the residents of this household. You may give your thanks to the kitchen." Tom grinned at her smartly.

"It does it's job well."

"That it does." "

"One of the maids brought my festival dress in while I was sleeping. I put it in my bag in place of another one."

"Well then, shall we?" he asked, offering his hand. Molly took the whole arm, wrapping 'round him like ivy.

Outside a covered carriage sat waiting for them. The driver, waking from a short nap, stirred the horses with a gentle toss of the reins. The housemaids bade the two a temporary farewell. "*Adiós!*"

Tom waved to them and helped Molly into the coach.

"Ha!" exclaimed the driver with a sharp snap of the reins.

"Pamplona is northwest of here. We'll be stopping only a few nights and will be in the city just in time for the festivities."

Molly nodded, flattening out her dress with her spread fingers.

Thomas took one of her hands and threw his up in a cheer.

Thomas Crowe created several lives and identities for himself, and perhaps it was because he did that he was not captured or discovered as easily as the English authorities would have liked. In London, he was the upright businessman and gentleman, Charles Walsh; in Barcelona, he was the secretive lady-charmer, Benito Garcia. As far as I know, he may have had a hundred other identities and homes scattered across Europe, but those in London and Barcelona were the ones he most enjoyed. I knew many other werewolves who chose a life of secrecy in order to avoid conflict with the authorities during times of lupomorph persecution. In this sense, Tom was nothing out of the ordinary.

In Spain at the time, Thomas would not have had to try to blend in as much as in England. The Spanish Catholic Church was much more concerned about the sinful abuse of magic. The Church also despised the Spanish cults much more than the clans, so a werewolf like Thomas need not have kept his head down too often. He wasn't a prime concern of the government's or God's wrath. Ironically, the largest magic trade in Europe at the time was in Spain. Italy was second. Molly Bishop's father, a Spanish gentleman, had attempted to keep his *daughter far from Spain. He knew a life lived in and around the magic business was no environment in which to grow up. He dealt with the lowest and evilest men at times, and every time war reared its head in Europe, the shadowy customers came pouring into his shop, looking to procure the most potent and deadly varieties of magical artifacts. Even a few priests came to him looking for ways to protect their churches. They had given in and were ready to fight fire with fire, and sometimes in the most literal sense.*

Spain has long been home to a number of clans and cults. The origins of its werewolf population are uncertain, but I believe lupomorphs migrated from France into northern Spain; they have never been seen in the south of Spain. There are only a handful of Spanish clans, including the Luna Nueva Clan—a rather quiet bunch— and Los Podencos de Seville. The latter clan is a rather bitter lot. They are often thought of as the Spanish equivalent of the British Grey-Reivers—a temperamental clan that has no objections to being a nuisance to civilization if they feel justified.

Spanish cults are more numerous and varied. Historically, they've maintained a very cold relationship with the Spanish churches. The Catholic Church considers *La Familia*—a fierce and extensive cult—to be its foremost antagonist. *Virgenes de Muerte*, an all-female cult, is looked upon with scorn, but compared to *La Familia*, they are merely "unholy miscreants." The *Virgenes* did sometimes associate with *La Familia*, but its members often preferred a safe and silent existence to a public, unstable one. They, like only a few cults and even fewer clans before them, tried to appease mortal society by integrating themselves into it. It was rumored that one of the young *Virgenes*, a girl of fifteen years, was, at one time, a member of a local choir in Valencia, but when she was discovered she was excommunicated and banished from the church.

Unknown to Thomas, an associate of the Black Coats had an eye set on Molly Bishop, and though Spain was not at that time Black Coat territory, it was not far enough away to evade the interests of the Black Coats if they wanted someone badly enough.

Geoffrey Mylus,

April 30, 1833

᭞᭞᭞

After three days and three nights of paced travel they were within sight of Pamplona. The festivities had already begun, and the roaring of the festival-goers could periodically be heard from the carriage—a jubilant, collective song of celebration. The city dwellings were stacked high upon one another, the streets quite narrow and crowded. Large red, white, and yellow ribbons adorned the market places, and flags waved in the midday wind. Men and women lined the streets with dresses and hats matching the colored flags and ribbons. The blast of instruments filled what space was left in the air underneath all the cheering and bellowing. Tom and Molly's coach stopped before an inn, and the driver helped Tom carry his and Molly's belongings indoors to a room.

"Shall I get ready?" Molly asked Tom once they arrived in their room.

"I'll be waiting outside for you," he replied with a smile.

Molly changed quickly, inserting a silk carnation into her hair that had come with the dress. She spun around, watching the dress flowing about her in a magnificent array of red and white. The skirt was in tiers, white over red over white over red. White, puffy sleeves left her shoulders bare, and a tight red bodice showed off her tiny waist. Molly looked like a sweet treat, perhaps a little strawberry and cream torte. Sofia had made an excellent choice. Molly quickly headed outside to meet the captain, taking one final look at herself in a mirror before doing so.

Tom took Molly's hand, and they ventured out into the streets. Throughout the city there were large group dances, plenty of food, and seemingly more and more decorations as they walked. Overhead were small, independent celebrations on balconies of the multiple-story homes and inns.

Turning her head this way and that, Molly gazed in wonder. "This is incredible. I've never seen such a celebration."

"I've been only once or twice before, and never has it been so large and noisy," said Tom. The crowd began to shift, and most of the people moved into doorways and up into the higher balconies of the buildings. "Follow me, quickly," Tom instructed, leading Molly into a nearby building and following a group of people to a second-floor balcony. "They should be beginning soon." He kept an eye on the streets below.

Following Tom's gaze, Molly was unsure of what to expect. A small tremor in the ground reached the balcony, steadily growing to a rumble. Swiftly it escalated to a quake. A smile spread across Tom's face. The crowds began to shout and raise their glasses and hurl hats into the air. Tom shouted in unison with the crowd at the first sight of the rush of white shirts and red sashes in the street below.

"*Olé!*"

Dozens of young men sprinted quickly and swiftly past the doorways below, hopping over carts and tripping over themselves and others. The quaking grew intense, and the vibration rattled a glass of tequila off a table and onto the balcony floor. Just as the men in the streets rounded the corner, a stampeding mass of horns and hooves appeared around the other. Shaking their large heads irritably, the bulls overturned carts and straggling sprinters alike in an aggressive rampage. Upon seeing the animals, Molly jumped in surprise. The crowd shouted and rained ribbons and paper confetti down on the street below. Those brave enough to stand in the streets ducked into doorways and cheered from the sidelines. One unfortunate gentleman met one of the animals headfirst and landed upside down in some fruit baskets. While others were watching that event, Tom spied something else.

"Uh-oh." Tom muttered, hopping over the balcony and landing hard on the stone walk below. As he attempted to get to a cornered individual trying to ward off the beasts behind a stack of crates, another herd charged around the bend.

"Thomas!" Molly screeched. "Get back here!"

The trapped stranger squeezed himself up against the side of the building, making himself as small a target as possible. Tom leapt up quickly, running across the back of one bull and vaulting over another, landing in front of the man and spinning about to meet the next bull head on.

"Oh, why bother," Molly resigned, flipping her wrist and rolling her doll eyes.

A familiar gold tint flashed in Tom's eye just as he caught the pair of horns in his hands. The weight of the animal traveled through Tom's arms and down his legs, cracking the street beneath his heels. The bull's legs gave out, and its back arched skyward. Pivoting one foot and raising his arms in synchronization, Tom tossed the charging bull overhead and into the crates, smashing them and creating quite a mess. There was an instant, enormous "*Olé!*" from the bewildered crowd. The man behind Tom stared in disbelief and laughed nervously. Tom, of course, was absorbing the crowd's cheers, too busy to acknowledge the man's timid *gracias* before running away. A fuming Molly glared at Tom from the balcony.

"Is this your idea of peacocking?" she shouted at him from the balcony.

Tom reappeared on the balcony moments later, with a large glass of tequila in hand. "Exciting," he said, taking a drink.

Molly walked over to one of the tables, grabbing an untouched tequila before it, too fell and joined the other glass on the floor. She stared at it momentarily before raising it to her lips and taking a large gulp. "Oof! Bless me!" She stretched her neck and smacked her lips. "I don't know if I care for...whatever *this* is."

Tom watched her expression after downing the drink and stifled a snort. *What a woman!* he thought, laughing to himself. Molly's eyes narrowed. She grinned, but wouldn't look at him.

The last of the bulls were herded along manually to the large ring at the end of the enclosed course, and the bullfights began. In the distance, a large crowd cheered.

"Better hurry and get back out there. You haven't managed to get yourself killed yet," Molly said.

"Yes, and while I'm tending to that matter you may want to have yourself a few more tequilas. You're not entirely drunk out of your wits yet."

Molly growled and chased him from the room.

Leaping down the stairs three at a time, Tom whipped out a pistol and blew a hole in the inn roof. "*Olé!* Ha, Ha!"

Molly hastily downed the rest of her tequila and went in search of another one. The drink was powerful, and growing on her. She grabbed the first one she came across, which was in the hand of an unsuspecting stranger. Walking outside and standing by the door, she watched confetti continue to rain down from the buildings and onto the dusty streets. Tom was almost out of sight, walking briskly uphill back toward the inn, spinning the pistol around one finger. The heat of the day or the tequila, or both, worked sorcery on Molly's eyes. She grabbed hold of anything and anyone she had to in order to stay on her feet. Tom's figure danced back and forth and schmoozed with the crowd. His voice echoed in her head. "Coming, Miss? Miss? ... mizz ... mizz bizzup?"

Molly next woke to see Tom snoozing in a chair across from her in their inn bedroom. A new bottle of tequila had conveniently been placed on the table next to her bed, along with an empty glass, a small red ribbon tied around it, and the cork pinned to the table with a throwing knife. A scrap of paper under the cork read, "*Buenos noches!*"

Molly glanced at the inviting bottle of tequila and then to the window. It was almost dark, the sun just setting. She looked at the note and then at the captain, suddenly remembering her irritation toward him. Glancing at the dagger with a smirk, she debated whether or not to test if he really was as invincible as he seemed. She quickly decided against it and, instead, poured herself a glass without hesitation. The effects of the previous drinks had not yet vacated her brain or legs. Incredibly, she did not have a headache.

Tom, abusing his talents again, decided he'd catch her off guard, whispering a sly "Good evening" in her ear just as she contemplated reaching for the glass. Molly jumped, letting out a yelp. He picked up the bottle and filled the glass, offering it to her with a smile.

"Thank you," she said curtly, taking the glass from him and placing a hand on her thumping heart.

"Sofia is very good at selecting dresses, don't you agree?" He pointed at her dress. "Red and white. Just as beautiful as I expected."

Molly turned away, moving toward the window and looking out to the street. The scene was entirely different—dark, hushed and romantic.

Stepping halfway out onto the balcony, Tom opened the curtains and doors to allow some music and cool air to drift in. "Pamplona. My kind of people."

Molly looked down into the street where people danced in a blur of color to cheerful music, their shouts and laughter filling the air. Tom simply closed his eyes, still smiling, face to the breeze. Molly sipped her tequila one grimace at a time.

"The first time I came to Pamplona, my father brought me," said Tom.

Molly turned to Tom with interest.

"Five or so years after we lost Harlan and my mother. He told me he had promised my mother he would take her to see the bullfights one day. But only he and I were there. I remember he put one hand on my shoulder and pointed down into the ring at the matador swinging his cape and dodging the bull. He told me to take note of the matador and his courage. He told me somewhere in the crowd was a woman he had in mind. With every rush of the bull the man knew he risked never seeing that woman again, and she—watching from the crowd—knew he intended to leave that ring alive. For *her*. My father, after the accident, made a point of that every so often. 'When you find her, don't lose sight of the bull just yet,' he would say. 'You will be a man someday, and you will fight for two lives—yours and hers—but always ... *always* for hers, first.' His words never took hold of me, never made much sense, until much later in my life. I realized one day recently that I am now standing before the bull, fighting for two."

As she turned her head away from Tom, Molly realized her heart was playing her ribs like a piano. She opened her mouth, but no words came out, so she filled it with more tequila. She covered her mouth, choked on the last sip. Her head spun and she felt as if the world bounced with every beat of her heart.

Leaning against the rail and watching the festivities, Tom laughed. "One bull or ten thousand bulls ... let them come! Ha! After all, I have a thousand lives to give, don't I?"

Molly looked at his face, studied it. His words were sincere and sweet. In the breeze the silk carnation suddenly jumped from her hair, floating down into the crowd below. Her gaze followed it, her hair flying gently in the cool air.

"Oh, no! Like an angel cast out of Heaven..." Tom's eyes followed the bloom as it floated away, then shifted his weight and looked at Molly, still quietly lamenting her carnation. He silently questioned whether the tequila had a hold on him, or if her hair was really moving the way it appeared—light and quick, shining in the scarce light of dusk like thick ribbons of liquid cocoa. The dress moved in the same fashion, strawberry red and creamy white tiers of soft cotton darting away from her feet and snapping back again. Tom realized she was dancing.

As Molly floated about, the music slowed. She held out her delicate arms and wiggled her hips and tossed her hair.

Mesmerized, Tom traced her contours with his eyes and tried to imagine the smooth legs beneath her skirt. Thick, toned and glossy, they peeked at him every now and then when she twirled and her dress flew up from the floor. Her light blouse inflated with the rush of air she created, complimenting the softness and curvature of her shoulders and chest. She closed her eyes. Tom reached out and caught one of her little hands in his.

Molly stopped abruptly at his touch, sleepily making eyes and touching his chest. Molly's hand tightened around his, and she moved close, resting her face in his neck. Gently she directed his other hand to her waist. Tom followed her lead as she began to dance again.

"Your father ... he was a good man, wasn't he?" she asked quietly.

"A nobler man than I am fated to be. He loved his wife and both his sons. And he died, as far as I know, without a breath of regret."

"And you believe you're not capable of being like him?" She looked up at him. "Mr. Crowe, you have saved my life on more than one occasion. I was a stranger. You could've left me in Bermuda, or London, but instead you heard the wishes of a young, lost soul and made a hobby of trying to grant them. "If that does not make you noble, I do not know what does."

"I wish I could've done so with more grace, and the only danger I shield you from is that which I also lead you toward. I wish I didn't have to protect you from myself.

But I will do so yet. You are the very thing that keeps my monster in check or makes heroic use of it, Miss Bishop. For that I am grateful."

"How can you…how can you give…*hic*! Give me so much credit? All I'm capable of is cooking and, per…perhaps reading star charts. Why do you trouble yourself with me?" She slurred and pouted and clutched at his open shirt dreamily and wantonly.

"Because I've found a reason to face the bull besides saving my own life." Tom fidgeted anxiously as her fingertips crept over his collar like thieving rabbits into a vegetable patch. "Until recently I've been chasing my brother into Hell, with my enemies biting at my heels all the way. You appeared like a dove through a hail of brimstone and turned my gaze toward a ray of sun."

Molly pinched her bottom lip in her teeth.

"I … I apologize, I…" Tom couldn't finish his thought. Stuttering and fidgeting, he frantically ran a hand through his hair.

Molly felt something rise within her—a new feeling, something she couldn't explain. The tequila weakened her. Without a second thought, she brought a hand up to touch his face.

Tom flinched. He wanted to touch her but didn't know just how. Her eyes softened, getting lost in his features. Thomas breathed slowly and heavily. The touch of her hand drained all the strength from his neck and shoulders.

Tom's bravery returned, and he raised both hands to cup and beckon her face closer. Molly closed her eyes. Her red lips brushed his. Following her heart's feverish decree, Molly finished the path, gently pressing her lips against his. Tom allowed his hands to find and rest on her neck. His arms felt as heavy as waterlogged Persian rugs and his heart filled with goose down.

"Do you want to know something?" she whispered.

"Hm?"

"It's you. The whole time I thought I was looking for a purpose. It's been you. I want to stay with you, Thomas."

"As long as fate deems me fit to deserve you," he replied. An odd assortment of feelings boxed Tom's thoughts around. Perhaps...no, this feeling was entirely the tequila welling up in his brain. The walls and balcony turned around him like satellite, while Molly, his little bright star, remained in place. The room felt circular and bowed like a coach's undercarriage springs.

As for Molly, she felt absolutely weightless. As she looked into his eyes, she felt a rising warmth, like hot bathwater, spilling over her heart and pleasingly rolling down her arms and legs. She looked fondly into Tom's eyes, "Will you stay with..." Her eyes shut and her lips hung open as she fell straight asleep in his arms.

Thomas carefully lifted her off her feet and pulled back the covers of her bed, never waking her. Lying her down, he draped the covers over her. He shut and locked the balcony doors and closed the thick curtains. After feeding the fire the last of the wood from the hearth, he corked the tequila. He removed his gun belt and tossed it over a chair, then swiveled around several times like a puppet, realizing he'd left himself nowhere to sleep and gawking drunkenly at nothing. Arms crossed, he paced around the room, occasionally running a hand through his hair and rubbing his dry eyes. Not having any better ideas, he returned to Molly's bedside, set himself on the floor and rested his head against the mattress next to her arm. When the room stopped spinning, he knocked out cold.

Molly slept easily, then rose to open the balcony doors. It was unusually dark outside, and much too cold for a Spanish summer. Was she dreaming?

She shivered slightly. A pair of arms wrapped around her from behind, and she relaxed. She smiled, guessing who it was before he spoke.

"Good evening, Captain." As she turned, she gasped, her eyes widening in horror. She had guessed wrong. The arms belonged to someone else. Someone she hadn't seen since her life in Barbados.

Molly awoke with a start, her eyes fluttering open. Tom lay asleep on the floor, his face covered by the sheet she had thrown aside. Standing, Molly moved the sheet, draped her blanket over Tom and placed a pillow by his head. She walked over to the balcony and peered through the curtains outside. Still low in the sky, the sun afforded just enough comfortable morning light to touch the tops of the city, capping them with a golden hue.

A pair of arms slowly wrapped around her waist. Molly's arms developed goosebumps. The nightmare she'd had was still fresh in her mind. Tom's voice whispered, "Good morning," into her neck.

She relaxed. "Good morning. I hope you slept well, despite your choice of bedding. I did not intend for you to sleep on the floor."

"It's alright. There was nowhere else."

Yes there was, thought Molly.

"Our carriage arrives in an hour. If anyone arrives looking for me—not Benito Garcia, you understand, but *me*—then we'll have reason to leave much sooner." He laughed.

"Let us hope that won't be an issue."

"If that is the case, which I have considered, then you may want this …" Tom retrieved a case and presented it to her. "I found it yesterday after the festival. It's rather beautifully made, but don't let that lead you to underestimate it."

The box contained a Spanish-made pistol. The metal of the barrel had been shaped to appear to have ivy snaking around it. The hammer was shaped to look like a rose bud; the trigger, a smooth leaf. Tom smiled proudly. "I already gave it a name. La Flor."

"This is beautiful! You *found* this?" Molly looked up at him skeptically.

"Deadly accurate too," he added, ignoring her question. "I put it through a few trials. And, it's easily hidden." He gave her a small, leather holster, not meant for wearing around the waist. He started forward, and then paused.

Molly cocked her head in question.

"You'll have to excuse me," he murmured with a blush. "Right, then." With the holster in his hand, Tom knelt down and raised her dress to the thigh. "Right or left?"

Molly blushed. "Uh ... er ... right. The right one." She cleared her throat in embarrassment.

"Right it is then." Fastening the holster high around her right thigh, Tom twirled the pistol and pocketed it within the holster, buckling it down securely before sneaking a kiss to the inside of her thigh. Molly drew a quiet, sharp breath. "I pity the bastard that provokes you to use *that* thing," Tom said with a rather devious grin. "It's enchanted with deleterious magic, like a poison."

"Yes, well I hope that won't be necessary."

"Hm, but it would be a shame not to ever hear it fire, yeah? A waste, I should think."

Molly hid her own grin. "You and I clearly think differently of waste. And you *found* such a fine gun?"

"I have a habit of finding *many* things, whether I mean to or not," Tom replied with a smirk. "Most times I'm quite lucky, such as when I found you."

Molly turned her face from view, biting her lip and smiling. "I think you're mistaken. Twas I who found you, Thomas."

"Well," he said looking at her, "let's split the blame." Tom retrieved his things from underneath the bed, slinging a leather belt over his shoulder, filling it with knives, and wrapped a pistol bandolier around his waist, covering both with an inconspicuous, loose white shirt. "Beautiful day," he said, squinting out the balcony doors.

"Lovely," Molly agreed, looking at Tom rather than the scenery.

Placing a hat on his head, Tom asked if she needed anything before the carriage arrived.

"I'll just need a moment to change. I don't want to risk ruining such a lovely dress." She was still wearing the red and white dress from the night before.

He nodded. "Of course. I'll wait outside the door then."

After a moment, Molly met him outside the room, dressed in a simple, cream-colored skirt and white blouse, held tight by a black bodice, her mahogany hair sitting freely on her shoulders. "Shall we?"

Tom smiled and led her downstairs. He noticed that in addition to her everyday attire Molly had put on a belt he'd never seen her wear, he assumed it hid a pistol and some knives. It was pretty, stamped and riveted.

At the bottom of the stair they heard a commotion coming from the first floor of the inn. Tom quietly suggested they stop near the base of the stairs.

"Return to the room for a moment, please," he whispered to Molly.

A distinct English accent rang out from downstairs: "Sir, if you are lying you will suffer the wrath of the law and His Majesty's Royal Navy!" Molly's eyes widened in shock.

The Spanish voice of the innkeeper responded, sounding confused. The officer spoke again.

"Do you realize you are harboring a criminal? Reveal him to us or be arrested!"

Tom whispered to Molly again, more urgently. "Go now, please. Hide."

Molly gazed at him hard. "I'm not going to stand by while they take you away."

"What makes you think they can?" He smiled mischievously and started down the stairs. "Go."

Molly hurried back inside her room, listening intently through the door.

"Has anything been found upstairs?" Heavy footsteps patrolled the hallway.

"Sir, I have only so much patience!" The voice called upstairs. "Search the rooms!" Along the hallway, doors were broken in.

In a panic, Molly searched around for an escape. There was nowhere she could hide. Thinking quickly, she slipped behind the curtains and stepped out onto the balcony, closing the doors behind her. The bedroom door crashed inward and two British Royal Navy soldiers stomped in. Instinctively, Molly held her breath. The voices were muffled behind the door: "Turn over the bed!"

The balcony was too high to jump down from. Below patrolled a group of another ten soldiers. Molly's heartbeat quickened. One of the men in her room pulled back a curtain and saw her on the balcony.

"You there, ma'am!"

Molly turned, startled, but quickly composed herself. As the soldier spoke to a guard next to him, Molly saw five armed men rush into the inn downstairs. Another voice from inside on the first floor cried out.

"Sir! I'll ask only once mo—" *Crash!* She saw a soldier, presumably the one interrogating the innkeeper, hurled through a window into the street.

The squad of soldiers in the street shouted and entered the building. The balcony doors flew open. "Miss! Come with us for your safety!" The soldiers who'd turned over her room approached, with muskets in hand. Molly looked back over the rail, contemplating a jump.

"Pardon me, gentlemen," a voice began. The guards came to a halt. "I'll take her with me."

Both guards spun around. "Who are you—Agh!" One of the soldiers fell to the ground before finishing his sentence, having received a pewter vase to the forehead. The other soldier wheezed as Thomas thrust a palm into his chest. A burst of bright green magical light propelled him over the balcony. He flipped backward, musket firing into the air, and landed in a rain barrel below.

"About time to leave, yes?" Tom hurried Molly to the railing.

"Breakfast would have been nice, but yes, I do agree," she stammered, taking his hand.

"Don't scream." He wrapped his arms around her and leapt off the balcony. Landing with a grunt, Tom rushed Molly to their waiting carriage and set her inside. The driver gave a forceful "Yah!" and the horses charged forward. The soldiers in the inn scampered out into the street and raised their guns to fire. Tom swung himself up on top of the carriage while Molly ducked to the floor. With an annoyed sneer, Tom climbed to the driver's seat and tossed the driver out of his way, sending him tumbling into the street, shouting in surprise. Tom snapped the reins furiously. "Yah!"

The horses got the message. Musket shots rang out and woke up everyone in the neighborhood. Swearing, the soldiers lowered their guns. The carriage tore through the streets of Pamplona and left the town, disappearing from sight.

"Carriage rides, tequila, dresses, guns..." Molly shouted, poking her head out the carriage window, "I do believe you are trying to court me, Thomas Crowe!"

Tom drove the carriage straight through the night and stopped only to allow Molly to sleep peacefully for a few hours while he kept watch. The soldiers caused them no more grief during the night, and by noon the next day Tom began to relax. When they were safely back at his home in Barcelona, Tom carried the sleeping Molly from the carriage into her bedroom, placing her beneath covers on her bed before hastening to his own bedroom, where he immediately collapsed.

Molly shuddered violently in her sleep from a searing pain in her upper arm. She awoke suddenly, touching her arm and wincing. Part of her sleeve was caked in blood. She realized the misfired bullet from the soldier on the balcony must have nicked her upper arm, and she had failed to notice in all the chaos. The pain had finally caught up with her. It was nothing serious by any means, but she decided it would be best to clean it. She peeled off her blouse and pulled her chemise out from under her skirt and over her head. The pain caused her to suck in a breath sharply. How did Thomas shrug off such terrible wounds? Molly thought she'd rather be dead than shot again. Blood began oozing, and she laid a soft cloth over the wound. The contact, delicate as it was, made her see stars and for a moment she became sick. It would've surprised Thomas to know it wasn't the first time she'd been shot, either. She didn't like to think about the first time, and put it out of mind.

Finding a silk robe in her room, she quietly made her way downstairs. She thought about washing off in the kitchen but decided against it, thinking it would cause too much noise. She wanted to avoid waking the captain at all costs, and didn't want to worry him. Instead, she headed into the garden and sat by the fountain.

Beyond the fountain two maids were tending the garden on the patio. Molly, noticing them, hesitated. She couldn't have the maids knowing, because they were sure to mention it to the captain. She headed back inside, knowing she would have to take her chances in the kitchen. The kitchen was empty; the next meal wouldn't be served for two or three hours. Molly prepared a bowl of water with a rag and sat down at the kitchen table.

Tom writhed in his bed, biting down onto a pillow to suppress any shouts of pain. Standing up defiantly, he unintentionally ripped the sheets on his bed. He tore a sleeve off his shirt, rolling it up and substituting it for the pillow in his mouth. Unlacing the shirt and casting it aside, he examined the full extent of the damage done to his ribs and left arm. He hadn't gotten away clean. The mark on his back burned red hot. The rag fell from his mouth, allowing a shout to escape. The pain intensified, and his shouts became barking, growling and snarling. He quickly covered his mouth again. The numerous sword slices in his abdomen slowly hissed and sealed themselves shut. *At least I'm not bleeding*, he thought.

Molly, downstairs, heard the noise coming from upstairs. Setting her wound dressings aside, she got up and went to check on Tom.

Tom bit down onto the rag again and swore. The wounds burned and hissed insufferably. Attempting to cross the room and lock the door, Tom fell to one knee.

"Aaaah!" He wrapped an arm around his stomach and reached out to the doorknob. His fingers fumbled with the lock and finally flicked it into place. Through gritted teeth he breathed furiously. The gashes across his body slowly disappeared, hissing and producing a dark smoke, which rose from the severed edges of his skin. Why did it hurt more than usual? The blade hadn't been silver, had it? The thought frightened him and he tried to calm himself.

Molly came to the door and tried to turn the knob. It wouldn't budge. "Thomas!" She wrestled with the door handle. "Thomas, are you all right? Please answer me!" Molly's own wound began to bleed again but she hardly noticed. "Thomas! I need to know you're all right!"

Accidentally Tom bit into his own tongue with an elongated fang. His wounds sizzled shut and he lay still, breathing heavily. Angry at himself, he lifted both arms, thumping the floor with his palms and willing himself to stand. His footsteps assured Molly that he was up and walking. Molly backed away from the door as Tom sighed and unlatched the lock. His voice was soft and tired.

"Good afternoon." Folding an arm in an attempt to cover the temporary scars, which were tinted a pitch black along the sword lines, he allowed her in. "Have you eaten?"

Molly sighed deeply, looking away, but happy to know he was all right. "You've a bad habit of trying to distract me with food, Thomas. You should learn new tricks."

"Did you hurt yourself?" he said, noticing the blood coming through the sleeve of the robe. He reached toward her shoulder.

Molly flinched, turning away. "It's nothing. The first of many to come, I'm sure." She tried to laugh about it. "I guess it's rather special, in that case." She didn't want him to worry. As much grief as he normally gave himself, she did not want to know, of all things, he'd gotten her shot.

"It's still bleeding. You don't want to lose any more. You only get so much, you know. I'll find you a better bandage." Tom exited to the hallway and motioned for her to follow him. He seemed to forget his stomach and failed to notice when he stopped covering the black scars on his body.

"I'm sure I can take care of it," she said meekly as she followed him into the hall.

"I have medicines. I'll treat it so there is no scar." Taking her arm, Tom led her onward.

Molly winced.

"Sofia!" Tom searched the main hall. Sofia entered from down the kitchen.

"Yes?"

Tom instructed her to retrieve particular medicines while he found bandages. Seeing Molly's bloodied sleeve, Sofia released an "Oh!" and hurried to find the medicines. Tom came back with the bandages, followed by Sofia, who handed him two glass jars.

"*Gracias*, Sofia."

Sofia, not much older than Molly herself, but shorter, with green, feline eyes and ink-black hair, nodded and wrung her hands nervously. Tom sent her away and then took Molly's hand again. "All right then, follow me." He guided her to her room. She followed him reluctantly, thinking it best not to protest. Tom closed the door behind them and set her on the bed.

"Don't worry. With this treatment the wound will disappear entirely." He smiled at her reassuringly.

Molly frowned, seeing Tom's wounds, which were much more numerous and severe. "What about you?"

"Me?" He chuckled wholeheartedly. He had completely forgotten about his own pain.

Her brow furrowed in confusion. "Captain, I've never before heard anyone in such pain."

"My pain is an inescapable fact. It's routine. Yours is of much more concern to me. You're always nursing me. It's about time I reciprocated." Picking up a rag from the table next to him, Tom pulled up a chair to her. He slung the rag over one shoulder, partially obscuring a trail of the black scars, and opened the larger of the medicine jars. Setting the lid aside, he took out some of the light green ointment with two fingers, spreading it across both hands.

He then held his palms face-up. "Could you ..." He gestured at her robe with a very subtle nod, eyes darting down to his hands awkwardly and remaining there, then attempting to meet hers again. Molly nodded, letting the robe slip from her shoulders, folding one arm across her chest to catch the fabric as it bunched up at her bust. Tom fumbled the jar back to the table and shakily slid the chair closer. "It won't hurt."

Molly watched as Tom gingerly placed a hand over the wound and applied the strange medicine to her skin. The sensation left by the substance was soothing and cool, creating a numbing effect on her shoulder. Once more, with the other hand, Tom coated the wound. Molly closed her eyes with a sigh. After cleaning his hands, Tom opened the smaller jar and poured a fine, black powder into one hand, but only very little. "This will seal it and prevent a scar," he explained.

Molly opened her eyes once more and watched as Tom sprinkled the grains evenly over the ointment, then brushed off his hands before sealing the jars and setting them aside.

"Allow it some time to dry, and then I'll wrap it for you."

Molly didn't immediately pull the robe back up to her shoulders. She liked the way Thomas looked at her.

"I'll leave you in privacy so it can take effect. When it feels like it has settled properly ... I'll ... would you like me to wait outside the room for your call?"

Disregarding his question, Molly reached out to touch his shoulder, touching the tip of one of the black scars. "Are you sure you're all right?" she asked quietly.

"I promise." He forced a comforting grin, his blue eyes dashing back and forth between her face and her deep cleavage.

"I know this must be normal for you. But *I* am only human. I can't help but worry about you."

"I don't mind your concern at all." Allowing her fingers to slip away, he turned to leave. Tom stopped at the door, head tilted toward the ground, turning slightly toward her. "You're sure this is the life you want? The purpose?" he asked.

"Absolutely."

Tom swallowed hard, keeping his head tilted away, hiding his face.

Molly stood, moving to look at him. "Why do you say such things?"

"Because I can't forgive myself when you get hurt. I can stand in front of a gun and laugh at its wielder knowing I run no risk of death. You don't have that luxury, and yet you should be the one who is impervious to pain and death, not me. It's all a part of the curse, I suppose. I'll wait outside for your call." Trying to keep his eyes averted politely, Tom tripped over a rug on his way out. "Be sure to tell me if you begin to feel any pain, yeah?" He opened the door and left.

As he vanished, Molly frowned. "What is he thinking?" she asked aloud. Sighing, she approached a mirror in a little boudoir off to one side of the room and fussed with her hair. She let her silk robe fall to the floor. Before putting anything else on, she locked her door and went to her bed, lying on her back. Shutting her eyes, she thought of the night before, being in Tom's arms again. Rolling over onto her stomach like a cat, she stretched, reaching over the side of the bed and rummaging through the bag containing her personal effects.

Tom called down to the Sofia, requesting an early dinner. In no time, the house was filled with the scent of rice, flour, spices and beef. Molly could smell dinner from upstairs and decided to call the captain for the bandage before she ate. Getting up from her bed she quickly donned her silk robe. Tom arrived at her room promptly, bandages piled in his arms. "I had the kitchen prepare dinner so you could eat as soon as the medicine set in."

Molly smiled in thanks, letting him in. Tom slid the chair over to her bed once more. "I promise I'll be quick this time," he said, waiting in the chair, unfolding the bandages.

Molly exposed her shoulder and arm to him, turning away so she couldn't see the ugly wound.

"It may be tight, but you won't have to be concerned about bleeding. The medicine is working very well," he continued, unraveling a bandage and looping it over her shoulder, tying it and then securing the first bandage with a second that overlapped it. He repeated the process with three lighter bandages, tying off the last and gathering up the spares.

Covering herself, Molly turned back to him again. "You're much better at this than I am."

"Well one does become accustomed. I gave up the effort to care for my own injuries. The medicines take away the pain of the rapid healing, but I simply stopped after a year or two. The scars hurt a little, but only until the next visible moon. It isn't so bad. Tending to all of them became tedious. There's no point when they'll just go away by themselves."

Molly reached out to touch his face tenderly. "You'll find Harlan and make things right again. I know it. I have a feeling there may be a peaceful solution to all of this."

Tom closed his eyes, toying with the bandages in his hands. *No, there won't*, he thought.

Molly wrapped her arms around him, embracing him tightly. "Whatever happens, I'll be here." Despite Tom's best efforts, he couldn't say anything in response. The darkness inside released him as she squeezed, and solace was all he could think about.

"Let me change and we'll go eat." She kissed him on the forehead.

"You don't think the Royal Navy will find us here, do you?" Molly asked Tom as she dug into her beef and rice.

"Not for another day or two, and when they do, I'm going to make sure they never come looking for us again," he promised her. "This afternoon we're going to go out to a shop. It should benefit us to pay a quick visit. I'm going to get dressed. As soon as you finish, fetch anything you wish to bring and come get me in my room."

"All right." Molly soon finished with her dinner and climbed the stairs up to her room. She strapped La Flor to her right thigh before heading back downstairs and knocking lightly on Tom's door.

"You have the ring, yes?" asked Tom, meeting her at the door.

"Yes, always," Molly replied, glancing at her hand.

"Then let's be off."

Tom led the way as they walked along Barcelona's curvy streets, heading westward across town. He said little, but when he did speak it was to make comments on the dry weather and the meal the maids had prepared. Simply listening, Molly inserted a few words here and there, but she was more concerned about Tom's odd behavior. He always acted as though he knew more about where they were going and what they were doing than she did. But there was an unusual degree of hidden knowledge Tom kept locked away behind his deep blue eyes. He appeared to know more about complete strangers than they knew themselves, and more about his own future than any man or woman could know. How?

After twenty minutes of walking, Tom paused before a tiny building with one door, its single window shaded by a small awning.

"Here it is." He walked up the three steps leading into the doorway and hesitated. "Wait here for a moment."

"What is it? Is something wrong?" Molly asked warily.

"Oh, no, just … one moment, if you please." He disappeared through the doorway.

Standing nervously outside, Molly kept her eyes on the door and occasionally peeked over her shoulder, feeling as though she were being watched.

Tom strolled into the dusty old shop. There were several long, tall shelves lining the walls, built to such a height they touched the ceiling. They were lined with oddities and trinkets from many far-off kingdoms, empires and tribes—small knives, crystals, jewelry and navigational items in abundance.

A short, Spanish man of about fifty years emerged from the back of the shop, eyeing the grinning Tom.

He swept his thinning hair back and scratched his chin.

"Gabriel Vasquez?"

Gabriel squinted in curiosity and then burst out in glee. "Thomas! *Dígame, cómo está usted?*" He rushed forward and threw his arms wide.

Tom allowed himself to be embraced, and then quickly stepped back. "How have you been, Mr. Vasquez? How is business?"

"Not so much business anymore. I travel now. I got away from the dangerous crowd a long time ago, Thomas. And you?"

"Traveling as well. I came across a particular navigational piece you crafted for my father years ago, and I'm curious as to how it works exactly."

A knowing look fell upon Gabriel and his eyes widened. "Oh, yes, yes, the rings?"

"Well, yes, one ring. I can't seem to find the other."

"Ah well, a shame, but you do have at least one?"

"Yes, yes, with me. I would also like to offer you something quite unique in exchange for a tutorial on the ring's magical functions."

Gabriel waved the notion off. "Oh, well, anything will do Thomas. In fact I believe I'm still in debt to your father. Consider it a favor."

Tom grinned. "Well, I have no money with me at the moment anyway, but what if I offer you a memory?"

A puzzled expression crossed Gabriel's face. "A memory, you say? Your father liked to play these kinds of games with me, too." He shook a finger and chuckled. "What do you mean, a memory?"

"Let me show you. One moment."

Tom reappeared in the doorway outside and beckoned to Molly.

"What is it, Captain?"

"Would you like to come in?" he asked, gesturing for her to step inside.

"Um, yes. Of course." Cautiously she followed him inside.

Tom led her to the middle of the room and stepped aside. As Gabriel studied Molly, any distinguishable expression faded. He looked as though he'd heard thunder on a sunny day, or as if he'd woken up in a stranger's bed. His small mouth parted, but he didn't speak.

Molly stared back blankly at the man before her. Thomas hadn't told her who he was, but she knew. She could feel her heart beat in her throat, and the blood seemed to drain from her face.

"Gabriel Vasquez, allow me to introduce you to Molly Bishop," Tom said needlessly.

When Tom spoke the man's name, Molly felt a prickling the skin of her arms and the nape of her neck. She looked into the man's startled eyes, never before having seen a pair so identical to her own. She knew not what to say or do. There he was, just steps away. Her father. *Real.* This was her father, the man who had left her for others to care for. Her father, who had given her a gift that would erase all memories of him from her mind. Was he stunned by rejoice or remorse?

When Gabriel spoke, his voice was barely audible. "Lucia?" He slowly smiled and took her in as if she'd just been born again before his very eyes.

Tom looked at Molly curiously. "Lucia, is it?"

"You look like your mother. I thought ... I thought I was seeing a ghost." Her father stepped toward her, his voice cracking.

"My mother?" Molly repeated blankly. Tears glistened in her eyes as her lips curved in a tremulous smile. She took the compliment as if he'd called her Aphrodite, despite having never seen her mother.

Gabriel hobbled over to Molly and hugged her tightly.

Molly stood in place, unresponsive for a moment as conflicting feelings warred within her. Then with a great sob she returned his embrace, tears streaming down her cheeks.

Gabriel stepped back. "Let me look at you, Lucia. I can hardly believe it is you."

"Nor I, you," she replied. "Thomas has told me fascinating things about you. Has he said anything to you of me?"

"Nothing at all, Lucia. I have not seen him in ages, and he surprised me today."

Again they embraced. "I thought I would never see you," she said, her voice trembling. And then when

Thomas said I would find you in Barcelona, I was afraid you would not love me."

Again Gabriel stepped back, this time with an alarmed expression on his face. "Not love you? But that would be impossible, my beautiful child! I am the one who fears not being loved!"

"Fear not," She took his hands.

Tom paced the shop, studying the items on the shelves. "Oh, *señor*, I meant to tell you, she's inherited your talents. She says there is a map within the ring that I mentioned."

Gabriel gazed with wonder at his daughter, bringing her hand to his lips. "Can you see it, Lucia?"

"Oh, yes. When the sun hits it just right, I can see the constellations. It's a beautiful ring..." She wanted to say 'Father,' but awkwardly withdrew the term from her sentence.

"And you've never been taught this by anyone? Not a magesmith?"

"No. I was just able to see it."

"Strange. But very fortunate, and rare. I always knew you would be a special girl," Gabriel said with a gleam of admiration tinged with an undercurrent of guilt in his eyes.

Tom intervened. "I can't see it at all. I was hoping you could teach me."

Gabriel dropped Molly's hand. "I don't want to disappoint you, Thomas, but you may never be able to read it." His tone was sympathetic as his smile faded and he turned to the young man.

"Why's that?"

"I always purposely protect my gems from the abuses of people who carry the marks such as the one you carry on your back, Thomas, ever since the Order of the Blood Moon came back into power. Not to mention many other such people and..." he paused "...things."

"How could you tell? I—"

Gabriel cut him off. "A magesmith has ways of knowing many things, Thomas. I've done business with many men, werewolves, vampires and even stranger beings than you would believe." From his finger he took a ring fitted with a simple grey pebble and handed it to Tom. The pebble changed to a glassy yellow, like a wolf's eye. "That ring spotted you before I did. Yellow indicates any person nearby carrying a mark. White reveals those lacking any," he explained with a grin. "Red for vampires and black..." he shuddered.

"What's black for?" Molly asked.

"Demons," said Gabriel.

"I should have guessed I couldn't surprise you," Tom remarked with a laugh, "So there is no way for me to read the ring, then?"

"As long as you carry a mark, I cannot help you, Thomas. I am very sorry," Gabriel said, apologizing and frowning. "I know you did not choose your curse, but I cannot reveal any secrets to you or anyone else who is cursed in such a way. I promised myself that a long time ago, after the Highland Wars in Britain, the ones your own father fought in. The horrible things the Grey-Reivers did with my magic and so many others' ..."

"If I can't follow the map, how am I supposed to find Harlan?"

Gabriel shrugged. "Your brother cannot read his either, Thomas. You may never find him, but listen to me. It is a lost cause either way." He lowered his voice for Tom's ears only. "Your father would not want you and your brother to behave this way." Gabriel knew exactly why Tom wanted to find Harlan.

"I have good reasons to find him!" Tom fumed.

"Good enough reasons to do what must be done to cast off a curse?" Gabriel challenged him sternly.

Molly stood aside, a pitying expression on her face. She avoided eye contact with Tom.

Gabriel glanced at Tom and then at Molly. After a moment he smiled and looked down to the floor. "I can sympathize, Thomas, but I cannot teach you. I have long disassociated myself with your kind. But perhaps Lucia could."

Molly grabbed her father's left hand in both of hers. "I'll do anything to help him, Father." The word was not so difficult to say.

Gabriel felt the sincere love of a daughter in the warmth of her palm. "You have the ability," he assured her before she could finish. "You are younger and sharper than I, Lucia. You are of much more help to Thomas than I could be."

"What must I do?"

"If he must know, you have all you need to teach him. All you must do is figure out how. I cannot tell you. It is a family secret. Bestow it upon whomever you wish, but it is not so easily given."

Tom intervened again. "I do appreciate it, *señor.*"

"Always an honor to assist a Crowe," Gabriel replied with a smile. Reluctantly he withdrew his hand from Molly's. "It's getting dark. I trust I'll see you again, Thomas? Lucia? Thomas, I know you will watch after my daughter, yes? I would love nothing more than to catch up, but not in this place and especially after nightfall." He gave Tom a stern look.

"He's been doing a fine job," Molly affirmed, feeling something she'd never been able to before— the need to win a parent's approval.

"Very well, then. Make sure she returns to her bed tonight safely. I must send you both off before the streets begin to swarm with unpleasant characters. Lucia, goodbye." He hugged his daughter once again with great strength. "Come and see me again soon, my daughter. I will not sleep until you do."

"I'll come back as soon as I can. I have much to tell you." Molly said with a long-lost girlish excitement.

"I am glad! Return before my old ears are no good!" He chuckled to disguise his lingering regret over all the years lost between them. "Oh, Thomas, before you go, I must give you something. I'm certain it's in the back of the shop." The old man entered the back of the shop to retrieve the item, returning after several minutes of digging through boxes and jars. "Take this with you." He placed a locket in Tom's hand. It was simple and golden, smooth like a butterscotch candy. A single stone, like the one in Molly's ring, was set into it. It contained a small amount of light that swirled and glimmered deep within the gem. "Keep it. Guard it. Do not open it. Do you understand? Your father had but one to give and he gave it to you, not Harlan. He instructed me to find you and give it to you only on the condition that you were determined to find your brother and there was nothing stopping you. I can see there is not, but still I urge you to make your choices carefully."

Tom's eyes grew curious. "What do you mean?"

"You will know. I cannot tell you. It was your father's wish."

Confused, Tom accepted the locket and tucked it away. "Well, thank you."

"No trouble at all. You two had best journey back home." A bittersweet smile crossed his face.

"Molly." Tom motioned her toward the door.

She started toward it, then ran back to hug Gabriel again. "Until we meet again ..."

A great sigh escaped his lips. "Daughter. Now. You must really go. The streets harbor danger."

She let go of him and rushed toward the door, not looking back as she said, "Good-bye!"

"Goodnight Thomas, Lucia."

Tom waved as he followed Molly out of the shop.

Once outside, Molly paused. "No words can express my gratitude, Thomas. You've helped me, so I promise I'll find a way to help you."

"Then tonight begins a long journey, Miss Bishop."

Gabriel Vasquez practiced in the magic trade for most of his life. He lived in Spain where, as I have said, the magic trade was everywhere, but well hidden. He'd sold his share of magical goods to both noble and untrustworthy men and beings, and once, after a sour deal between himself and some non-European traders (rumored to have been a shamanic tribe of some kind), Mr. Vasquez began to practice much more selectivity. After the Highland Wars, Mr. Vasquez vowed to never again sell to werewolves or vampires. At that time clans and cults were far too numerous, volatile and ambitious to trust with magic.

The Grey-Reivers in Britain were a particularly abrasive group of lupomorphs, responsible for creating a sore tension between mortals and non-mortals in the Isles. The clan was composed of the descendants of early reivers, mostly human Scottish families, who, during the late thirteenth century, joined numerous other families (some English) in stealing cattle as a preferred livelihood. They had to be quickly and violently dealt with decades ago after they nearly burned down a large English town using particularly potent fire-based magic. The clan had consulted a small community of Welsh druids sympathetic to the Grey-Reivers, and with their help, called forth a helldog—a fiery hound spirit—over which they soon lost control, thus beginning a war from what was meant to be an act of outspoken vandalism.

The Grey-Reivers' actions were foolish. Mr. Vasquez was particularly fortunate that the magic he had sold the Grey-Reivers was all spent during the creation of the helldog. Otherwise he would have been discovered and most likely blamed for some of the havoc. Mr. Vasquez was certainly aware of his buyers' plans when he sold them the magic they requested. It was so specific that anyone with any degree of magical knowledge would have spotted the intent to summon an archaic being—a practice that has for so long been taboo that the idea of anyone's attempting it now is almost too difficult to believe. Mr. Vasquez just saw the opportunity to make a strong profit, and most likely assumed the Grey-Reivers would never be able to achieve a summoning.

The locket Gabriel gave Thomas was an incredible artifact that would eventually affect the lives of more than one person—indeed, thousands, if we consider the greatest and farthest-reaching effects. Thomas did not know exactly what the truth behind the locket was, but his assumptions were close enough to lead him to use the locket in such a way that its purpose was served as intended. But the locket must wait for now. There is much that is important to tell before we come to that.

It is also an interesting coincidence that Thomas gave La Flor to Molly shortly before Gabriel handed Thomas the locket created by John Crowe. The two items would join together to greatly affect the events of this tale. La Flor was a soul well, something Thomas had failed to tell Molly. Thomas had nicked it from Henry Bardow after killing him in the Caribbean. He did not find it in Spain, as he had told Molly. Henry Bardow, like many desperate werewolves, had intended to find and kill his infector, but he never got the chance.

This reminds me of something Thomas once said to me during one of our many conversations: "That's what all people have in common, Geoffrey—each of us is out to kill something, whether it is a man, a moment or a memory."

Geoffrey Mylus,

May 3, 1833

❦

Once back in east Barcelona, Thomas led Molly into the house and hung up his hat. "I had originally planned to sail again sooner, but I'm going to assume you would like to stay in Barcelona just a bit longer."

"I would much like to talk with my father at least once more, if that's all right. It's still baffling just seeing him in person." Her voice held a mix of excitement and anxiety.

"That can be arranged. I am greatly concerned about the Royal Navy, but I can send you in a carriage tomorrow morning if you like."

"That will be fine. We don't have to linger any longer than we have to."

Thomas looked her over carefully. "How is your shoulder faring?"

"It's doing well, thank you. Your nursing is very effective."

"No pain, I hope?"

"None at all."

"Would you like new bandages?"

"If you think that would be best."

Tom exited the main hall and called to Sofia as Molly headed upstairs. A new fire grew brightly in the fireplace as Molly sat on her bed. Pulling down her dress to expose the bandages, she peeled them off.

Tom knocked on the door. "May I come in?"

"Come in," Molly answered, inflating her chest.

"While we were out Sofia purchased some much better cloth for wrapping your wound," Tom said, stepping inside.

"I give her my thanks."

"*De nada, señorita,*" chimed Sofia.

"Oh!" Molly hadn't seen her come in behind Tom, and tugged her dress back up. Sofia excused herself shortly after.

"I see you've already removed the old bandages. All right." Tom unraveled the new cloth, tearing it into strips and then wrapping them as he had the earlier ones, using extra bandages for padding. "The medicine I gave you earlier today tends to thoroughly exhaust one. I recommend you let it do its work and sleep until it wears away."

"Of course."

"I had my maids purchase a small sleep-aid for you today, as well. I'll be right back." Tom hurried down to the kitchen and returned quickly. He placed a new bottle of tequila on Molly's bedside table.

"*Just* a sleeping aid, of course. I'm glad you amuse yourself."

"It works quite well. You have to trust me. After all, I did witness it put you out rather quickly a few nights ago."

"Honestly, I usually don't drink as often as I have been lately," she mumbled, embarrassed at her behavior and wondering whether it changed Tom's perception of her.

Tom raised a hand. "It was only a gift. Do with it as you see fit. I will see you in the morning," he said, standing.

"Thank you, Captain," she cooed.

Molly stared after him, her eyes alight. As he shut the door behind him, her gaze fell upon the ring, shimmering in the firelight. "It may take some magic, but I'll find a way," she said softly.

A large clock in the dining room rang twelve times. Aching all over, Tom restlessly strode down the upstairs hallway. He paced furiously. One of the maids had passed on the tip that the Royal Navy was present in Barcelona, actively searching the streets for a man named Thomas Crowe.

Word had travelled from Pamplona to a certain Captain Robert Locke, who otherwise would never have docked in the port of Barcelona, and now thought himself to be having quite a turn of luck. Locke had sailed a ship-of-the-line through the Strait of Gibraltar not long after the *Scotch Bonnet* had come through. It had taken a tour to Marseille and was passing Barcelona when it spied the *Scotch Bonnet*. Thinking the ship stood out from the rest of the vessels in the harbor, Locke decided to snoop. Locke's ship was a titan, capable of holding three hundred, four, maybe five hundred men, and three times the cannon strength that Tom's vessel could boast.

To make sure Tom couldn't rely on guile and escape to sea, Locke had his men vacate the *Scotch Bonnet* of its watchmen, and did so while Tom and Molly were away in Pamplona. Royal officers had been milling in the streets all night, their torches lighting the dark windows and doorways of Barcelona. Tom tried to avoid drawing attention to the house, snuffing out every candle and shutting the window latches securely. Outside the moon was full and rising swiftly.

Tom never ceased pacing as he began to ache, wild sensations plaguing his body and mind. His eyes gave off a particularly bright, yellow glow that night. Sofia approached him, warning that Royal officers were very close by. There came a loud pounding on the front door.

"Helloooo! You are commanded by His Majesty's Royal Navy to allow us into your home to search for a wanted man! He is to be extradited to England upon his discovery and capture. If you do not comply, we will forcibly enter!"

Tom tried to distract the men by shouting from upstairs, asking them what business His Majesty had so far outside his jurisdiction. The man quickly rebutted, explaining that a man withholding "property of His Majesty" (any privateer vessel, by law, was technically such) was hiding illegally beyond English borders with "stolen goods." Tom knew this was a lie, and even if it were true, the *Nymphe Colère* was at the bottom of the Caribbean. He also knew there would be Spanish soldiers in town soon to confront the British intruders. The soldiers were not stupid or patient, though. They would break his door down before long, in order to avoid butting heads with the local militia. There was plenty of time for

Tom to be captured or shot. He fumed. They were fools not to leave him alone.

Molly stirred in her sleep, the medicine and tequila muddling her senses.

Thomas turned to Sofia. "Answer the door for me, please, Sofia." A wicked grin spread across his face.

"*Señor?*"

"Answer it. It's fine. Go on, then."

Sofia scampered downstairs to the front door and opened it. Outside stood a Royal Navy officer holding a torch and musket.

"Ma'am, if you cooperate, this will be dealt with quickly. Where is Crowe?"

"*Lo siento, señor, pero este es la Casa* Garcia." Sofia didn't dissuade them, and backed away as they marched inside.

"I will search the premises and decide that for myself, thank you. Do not interfere."

The man stopped just beyond the foyer. Immediately he was met by a hulking beast, half cast in shadow. Its deep golden fur bristled and its long white teeth parted like a deadly picket fence just waiting to close itself shut around the soldier. They dripped saliva on the floor at its feet. A rumbling noise in its throat almost sounded like a chuckle, but deeper, a canine grunting. The officer dropped his torch and bolted to the front door. The werewolf sprang after him, barking like a hound of the Pit. Just outside the front door, the soldier signaled ambushers.

"Drop the net!"

Molly finally woke.

Two men waiting above the front door had released a net, weighted down by iron balls. Tom was snared underneath. Clawing at the net, he managed to slice open several large holes. The net, made of silver links, seared Tom's skin through his fur and he thrashed. Acting quickly, the officers bound his wrists and ankles with irons. More officers gathered and collectively dragged him toward the harbor.

Molly had seen everything from her bedroom window, was already dressed to fight, and slung her two pearl grip pistols around her waist and holstered La Flor at her thigh. She rushed to the balcony window, careful not to expose herself, but close enough to see the soldiers and Tom.

A crowd of spectators grew in the streets, following close behind the officers, gawking at their catch. Tom roared and snapped and fought against his captors wildly, actually rending one soldier's leg completely off. As the man screamed and writhed in the street, his companions jabbed at Tom with sharpened, silver-tipped prods.

Molly opened the window, aiming one of her pistols at the men surrounding the net and firing into the mob. Tom's attention was drawn to the balcony window as the guard next to him quit thrashing, presumably dead. Molly ducked quickly by the window, preparing another shot. She likely wouldn't hit a thing, but if the mob panicked, or she could alert the militia, that would be as good as any plan.

"Show yourself!" The soldiers spun about, rifles sweeping the air. They could not find the source of the shot that had sent the spectators into a riot.

Molly's hands shook, making it hard to manage her accuracy. She took a deep breath. It was too risky to get a good look out the window, so she used her better judgment, firing blindly out the window.

The crowd grew larger. Some people thought the town was under attack. The soldiers pushed them back, still scanning the bodies for armed foes. "Keep 'im moving! There are too many people in the street! Get 'im to the docks!" a soldier shouted.

Molly swore under her breath. Taking a risk, she peeked out the window and aimed at the soldiers handling the net. The soldiers moved double-time, hauling Tom along with not far to go. They huffed and panted and wheezed. It was like dragging a floundering bull. Molly concentrated on steadying her hand. Two more shots. She ducked down again. No good, she'd have to give chase and figure out something else.

Sofia snatched Molly's hand as she came running through the first floor hallway, leading her out through a hidden gate.

"Oh! Sofia! Thank goodness you're safe," Molly said, panting.

Once outside, the young woman pointed Molly down a private footpath headed to the shore by the harbor before taking refuge with the other maids in a secret cellar behind the house. Tom had it dug a long time ago, just in case.

"Thank you," Molly called after her softly as Sofia vanished into the dark.

A commanding officer's voice was distant but audible: "Move these crates! Take them onboard to the captain!"

Molly raced down the path and toward the voice, desperate to catch up.

Robert Locke's regal ship-of-the-line, the *Horse of Neptune*, sat close in Barcelona harbor—a giant among the Spanish ships. Half the town must have witnessed the capture by now. The citizens lined the seawall at the docks, but British soldiers prevented their further approach. At least Molly had helped cause a scene. Tom was dragged up a boarding ramp and onto a boat opposite Locke's. Then Locke's voice sounded out.

"The Royal Navy, under order of His Majesty the King and the British Empire, places you, Thomas Crowe, under arrest for egregious crimes against the Crown. You are charged with transgressions that are undeniable and incorrigible—scores of murders, more than one hundred thefts, treason, piracy and innumerable petty criminal acts against England and its citizens and colonial subjects. Thomas Crowe, the High Court of Britain has produced a warrant for your execution upon capture, and, though I have a penchant for proper procedure, I am also overdue to return to London."

The commanding officer's voice boomed out once again. "Drop the anchor on the execution boat!"

Without hesitation, Molly fired at the nearest soldier. Anything to distract or delay them was essential. The crowd scrambled for safety. Molly quickly hid herself among them. The soldiers at the dock became disorganized. Some were trampled by the mob. From up the street, the Spanish authorities approached. Their leader shouted from up the hill for Locke to stop and disperse immediately.

"All officers clear off the execution boat! Launch the boat!" the commanding English officer ordered.

Obediently following the commander's instructions, Tom's captors leapt off the small, ownerless fishing ship onto which Tom had been dumped.

Tom lay bound in his irons on the small vessel. On its deck were piled large stacks of gunpowder kegs and oil barrels. Locke meant to burn Thomas alive—something his curse couldn't fight forever, and if it tried, it would be unthinkably agonizing for Tom. In the chains, Tom awkwardly struggled to a standing position, bumping into a mound of the kegs. One toppled over and broke open, spilling the powder around Tom's feet. Locke, standing safely aboard his own ship, was handed his hunting bow, an arrow and a jar of oil as a soldier with a torch stepped up next to him, ready to ignite the arrow. Through the dark, Tom could see the smiling face of the young captain—his neat, tidy brown hair, decorated crimson uniform and arrogant demeanor. Tom would not die at the hands of a man of privilege, titles and excesses. Inciting his curse to thrum through his veins, Tom's body grew and his muscles surged. The irons, not able to contain his legs and arms, warped and snapped off. Locke raised the bow and arched a flaming arrow into the midst of the gunpowder barrels. The powder around Tom flashed and crackled. Inhaling nasty smoke, Tom gagged and snarled. All the while, Molly stood at the head of the crowd on shore, her pistol at her side, as she watched in horror, unable to do anything for Tom. The English soldiers forgot all about her as they squared off with the armed Spanish militia.

Tom seized a boarding hook near his feet and, with a furious roar, tossed it onto the railing of Locke's ship. The hook snagged the railing, and with inhuman strength,

Tom began tugging his boat toward the English ship. The soldiers onboard Locke's vessel detected Tom's intentions quickly and abandoned ship, ignoring Locke's commands to sever the line. As the English ship and the execution boat met with a crack and the hulls bounced against one another, Locke and the last of his men ran about the deck. The execution boat erupted like a firebomb, blowing itself to splinters and opening a fatal, gaping hole in the hull of the *Horse of Neptune*, which lurched and collapsed inward. Hundreds of gallons of burning oil set fires to the belly of the ship and incendiary droplets clung to the sails, creating an inferno above and below. The night sky was freckled orange and yellow with hot ash, and shards of wooden beams and planks rained down on the onlookers.

The crowd of civilians was in a panic, tripping and falling into one another. Spanish soldiers apprehended the British naval officers littering the churning, dark water below the docks and corralled the ones causing disorder along the waterfront.

Molly wiped tears from her cheeks and kept a hard expression. Pushing her way out of the crowd, she ran to the beach and began to wade out into the water. Tom had been stabbed and shot and who knew what else. She wasn't ready to believe he was dead yet.

"Thomas!" she cried loudly, searching for a sign of life, movement, anything. If he were alive, she needed to get him out of the water and back to his home. She'd had enough of Barcelona. It had already made her experiences in London seem cheery.

Smoldering junk from the explosion littered the water. The soot rained down onto Molly's shoulders and face, mixing with her tears and streaking her cheeks a mournful grey.

Sofia, arrived shortly, wrapped in a shawl and out of breath, seized Molly by the arm and tried to draw her away to safety.

Molly jerked away forcefully. "No! He's coming! I have to wait!"

"*Señora! Por Favor! Vamos*! *Es demasiado peligroso aquí*."

With the maid holding tightly to her arm and the Spanish militia lurking, Molly had no choice but to go. Sofia guided her home.

Once in the main house Sofia locked the front door and released Molly, who collapsed, leaning against a wall, huffing with exhaustion. Bereft of hope, she fell to her knees and buried her face in her hands. The clock rang out two o'clock. Molly, defeated, climbed the stairs to her room. She couldn't just sit still, and began to pack her things. Tom would come home, or she'd sneak back out, and they would leave Spain the first chance they got. *Right? Won't we?* Molly shook her head and sprinkled the floor with tears. She needed desperately to talk to someone.

Sofia sat outside on the patio in the dark, staring into the fountain with a rosary in her hands. She squeezed the little beads tightly, muttering to herself and drawing lowercase "t"s on her breast. Molly approached the maid and announced herself.

"Sofia, I have to go back out."

"Molly..." the maid turned around. "*Por favor*, do not go. He made me promise not to let you go after him if the soldiers come for him."

"But Sofia, I know he's not dead. He can't be. I—"

"Yes, I know, *señorita*," Sofia interrupted, "Nothing can kill that man. I don't know why, and that is why I pray for his soul. But you, Molly, you could get hurt. Please, wait for him to come home."

"I will tell him you could do nothing to stop me, Sofia," Molly said.

Sofia looked at her for the longest moment. "Be careful."

The streets were nearly empty, swept clean by the local authorities. A few soldiers were still ushering people back into their homes. Molly avoided looking out to the sea as she rushed through the streets toward her father's shop. As she ran, the bright moon above caught her ring and constellations burst forth, rearranging themselves and dotting the path before her like glittering jewels. She'd never seen it behave in such a way. A string of particularly luminous points projected by the ring began to align and glow brightly. They created a path pointing southeast, toward the docks. She knew exactly what it meant somehow, and beamed with joy. Tom was alive, and the ring was showing her the way to him.

The moon came out again and her heart jumped with hope. She quickened her pace in the opposite direction, away from her father's shop and toward the docks, breaking into a full run. The ring gave off a warm, pink glow, its brilliance reflecting strongly in the black windows of houses and shops. Molly came to an abrupt stop when she reached the edge of the docks, her heart pounding. Her eyes searched the black face of the waves.

"Thomas!" Her ring glowed brighter still.

Tom shivered weakly, feeling his hair slowly flowing above him in thick ribbons, occasionally brushing his forehead like delicate, lacey fingers. It was dark. Strange shapes fell around him, disappearing below into the abyss. Above, the surface changed shape erratically, and a single white light source peered down at him. The eye of Luna Mater, he guessed. She blinked again and again, crying for her fallen child. Tom heard whispers. They reminded him of his contract and his body's unconditional bondage to life. A flock of sparks swarmed through his nerves. The mark on his back burned like a hot iron. His skin stung, ached, fought against Death's groping clutch with all the ferocity of a hunted buck. Throbbing incessantly, a large bruise on his forehead was all that kept Tom conscious. His surroundings grew darker. He sensed he was falling slowly and was reminded of a dream he'd been having for years, a dream in which he lay on a stone street while white flowers fell to the ground all around him. That place was where he was meant to die. Not here. He wasn't supposed to die yet.

Tom heard the whispers again.

You may not die here …you are marked … your pain compels you to serve your eternal mistress …

Tom blinked in a half-conscious daze. He thought he saw a glowing, white woman—an ivory, silky-haired goddess—diving toward him through the blackness, taking hold of his soul. Her dainty arms towed him upward with the strength of a hurricane tide.

Tom's head made contact with a hard, gritty surface. He'd lodged into wet sand. Water washed over him periodically, the salt stinging his wounds. The face of the moon goddess stooped over him. Cool air poured forth from her pale lips and filled his lungs. Wet sand clung to him and weighed down his clothes. The inland breeze was the only mercy he received. The vision of the white woman had left.

Hanging in the clouds above, Luna Mater watched. Thomas would be fine. She'd sent a little star, Molly, to help him, just in case.

Tom's wounds reawakened, and the curse began its tireless work. The cuts hissed and slowly sealed themselves. A dark, wispy aura rose from the numerous injuries, creating a cloud around Tom's form. Bones mended themselves, bruises diminished like evaporated rain puddles, and splinters were ejected from their deep burrows in Tom's skin. He coughed several times but could not manage a shout of pain. Looking at his arms and hands he saw lots of blood.

Blood! He thought. *Who's bleeding? Am I bleeding? Don't let it out!* He hugged himself and writhed. The shore waters washed over him again. Blackened planks, sections of masts and shreds of Tom's own clothing washed up next to him. Littered with debris, the soft shore cradled him and the few dead whose bodies the Sea rejected.

The path of Molly's ring suddenly bent and changed direction ever so slightly, leading her to the shore nearby rather than the docks. She stopped abruptly. Tom had moved quickly somewhere else. The first sight of him was painful to see. She walked to him. Relief, happiness and grief accompanied her.

Falling to her knees next to Tom, she spoke hoarsely. "Thomas?" Her words were as frail as Tom's broken body. "Thomas? Can you hear me?"

Tom lay still, breathing gently. The injuries continued to hiss and close, the black aura escaping in a smoky stream. Molly closed her eyes, unwilling to witness the crude healing process. Tom offered no resistance to it. His chest simply rose and fell in silence. Tendrils of soaked hair lay across his face. Half-buried in sand, his arms appeared to be missing, but Sea slowly unearthed them, as if pulling back the covers of his would-be deathbed. Molly removed the hair from Tom's face.

"You're going to be all right, Thomas," she whispered, not quite sure whom she was trying to reassure more. "Thomas? Thomas, you have to wake. Please." She placed a hand on the side of his face.

A fresh wave washed over Tom's lower half. He coughed quietly.

"Thomas? Can you hear me?"

Tom mumbled something in intermittent, nearly inaudible whispers and coughs. Then he managed to make words. Where ... she? Molly ... the woman?"

Molly squeezed his hand. "I'm here, Thomas. There's no one else."

"Can't find her ..."

Molly immediately took off her coat, draping it over his body. Had someone come along and pulled him to shore? Why would they leave? "Settle, Thomas. I'm going to help you. You just need to stay awake."

"How long was I gone?"

"An hour, perhaps."

"Molly?"

"Yes?"

"Did I die?"

Molly was shaken by his words, unsure of how to reply. "I-I thought so at first, but here you are. Perhaps an angel was with you tonight."

"I was gone for a long time. Who was whispering?"

"Whispering?"

"How far is home?"

"Not far."

"Let's go, please."

Seven chimes of the clock woke Molly the next morning. When she opened her bedroom door, Thomas was pacing in the hallway. His body showed no sign of damage at all. Oh, how taxing it was to have to become an audience accustomed to another's immortality. Tequila and blood were making one hell of a drunken dream out of their Spanish excursion. Molly again questioned what she'd gotten herself into.

"How are you feeling?"

"Not a scratch," he answered, spreading out his arms and turning them, examining his skin.

"That's good. Can I get you anything?" Molly asked.

"You have done everything that needed to be done for me. I asked Sofia to tell the kitchen to prepare something for breakfast. I'm sure you're hungry. *I'm* hungry..." Tom stared through a wall for a long moment. "Thank you, by the way. Sofia told me she could not convince you to stay in the house when the soldiers came. I don't remember much of anything."

Was he thanking her sincerely or just trying to comfort her, Molly wondered. If he had never been worried about dying, did her efforts make any difference? Molly couldn't shoo the feeling away. She couldn't even prepare breakfast, because Thomas had Sofia for that.

Tom leaned in closer and whispered. "Please don't be sad. Don't be afraid or angry."

"I was so worried about you."

"People die only when they don't have anything left to live for—when they no longer have a purpose. I have plenty to attend to before the day of my death."

Molly thought for a moment. "Is that the secret to immortality?"

"You don't have faith in a word I say, do you?" Tom asked, releasing her shoulders and stepping back.

Molly looked down sadly.

"Anything the matter?" he asked.

"Not at all."

Tom leaned against the door frame, folding his arms. "No need to lie, I've already caught you sulking."

Molly squirmed in irritation, but replied matter-of-factly. "I'm ready to put Barcelona behind us, that's all."

"We'll be leaving soon, but I don't expect any more trouble from our English friends."

You said the same thing in London, Molly thought, sighing and folding her arms.

"I'm going to go out for a bit. Sofia should bring your breakfast up shortly. I'm going to take mine with me."

"First, could we just—" Molly placed her hands on her hips. The man had a habit of walking off when he assumed conversations were over and was almost out the front door. "Can't we just spend one day in a couple of chairs with some tea?" she whined, going back to her room and opening her windows.

Boom! Tom strolled down the street outside, whistling and firing a pistol into the air.

"Wake up!" he yelled, laughing maniacally.

Molly flinched and covered her head, and she knew without a doubt that the neighboring households couldn't have missed the noise either. "I have pledged my company to a madman," she mumbled.

Tom strutted toward the docks as neighbors filled the windows of their homes, yelling and shaking fists.

"He's not leaving me here again while he gets himself into trouble," she resolved.

Ignoring the breakfast left on a tray for her outside her bedroom, Molly pulled on a fresh white chemise and a voile dress. A red sash matching the flowers on her dress concealed the leather belt underneath which contained her pistols. Patting her thigh, she made sure La Flor was snug, and then made her way downstairs. Sofia was at the bottom.

"*Buenos dias*, Sofia."

"*Buenos dias, Señora.*" Sofia smiled sweetly.

Molly took an apple from the dining room with a thankful nod. Sofia offered her several more to take along.

"*Gracias*, Sofia, but this will do fine. I have some business to attend to in town. I shouldn't be gone long. Should Mr. Garcia"—she grimaced, not in the mood for theatrical facades—"come in search of me, tell him not to worry, and that I'll be back."

"*Sí Señora. Adios.*" Sofia smiled again and waved as Molly left.

With a final thanks, Molly headed out. She started westward, munching on her apple as she walked. The townspeople looked annoyed and disheveled and underrested that morning for reasons obvious to Molly. No one had slept the night before, and they had one man to thank. Molly bit into her apple harder.

Tom strolled easily down to the docks, delightedly ignoring the angry complaints following his morning greeting to the city. He reached the fish market, and a scroll of paper hanging on the wall of the fisherman's shack caught his eye.

"Ha. Heh-heh." Amused, he read the paper, then folded it and stuffed it into a pocket to take home later.

Molly knocked on the door to her father's shop before entering. "Father?"

There was a shout from within. "*Un momento!*" Gabriel's slow footsteps shuffled toward the door. Opening the door for her, Molly's father welcomed her. "*Hola, Lucia.*" He smiled from his mouth to his big ears.

She replied with a hello, embracing him gently. "I don't suppose you received the wake up call?"

"He is very well his father's son, isn't he?" A gruff laugh escaped the old man.

"I wouldn't know, actually."

"Speaking of which, John stopped by my shop not six months ago. I hadn't seen him in years. Asked about Tom, and said he'd been missing for a long time. Then he made that locket to give Tom, right here in my shop. He said Tom was set in his ways, so he needed something to ensure Thomas didn't do anything he'd regret. Can't imagine where John was off to, but he left in a hurry, eastward."

"John Crowe is still alive? Thomas thinks his father is dead! Or … at least, he gave me the impression that his father is dead."

"No, he's alive as far as I know," Gabriel said, shaking his head. "How are you today, Lucia?" He smiled again, clearly happy to see his daughter.

"I suppose a bit worn from last night's events," she admitted.

"Thomas gave them quite a show, *si*?" Gabriel laughed.

Molly didn't think it was funny.

"Lucia, my dear, there are plenty of eligible men with less exciting lives who would throw themselves at your feet, if you do not want the kind of life Thomas leads. I would understand, but I assure you Thomas is a good man like his father."

"I am curious about what occurred with this ring last night." Molly decided to steer away from the former topic.

"Yes, go on."

"It was strange. I was looking for Thomas, and the stars emitted by the ring formed a path. It's never done that before."

"It was doing what it was meant to do, Lucia. The twin rings I created seek out their owners as a first priority and seek out the other ring as a subordinate priority. The celestial maps they emit do not align north. Each aligns to point to the sister ring."

"I see. If that's so, wouldn't I be able to seek out the other ring if need be? Since Thomas can't read it, what does that mean?"

"The ring seeks out its owner first, and then the other ring. It is a nuisance, yes, but Thomas must be near in order to search for the other ring."

"But it is possible?" Molly persisted.

"You can indeed read the map as long as it points to the other, yes. You can see the map, can't you?"

"Well, I can see the stars, but—"

"Then you can read the map," said Gabriel, shrugging his shoulders and lifting his hands, palms up.

Molly nodded in understanding.

"Very well, then," he said.

"I was also wondering about these," Molly began, taking out her pearl pistols.

"Yes? Those are my handiwork as well." Gabriel pointed out the initials carved in the handles.

Molly grinned sheepishly. "I'm afraid I'm in need of some ammunition."

"Really? Why?" Gabriel replied, his brow furrowing.

"Well, so I can use my pistols?" Molly laughed.

"I told you, those are of *my* making, Lucia. Does that not tell you anything, or has Thomas not explained my line of work?" He laughed. "I guess you've been using them like ordinary guns until now?"

"Should I have not been?"

"Well, you can if you wish, but these pistols were made to use spells as ammunition. This is why I fitted them with pearls. The wielder is meant to speak an incantation, converting magical energy into bullets."

"I see. Thomas told me something else about the pearls in the handle. Something I would prefer that my father had explained first," Molly said, her voice growing quiet as she waited for his reaction.

"Also intentional. Did Thomas explain why? I'm sure it did not puzzle him. He is familiar with gem magic."

"He did, but all those years ... you were doing business?"

"I would not risk your life and have you live with me during those times, Lucia. You, a child, among *those* kinds of people and that kind of dangerous magic? What kind of father would I have been?"

"I understand. It's just difficult—growing up without a father or mother. Couldn't you have found business elsewhere?"

"Are you angry with my decision?" The old man's voice revealed guilt. He'd given up easily.

Molly looked up into her father's eyes, startled at his question, not wishing to upset him. "Of course not. It was for my own well being. I'm just glad I finally found you."

"I had always hoped you did not believe I and your mother did not want you, Lucia. That is another reason for the pearls. I wanted to spare you the doubt. Of course, now that truth has settled upon your mind, the spell is broken."

"I had suspicions. I knew you were out there, somewhere." Turning the pistols in her hands, Molly tried to remember if she'd ever even seen her father before this time. "My mother. What was she like?"

"Everything about you reminds me of your mother. Does that answer your question?" Gabriel grinned at her. "The same features, the same noble personality. Very proud, very kind, very stubborn." Changing the subject,

Molly's father stood and began dusting off his shelves. "How did Thomas find you, Lucia?"

"I suppose it was I who found him, actually," she corrected.

"Oh?"

"I needed to get away from Barbados, and he allowed me onto his ship."

"Barbados? That is a very long way from Samuel Bishop's farm."

"After coming of the proper age, I went out to find you. I knew something so much more was out there for me. I wasn't meant to live on a farm my whole life. Samuel and my mother's relatives were all I knew. I had never met anyone other than them, that is, until I was to be married. But the young man I was meant to marry was involved in an accident. I was alone and purposeless, so I began to travel." She avoided admitting to her father that she had originally held other intentions upon travelling to Barbados.

"Your mother lives in you," Gabriel commented, smiling at his daughter's words. "I expected you were not one to grow roots in any one place. How fitting that you crossed paths with a Crowe. Ha! I just hope that that man stays clear of his brother. Harlan is not like John and Thomas. The boy fell in with an evil crowd. Perhaps Thomas has more than one motive in seeking him out, though. I cannot say," Gabriel admitted, sighing and shaking his head, He paced about the shop, hands folded behind his back. "Maybe he'll give up and want to settle into a decent life now that you're on his arm."

Molly's smiled and blushed.

"Ah, I knew it," Gabriel wagged a finger. "But listen, Lucia. Thomas may try to give you the locket as a gift, eventually. The one I gave him the other night. Do not take it if he does, but insist he keep it around his neck. Do you understand?"

"Yes, but—"

He cut her off. "And ... do ... not ... open it. Not before it's time. Do not ask me further questions about it. It is best that way."

Molly nodded in understanding.

"Sometimes answers will lead only to your trying to change what is to come, and you cannot. The world itself is changing as we speak," Gabriel whispered cryptically, "and there is a great deal of magic involved. Many lives are being linked in curious ways and under frightfully fateful circumstances. Thomas and Harlan are but one pair of men who have become subject to the times. The clans are beginning to change. The cults are changing, too. A few famous magesmiths have disappeared. Only a few years ago, something happened to a large gypsy society far east of here and they vanished. Many powerful artifacts vanished with them. Each day I wake from nightmares, and the morning air smells like war—no, like the very brink of war, like the smell of a flame before it is touched to a wick. I can't hope to explain this all thoroughly to you. It's taken a lifetime of magecraft and experience for me to learn the nature of time and ambitions. But be brave, and all will fall into place as it should, and you will have no reason to worry," he assured her.

Molly's eyes uneasily moved to the floor. "If you're sure."

"Have faith in Thomas. If he is his father's son, he is an honest man, and he wishes only the best for those he loves. We cannot judge Thomas for hunting his own brother like a dog. A curse will make a man do almost anything to rid himself of it or be devoured by it. These are not happy times to be a werewolf. There are many places across Europe where persecution is severe. I believe, ultimately, that Harlan will be the smallest of Thomas's trials." Gabriel took a deep, weary breath and continued. "And you, Lucia, must have some part to play as well. The only reason the pearls in those pistols could have failed their purpose—to keep you from me—is because of fate. I tried to keep you in England, but my wishes apparently clashed with the greater design."

There was a knock on the door. Molly looked over curiously.

Gabriel called out. "Yes, we're open!"

The door opened wide, and Tom stepped into the shop. He was soaking wet, and smiling. His mood hadn't changed a bit.

Molly's eyes widened. "Thomas?"

"I apologize for the mess, I won't be long," Tom apologized.

Gabriel tried not to look surprised. "What can I help you with, Tom?"

Molly shook her head, hiding a grin, unwilling to let him see that she wasn't still angry with him.

"Well, I need to pick up a few things, that's all. I've just been for a refreshing swim." He wrung out his sleeves. "An ill-tempered woman down by the docks pushed me over the storm wall. "Englishmen will not be welcome here for some time, I think."

"Well, what can I do for you, Thomas?" Vasquez choked on a laugh. "Come to the back. I'm sure it's not the trinkets on the shelves you're after."

"Not at all. It's something special ... rather, for uh ... well, it's a special day, you see." Tom winked at him.

"Ah, right, right."

Both men retreated to the back for a moment. Tom returned with a small box and spoke to Molly. "Shall I take you home?"

"Very well," agreed Molly, not at all anxious to leave.

"I will expect you again soon, Lucia?" Vasquez asked with a smile.

"Of course, Father."

"I have some things to show you," Tom told Molly, "I think you'll enjoy them."

"I have taken it upon myself to buy you a birthday gift!" Tom announced. The two sat alone at a table in the back corner of a tavern across town.

"Birthday? It's not my birthday," said Molly, shaking her head.

"I know. It's the eighteenth of August, yes? It's a little early, but I couldn't wait to give you this."

"Captain, really, I haven't celebrated my birthday in years. This isn't—"

"Oh, stop complaining. Just smile and thank me."

Molly sighed, defeated, but couldn't help but smile.

Tom threw open a rolled bundle of fabric and spread it out on the table. "Oh, look at this." He took a folded piece of paper from his pocket and handed it to Molly, who unfolded it and looked it over. Tom arranged the items from the bundle while she read.

The news notice had a large drawing of Tom on it, framed by thin lines that read: "Thomas Crowe: wanted, in any condition, by the British Royal Navy and the French Colonial Guard in various territories of the Caribbean. Reward: generously negotiable depending upon condition of subject upon capture." There were two bold paint stripes across the picture of Tom in the shape of an X. Below it read: "Executed."

Molly sighed, throwing the paper onto the bed. "How lovely."

"Do you see the humor?" Tom asked, laughing. "Well, I'm amused. Captain Locke is a hero and I'm dead. Ha!"

He picked up a small, shining object from the wrappings. "Here we are ... more jewelry. I hope you don't mind much," he said, grinning proudly. "Try it on."

The small gold band he handed Molly was shaped like the scaly body of a dragon. A squared, beautifully cut ruby was set in the open mouth of the dragon, clasped in place by four long golden fangs. Its tongue hung out below the gem and curled to one side. The legs and arms of the serpent seemed to cling to her finger like the limbs of a little perching bird. Something about the light the ruby reflected was reminiscent of the behavior of flames.

"Under any other circumstance I would have to refuse," Molly said, taking it carefully before slipping it onto her finger. "But I *am* a magesmith's daughter and a woman of impeccable taste, aren't I? It's beautiful, Thomas."

"Yes it is, but that's not the point." He scooted to his left, snuffed the candle on the table and put it between them.

"And what's the point, then?"

Tom hid a grin. "Aim your ring at that wick. Make a fist and point the ring at the tip of the candle."

Following his instructions, Molly raised her fist.

"Now," he began with a coy grin, "Repeat after me, all right?"

"All right."

"*Spuere ignis!*" he cried.

Molly took a deep breath. "*Spuere ignis!*"

A blazing stream of flames burst forth from the tip of the ruby ring. The fire illuminated the entire back corner of the tavern, roaring loudly and then hissing to a stop. Molly gasped loudly, using her other arm to steady her hand. The flames vanished, and the ring emitted small wisps of smoke.

"It *is* a beautiful ring, isn't it?" said Tom, touching the blackened wall behind him. The candle in the middle of the table was reduced to a waxy blob and ran off onto the floor.

Molly stood in place, eyes wide. "That is why I don't celebrate my birthday, Mr. Crowe!"

Thomas stared at her, trying not to laugh.

"I hate surprises!"

He frowned.

"But I love this ring!" she squealed, scrunching her nose and smiling. The two looked at each other across the table like a couple of adolescents.

"Oh, I purchased something else as well. I've been meaning to get one but just didn't have the money." Tom took a golden necklace from the bundle and dangled it for her to see. A teardrop shaped onyx hung from it. Tom looped it around his neck and vanished from sight.

"Thomas?" Molly gripped the table and looked around. Where the devil had he gone?

"Wonderful trick," Tom whispered, his voice right next to her ear.

"Ah!" Molly scooted away from the chair beside her.

"Amazing, yeah?" One of the wine glasses rose from the table and wafted to her hand, waiting to be taken. Tom's sword appeared as well, balancing the other glass on its tip. Its contents sloshed and the glass tilted over but did not spill. The wine simply vanished as it fell from the lip of the glass.

"Not bad stuff," Tom's voice said.

"Thomas? What is this?" asked Molly, watching the ghostly phenomena occur all around her.

The empty glass settled on the table and the sword found its sheath as Tom reappeared before Molly's eyes, in the chair right next to her. In his hand he held the gold and onyx necklace.

"How—" Molly began.

"Don't ask me, ask your father," Tom replied quickly. "I wouldn't know what kind of magic causes such an effect. I can appreciate how expensive it is, though." He looped it around her neck. "All you have to do is touch the stone and whisper, *'absconde me'*, and you're gone."

"This is marvelous. Are you sure I can have this?" She was completely enamored with her gifts.

"Of course. I don't need it. If I need to do any spying I'll stick to the hole in the cabin wall. It's much simpler and cheaper," he said, quickly getting up and cackling as Molly gasped, blushed and swatted him.

Thomas often spoke to me about an unusual fear he had developed over many years. The idea of bleeding frightened him. Not the sight of blood or the spilling of it, but the concept of losing blood was what concerned him.

His fear reminded me of vampires and the ill-willed nickname used against them by mortals and sometimes werewolves. Vampires often have been called "cowbloods," or cow-blooded, because most of them choose to sustain their bodies by draining the blood of livestock instead of humans. Living off the blood of livestock doesn't seem to disturb most vampires, but many often develop a certain dreary disposition when realizing they possess no real blood of their own. I believe Thomas was bothered by the notion of living a borrowed life through his curse, but the only way he could describe his fear was through the concept of "bleeding." He told me he felt as though the "haunting possibility that he was immortal" sometimes made him feel dead, or imaginary. He didn't feel like a beast or an immortal. He felt like a man who was sentenced to facing the punishment of eternal life while on earth—a horrible fate, in his eyes. "Man was not meant to live forever while still bound to a body," he would say. He so hated the persecution—the fact that his fellowmen never looked upon him as human.

What is it then that makes us human? Is it because we bleed? Is it because we are so frail? Thomas Crowe believed mortal frailty was the most precious of gifts.

Geoffrey Mylus,

May 5, 1833

❧

After leaving the tavern, the pair spent the remaining afternoon shopping in the markets nearby. In particular, Tom was on the lookout for an apothecary. Much time at sea and a handful of run-ins with the authorities had exhausted his medicinal supplies. As luck would have it, he was able to find a small place, and left Molly outside, letting her know he'd only be a moment.

Molly wandered close to the apothecary, eventually standing off to the side of the foot traffic and happily examining her new ring and necklace. How she longed to be a magesmith or magician more and more each day. *And to think,* she told herself, *I could've been cleaning stables or plowing fields or mending dresses should I have stayed at home. Ha!* Molly wandered next door and discovered a man selling flowers. She began to ask how much he wanted for a carnation, but then a voice she recognized interrupted her.

"Hello! Molly! Molly, is that you? I thought I'd never see you again!"

Inside the apothecary's, Tom paid what he owed and reached to take his satchel of medicines. He stopped, and inhaled, turning his head this way and that. A scent of death—*old* death—had crept past his nostrils. He also detected another scent. *That's blood,* he knew.

"*Gracias, y buenas tardes, señor.*" The apothecary bid him farewell.

Ignoring the man, Tom put his satchel in his pocket and moved to the door. Someone or something unpleasant was about.

"I've been looking for you, Molly."

Thinking herself to be dreaming, Molly pivoted in place. Her chest filled with bricks, heavy with dread.

"Christopher?"

A handsome young man stood before her, his lightly stubbled face half hidden in a black bandana and long, brown hair tied back neatly and hidden beneath a hood. A distinctive silver hoop dangled from one of his ears. His frame towered above her as he embraced her.

"I was begining to wonder when I'd find you. Ever since you left Bridgetown all I've done is wish to hold you again," he told her.

Molly could hardly believe her eyes. "Well, this is certainly a surprise." She tried not to act entirely repulsed. "What are you doing here?"

"Looking for you, of course." He kissed her cheek.

Molly was taken aback. "Christopher, I don't think I understand." She took a step away from him. "Perhaps we can speak some other time." (*Never is a time, right?*) Molly put on her best smile. "I need to finish my shopping. I have a prior engagement and I'm already late."

Christopher feigned a hurt expression. He'd always been a bad liar. "Nearly a year has separated us and you leave so quickly?" he said, placing a gloved hand on her shoulder. "I'm quite curious as to why you left, but I suppose that can be left for later. It's just fortunate that I found you. Wonderful things are happening back home, and everyone wants you to be part of it."

Molly again put one stride of distance between herself and Christopher. "Why have you been looking for me?"

"My associates and I have made significant headway in the Caribbean, and soon I'll be able to have us our very own home built to any specification you wish," he replied, avoiding the question.

Molly glanced over her shoulder anxiously. "I really need to return—"

Christopher grabbed her hand suddenly, cutting her off. "If you come with me, love, I can explain everything on the way to Barbados."

Molly looked down at her feet, "I'd rather stay here."

Christopher reached out to move a strand of Molly's hair behind her ear. "Please, Molly, I'd like to take you home."

Molly pulled her head away, but his grip remained around her wrist. She refused to placate him. "Why are you *really* here, Christopher?" she demanded to know.

"I thought you'd been kidnapped, or arrested, or worse! I had to come after you and make sure you were safe!"

Molly tore her hand away from his cold claw. "You never were a good liar."

Christopher chuckled darkly. "For once, love, you're wrong. I'm not lying." He grabbed her hand again, this time holding it painfully tight. "The Society is growing, and you are to play a wonderful part in it. I volunteered to fetch you because, in my company, you'll be safe. We'll return, and you'll be looked after closely. You'll never again need to worry about anything. And I'm sure this time you'll accept an invitation to join the Society as my wife. Yes, there are risks, but you can have life everlasting, Molly!"

Molly tried to jerk away. "It would not be wise to make a scene here, Christopher, wouldn't you agree?"

Tom had been watching the two from the shadows of the apothecary doorway, his keen eyes gazing over the heads of the crowd. Seeing fear in Molly's eyes, he could not delay any longer. His instincts had led him to assume danger was prowling, and sure enough, they had led him to the source. His body ached. The blue in his eyes faded and died. They turned deep gold, then a pale yellow. The pupils shrank and became void of humanity. Stitches from old wounds in his arms and torso split and popped, falling away. Newer injuries hissed and sealed within mere seconds. His head throbbed painfully.

A thirsty smirk remained etched into Christopher's face. "It's probably best you come with me, so we don't draw any attention, love. Come, let's get out of this wretched sun," he urged her, tugging at the hood on his head and pulling his bandana up, keeping his face turned away from the daylight.

"I don't think so. In fact, I think you ought to slither away before my *friend* chews you in half." Molly spat the words.

Tom's senses sharpened tenfold. He could hear Christopher's breathing and Molly's protest. He smelled traces of blood on the man—blood not his own.

Christopher moved closer to Molly. "You think to frighten me away? I know who you are with. He is also of great interest to the Society, and my superiors. Especially Harlan."

Tom's terrifying presence divided the crowds and opened a path straight to Molly. His teeth grew long and razor sharp, hidden behind his lips.

Molly's eyes widened. Harlan was Christopher's superior? What was the Society up to? A creeping horror filled her mind.

"So you are with Thomas. I thought so." Christopher read her face like a book.

The bones in Tom's spine cracked and popped. Growing taller, his body stretched his white shirt to its limits and tore it in the back.

"I can only imagine what you'd like to do to Thomas," Molly said bitterly, "but whatever it is, you're a fool to think you could. He can kill men as a horse's tail swats flies. Harlan should have come here himself. I won't tell you where Thomas is, because if you find him, you won't leave here alive."

All traces of Christophers grin disappeared. "Oh? But I believe you *will* tell me." He reached for something in his coat.

Tom moved fast, his large steps beating on the dusty street with increasingly heavier thuds. Several people screamed, frantically getting out of the way of the giant in the crowd.

Noticing the disruption, Molly looked around her. Christopher was momentarily distracted, but as he glanced about he kept a painfully firm grip on Molly's wrist.

Tom sensed Molly's discomfort and roared in anger, releasing a sound Molly had never heard from him before. His demonic howl drove the rest of the crowd into their homes and shops. The shoppers dispersed, dropping their goods in order to flee. Molly trembled, her eyes watering. Breaking into a lightning sprint, Tom's transformed legs propelled him toward Christopher, who gaped at him in horror and pulled a pistol from within his coat. Molly shoved Christopher's arm as he pulled the trigger. Roughly, he flung her away, swearing. Tom received the bullet as a mere brush on the cheek. He charged, growling and winding back one arm to bash Christopher sideways off his feet.

Getting up quickly, Molly backed away to safety. Tom moved behind Molly, looming over her and maintaining a wide stance in order to surround her with his protective presence. He watched Christopher struggle to stand and dared him to touch Molly again. From the ground, Christopher sneered at Molly and the beast. Molly moved closer toward the monster, making Christopher furious. Hatred marked his expression as he stood and fled. Tom's dark eyes asked Molly to make the next decision. Would the stranger be allowed to escape? He hunched down, awaiting any indication and kept Molly shielded.

Molly spoke hoarsley. "Let him go. He's not coming back."

Tom obeyed, but his attentiveness did not wane.

"I'm fine, Thomas," Molly stammered, touching the beast's arms, her hands disappearing in the thick, dark golden fur.

Tom's breathing hushed. The yellow eyes became bluer. While the wolfish traits receded, Tom's eyes blinked sleepily. After walking back home with Molly, Thomas slept, knowing Christopher would be back when the daylight was gone, and with the disappearance of the sun, Tom knew he'd have a deadlier fight on his hands. He did not alarm Molly, but when she refused his advice to go to her father's shop for the night, he asked her simply not to leave the house.

With the setting of the sun, Molly prepared herself to sleep, but slumber would not come. Her mind was on Thomas, Christopher and her old life in Barbados. But she mostly thought of Thomas. Life wasn't fair to him. Despite having witnessed the man kill and steal, she felt nothing but sympathy for him. He was not the bad person whom the bounties depicted. He was not an animal. He was a young man with nowhere to go but further and further away from himself—further and further away from normality, grace and peace. Becoming a wolf wasn't the real curse, Molly thought to herself. Unable to sleep, she left her room, knowing she'd find Tom on the roof, where he'd been sitting for about an hour since waking from his long hours of sleep.

Tom did not speak when Molly appeared on the roof. His eyes looked out to sea as the sun sank lower and lower. In another hour or so, the light of the day would be gone, and darkness would come looking for him. When Molly sat next to him, he broke away from his thoughts and smiled for her.

Molly lay against Tom. He seemed so happy, and it showed in his eyes. It was something she was unable to see often.

In the short time elapsed sitting there with Molly, all Tom's pain ceased, and life seemed to greatly simplify. The world and its vices were far away.

Molly lost herself in his features. She had never before seen such contentment and peace in his eyes. There was a new, serene beauty to them—a beauty she had longed so badly to see on the surface. Something within her chest began to flutter, and an electric chill rolled across her arms to the tips of her fingers. She wanted to become much more familiar with that sensation. She wanted it to last.

Tom's eyes watched the sun intently. Against expectation, he had always felt a closer kinship to it than any other celestial object. Like the sun, he felt, he rose and fell each day—was born and died again like clockwork. But neither life nor death was permanent. Neither life nor death ever lasted, and that's why his existence was everlasting—because he was always being born again, always dying. His curse and punishment were regular, inevitable and powerful, like the light of day. They were never waning or waxing; never new, full or halved like the light of the moon.

He stood suddenly and pulled her up with him. "Time to go inside."

"Why?"

"I must be ready. Christopher will come. Trouble comes in threes, and he makes the third plague to have found us in Spain."

She saw that the contentment in his eyes had fled.

Together they spent hours upon sleepless hours in the sitting room. Midnight passed, then one, two and three o' clock. Molly sat watching Tom as he paced about the house, moving from room to room with no apparent mission or reason. It was well after four.

"What are you doing still up?" Molly asked. She'd dozed on and off all through the early morning.

"What am I doing? Nothing really, I'm just restless. I slept all day, after all." Tom toyed with an empty jewelry box, fidgeting and looking into Molly's eyes with the expression of a child who has been caught red-handed knocking over a valuable vase.

"Are you feeling well?" Molly persisted.

"I'm fine," Tom said with a forced smile. "Why don't you try to relax? Get a fire going in your room?" Distractedly, Tom kept looking out each window he passed. Night had long fallen and morning approached, and yet, ever since he'd left the roof, Tom had been acting perturbed.

"All right," Molly surrendered, "I'll go to bed again, I suppose."

"Very well."

They had just entered her room to build the fire when Sofia called from downstairs. "*Señor*! Visitor! A gentleman here! *Dice necesita hablar con Señora!*"

"Do *not* invite him inside!" Tom's head snapped toward her voice. His eyes were wide and still. "All right, Sofia?"

he called back. Turning to Molly, he said, "Maybe it's just your father. Wait here."

"Thomas?" Molly felt uncomfortable. Why would her father come to visit so early?

Tom walked down the stairs and strode to the door with haste. Molly followed closely behind him. Sofia left them, but her expression and the way she kept her eyes on the visitor at the door made Tom apprehensive.

"Good evening sir," Tom said, meeting the visitor, "I understand you need to see Miss Bishop?" He smiled and offered his hand. "I'm Mr. Garcia," he said curtly.

The gentleman, though smiling from beneath a broad hat, did not accept the offer. Tom could see his face well enough to determine that he was not Christopher.

"Miss Bishop, may I speak with you *outside?*" the man asked, looking past Tom.

"What was your name again, sir?" Tom asked calmly.

"We'll be but a moment, Thomas," Molly interrupted, trying to form a convincing smile. "I'll tell them to leave," she whispered, touching his arm and hoping things wouldn't escalate for once.

Tom nodded. Molly didn't appear concerned, so he allowed her to go outside. Molly's smile faded as she passed through the door. As she exited, two men in black coats traded places with the first gentleman. "You people find me anywhere I go, don't you? Well, don't loiter in my doorway. Won't you *come in*?"

The men smiled, their veiny, rose-stained eyes glowing.

"How might I help you, Christopher?" Molly asked, glaring at him as his associate led her to his waiting arms. "I thought you would be more intelligent than to ..." She trailed off, seeing murderous intentions inscribed his gleaming eyes. "What do you want?"

"Simply to protect you, love," he responded. His pale face brought back awful memories.

"Well, gentlemen, we all know what happens next, don't we?" Tom said darkly, looking back and forth between the men in black coats standing in his foyer. As the men drew long, thin, silver blades from beneath their coats, Tom's eyes turned yellow. A shiny, golden coat of fur spread over his body. "Very well then, just promise you two won't shame yourselves by screaming, yeah?"

Molly's eyes cut to the front door.

Christopher chuckled. "I wouldn't advise going back inside, love. It's bound to get unpleasant."

A pair of yellow eyes blinked in the darkness behind Christopher's head.

"I think it's already finished," Molly corrected him, seeing Tom's large body looming behind the oblivious vampire. One of the men in black coats threw open the front door of the house and staggered outside. His own, long blade was buried in his stomach and twisted into a corkscrew. A broken table leg protruded from his chest precisely where his immortal heart once beat. Christopher remained eerily calm, watching his associate fall to the ground.

"No, it's not quite finished yet," he snarled, seizing Molly's wrist as she attempted to run, holding her in front of him and revealing a large pistol. Molly gasped and imediately reached for La Flor. Tom barked harshly and poised low to spring. "I wouldn't do anything brave, Thomas," Christopher warned, cocking the hammer on the pistol, holding it threateningly close to Molly. "I learned something during our first encounter. You may take your own life lightly, but you value hers," Christopher grinned. "Not that it's anything to you, but this is all simply a concern of the Black Coat Society. I really hate all these unnecessary measures. I advise you to back down, Thomas. I do not wish Molly harm. But I cannot leave her here. She belongs with her family."

"Family?" Molly spat the word out like a piece of gristle.

"She is too talented a sorceress to be left in the hands of a self-destructive pirate, and too rare and beautiful a woman to lay with a dog," Christopher insulted him.

"You pig!" Molly screamed, kicking and wrestling against Christopher's hold.

Tom's black pupils contracted. Christopher, some of his confidence diminished, held Molly tighter. Molly flinched in pain, losing her grip on La Flor. Sensing her distress, Tom bellowed a booming howl. The front windows of the house cracked. Christopher yelped, loosening his grip on Molly and clapping his hands against his head to stifle the ear-splitting noise. Tom writhed, growing into full form. Breathing heavily and lowering his clawed hands, Tom bore his yellow eyes down on Christopher from a height of nearly three metres. Molly struck Christopher in the face with her ring hand. The vampire recoiled and released her, misfiring his pistol.

The round shot from Christopher's pistol emerged from Tom's right leg, but the entry wound did not immediately heal. Tom wailed. The wound, instead of sealing, began to burn and smoke. Molly gasped in horror, and Christopher backed away cautiously. The beast before them raged and bared its teeth before rushing Christopher. Molly made a grab for La Flor, but Christopher intercepted her. A clawed fist caught him in the stomach, projecting him through a window and into the house. Tom leapt after him, jaws wide open. Christopher raced upstairs, overturning a large bookshelf and hurried into the darkness of the hall. Molly rushed inside after them, loading a shot into La Flor. Tom jumped the main stairs with ease, landing in the upstairs hallway. It was silent and empty.

Molly stood at the bottom of the stairs, her pistol at the ready. She wished she had asked her father for a spell or two, because otherwise her pearl pistols would do her no good at the moment.

Tom crept forward, his frenzied eyes scanning the upstairs hall. A strange shadow materialized on the wall behind him and moved like liquid, mimicking his movement.

From her place at the bottom of the stairs, Molly saw it before Tom could. The shadow's dark hand peeled away from the wall. Molly could see that it held a dagger. Tom crept along, unaware. A black pair of wings appeared after the hand, followed by a body. Christopher, in his true devilish form, raised the dagger high.

"Thomas!" Molly screamed.

The shadow let out a piercing shriek and stabbed at Tom, who leapt aside and beat the shadow backward down the hall. Christopher stood again with an insane smile on his face. Large black wings spread and fluttered behind him. Molly raced upstairs but froze before Christopher, who stood between her and Thomas.

"Mr. Crowe, I am just as determined as you," Christopher said, laughing. "Ah, there you are, Molly," he exclaimed, turning his blood-filled eyes on her. "Don't be afraid. I will kill him quickly, and you will be safe with me again."

"No." Molly's voice felt dead in her throat. She trembled violently.

"And maybe," he continued, "you will come to your senses and allow me to share this wonderful immortality with you, love. *Forever.* Imagine that." He smiled again.

His teeth were thin, straight and as pointed as needles. Two, much larger fangs protracted over the top of them.

Molly attempted to steady the gun in her hand. She had no way of knowing if it would do anything.

Tom suddenly pounced and dug a handful of three-inch claws into Christopher's forehead.

"Aaah!" Christopher screamed, tumbling over the second floor railing. Molly shrieked in terror. Standing, Christopher gave a forceful snap of his wings and soared upward, catching Tom and rocketing the two through the second floor ceiling and onto the roof. Molly scrambled to the roof stairway, cursing her cowardice. Loud thuds from Tom's fists connecting with Christopher's body echoed down into the house. Shrill shrieks vibrated the windows and floors. Glowing brightly, Molly's map ring guided her up the stairs to the roof.

"Thomas, I will protect her! Just give her to me! You know you are a danger to her! I can make sure she lives forever! The Society is strong, and when our new leadership decides it, we're going to erase our enemies from the world. You don't want Molly to be among the dead, do you?"

Tom responded with another quick pummeling. Christopher dug his nails into Tom's lower back. Lifting himself skyward with a flap of his wings, Christopher looked down at Tom. "The clans can't survive what's to come, Thomas. You won't survive. None of your kind will. Don't curse Molly by forcing her to share your grim destiny!"

Tom leapt from the roof, catching Christopher's ankle. The vampire hissed loudly, savagely swiping at Tom. Christopher's needle teeth snapped and gnashed together.

Tightening his grip, Tom swung his body hard and released. Christopher plummeted to the street below, cracking the stone.

Molly crashed through the open roof door, La Flor raised above her head. She spotted Christopher on the ground and didn't hesitate. Pointing her ruby ring downward, she shouted, "*Spuere ignis!*"

As Christopher raised his head, his attention was immediately drawn away from Tom by the fireball racing toward him through the dark. He opened his mouth to bellow a shrill shriek before he was consumed. Rising to his feet and screaming in pain, the blazing vampire lifted off the ground, his wings sizzling. Molly tried to fire a shot at him. Reacting quickly, Christopher dodged the shot, retreating up the street toward a church. Tom's eyes locked onto him. The winged shadow climbed the steeple of the church like a giant bat and disappeared into the belfry. Tom sprinted after it.

Molly fired again, the shot ringing loudly in the darkness as it struck one of the bells inside the tower. Her map ring radiated a violent white light. Realizing it was a warning, she hurried back inside the house. "Sofia!" she called out.

The confused maid rushed to her. "*Señora!*" She exclaimed, pointing out the wreckage in the main hall and stairway.

"Are you all right?" Molly asked.

Sofia, unharmed, asked where Tom had gone, trying to explain that she and the other maids had been asleep in their rooms when they heard the ceiling cave in.

"I'm going to find Thomas now," Molly told her. "Keep youselves together and stay safe." Molly, equipped with her three pistols, ran outside and down the path toward the church, her map ring showing her the way to Thomas.

Tom reached the church and gazed up to the steeple, leaping onto the building's exterior and digging his claws into the stone. He climbed to the top of the tower and into the belfry. The deep, unbroken darkness surrounded him, disoriented him, stuck to his skin. Christopher's laughter sounded out in the blackness. He coughed and groaned through his pain.

"Thomaaaas ..."

Tom spun around. His ears perked up and his pupils ached as he tried to capture the scarce light as a moth might do.

"You do not understand, Thomas. Your kind is inferior. Your brother is clearly the wiser of the two of you! Look at you—so reckless and brutish." A dark hand emerged from beneath Tom and slashed his ankle with a dagger, then vanished quickly again, retreating into the solid stone.

Tom stumbled and roared, swatting at the dark.

"I can kill you as you are now, despite our respective physical strengths, Thomas. How pitiful you are in the dark." The hand leapt from the stone wall again, tearing a gash in Tom's back before vanishing into the wall. "Does death frighten you? Where is the brilliant light when you need it?" Both hands appeared and shoved Tom backward. He stumbled into a large bell. It rang and echoed deeply in the tower. His wounds burned horribly. Christopher's dagger was silver. He'd come prepared.

The light from Molly's map ring was blinding. As fast as her legs could carry her she climbed the stairs to the church belfry.

Christopher's shadowy form lunged from the wall. He reared back, brandishing his short, silver blade. "I want you to die before the sun rises! All you will see is blackness before you go!"

Molly appeared in the belfry, the light from her ring filling the entire church. Christopher released a harsh gasp, gagging and choking on his shrieks. He covered his eyes. Although his body began to burn away in the light, he advanced forward, the tip of the silver blade one short thrust away from Tom's heart. Molly drew her pearl pistols and fired. The shots beat against Christopher's body, forcing him backward. Pushing off of the bell, Tom charged Christopher, tackling and shoving him into the wall of the belfry. Throwing Tom away, Christopher lunged at Molly in desperation, too late remembering her other ring. Trying to slow himself in time, he propelled himself backward with a strong flap of his wings and shielded himself with his bare arms.

Molly, without hesitation, raised her fist. *"Spuere ignis!"*

Bursting into flames, Christopher tumbled out of the belfry. Tom leapt after him but stopped abruptly at the ledge, watching Christopher plummet toward the ground, wings blazing. The rush of wind extinguished him as he fell. His right wing snagged the outstretched hand of a stone angel carved into a lower tower ledge. His body jerked to a stop as his wing was pierced by the hand of the statue. A faint orange glow appeared on the horizon. Simultaneously, the light from Molly's ring grew dim.

Tom huffed and puffed wearily. The sky outside grew lighter, orange blending into pink and yellow—black, blue, and violet receding. Molly sat motionless on the floor of the belfry, her eyes void of emotion as she stared at the horizon. Christopher stirred. He tilted his head up to gaze at the sea. Squinting with one eye, he drew in a gasp and struggled to free himself. The red in his eyes became pale and faint. The morning sun rose slowly, and the night was driven from the city streets. The color faded from Christopher's body, turning him the color of ash. In defiance he stretched a skeletal hand outward and gritted his teeth before ceasing to move altogether. As he froze in that position, his limbs and face crumbled to dust. A light breeze carried him away one particle at a time like a sandcastle in a rising tide.

Tom placed one hand on the floor of the belfry to raise himself to his feet. He limped to Molly and hunched down with his back to her, offering her a ride back to the house. Standing, Molly grabbed onto Tom's shoulders for support; he gently took her hands to help her onto his back. Leaning a bit, he looped her arms around his neck. The fur was thickest there and easy to hold onto.

Tom descended swiftly down the exterior edifice and landed as softly as possible. He hurried down the empty streets before the city dwellers rose to begin their day. Carrying Molly inside, he motioned for Sofia to follow and carried Molly into his room, where she would no doubt be safest. Sofia stayed by Molly's side while Tom returned to his normal form. Afterward he excused and thanked Sofia, watching Molly while she lay in his bed. Eventually he fell asleep on the floor beside her.

Tom opened his eyes and blinked them shut several times. Sofia's happy face hovered above his as he lay on the floor.

"*Buenos dias!*"

"Yeah, yeah." Tom stood up.

Sofia told him Bart had come to the house to tell him the *Scotch Bonnet* was set for sail, and that word was a local vampire cult had run off the Black Coats earlier in the morning.

"*Gracias*, Sofia," said Tom gratefully. He stretched, stripped and put on a clean white shirt and new pants so Molly would not be reminded of the night's events too soon. As he quickly dressed, he took extra care to be silent, constantly glancing back at the bed where Molly lay asleep. Sofia called them to breakfast. Tom tied his right boot and hunted for the left. Molly stirred slightly.

"It's here," she mumbled. Her hand pointed limply toward the corner of the bed on the floor.

"Ah, so it is," Tom said, sliding it on and tying it quickly. "So, just now awake, eh?" He asked with a grin.

Molly tucked herself comfortably back in her blankets, mumbling something incomprehensible.

"Hm? You were saying?" Tom persisted, throwing off her covers.

"Perhaps."

"Perhaps what?"

"Perhaps I *have* just now awakened. Not a problem, is it?" She sounded cross.

"Oh, no, depending on when you woke I may consider you a very lucky woman. Ha ha!" He headed toward the door.

Molly's brow furrowed. "What?"

"Nothing! Are you coming to breakfast?"

Glaring at him, Molly pulled the covers back over her head. "No."

"Why not?" He leapt onto the bed.

Molly yelped in surprise.

"Ship's in port, sun's up, sea's waiting impatiently. And I've done more than enough to lure you out of bed already, I believe."

"We're leaving?" Molly asked.

"Yes, we are. Well, *I* am."

"I'll just be a moment." The way Molly rose from bed would have made a corpse look vigorous.

"I'll just wait here." Tom lay across the bed, his head hanging over upside down and looking up at her with a grin. "*Not a problem, is it?*" He tried not to smile.

"No, but let's pretend I would like some privacy just this once." She grumbled and put her hands on his chest and walked him backward out of the room.

"Temper, temper," scolded Tom, following her. "I've been meaning to ask you something."

"Hm?"

"Well, I'm sure you can guess. But nonetheless, who is, er … *was* that man, Christopher?"

Molly sighed deeply, turning her gaze to the windows. "His name was Christopher Jonathan Barnes, and, though a Black Coat, he was an otherwise excellent gunsmith, among other things. He was the one who taught me to shoot." She paused. "He was also the reason I was so desperate to leave Bridgetown."

"How did you meet such a man? Or is that none of my business?" Tom asked carefully.

Molly's eyes narrowed. "It was nothing of the sort you are implying, I assure you. I had nothing in Barbados. I had spent everything I had to receive transportation to the island, and I couldn't afford an inn. Christopher happened to find me and offered me a place to stay at his home at no expense. It was an offer I could hardly refuse. He took interest in the fact that I had two pistols and no knowledge of how to use them, which led him to educate me on the proper technique of handling such weapons. He seemed like a good man."

"Many do, at first. Molly did he and you—" Tom struggled to phrase the next question.

"No! Of course not! I would never—" Molly exclaimed.

Tom blushed. "You didn't let me finish."

"Oh ... I apologize. What were you going to say?" Molly looked away, flushing.

"Did he ever mention the Black Coat Society to you before you found out on your own? Did he ever offer you an invitation to join?"

Molly glared out the window. "I fled long before that."

"Did he ever take it upon himself to make the decision *for* you? Or try?"

Molly wrung her hands. "It's hard to explain."

Tom approached her. "I need to see your neck. Unless you're certain he didn't bite you, perhaps, in your sleep?"

"Thomas, I assure you, I fled before he had the chance. Surely you would've noticed something like that by now, anyway."

"Move your hair, please," Tom asked firmly.

Molly fumed, pulling away. "I will do no such thing! I think I am capable of knowing what I am."

"Then you have no reason to get upset. You're in no danger either way. Mr. Barnes is dead, Molly."

"I'm well aware," she snapped.

"Well then?"

"Then check if you so desire. You'll find nothing," Molly said angrily.

"No." Tom turned away from her. "How long were you in Barbados? Did Christopher tell you immediately about his affiliations, or did he wait? Or, did you find out for yourself?"

"I remained in various towns in Barbados for almost three months," she replied. "Unfortunately I found out about everything myself. One night as I slept upstairs I awoke hearing voices from below. I crept out onto the upstairs landing and looked down. There was a group in black standing downstairs, with Christopher among them. They had captured a woman. They seduced her, and I don't know what else. She died after."

"Someone you knew?"

"Not very well. She worked a sugarcane field nearby."

"I see. You must understand that despite your strong-willed nature, it wasn't average men you were living amongst. They can be persuasive to *any* degree they have to be. Any—physically, mentally, emotionally. I know what Mr. Barnes would have resorted to, but luckily he never had the chance. I assume from your earlier outburst that he tried, nonetheless, yes?"

"It was cruel," Molly nodded. "I would receive visions in my dreams. Horrible ones." She shuddered. "That was when I decided to leave immediately. I didn't know how they were doing what they were doing to me. I knew it was something supernatural, and it frightened me."

"Yes." He nodded in understanding. "I'm not unfamiliar with that method. Lucid hypnosis. The dreams," he said, looking at her solemnly, "they seemed so real, didn't they? As if you were waking up in another place altogether. But you weren't."

Molly's eyes began to water in rememberance. "It was as if I could feel them touching me in my mind's eye. I had no idea who they really were. I never would have suspected them to be vampires. That would have seemed silly."

"I've always had unusual visions in my sleep," Tom began. "I am not sure, however, that it's the mark of the curse that allows me to have such dreams—to create a reality in my sleep and see the events of days and years yet to come."

Tears hanging in her eyes, Molly listened closely.

"Molly," Tom said quietly, "I dreamed of you before we ever met."

Molly's eyes widened.

"That's why I took you aboard my ship in Bridgetown. I recognized you from a dream in which we were dancing. Although you seemed so real in the dream, I thought you were something purely of my imagination until I saw you that night on the docks. Normally I have complete control of my dreams, but you acted independently of my will. You had a personality. I never forgot that dream."

After preparing the remainder of her things, Molly paused at her bedroom door, breathing deeply, trying to memorize it all so her imagination could comfort her once she was out at sea again.

"Sofia! *Tengo hambre!*" she heard Tom downstairs, happily eating his breakfast. He'd left abruptly after their last conversation.

"*Silencio, cerdito!*" Sofia called back. All the other help laughed.

Molly wandered into the dining room and prepared herself a small plate, sitting down near the end of the table. Beginning to eat her breakfast, she saw Tom hurrying up and down the main stairs over and over. In no time at all, he had packed and was at the front door.

"Ready, Bart?" she heard him say.

"Been ready, Cap'n!" Bart replied enthusiastically.

"All right then. *Adios*, Sofia! Molly? Are you coming? *Adios*, everyone. *Muchas gracias!*" The two men stepped out the front door, and the maids bid farewell to them.

Molly looked up at the door and her jaw dropped. Where did Thomas think he was going without her?

Sofia brought out more food, puzzled that Molly was not following them out.

Molly looked long at the food on her plate. Why shouldn't she stay? She would be with her father here. She had found what she was looking for. Feeling uneasy, she looked up again toward the front door. The girl inside her was telling her that the life she wanted was walking down the street away from her.

"I'd best be off or they'll leave without me," she told Sofia. "Thank you for all that you've done."

"*De nada, Señora Bishop. Adios.*" Sofia smiled sweetly.

Molly offered one last farewell and made her way hurriedly out the door, only then noticing how young and beautiful Sofia looked. She'd paid the girl little mind since arriving. Molly suddenly found herself unable to resist wondering where Thomas had found her or what kind of past they'd shared. Had it been similar to Thomas and Molly's? As Molly turned away, Sofia, still smiling, shut the front door.

Tom reached the ship and admired it for a moment. "Gentlemen, let me see those white sails fly!"

"Cap'n…" Bart stopped him for a moment and cracked a bittersweet smile.

"I already know," said Tom. "You've decided to stay, yeah?"

"I'm gettin' old, Thomas. I may return to Isla del Sol some day, but for now I need to rest my bones here. I took the liberty of recruiting you a new quartermaster. He ought to do fine by you."

"No worries, old friend." Tom clapped a hand on the old shipbuilder's shoulder. "May we meet again when times are better."

The crew—some new, and some old survivors of Tom's past voyages—prepared the rigging, weighed anchor and raised the sails.

Tom strutted along the main deck, barking out stern commands. "How does Morocco sound, gentlemen? We can stock our kitchen for less coin than we can here if we make it a quick excursion."

The crew gave a cheer.

"Then make haste! We haven't until the new moon, boys! Chop chop!" Tom had certainly seen the crew work faster on worse days than that one. "Now where did my map get to?" he asked rhetorically, gazing back up the streets into Barcelona. He saw a speeding figure approaching the dock.

Racing to the docks, her legs flying beneath her, Molly saw the white sails of Tom's new ship.

"Ah, there it is," Tom said, grinning. Leaning over the railing of the ship, he waved his hat at Molly. "Good day, beautiful young stranger! Join me!"

Bart dropped a gangway down to the dock.

"Room and rations enough for just one more!" Tom called to her.

Resisting the urge to push him overboard, Molly scampered up the gangway with a small trunk and books in her arms.

Tom snatched her up in a hurry, catching her in one arm and lifting her aboard. Tipping his hat and placing a kiss on her neck, he left her for the quarterdeck after helping her to her cabin. "Helmsman!" he cried.

The helmsman nodded and spun the wheel around, maneuvering the ship away from the dock. The crew lifted the anchor into place and locked it against the hull.

"Morocco!" Tom shouted, throwing an arm forward. As the ship sped out of port, Tom searched his coat and retrieved a fresh bottle of tequila.

Molly collapsed on her bed, breathing deeply. She was flustered and in total disbelief. How dare he test her patience?

Outside, Tom's eyes swept the deck as he called out for Molly. "Miss Bishop?" He stood on the quarterdeck, directing the helmsman, tossing the bottle of tequila from hand to hand.

Molly glared at the door of her cabin as she heard her name.

"Never mind! I've set the course already." Adjusting the helmsman's course, he turned to the rest of the crew. "We will stop for only a day in Tangier, but we will not enter the city past the waterfront! In five days, be prepared to anchor." He consulted his assistant navigator and paired him with the helmsman before moving to his cabin.

Molly sat on her bed gazing at the constellations emmitted from her ring. She sighed, realizing she had not had a chance to give her father a proper farewell, though she was sure he would understand. As she continued to stare, other thoughts entered Molly's mind as well. She left her cabin in search of a distraction. She set herself on the railing at the top of the forecastle—allowing fresh air to clear her head. Looking over her shoulder to ensure she was alone, she took out her pistols. She needed to practice her marksmanship. Her map ring gave off a faint glow. She wasn't sure if it was a trick of the light or if she really was seeing it. She shrugged it off, deciding it was nothing to concern herself with.

Tom stowed all his bags beneath his bed and tossed his heavy coat on a desk, on which a map of the Atlantic lay open. Tom loomed over the map, hands planted on the desk. "Where are you, exactly, and what are you up to?" he asked the emptiness of the room. Frustrated, he twirled a small throwing knife in one hand then stuck it in the desk, making steady circles in the wood grain. "You have five more days to run. Then I begin hunting. See you in the sunny isles, Harlan."

Molly never asked Thomas about Sofia. She explained to me that just as she left Spain with the captain, it occurred to her that she could not have realistically been his one and only woman, considering how often he traveled and how many places he'd seen. However, it was not the possibility that Thomas had once felt strongly for Sofia that bothered her. Rather, the idea of past lovers reminded her of one of her own—a man named Eli Wilks. He'd died at the hands of ruthless pirates several years before she met Thomas. She was a young girl then, and on her way to the New World, where she was to marry Wilks and live a simple life. When Eli was pronounced dead, there was an argument between Molly and Eli's family, and she left the colonies on a merchant ship headed into the Caribbean, where Christopher Barnes soon discovered her and her yet-to-be-realized skills as a powerful sorceress.

Christopher, as Thomas suspected, had left the Caribbean by request of his brother, Harlan. It had been obvious to Thomas since leaving London that Harlan was associating with the Black Coat Society. As strange as it was that a werewolf could have climbed ranks in a vampire cult, Thomas was sure he'd find Harlan in the Caribbean. Thomas knew after leaving Spain that he'd have the upper hand. Harlan would be waiting for Christopher to return with Molly, unaware that Christopher was dead and Thomas was homing in with the intention to strike.

Soon Thomas would sail to Tangier where, once again, his life would face the threat of bounty hunters—namely mercenaries of Fahkir ibn Abdul-Hadi, a temporary steward of the Alaouite Sultanate. Fahkir, unbeknownst to Thomas and all of Morocco at the time, was in fact not a man. The rightful sultan had fallen into a cursed sleep, and a dark being called a qareen—an evil, shadowy double—had replaced him, ruling the territory as a vicious tyrant in the sultan's stead.

Molly related most of this part of the tale to me. She told me Tangier had been a great trial for her. She felt as though the third time she was called to guard Thomas's life, during his imprisonment in Tangier, was a sign. It would change her perspective on her own life, and, she told me, though nearly losing Thomas again terrified her, it gave her purpose. The only grace granted to her was the aid of an unexpected ally.

Geoffrey Mylus,
May 9, 1833

❧❧❧

Three days from Barcelona, Tom's ship anchored within the port of Tangier, Morocco. Even from a distance it was clear the North African city flaunted its wealth, and its buildings revealed a prominent Islamic aesthetic. The kingdom was currently under control of the Alaouite Dynasty, which was friendly to the merchant ships of the New World and hostile toward the regional Barbary pirate ships.

Tom walked out on the main deck. "Launch a small shore boat. Five of you come with me. Quartermaster, we will return by dusk."

The *Scotch Bonnet*'s new quartermaster nodded and took charge of the rest of the crew. Tom and five others boarded the shore boat.

"Lower it!" Tom commanded. Soon he stepped from the shore boat onto the docks in Tangier.

Molly watched through the window of her cabin as the captain and crew departed. She hurried out onto deck, wondering why her ring maintained its faint glow in the broad daylight.

Tom and the others stayed close to one another as Tom countered every passing look with one of his own. They entered the bazaar along the waterfront, and as they approached a little stand situated at the very edge of the market, shaded by a cork oak, Tom greeted a merchant.

The young Moroccan man smiled and invited Tom to purchase an item or two.

"I'm looking for special ammunition," Tom explained.

The man nodded and retrieved a hidden box from behind a stack of large rugs.

Tom opened it and inspected the selection. "Yes, thank you, this will do," he said, handing the man a few gold coins in exchange. Tom sent the crew back into the central bazaar to collect some large barrels of fish and fruit, while he ventured deeper into the city against his own orders. He cruised through the dry, dusty streets, searching for a particular sort of artist who might happen to be able to help him. The crowd was thick and noisy. Strangers walked by carrying large pots, racks of cloth and tobacco. Tom stood out among the robed and veiled. He tried to hide his pistols beneath his light cotton shirt, although they clearly bulged through the thin material.

Soon Tom came across an old man busy moving empty pots and brushes around his shop. Tom approached the man and, revealing a handful of gold coins, explained his dilemma to the old artist. The man, uninterested at first, did not object as soon as Tom offered another handful of gold. The man told Tom to wait as he went to fetch a small pot of ink. Upon his return Tom wrote out exactly the words he needed the man to translate and copy onto his skin. The man scoffed at the relative ease of the task before him. When he finished, a neat circle of Arabic script surrounded the cursed mark on Tom's back. Roughly translated it read, "In the name of God, and to calm the beast." Tom's hope was that the finished product would help lend him control of his transformations and the consequential fits of rage and hunger.

When the artist finished, Tom asked to be directed to a holy man or any individual capable of assisting him in the second phase of his request. "Can you take me to an *imam*?" he asked the old man.

Being cautious and quiet, the old man surreptitiously pointed Tom in the right direction.

Tom thanked him and left the shop. Wandering once more through Tangier, Tom found his destination without difficulty. He entered a dark, candle-lit parlor and approached the holy man inside. "I've been sent—"

The *imam* raised a hand to silence Tom and assured him he was well aware of Tom's purpose. Before reciting the prayer Tom needed, the *imam* warned Tom against staying in Tangier too long. Tom's kind were not welcome in the city. After the man prayed over the fresh ink in Tom's skin, the script seemed to come alive, shifting and turning round and round. Thanking the man, Tom returned hastily to the docks, where the other five crewmen awaited his arrival.

"Time to be off! I can't believe—" Tom began to address his crew and then saw their uncomfortable lips turned up. They glanced around uneasily as droves of armed men dressed in long pants, long sleeved shirts, and scarves disguising their identities appeared all around Tom and his men.

"Sorry, Cap'n. There are too many of 'em. We didn't see 'em coming," one of the crew apologized.

"Oh, it's no trouble, boys," Tom assured them, beginning to take on his monstrous form, "Let me handle them and we'll be on our wa—"

Wip!

"Agh!" Tom put a hand to the nape of his neck. A long, thin dart was stuck in his skin. An assassin in league with the armed strangers had stuck him with the projectile from high up on a nearby rooftop. Before Tom could react, he fell asleep where he stood, and collapsed face-first to the ground.

Watching the sun setting in the west, Molly slammed her fist down on the deck railing and let out a shriek of anger. She'd known something was wrong when the shore boat returned with five men and no captain.

"They were mercenaries, dozens in number," one of the men had tried to explain to her when she demanded to know what had kept them and where Thomas had gone.

"They told us if we handed over the captain, they'd let us go," said another.

"Which we did," continued the first, "Because how else could anyone have returned to the ship to tell you about it, Miss Bishop?"

"I don't mistake your cowardice for cunning, any of you!" she scolded them. Going to her cabin to retrieve her pistols, she stormed back out on deck. To no surprise, the stars in her map ring formed a neat line and pointed to Tangier.

Molly shouted out to the crew. "All hands!"

The men winced at the sudden bark of Molly's voice. Obediently they assembled on deck. The quartermaster approached Molly angrily. "And who gave you the right to order this crew around, eh, Miss?"

Molly retaliated with a dark glare and sharp tongue. "Apparently, *sir*, none of you are worthy to take charge, considering the lot of you allowed your captain to be taken away."

The quartermaster failed to reply. The crew fidgeted nervously.

Molly continued, firmly. "I will go ashore and find the captain myself! A few who are man enough to assist me will follow me to shore!"

The quartermaster shrank to the background.

"Five of you will come with me into the city! Bring any weapons that are available but easily concealed! I need men below deck to ready the cannons! Upon return, we must be ready to sail!" Her eyes found the quartermaster in the crowd. "I trust you, sir, will be able to make sure this is done?"

A crewmate approached Molly. He was young and fit, with wild, short brown hair and a pair of hazel eyes that looked much older than they should. "Ah ... Miss Bishop?" The man threw a hard look at the quartermaster. "Allow me to oversee this operation. The name's Morgan Shaw. I've served under Captain Crowe for much longer than *that* cowardly runt," he said, cocking his head at the sulking quartermaster. "I'll gladly have this vessel ready for quick escape and battle if necessary, Miss."

Nodding, Molly agreed. "My thanks, Mr. Shaw."

"It is my duty, Miss. You must hurry now if Captain is to live." He turned to the crew. "Prepare the guns! Man the rigging and sails! Five of you go with the lady! Make haste!"

Congregating like hungry vultures, Tangier's citizenry followed the mercenaries and Tom through the streets. Tom half-consciously heard mockery and insults directed at him from the crowd of spectators. His captors hurried him to the palace while the people began to throw stones and food at Tom. His mark began to burn, and he gasped hoarsely. Receiving a sharp blow to the ribs, he shut his eyes and blacked out upon arrival.

"Is he alive?" Tangier's surrogate sultan, Fahkir ibn Abdul-Hadi, growled as Tom was toted into the throne room. The thin, lavishly dressed man's scholarly eyes examined the catch from behind the tiny bifocals resting atop his nose. Dark and secretive, they hid in the background of his tan and bearded countenance.

"Yes, Your Excellence, but only clinging to life, I'm afraid."

Easily irked by the news, Fahkir became impatient. "See to it that he is sent away by dawn tomorrow! If he dies before I receive my bounty, your neck will pay the deficit!" The man's permanent wrinkles emphasized his already exaggerated displeasure.

"Yes, Your Excellence! At once! Take him to a cell!" ordered an officer. The subordinates filed out of the throne room. Tom was thrown into a small cell within the lower levels of the palace. The soldiers shut the door and put out all the lamps, leaving him alone in darkness.

Molly and the crew crept through the streets of Tangier and distributed themselves throughout the crowd; with

Chad T. Douglas

calm and cool finesse they followed Molly as she, in turn,
followed the light of her map ring toward the palace.
Discovering guards posted at the gates, Molly took a
different route around to the gardens outside the palace,
avoiding the patrol. She kept a tricorn hat—one borrowed
from the crew—low over her eyes to conceal herself. She'd
crammed all her hair up inside the hat and loathed how it
made her sweat. She felt like she had a raccoon perched
on her scalp.

The guards apparently did not intend to keep Tom's
capture a secret. They discussed him loudly.

"He was dead when he arrived?"

Molly's attention was drawn to the voices, though she
did not understand Arabic.

"No. Almost. They're treating him with just enough
medicines to keep him alive."

"Medicine? For that kind of poison? Shouldn't it have
killed him?"

"It would have killed a man, but the captive is a skin
changer. He is cursed. Evil magic protects him, though I
am sure it will not keep him alive for too long. That must
be why His Excellence ordered the sorceress Udbala to
watch him. She was giving him medicines from a tiny

374

vial." The soldier exaggerated its small size with his fingers.

"What's in it, then?"

"I don't know. It's very potent and unusual magic Udbala uses."

"To be honest, if I were His Excellence I would have some fears concerning her. She is not Moroccan. She never speaks. She always seems to be conspiring, but His Excellence trusts her nonetheless. She keeps to herself in that small, dark room, high up in the palace."

One guard pointed up, and Molly noticed. The second guard shuddered. Several other soldiers approached. The two guards hushed themselves and stood upright again, plumed spears resting properly on their shoulders. Molly made haste to the back gardens, attempting to lift the great weight in her chest.

Appearing from out of the shadows, the sorceress Udbala ascended a large staircase at the other end of the garden. Her heavy, tight black robe and *hijab* flowed strangely in the breeze. The ends of the cloth looked like vapor, wafting on the air like hookah smoke. Molly spun around, drawing her pistol, startled by the woman's presence. Stopping momentarily, Udbala looked directly at Molly. Her gaze was not threatening. She turned her head again as if to make sure she was not being watched by any of the guards and continued up the staircase. Staring after the woman, Molly lowered her weapon. Somehow she felt at ease with the stranger, but she maintained her distance. Motioning for the crewmembers to stay hidden in the shadows, Molly followed. The last wisps of the Udbala's robes inconspicuously curled into the shape of a beckoning hand. She glanced back once more at Molly before hurrying into the tower as guards passed by the staircase. Molly hid herself as the guards passed, then moved to the stairs.

Tom squirmed in his cell. The small dose of medicine the sorceress gave him healed him to near health, but as quickly as she left him, the toxin in his veins came back out of hiding *What are they planning?* he wondered. What had the sorceress meant when she told him, "Suffer a while longer and you will live"? Why did she come and go so hastily? Where was he being held?

Making her way up the tower, Molly looked around for the mysterious woman she'd seen only moments before. The staircase spiraled higher and higher, ending at a single door, which had been left slightly ajar. Molly entered quietly. Her map ring glowed and revealed every scintilla of dust in the room. The small room was filled with large wooden shelves holding books written in hundreds of languages and dialects. Small bottles, vials, and bowls crowded a dozen or so tables of disparate sizes. Mortars and pestles covered tabletops as well. Small fires burned in dishes beneath pots full of liquids. A soothing smell permeated the air—some kind of perfume.

"You have come for the vagrant wolf, yes?"

Molly flinched, looking around for the source of the voice. "Yes."

"Why?" The veiled woman stepped into view, holding an open book in one palm.

Molly looked the woman up and down, detecting no concealed weapons. "He does not deserve the fate these people have chosen for him."

Udbala shut the book. "Many people do not deserve the judgments exacted on them by men in positions of unquestioned power. But what is to be done about it is a quandary as old as civilization, and irrelevant. Why does this man deserve to live more than anyone else?"

Molly eyes hardened. "Why does he deserve to die?"

The sorceress's mouth formed a smile. "If you wish him to live, I can help you save him. But you must help me as well, for his escape will cost me my life otherwise."

"What must I do?" Molly asked without hesitation.

"You must help me overthrow Fahkir ibn Abdul-Hadi. He is not what he appears to be, but the people of this kingdom are unaware. Their rightful ruler is in the throes of a dark enchantment."

"What do you mean?" asked Molly, warily.

"Fahkir is not human. He is a *qareen*—an evil *djinni* and shadow double of the true sultan. He has been reigning in place of the real sultan, and it is a wrathful tyrant."

"How do we overthrow him?"

"I require only the Alaouite family earring. It belongs to the sultan and has been passed down through the Alaouite family line as long as anyone can recall. It contains a *djinni* named Ghazi Al-Shereh, an ancient advisor to the Alaouite line, and the being masking itself as Fahkir. With it, my task will be absurdly easy. You must understand first, that the *djinni* Ghazi is a magical being. I do not serve beneath him. I am not a native of this kingdom or of this country. I was sent from a place far east of this land. I am here to usurp Ghazi and place his powers back into the hands of a capable wielder. The so-called sultan Fahkir is immortal as long as he wears the earring, which houses Ghazi. If I attempt assassination or escape, it will be my own life that is sacrificed, not his. He will have us both executed along with your friends if we are caught. He disposes of anyone he dislikes or feels threatened by. Your friend is especially dangerous to the *djinni*, and it fears his kind. Your friend has no intention of threatening this kingdom, I know that, but the *djinni*, having freed itself from bondage, is corrupted by paranoia. If you can bring me the earring, I swear on my own life that you and your friend will leave this city unharmed."

Molly gazed down in thought for a moment.

"I created a medicine that can cure the effects of the silver-laced poison eating away at your friend's life," Udbala continued. "I cannot do everything myself, for if I am captured you will be also, and you will have no chance of succeeding. I must mix a new batch of ingredients. The last dose I gave your friend emptied the only vial I had.

We have no time to spare. If we do not conduct these tasks quickly and conjointly, your friend will not last through the night."

Molly nodded. Afraid for Tom as she was, she had no choice but to trust the woman. She neither had time to care about the sorceress's dealings in Morocco, or with the Alaouite family.

"Fahkir will soon be asleep in the royal bedroom. At all hours of the night there are armed guards outside his room, standing at every entrance. Fahkir will remove the earring before he sleeps. That is your opportunity. I know you cannot trust me, and for that reason I think you are wise. However, there must be trust between us." She handed Molly a vial of light green liquid. "Drink this and stay out of sight, and you will pass the guards unnoticed. It will silence your steps and movements. Use it with that onyx I spy around your neck, and you will be no more than a ghost."

Molly took the bottle delicately into her hands. "You can promise that he will be safe?"

The sorceress's eyes were solemn. "Unfortunately at this point neither one of us has a choice other than to proceed with our set tasks. The guards now know you are here, for they heard you ascending the stairs. They are looking for both of us." Something about her eyes was unnatural. "I can see them. You must make your decision quickly."

Molly did not need time to think. "Where does Fahkir sleep?"

"The fifth floor of the palace, in the central hallway through the grand doors. You will recognize them easily, for they are the only pair made of carved ivory. Take the courtyard balcony and climb the fourth floor ledges as extra precaution. Nonetheless no one will detect you as long as the contents in that vial last for you." The hue of the woman's eyes changed to a misty violet. "Your men have moved into the west garden. It is on your way. They won't be able to see you, but I will protect them from here."

With that she uttered an incantation, closing her eyes and lifting a hand in the direction of the west garden. "It is done. Drink the entire vial, and hurry. I will prepare the medicine." Her eyes shifted again. "Guards are coming! Swallow it and go!"

Molly wasn't entirely comfortable drinking the substance and the sorceress noticed.

"Look," Udbala said, fetching some more of the stuff and drinking it herself, "Harmless. See? Now, hurry!"

Molly quickly gulped down the contents of the vial and slipped out the door, mouthing a silent thank you. "*Absconde me*", she whispered, vanishing from sight.

The Sorceress hurried to a large cabinet and picked through jars frantically. Several soldiers moved stealthily up the stairs toward the room. The first few ran straight past Molly. The last two collided with her and spun around the staircase in confusion, blind as to what caused the blunder. One soldier looked directly at Molly and then away, shrugging.

An odd sensation lingered on her skin as Molly realized she truly could not be seen. She dashed through the gardens, noticing the crew where Udbala said they would be. Seeing the balcony on the far wall, she made her way to some thick vines that grew nearby, ascended them and closed in on her destination. After much struggle, she finally made her way to the balcony and headed up the nearest flight of stairs to the fifth floor. To her right, at the top of the stairs, was a long corridor where she spotted the two large, ivory doors of Fahkir's bedroom, a guard on either side. The guards stood, watchful, turning their heads at every whisper of the breeze. Nervous, Molly wondered how on earth she would be able to gain entry unnoticed.

A burst of shouts suddenly came from the sorceress's tower. A pair of armed men rushed up to the startled guards as Molly watched. It was clear to her that they were expressing severe concern by their gestures and because the guards left their posts to assist in the scene unraveling at the tower. Molly pressed herself against the wall as the soldiers passed, holding her breath. The soldiers hurried by without any acknowledgement of Molly, standing in plain sight. The ivory doors were vulnerable. Wasting no time, Molly reached out to one of the large handles, taking a deep breath before pulling it open and quickly slipping inside. Inside the large bedroom Fahkir lay asleep. The sheer curtains in the arched windows blew back and forth lightly and shaded the floor beneath. Fahkir's massive bed sat in the center of the room. A small box lay on top of a trunk next to the bed. Molly put a hand against her chest to silence her steady breathing, making her way over to the trunk as quietly as possible. Fahkir showed no sign of being disturbed. The golden box on the trunk was open, and held an earring in its cushioned belly. Molly glanced at Fahkir uneasily, her hand lingering cautiously over the earring. His light snoring reassured her, and she quickly took the earring and placed it in her pocket.

"You!" Fahkir sat upright, his dark eyes burning. They saw past the sorceress's magic and told the *djinni* possessing Fahkir that Molly was looming by his bedside.

Molly turned to run.

"Stop!" he cried. "Agghh!" In attempting to spring from the bed he had fallen to the floor.

Molly pushed her way through the heavy doors and raced down the corridor. A low, powerful humming noise filled the air outside in the garden and east courtyard. She looked down to see the palace guards encircling Udbala. Standing calmly in the midst of her attackers, the sorceress stood poised, a violet aura seeping from her body. One soldier rushed her from behind, sword drawn. She raised a hand without turning around. The soldier stopped immediately, the violet aura swirling around him. The sorceress thrust her hand forward, and the soldier was sent sailing through the air and into several of his comrades. She turned to look at Molly and opened her hand. "The earring! Quickly!"

Molly tossed the ring down to her over the balcony.

Fahkir approached. "Stop her!" he yelled, just as the ring was tossed. As it arched through the air, Fahkir leaned over the balcony in a desperate attempt to catch the earring.

Udbala's violet aura stretched beyond the sultan's reach to retrieve the ring before he could get it, bringing it to her open hand. The guards charged once more and were swiftly deflected in all directions with a few flips of the mysterious woman's wrist. Placing the earring in her open palm and holding her other hand directly above it, the sorceress recited a spell in a strange language. A heavily tattooed man rushed to her side and threw off his concealing wraps and robe. Standing beside Udbala, he began to chant, and as he did, Udbala placed the Alaouite earring in the lobe of his right ear.

Fahkir shouted furiously to the guards. "Don't just stand there idly! Kill he—" His mouth ceased to move. As the moonlight illuminated his face, Molly could see that it was different now—his skin darkened and his eyes became inhuman. His complexion then paled again, and he developed the features of a tusked, porcine imp. Molly backed away as the *djinni* thrashed and squealed.

Compelled by a curse, his form became like a liquid shadow and leapt down to where Udbala and her assistant stood, and was drawn into the earring. The tattooed man breathed a heavy sigh and his eyes flashed with supernatural fire as he contained and seized control of Ghazi Al-Shereh's powers. The remaining soldiers turned their backs and scurried away.

Molly hurried down to the garden, running up to the sorceress. The tattooed man said nothing, nodded to Udbala, threw a hood over his head and slipped away. Molly didn't bother to inquire after him; her only concern was finding Tom.

The sorceress, radiating the violet aura as strongly as ever, turned to Molly. She took a small vial from her robes and handed it over. "Give him the entire vial. He must drink it. I can sense that he is beginning to weaken." She pointed toward the staircase leading down to Tom's cell. "None will oppose you now. Hurry!"

Molly raced toward the dungeons, Tom's crew trailing behind as she sped foward. The light of her map ring dimmed in and out. She followed its waning guidance, finally coming to Tom's cell. Taking out a pistol, she broke the lock with one shot and raced inside. Tom lay very still, sprawled on the cold cell floor. Breathing out his name, Molly knelt beside him. As she took out the vial, her eyes watered at the sight of his horrible condition. She administered the medicine, trying to steady her hands as she pried open his lips and poured it over his tongue. In that moment, the contents of the vial were more precious than anything she had ever held in her mortal hands. "If I spill even a drop," she whispered, "Thomas's life is over, and so is mine."

Tom's weary eyes opened. When he gasped suddenly and sat upright, Molly flinched. She saw that the medicine was working quickly, beating back whatever noxious poison that had compromised his health. Then all energy seemed to drain from him. He exhaled slowly, and then limply lay back down. Color returned to his face gradually, but he turned a feverish pink.

The sorceress entered Tom's cell. "You must leave," she told Molly. "I can protect you until your ship is away from the city, but beyond the port I cannot easily shield you. My abilities have their limits. Leave before the authorities retaliate. Fahkir's fleet will be looking for intruders until the confusion is cleared and the people learn of the truth."

Molly nodded, her voice hoarse. "I understand."

The crew lifted Tom and led the way out of the palace. As they boarded the ship, Molly instructed the men to place Tom in his cabin, then shouted out to set sail. "Mr. Shaw! Get us out of here! Aim for Gibraltar!"

"Aye, miss! Raise sail! Man cannons!" shouted Morgan.

The *Scotch Bonnet* instantly came to life. Spinning the wheel clockwise, the helmsman strained the rudder, and the ship sluggishly turned about. "We may have trouble soon!" he said, pointing toward the waterfront. Fahkir's fleet was hastily maneuvering toward them. "Wha-?" The helmsman looked up to the sky above Tangier.

Molly's eyes followed his gaze. An ominous violet cloud was rising from behind the city's rooftops. The aura grew and moved like a living fog as the Moroccan ships continued to gain on them. Suddenly a figure took shape and climbed high into the night sky. The Sorceress's face manifested itself in the cloud. The figure stood like a colossus over the city and its port. The figure of Udbala extended and formed an arm, then a hand. With one powerful sweep, the hand summoned a fierce wind, shredding the sails of the Moroccan ships and pulling them apart by the plank, sinking most of them in the process. The gust of wind blew Morgan and the crew backward across the deck of the *Scotch Bonnet*, but the ship was otherwise unharmed. The figure of the sorceress seemed to smile before leaning forward, pursing its lips and exhaling another monstrous gust of wind, propelling their ship quickly and smoothly out to sea. In the distance the massive aura shrank and raised a smoky hand in farewell before dissipating into the air altogether.

Astonished and pale, the crew tended to their duties, trying to ignore the odd and seemingly impossible events that had taken place moments earlier. A few of the men looked at one another in utter bewilderment, dumbfounded laughs escaping their mouths. Molly smiled as the ship raced foward.

As soon as Molly saw that all was well on deck, she hurried to Tom's cabin, entering quietly. Looking over at Tom's form, she saw that he slept quietly. The effects of his poisoning had been subdued. Silently Molly walked to his side, making sure he seemed comfortable. She looked at him solemnly for a moment before making her way back out, going down to the galley to fetch Tom a cup of water for when he awoke. As she descended toward the galley she glanced down at her ring and smiled. It was glowing radiantly once again. With water in hand, she made her way back to the captain's cabin, avoiding the looks of the crew, embarassed over her unabashed fury earlier that day.

She entered the cabin and set the water down on the desk. Pulling up a chair quietly next to his bed and taking care not to wake him, she watched the steady rise and fall of his chest as he slept. Molly frowned when her eyes fell upon her ring again. She'd had enough of danger, and she didn't know if she could bear to go on living Tom's way of life. It was fast and crude and cruel—a never-ending woe. She placed her hand gently on his, wondering hopelessly why such things had to happen. After a moment, she stood, leaving Tom to sleep undisturbed for a while.

Later that night Molly crept quietly from her cabin out onto the deck. She had awakened after trying in vain to sleep, feeling it would help if she knew Thomas was still sleeping soundly. She paused momentarily to allow the gentle sea breeze to waken her senses and refresh her lungs. Stopping at Tom's cabin door, she gingerly tugged at the handle and let herself in. Shutting the door behind her, Molly turned to discover Thomas was not in bed.

Taking several more steps into the room, she jumped in surprise, spying his silhouette by the stern windows, facing out to sea. "Thomas," she sighed, putting a hand to her chest, "You frightened me. What are you doing up in your condition?" she asked.

"Condition?" he asked innocently. "I'm perfect. Look at me," he said happily, stretching out his arms without turning around, smiling at Molly from over one shoulder.

"The medicine must have worked." Molly realized it was a gross understatement.

"Like a dream," Tom added, turning to her and taking a few steps.

Molly's eyes nearly jumped from their sockets when faint light revealed that Tom was covered only by the ragged remains of his clothing.

"Sorry. Tangier wasn't the holiday I had hoped," he apologized, his blue eyes charming her like sapphires. He was standing very close. Molly could feel his body heat. It was intense.

"I haven't exactly come to expect holidays in your company, Mr. Crowe." She reached out to touch his chest. Her fingertips blazed, as did her frantic heart.

"Then we should take one in the scarce time we've been allowed." Thomas flashed his white teeth, touching a hand to Molly's cheek and craning down to brush her neck with his lips. The medicine had done much more than repair his flesh. It had invigorated his spirit and unchained his bravery. He wanted to know, right then, if tequila had had anything to do with Molly's attraction.

"Thomas." Molly couldn't put a sentence together. She didn't know what she'd want to say if she could. Her hands spoke for her, moving over Tom's body excitedly, grasping at his arms and shoulders.

Tom spoke no more. His hands found her waist, and he kissed lightly at her neck, teeth grazing her soft skin.

Molly closed her eyes and clung to his arms, feeling his hot breath sweep down her neck to her shoulder. She gasped as it traveled lower, warming her chest. She squirmed her shoulders from the confines of her blouse and chemise, pulling her arms in so that her breasts heaved, nearly exposed, and placed her hands on Thomas's stomach, fingertips curling around the fringes of his ragged clothes.

Just as Thomas touched his lips to her again, a torturous pain struck his limbs. He had abused his recovery-high, and the curse was going to punish him if he didn't lie back down.

Molly felt Thomas wince and held him tight at the waist when he appeared to have trouble standing. "Thomas?" she demanded. "What is it?"

"Nothing. Please, don't upset yourself." He struggled to smile again, cursing the horrible onset of aches.

"No, Thomas. Lie down. Please, lie back down. You're in no condition. Don't strain yourself for my sake." Molly herded him to his bed despite his incessant refusals, straightening the sheets, fluffing the pillows roughly and yanking her clothing up above her shoulders in embarrassment. Above all she wanted him to be healthy again, but damn if she didn't despise his curse that night! Her inward frown could've been used as a pair of tongs...

Realizing she was quickly running short on restraint, Molly apologized for keeping Tom from his rest and scurried out the cabin door, bidding him a regretful goodnight. Before she could change her mind, she fled to her own cabin, shut and locked the door, threw herself on her bed and groaned as if she'd been punched in the gut.

Tom lay in bed for another half hour, staring at the ceiling. He kicked at the foot of his bed hard, trying to convert his tension to physical power and unleash his frustration upon the hapless wooden framework.

After that night the Alaouite Dynasty was returned to its prior state. The locals awoke from the illusion in which the qareen had cursed them to live, and the sorceress Udbala vanished from Tangier altogether.

Udbala, I have guessed from Molly's description, was born far from Morocco, just as she had told Molly that night. What I wouldn't give to have met her! I can only imagine what depths of magical knowledge she possessed. She was apparently an adept producer of potions, for she created things I've never heard tell of before, such as the concoction that aided Molly in her conspiracy, and the antidote that drove a silver-laced toxin from werewolf blood! What interested me most, though, was that Udbala could project herself, using the violet aura Molly described.

Elemental projection is not a common magic. I've never heard of its being used by a mortal. In fact, I've never heard of its being used in the modern world by anyone or anything alive, outside of legends. Elemental projection is often thought to be a fictional magic, for no one, not even a magesmith, has been able to describe to me how one could use magic to convert one's flesh into another pure substance. Most magesmiths swear that one can manipulate the elements only with a gem whose composition agrees with the substance being manipulated. None of them knows of anything violet in color that could not only command the winds but also exaggerate the spellcaster's form to such a large scale as what was witnessed in the port of Tangier. How strange.

Thomas was on his feet again soon after the incident in Tangier. I often think he would have fared better during his capture had he not been temporarily weakened by the effects of the curse-inhibiting tattoo on his back. Doing just as it was meant to, the holy Arabic inscription most likely caused Tom's body to fail to produce enough of the werewolf hormone to combat the destructive effects of the silver in his flesh. Tangier was simply an unfortunate and unexpected turn of events that no one aboard the ship could have predicted. They had been so careful, but then again, bad luck had always seemed to foul up Thomas Crowe's otherwise intelligent decisions.

Bad luck is an interesting thing to me, because it seems, like all things of a bad nature, to come in threes. In *this case, Spain and Tangier would be bad luck's first two strikes. Tom's ship was allowed a few days of peace as it sailed through the Mediterranean, through the Strait of Gibraltar and out into the vast Atlantic, but even far from land and the violent world of man, danger is never in short supply.*

Geoffrey Mylus,

May 15, 1833

III
Blackheart Reprise

Tom awoke on the cold, wooden floor next to his bed. The fire in the stove in his cabin had long diminished. Only a few hot orange coals were left burning. Groaning, he lifted himself to his feet and shed the sheets tangled around his legs. "Ugh." He stretched. A bad dream had kept him up all night. Weeks separated the ship from Tangier's waters. The closer Tom got to Barbados, the more Harlan appeared to him in his sleep. The tattoo on his back burned as badly as the mark whose darkness it was meant to suppress. Tom shook his head and left the cabin, crossing the main deck to rest on the railing of the forecastle. Animated only in body, his mind lingered in the dream realm. He hung his feet over and clung to a secure line for support. Below, the Atlantic sparkled calmly in the moonlight. He sighed, the weight of the universe keeping his eyes from opening.

Molly climbed the galley stairs, a fresh cup of water in hand, and crossed the deck to check on Tom. Noticing him up and awake, loitering on the forecastle, she turned and went to him.

Tom rose and stretched, moving about while fiddling with the lines. Looking up at the moon, he rested against the nearest yardarm, quite comfortable. He began to doze dangerously by the portside railing. The yardarm slowly swung back and forth in the wind. Tom's arms dangled over it like a ragdoll's, largely unaffected by the motion. The ship rocked, and Tom was tossed to the deck. He rolled to a stop and continued dozing.

Molly ran up to him, crouching down beside him and holding his face gently in her hands. "Thomas? Thomas can you hear me?"

Tom's eyes snapped open in surprise. "Hm?"

Molly laughed in amusement. She wrapped her arms around his neck. "Oh, Thomas."

"What?"

"Mishaps aside, you've done right by me. Thank you for keeping me along."

"Mishaps?" He grinned. "Oh yes, I remember." He tried to draw a smile from her as he continued casually, "Almost died again? Back in Morocco? You see, that's the thing—I tend to forget, it happens so often these days. Terribly sorry if I woke you, by the way. I thought I was being rather stealthy when I got out of bed. How did I give myself away? Or were you watching me walk in my sleep?" He smiled.

Molly let out a hearty laugh.

"Ah, I might have known!" He snuck both arms around her, holding her close. "I admire how your repertoire of roguish skills has grown."

Molly felt her cheeks turn pink and her heart quicken. Her lips were tempted. "You're very difficult to keep up with. There are only so many times I can save you, Captain, and only so many hours of the day I can keep my eyes on you."

"My little misfortunes sway neither myself nor my loyalties to my crew or guardian angels."

"That's not what concerns me." She struggled to her feet. "You were a mere moments from death weeks ago. Had it not been for that sorceress, you would not be alive to see me. I can't lose you, Thomas. That's what frightens me."

"My death is of no concern to me. *Your* life is much more fragile than mine. Molly," he said shaking his head and rising. "I'll gladly give a thousand of my lives to keep the one of yours. You didn't listen when I promised you that I will … not … die."

"Even if an assassin came upon you in the night with a silver blade?"

"Not even then."

Molly looked at him for a moment, her eyes swimming with uncertainty and concern. She shook her head sorrowfully. "You shouldn't make promises you can't keep."

"There are things you don't know, Molly. If I die, I will surely die before I ever break one of my *promises*. If I make you a promise, do *not* shake your head and tell me I'm lying. I know what is to become of me, and vaguely when and where it will happen, and I can confidently tell you that I will not die in vain any time soon!" He sighed. "I cannot explain to you how I know this. I barely understand it myself ..." He looked at her sadly.

Molly's eyes fell to her feet as she crossed her arms and held her shoulders.

Tom continued quietly. "I won't die. Not until everything falls into place, at least. If you cannot trust me, there is no man or woman alive you can trust." He turned and headed for the quarterdeck.

Molly turned her eyes away to the sea, her voice distant. "I trust you with my life, Thomas."

"What is destiny, Miss Bishop? Is it a place chosen for us before we take our first breath or first steps, or is it somewhere we've always been headed because of the choices we've made? Is it a spoonful of both? How would we ever know we were bearing down on a different conclusion yesterday, and how can we know we won't set our sights on another tomorrow?"

Molly felt her breath catch in her throat. His words became fainter as he continued.

"Why Barbados? Why you and I? Why are we both still alive?"

Something about his words struck deep within Molly's soul.

Tom climbed to the quarterdeck and hauled himself up the rigging and high into the mizzenmast. Frustrated, he leaned against the highest yardarm, addressing the night sky. His tone became harsh. "So, how much longer then, eh?" He laughed cynically at the clouds in the distance.

Molly flinched at the hardness in his voice.

"How many more times will Death tip its hat to me before I go?" He yelled angrily. "That's not specified in the contract is it? I can't know the duration of my curse, but I can know what its departure will look like. No matter what, it'll end when I say so!" He took a pistol from his gun belt, eyeing it in an amused fashion and aiming it at himself as a morbid joke. "Boom! Heh, oh no, think again! Thomas Crowe, the ever-living wonder! "

Molly couldn't stand seeing Tom like that. It wasn't often that he succumbed to such moods, but when he did he always looked far frailer than when he was smiling and looking upon the world with eyes that defied his fate. Molly stood in place for a moment before making her way unsteadily to her room.

Tom spoke ominously into the wind. "A man with only one life and certain death ahead of him seeks all the joy and pleasure in the world, but a man with a thousand lives and everything in the world eventually seeks only death," Tom thought aloud. "Have you had the dreams I've had, Harlan? Have you looked down the path and seen me standing in it?" Tom's anger subsided as he pocketed the pistol and stood straight to scan the clouds in the distance. "Now where did that come from?" he muttered.

In the distance, lightning played back and forth between the gathering clouds. The sea had become restless in the previous hour—the waves rocking the ship as a gentle warning. Below the clouds, several dark triangular shapes were barely visible. They swayed on the water's surface like toys. The sea all around them flowed in a slow, circular motion. It was not a natural pattern, and it was too dark to be the beginnings of a whirlpool.

"All hands! All hands!" Tom shouted.

Molly's tears dried up. With both hands she wiped her cheeks and grabbed her three pistols before heading back out on deck. She moved to the quarterdeck and rang the alarm bell posted by the helm.

The crew awakened. The fifty or so men below filed onto the main deck. Tom shouted orders from atop the mizzenmast. "Everything that isn't tied down goes below deck! If you can't swim, you may want to tie *yourself* down!"

Molly gazed up at the sky, awestruck. The black night sky bled back like an ink-soaked canvas being washed clean by a bucket of water. Darkness gave way to a congregation of thunder clouds amassing in crowded, towering stacks, stained and surreal, burnt yellow, stretched over the horizon in all directions as far as the human eye could see. Bright orange flashes crashed and rolled across the breadth of the sky like bursts of fire. The visible heavens on the horizon, beneath the lowest clouds, turned deep sienna, and the ocean beneath the ship churned rust brown, as if the bottoms of the sea were being pushed up from their resting places. Large schools of fish appeared at the surface, desperately throwing themselves to the air as if they had all gone mad. Molly heard thousands of them slapping against the hull and falling hopelessly back to the tumbling waves. Something terrible was going to happen, but Molly did not yet know what it would be. The crew hastily complied with their captain's orders, taking all guns, powder kegs, loose lines and cargo below. Several men reinforced the rigging supporting the sails.

"Expect to get wet, gentlemen!" Defiant and godlike, Tom fired a pistol into the dark sky and laughed loudly. The muzzle flash lit his face and painted harsh shadows against his handsome features. The devils in him shone through. The dark things inside were stirring.

Molly rushed into her cabin and rummaged through her trunk, grabbing her ruby ring from the bottom corner and placing it on her finger. Paying no regard to anything else, she braced herself against one of the walls of her cabin.

The crew—confused and apprehensive—scrambled to finish their preparations. Tom holstered the pistol again and breathed deeply as a strong rush of storm wind howled across the deck of the ship and strained the masts. Lightning cracked and split the sky. The crew mistook it for cannon fire. Most of the men scampered below deck to their quarters to secure personal items. The galley chef, who had been hired to take over for Molly, locked all his tools into chests and put out the cooking fire. The aides scampered about, collecting armfuls of utensils and loose cookware to shut away.

Molly yelped at the sound of her cabin doors being ripped from their top hinge and dangling freely from the wind pressure outside. She secured her pistols tightly around her waist, clinging to the wall. Star charts and other bits of parchment scattered along the cabin floor, her desk completely overturned due to the rocking of the ship.

Tom swayed along with the yardarm. "I never thought I'd see the day ..." The thundering clouds caught up with the ship. Streaks of lightning exploded from out of the blackness in rapid succession. The unlucky convoy of merchant ships Tom had spotted approached, tossed about like toys in a bath. Their crews rushed around the decks snatching at cargo that had broken loose and tumbled overboard. A titanic curtain of rain roared toward the ship. The blast of water slapped Tom, stealing his hat and casting it into the sea below.

The few men still on deck were frightened, if not totally petrified. They patrolled the railing, scanning the water at the ship's sides, looking for something but keeping their heads craned back as if something would bite their heads off at the neck if they leaned too far. A large, rolling wave rose from beneath a nearby merchant ship, raising it high above the others and sending it sailing dangerously close to the starboard side of Tom's ship. The crew stepped back and braced themselves, but the merchant slipped past. The crewmen were relieved, but Tom watched the merchant with solemn eyes, knowing what would happen next.

As the merchant slowed and the large wave shepherded it away from the others, the seawater beneath seemed to calm and isolate it altogether. Lightning cracked again, illuminating the merchant briefly before it disappeared into the dark. Thunder rang out, and another bolt lit the ocean's surface. There were only a handful of loose boards where the merchant had floated seconds before. Tom dropped to the main deck, ordering the crew to put out all lanterns and to smother all the fires. "All lights out!"

Crewmen responded obediently. "Aye, sir!"

Tom climbed to the quarterdeck once more, watching the six other merchants behind his ship, still frantically fighting the storm. Molly, mimicking the crew, smothered the bright embers in her fireplace and made her way on deck, clinging to one of the masts for support as she looked around and across the grave waters. The sea thrashed and tumbled over itself. The sky above was continually alight with electric bolts, and the clouds were painted a hellish yellow-brown each time lightning raced along their edges.

Tom looked on in disbelief. "Oblivious. They don't see it." He spoke in a hush, watching the helpless merchants. "Put out your lights, you—"

Lightning cracked again. Following the flash, a smaller merchant split in half, its lights quickly extinguished in the salt water. A few desperate shots from the deck guns rang out before the vessel sank.

Molly looked on in shock as the ship was swallowed up in the waves. The destruction was quick, and the cause unknown to her.

Tom yelled out angrily. "Now you're just *inviting* it!" He pounded a fist on the railing.

The crew had gathered on deck to observe the phenomenon. Molly spotted Morgan Shaw just a few paces away and called out to him. "What's happening out there?" Shaw looked at Molly strangely. He moved his mouth slightly, trying to speak as quietly as possible so the crew wouldn't hear. The storm winds and the hammering rain thwarted his attempts. Slipping through the gawking crowd, he approached her. Still, Shaw failed to deliver the words, his eyes constantly glancing back to the merchants and scanning the dark sea around the ship. Molly followed his gaze out to sea, spotting nothing.

Shaw grabbed Molly's arm to get her attention once more. "Leviathan," he said.

Molly's expression wilted. "What?"

She saw Tom shake his head at the merchant ships. "You're all dead men," he muttered.

Lightning ravaged the clouds. In the midst of the hapless merchant ships a titanic, pale, finned body snaked up and back down into the sea like a deathly rainbow. The vermicular form flowed slowly overhead, catching a few strikes of lightning that dissipated across its body and down into the sea. Tens of thousands of little points of light dotted the body like galaxies of stars arranged in straight rows. Fleshy stalks protruded from the body as well, topped by the same glowing spots. The beast's head descended back toward the sea, emerging from the lowest clouds in a swift dive. Its open mouth revealed irregularly positioned teeth that were long and thin. Two sets of four, sightless eyes sat along the high ridges of the serpentine head. As the body, covered in all manner of oceanic growth, followed the head down, the tail crashed heavily through the sea's surface, spraying a column of salt water high into the air as if to rival the pouring rain. The spray reached Tom's ship, further drenching the men on deck.

Molly stumbled back into Shaw from the force of the spray, her eyes wide in fear of what she'd just witnessed. Shaw unintentionally clung to Molly as he fell under the weight of the deluge. Standing once more and hoarsely clearing his lungs of the water, he helped her to her feet. Molly sputtered, coughing out the briny swill in her throat and clutching Shaw's arm to steady herself.

Tom looked on silently through the blasting rain as another merchant was taken, this time by a large, gaping mouth. Monstrous, translucent teeth snared the hull and a giant, clammy tongue collapsed the main deck like an eggshell. The merchant sank beneath the surface as the teeth closed slowly, and the sea poured back into the empty whirlpool left behind.

Through the blinding wind several more ships appeared. Outfitted with many more guns, they were escorts for the merchants. No light could be seen from their portholes or rear cabins. Tom took note of this and quickly moved to the port side of the *Scotch Bonnet*, clutching the railing and squinting through the downpour at the new arrivals. He shouted to everyone on deck. "A white cloth! Bring a white cloth!"

The new ships approached slowly. On the deck of each were gathered hundreds of crew, several waving signal cloths and flags. Molly dug into her pockets, finding a dull white rag she had used in the kitchen earlier. She rushed toward Tom, handing him the cloth. Tom looked at Molly, both concerned and apologetic, but he acted quickly, taking the cloth and holding it to the wind. Shaw ran to

Tom, his wild brown hair batting at his eyes. "They will cooperate with us?"

Tom nodded and shouted to the crew. "Load all cannons! We have plenty of ammunition to spare!"

Shaw echoed the order. "Load cannon! Orders, sir? Who is to lead?" Tom raised his hands and gestured in a series of precise signs. The captain of the distant ship watched carefully through a spyglass, nodded and signaled back.

"*We* are the lead, Captain?" asked Shaw nervously.

Tom turned away from the railing. "Turn full around, helmsman! Load one round shot per cannon! Move all powder to the second deck and await orders!"

Shaw's eyes went wide with alarm. "Sir, we can't possibly hope to fight—"

"Follow your orders, Mr. Shaw!" Tom barked.

"Aye." Shaw descended to the second deck.

Molly peered down into the agitating waters, her stomach filling with dread. Tom's ship turned about and the merchants' escorts followed close behind. Tom grabbed Molly's hand. "Stay with me." He ran with her to the helmsman. "Full ahead! Keep close to that ship!" The Leviathan burst from the ocean's surface again, rising into the sky above the merchants and crashing its weight down on them. Molly tightened her grip on Tom's hand, her eyes never leaving the thrashing waters. The larger of the merchants split under the impact of a pressure wave. The nearest escort ship kept very close to Tom's. Tom, spotting the captain, signaled him once more. Several of his crew began to line the deck, manning the swivel guns. The three warships sailed ahead, tumbling forward dangerously over the mountainous waves. Their gun decks opened, and the heads of the crew peeked from behind cannons. Those on deck loaded harpoons.

The three ships circled water. Tom ordered the helmsman to sail straight for the center of the stormy debris-ridden waters. "All hands below! Each man secure a barrel of powder! Wait for orders!"

The crew complied without question, though not a man among them thought Thomas was sane. The Leviathan exploded from the dark water and crashed down again, this time within perilous range of Tom's ship. The vessel rocked, and several men catapulted into the sea. Tom snatched a line and caught Molly's wrist again. Molly took deep breaths, masking her fear behind hard, determined eyes and pinched lips.

The three warships began to unleash a broadside assault on the monster. The heavy lead shots did little more than pockmark the thick, outer layers of its ghostly white hide. Lightning flashed again, striking down the foremast of the leading warship. The deck below splintered, and the vessel was capsized by a following wave. Tom let go of Molly's hand and leapt to the main deck, seeing their one and only chance. The Leviathan approached the starboard hull. A colossal bulge in the ocean revealed it was gaining on them. Thunder clapped, following another bolt of lightning. The rain came in sheets sideways across the deck as Tom's ship leaned toward the whirlpool opening below it.

"Molly!" Tom shouted, motioning for her to stand next to him. His voice calmed momentarily. "You have your ruby ring?"

"Yes."

"Trust me."

She nodded and stood close to him, trying her best to hide the terror in her eyes. The ship rocked up on its side. A gaping mouth reared up beneath Tom and Molly. The Leviathan's gums and teeth were encrusted with a few centuries of wreckage and the skeletal remains of human prey. Its throat was a catacomb of ruin and rot, the stench of which made several of the straggling crew keel over in sickness. The ocean's surface receded, and a ravenous, alien cry pierced their ears. Tom shouted to the waiting crew. "Powder!"

The men below shoved dozens of barrels at a time up and out the lower deck stairs, all eighty or so barrels tumbling out of the bowels of the ship. Tilting on its side, the *Scotch Bonnet* groaned, the barrels rolling faster, spilling out of the ship and plummeting into the hungry abyss below. Tom seized a line tied to the main mast and wrapped it around one arm. Gripping Molly's arm in the other hand, he yelled over the noise. "Do not let go!"

The deck tipped perpendicular to the whirlpool. The sudden rocking caused the rest of the barrels to fall rapidly into the widening mouth of the Leviathan. A few men tumbled out after them and vanished into the dark. Molly clung to Tom as she lost her footing.

Tom freed the hand bearing Molly's ruby ring and struggled to hold her as they dangled over the mouth below. "Use the spell!"

The last barrel whizzed by Molly's face. Gasping loudly, she struggled to speak.

"Agh!" Tom strained to hold on. "Say it!"

Molly's dangling hand formed into a tight fist. "*Spuere ignis!*"

Bright flames spouted forth from the glowing gem. The fiery stream crawled through the wind, catching the kegs and finding a home in the volatile gunpowder. The resulting flash of fire rushed into the Leviathan's dark mouth. A forceful, hollow thump erupted from a cluster of kegs lodged in the beast's throat, rocking the ship upright. The ship tipped backward just as a column of fire soared out of the gnashing mouth. Tom lost his grip on Molly as he slipped across the rain-soaked deck, crashing into the broken railing. The explosion of the powder kegs tore Molly from his grip. She was flung to the other side of the deck, colliding with the main mast before rolling to a painful halt. Tom shouted out Molly's name.

A piercing cry stabbed the crew's eardrums. The Leviathan regurgitated another plume of fire before sinking below the surface. Thick, red and brown rain pelted the deck. Tom lay in place, breathing heavily, repeating Molly's name, calling to her over and over. The blow to his head dulled his vision and hearing. Molly lay motionless across the deck from him. Above her left eye a deep gash was bleeding heavily down her face.

Tom got to his feet and immediately fell again. As he slid across the deck he sighted Molly from a disorienting sideways perspective. Panicked, he got up once more and staggered awkwardly to her. "Mol... guhk!" He coughed and spat sea water. "Molly!" he called, dropping on his knees next to her and rolling her over into one arm. The other hand touched her face, trying to wake her.

Molly coughed violently at the sudden movement, ejecting sea water from her mouth. She'd have screamed if her lungs hadn't been on fire.

Feeling the familiar warmth of blood, Tom followed the stream staining his arm up to Molly's injured forehead. "Molly?" *Bleeding...who's bleeding?*

Molly struggled to find the source of the voice; her senses became muddled and nauseating. The sounds around her were no more than muffled, dull moans. Her eyes could barely open, and the world felt far away.

Tom knew it wouldn't be long. She was mortal. Luck wouldn't save a mortal. A costly decision now rested on his mind, but he wouldn't consider it until he was sure it was his only choice. "Molly! Listen to me! Can you feel anything? Molly?"

She failed to reply. Her breathing slowed and grew labored, and a metallic taste welled in her throat. She stuggled to open her eyes. The rain pounding hard against her cheeks. Her voice was barely audible. "Thomas? Am … I hurt?"

Tom made his decision. "Molly, forgive me, but, you can't die here."

Molly forced her eyes open weakly, finding Tom's, though his face looked like a fuzzy apricot. She gasped for breath.

Tom's eyes flashed golden yellow, and his voice grew strong and hoarse.

"I'll make sure…"

His teeth grew long.

"…this is only temporary…"

His body changed shape.

"…and you won't suffer as I do." Tom opened his jaws wide. He tore open Molly's blouse at the shoulder and sank his gleaming white teeth into her.

Molly sucked her breath in sharply, holding back the urge to scream. Around the bite a small black mark appeared in the shape of a crescent moon. Tom reopened his jaws and pulled away gently, resting his head wearily into her neck.

Molly gazed up into the dark sky. The tumultuous, thundering clouds were the last thing she witnessed before darkness rolled over her.

Tom raised his head. With both arms he cradled Molly against himself, lifting her and hunching over her so the rain could not touch her anymore. He winced with every step. *Probably broken*, he thought, not daring to look down at his legs. Despite the danger, he employed the curse to carry him at least to his cabin. The crew returned to the deck, swiveling their heads about in search of the Leviathan. Tom's feet thudded like leaden weights against the planks. He held Molly close. In the cabin he laid her on his bed and wrapped her in every sheet and cloth he could find. The curse receded, and Tom collapsed to his knees.

Molly was murmuring to herself. "Not here ... please. Let's go home."

The previous chapter of Tom and Molly's story is one that would long after be told again and again by sailors young and old, from the ports of the Caribbean to the seaside boroughs of Europe. The reader is now familiar with stories of werewolves and vampires, but what I've just described was the tale of a true monster.

Never before has lived a beast as terrific as the Leviathan. It has been called the Devil's Lighthouse, the Atlantean Worm and the Great Mouth. Sailing men have told me that they would rather die where they stood than go out to sea again if it meant meeting the Leviathan. The monster, they say, is not of our world; too large to have been bred in oceans so small, they say; too powerful to have been unleashed upon the seas of the earth by coincidence, they say.

What distinguishes the Leviathan from all other oceanic horrors is its frightening cunning. Stretching its upper body high into the air above the surface of the sea on dark or foggy nights, it casts a bright light from the luminous ridges atop its head. Beneath the surface of the waves, its vermicular body whips round in circles, treading water and creating a violent whirlpool great distances in diameter. Simultaneously, its head rotates round and round, luring in ships with the promise of safe land, hence its common nickname, the Devil's Lighthouse. The cyclic current it generates not only draws in sailors foolish enough to come close, but also manipulates the elements high above in the sky, creating twisting tempests that tear vessels to scrap as the beast dives down, mouth agape, into the carefully crafted kill zone.

A sailor I once met in Sidmouth, an old, eroded fellow with part of his left jaw missing and little sight left in his eyes, told me, through haggard breaths, that he'd seen the Leviathan and lived. His ship was lost, his fellows drowned and eaten and his captain driven to hysterical suicide. "When I saw it," he said, referring to the swirling current, "I thought the Ninth Circle had opened up and was singing us our death song. The furious gales hushed as the ship was drawn toward the abyss. Just as silence fell on the thrashing waves, the clouds drew back and the beast came down from the sky, shining like the glorious sun, stealing from us our sight and blinding us to the most hopeless moment of the ordeal, in which we were delivered to the cold depths."

Being mortal, and already in a position of great vulnerability, we often ask ourselves, "Why?" Why must we constantly fight to protect our already endangered lives? Why are we so often called to protect others? Why must we sacrifice on each and every step we take toward our destination? Why so much pain?

Molly's brush with Death may not have been as unnecessary as we would like to think. Upon looking back at the events of this tale, I must admit that what happened that night and what Thomas was forced to do were necessary in the greater design of things. I can't imagine how differently things would be now if Thomas hadn't bitten Molly.

Bridgetown, in Barbados, as the carousel of fate would have it, is where Tom would face his "smallest of trials" as Gabriel Vasquez put it—confronting his brother, Harlan. At the time, the Black Coat Society was attempting to establish a safe and strong brotherhood far away from the interference of English and French authorities at home. Times were difficult, and most cults in London especially were suffering greatly. Disappearances, betrayals and inter-cult violence were common. Good relations with Parliament were weakening. As the population of the world grew, half-humans increasingly competed for room. The new Black Coat Society had an answer to this: amass a new cult of vampires, dominate the Caribbean isles, remove problematic clan settlements in Europe, and then reclaim territory one major city at a time. I suppose some of the Black Coats surmised they could win back the favor of civil mortals by doing these things, simultaneously removing the obstructing werewolf population as well, just to ensure that competition for space would never again damage vampire relations with humankind.

Sometime during the development of these goals, something else was suggested: hybridizing immortal curses. Initially rejected and ill-received as unthinkably taboo, the idea gained popularity when a charismatic young werewolf began to advocate hybridization to young Black Coats in Barbados. His name was Harlan Crowe. In order to demonstrate his loyalty to the Black Coat purpose, he voluntarily became the first known werewolf in history to receive the vampire bite. It made him into something terrible and great. He would be the new patriarch of the Black Coat Society, and an unforgotten symbol of the times.

Geoffrey Mylus,

May 17, 1833

❧❧

Harlan!" Tom screamed the name, sitting straight up from sleep inside his cabin. Molly was nowhere to be seen. Tom leapt to his feet. As the curse reared within him, he crashed through the cabin door, breaking it from the hinges. Outside it was bright, midday. "Molly!"

Several crewmen jumped. Morgan Shaw approached him cautiously. "Captain, what's wrong?"

"What's wr—?"

"The lady's below, sir. Cooking, I believe."

Tom breathed heavily. "Wh—"

"Yes, I saw her earlier. She should be there."

Molly set out the last of several meat pies on a wooden table, reviewing her creations with pride. She wiped her brow, and a bit of flour smudged her cheek. Tom descended the stairs to the galley, wide eyes focused on the happy and carefree Molly, busy at work by the stove fire. She looked up in surprise. Beads of cold sweat traced Tom's cheek. At the last second he ducked to avoid walking straight into a low wooden beam.

"Thomas! It's about time you woke. Good timing, too. I'm just about to put these in the oven."

"You're awake? You're all right?" he asked dumbly.

"Yes, of course. I used beef in these rather than the pork. I think the men are tired of pork. Is that all right? Thomas? I told the cook you hired to take a holiday."

Tom walked over to her, his eyes inspecting her thoroughly up and down for injuries. Still wide-eyed and shaky, he slowly embraced her and rested his weight on her in relief.

"Yes! Yes...pies are just fine. Ha ha!" His laugh was both frightening and joyful.

Molly was surprised by his sudden embrace. "Careful, Thomas."

"Oh!" He loosened his overbearing grip and apologized with an awkward smile.

Molly rubbed her shoulder, wincing. "It's all right. I'm just a bit sore this morning for some reason."

"I'll leave you to the uh ... the ... your pies ... I ... sorry." Tom tripped as he attempted to leave her in peace. "Ow!" he shouted, hitting his head on the low beam on his way out.

Puzzled by his exceptionally odd behavior, Molly watched as Tom exited quickly before she could question him. She shrugged, deciding she would ask him about it later.

The large tear in Tom's pant leg from the night before caught a nail and tore wide open. "She's fine. She'll be fine. But now what do I— agh!" he shouted, falling through the main deck trap door. The crew on deck stared at their pants-less captain. Tom strolled on, pretending he didn't notice a thing out of the ordinary. Returning to his cabin, he lay down, pants-less, and pondered the situation at hand. The crew shrugged off the incident, continuing to repair the leftover rigging and raising new sails.

"Drop anchor for now! We'll wait for the captain's orders to sail!" Shaw called out to them. With a large splash, the ship anchored in place. The storm had carried the ship safely to a large shoal off of Cape Verde. The wild storm whipped up by the Leviathan had forced them across the currents they were sailing before. It was not a serious redirection, for now they would have only to catch the boomerang current off the African Coast and sail up to Barbados from the southernmost reaches of the Caribbean.

The afternoon was quiet, and the crew worked busily on the various needs of the ship. The tranquility was shattered as Molly let out a loud cry below deck.

Tom jumped up and out of his bed. Shaw was the first to reach the galley. "Miss Bishop?"

"Molly?" Tom fell into Shaw on the stairs.

Molly leaned against a cutting table, clutching a rag to her forearm, a cutting knife at her feet. "I'm sorry I startled you. I was being clumsy with the knife is all." Molly, talking quickly, tried hard to conceal the shaking in her voice.

"Are you all right?" Tom asked.

"If you'll excuse me, please help yourselves to the pies," she said, quickly cleaning up the counters.

Tom was able to catch a glance of the fresh cursed mark on her skin, barely visible behind her right shoulder, just below the neck. He said nothing of it and ordered Shaw back to the deck as he exited the galley. Shaw lingered behind for a moment, leaving only after Molly shooed him away and reminded him he had other duties to manage. He apologized and stood quietly in place, watching as Molly left the galley, heading for the main deck and her cabin.

Molly clenched her teeth together as the cut began a slow healing process. She was trembling violently, in a mixture of pain, fear and confusion.

"Whatever you do, never touch it." Tom suddenly appeared in the doorway of the cabin. "That makes it hurt worse."

"What are you talking about? What's happening to me?"

Tom sighed. "What's happening now is you're paying for a decision I made for you."

"I don't understand. What decision?"

"It isn't permanent but you'll have to live with it for a while."

"Damn it, Thomas! Tell me what you did!"

"It's better I tell you how to *rid* yourself of it, but you aren't healed yet. So calm down."

Molly was more frightened than she had ever been in her life. She trembled, eyeing Thomas with fear.

He continued, "You need to cooperate with me. First, I need a direction. Harlan isn't running anymore. He's waiting. But we seem to be a bit off course. I have to have orders to give my helmsman before dusk. Tell me which way the map ring points so I can be sure he's in Bridgetown where I expect him to be."

Molly's eyes narrowed. "I need an answer before you get directions."

"If I give you an answer now, I may die later. Because you are infected and I must confront Harlan, things must be done in a precise order, or very unpleasant things may beset us."

Molly's eyes widened.

"If you do not *trust* me, I may die. And if I tell you what I will ask of you … after I find Harlan … before the time is right … I will most likely die, because you will refuse to cooperate. I've seen these things in my dreams. I promised you I won't die, and from this point on, your decisions will determine if I can keep that promise. If I told you what you must do soon, you wouldn't do it."

Molly flinched, her gaze remaining hard. "Do what?"

"I can't tell you."

Molly tried to speak again, but a cry of pain escaped her lips instead, followed by a violent shudder.

"If you want to live with that pain the rest of your life, you are free to do so. If my word means nothing to you, I cannot convince you to trust me. If what …" he paused. "If you think things happen for a *reason* ..." He stopped again, giving up. Throwing the door wide open and leaving the cabin, he headed for the main deck. "Helmsman! West, full speed! Use your instincts! Find Barbados! Gentlemen, eat sparingly. We're behind schedule!"

Molly sobbed quietly into her hands, unaware of the dull gray color engulfing the face of her once beautiful ring.

Molly awoke later that night, the pain completely gone from her arm. No scar was left from the cut. She walked out on deck and stared out into the ocean, spotting the North Star.

"I'm so frightened. I don't know what to do," she murmured, speaking to her mother's star. "I'm walking blind, allowing someone else to direct my life." She reached her hand up, tracing the mark on her shoulder. She closed her eyes, visions flying before her in a blur—a white flower, her father, a burning ship, Tom's embrace. "I trust him." Molly glanced down at her ring and then back up at the star. "I just hope it's not too late to save him from whatever he plans to do."

Tom stood atop the highest point of the ship, balancing himself like a bird on a clothes line on the smallest yardarm of the main mast. The sea before him was infinite. The stars collected in a great crowd, each and every one present. Tom could feel it waiting for him over the horizon—destiny. He had memorized the scenario of meeting Harlan as clearly as it had been shown to him in his dreams. It always played out the same way, so it had to be true—Harlan dying, the strange feeling in Tom's chest, a white flower, and a flash of light. But now more than ever he doubted the flower and the light. Maybe he had invented that part. Everything hinged on the flower. A white blossom, particularly moonbloom, was traditionally a prophetic symbol. A milky white flower with triplets of red spots on its petals, it was the sign of Luna Mater, according to many werewolf superstitions, and was not a vision to be taken lightly, especially if it appeared in one's dreams. Tom was positive that the flower was a crucial part of the sequence. He was absolutely sure. There was always one more person in the dream after Harlan was gone, though. Or was there? Did he or didn't he die in the dream? The light. What was the light, then?

Tom stood pensively, watching the stars turn in place until the night air became too cool for him. He descended the mast and decided to lie down on deck instead of going back to his cabin. He stared at the locket Gabriel had given him, which was usually dangling from his neck and was now lying on his chest. Was the locket in the dream? He didn't remember.

For the first time in years, Tom slept peacefully, without a nightmare or dream. For now, he would lie without a care on the deck of his ship, under the watch of the heavens, sleeping on an eternal bed between Sea and Luna Mater.

Molly, across the deck, paced. "This is what I've found, after all the searching," she said softly. "I've finally discovered what I was meant to live for. I just had to see it for myself, with more than just my eyes." She played with her ring, a soft smile on her face. The jewelry's dull white glow illuminated her features. "I just needed time."

She wasn't sure how late it was when she returned to her cabin. Her candle had burned down to the base. She diligently mapped out everything the ring would allow her to see, the path to Harlan, the path to Bridgetown and where she first met Thomas, neatly recorded on the parchment before her. It did not occur to her that she should not have been able to read the map, now that she, too, bore the werewolf mark. Either her curse had not matured, or other, dormant powers within her—fearsome powers she had still not cultivated—were too great to be stifled by darkness.

The sun shone brightly overhead; the sky, azure. Molly hesitated at Tom's cabin door before knocking. Inside, Tom was idly arranging items on his large desk.

Since awakening at dawn he had occupied himself by cleaning his pistols and rearranging various charts in his cabin. He had opened a window to allow the cool breeze to soothe the persistent burning sensation in his back, which he often turned to the window, standing for long periods of time in relief. A soft rapping sounded at the door. Tom called from within.

"Come in!"

Molly entered, clutching the map she had worked on the previous night, and placed it down before him. "That should do." She turned to leave again, feeling a pressure on her chest.

Tom hadn't moved since she entered. He stood facing the stern windows, the black tattoo on his back displayed for her. "Thank you, Molly. Did you sleep well?" A quaint and often meaningless question, it had become something of a mantra.

"I don't remember, actually." *Is that part of the curse?*

"Yes. Sometimes a dreamless night is a good one though, I suppose. Better that you sleep in silence than be disturbed by bad dreams, yeah?" He laughed softly and turned to look at her over one shoulder, smiling. The blue in his eyes glistened like a cool spring in direct shafts of sun.

Be there sunshine or rain and mud upon his soul, those eyes always shine like polished glass, thought Molly to herself.

Still smiling, he glanced down at the desk then back to her. "I've been thinking. One day I promise we'll go back to London. I can take you to the All Hallows Eve ball. You would like it. It's something of a gala for the supernatural. I've been only once before, and I went unaccompanied." He turned back to the desk, resting his hands on it, shoulders rising to head level as he shifted his stance.

"I would like that very much."

"Then you have my promise."

"You have my trust."

Tom, leaning on one arm against the desk, extended the other hand. Molly placed her hand in his, her deep, dark eyes never moving from his beautiful bright blues. Tom took her in the other arm, holding her close. "I'd like to ask you a favor."

"Anything."

"Oh, it isn't much. May I ask for a kiss, even if just one? I feel rude, having never actually asked your permission before."

"When you love someone, permission is completely unnecessary." Molly smiled sweetly.

"Oh...." She'd used a word to describe them that he had certainly felt but never expressed before.

Bright afternoon sunlight filled the cabin, warming them both. The beams of light pouring through the window revealed small particles of dust scurrying through the air with every breath of wind. Something in Tom's kiss was a thing of divinity, and must have been leading

Molly's heartbeat as a conductor leads an ensemble, because each time she felt his lips touch hers, her chest became a music hall thrumming with timpani that could've heralded all of creation.

Molly and Tom later sat comfortably in the galley, finishing an early lunch of meat pies. The crew left them to their privacy and impatiently waited above deck at their posts.

"So then you will go to the ball when I ask you some day?" Tom smiled widely, taking up a bottle of wine his men had procured in Tangier.

"I can't have you go alone again, can I?"

"Well, I believe you deserve a splendid night out in London after all the things I've put you through. I'll get you any dress you choose. Any jewelry. A personal carriage. And you'll dine like a queen."

"I would prefer this curse to be gone," she said, rubbing the sore mark, "and then, I assure you, all I will need is you by my side. Besides, what could possibly be more splendid than a night spent on the arm of Captain Thomas Crowe?" She teased him and spoke the name with slow and regal intonation.

"Please …" He blushed. "Oh, but would you still allow me to at least buy you the dress?"

Molly grinned. "If it pleases you." Her thoughts wandered as she stood to collect his dishes. "I would love to see London again." Molly paused and lay a hand on her breast. *And to stay in that beautiful house*, she thought.

Tom raised his eyebrows and stood behind her as she washed the dishes in the basin. "Well what's stopping you?" He asked, wrapping his arms around her. "I promise you will see London again."

"I know I will." She pulled back with a smile and retrieved a dish towel to dry her hands. "A place I would much rather *not* see again is Barabados. Why must we go? Why not be done with Harlan?"

"I dreamed I confronted Harlan in Bridgetown, and he's there now. And he's the one who cursed me, and took Samuel from you."

"I know, and I haven't forgotten," she admitted.

"My dreams are never wrong. They weren't wrong about you."

Molly didn't argue, but she looked away sadly. She wondered if his desire to find his brother outweighed his desire to be with her. *No*, she scolded herself, *don't think so selfishly*.

"You do not have to leave the ship. I must go ashore only for the day. I have unfinished business in Barbados. But I assure you I will finish it quickly and for all."

"What is it you plan to do exactly?"

"I plan to pay Harlan and some of his associates a visit. Associates who were once in league with Mikael Sehović, if that was your next question."

"Who's Mikael Sehović?"

"Mikael was the one responsible for what happened to Samuel, Molly. He was also the first sent to kill me, by Harlan's instructions. And not until recently did I suspect he was Christopher Barnes's mentor."

Molly shuddered at the name. Tom continued.

"I believe Christopher was supposed to be his successor and the Black Coat patriarch destined to spread influence to the Caribbean."

"So he taught Christopher ways to torture and manipulate the women he graciously took in," Molly muttered bitterly, shaking her head.

"Yes, and you had been selected by Mikael, personally, to stand at Christopher Barnes's side as he came to power within the Society."

"Why me?"

"You were to be a queen of sorts. Luck of the draw, I guess. You are the daughter of a powerful and respected magesmith. What power that would have given the Society—an immortal queen, doubling as an expert in the magical arts." He made a disgusted face. Molly frowned at the floor. "Of course, they were afraid of you. That's why you were given strong doses of nightmares. It was to keep you under control."

"What could I possibly have been capable of to deserve such torment?" Molly fumed.

"You do not know? The possibilities are endless in the wrong hands. Your father—honorable man—chose the other path. He chose to combat the Society as well as all would-be wicked wielders of the arcane. My father did as well, as did his father before and so forth. I am going to Barbados to ensure that the Society understands they will never have you in their possession again, and that they have more reason to fear you now that you know the truth. I'm sorry if all this is upsetting, but I think you ought to know now. I didn't tell you before because I honestly wasn't certain that you were being held by the Society for these reasons. You could just as easily have been one of their other captives, you understand. They do not discriminate or hesitate to abuse their power. I wish I could have known sooner and told you, but I've had to piece together the clues I picked up in London and Barcelona first. Can you forgive me?"

"Are these the things you refused to tell me before?"

"Not all. There are important things which are to happen during my confrontation with Harlan and immediately after. Those are the things I must still withhold from you."

"They killed Samuel." It was all Molly could think about. For the first time since being bitten, a golden sheen appeared in her brown eyes and made them look like tiny pots of honey. "If you must go to Barbados and find Harlan, do not leave without punishing the rest as well."

Tom gazed hard at Molly, then turned his head to look at the long blade—Brother—lying underneath his bed.

"That night Samuel was stripped of a terrible curse and freed," said Tom. "Mikael was the one who was *destroyed*. I made certain of that. The Society exists in significant numbers only in Barbados and Paris now, and I intend to do what I can to ensure that Barbados is wiped clean of them. Although Christopher Barnes is no longer living, they will still choose a successor to replace him; however, without a patriarch, they have no organization. Vampires draw a vital strength and guidance from their figureheads."

"I'm coming with you."

"I won't take long at all. If you go and are discovered, they will try to take you back." His eyes darkened. "You will stay on the ship."

"No. I can't let them get away with what they did to me and Samuel."

"Mikael is dead. Christopher is dead. I will dispose of the rest by myself. There is no need to risk yourself."

"And if they change like Christopher? What will you do?" she argued.

"None of them is as strong as Christopher or Mikael. They are nothing. What I plan to do is comparable to pulling weeds. The Black Coat Society of Barbados will be nonexistent by the end of the night."

"If it's so simple, there's no reason I can't assist you."

"If you use that mark and transform, the curse will overwhelm you. It will be difficult for me to stop you if you lose control of it."

"I don't need the curse to kill them," she scoffed.

"You cannot fight them with pistols alone. What would you hope to do? Tell me. I have *one* sword capable of doing what's necessary to kill and destroy a vampire, Molly."

"They don't seem very fond of flames or light."

"Flames are a nuisance. Light will kill them. Do not place too much faith in that ruby. Perhaps that other one"—he nodded at the map ring—"could be of assistance, but I am afraid I cannot explain to you how or if you can control the light within it. I can't even read the *map*."

"I *can*. I've controlled it before."

"Can you show me? If you can, I may have a change of heart. But first, demonstrate."

Molly confidently stood and aimed her hand at the door. She thought hard. The ring would react to certain situations Tom was in. It was brightest when Tom's life was in the most danger. She thought back to that night, and Christopher's silver dagger inches away from Tom in the belfry. She gazed down at her ring, still maintaining its calm glow. Now that she thought about it, she wasn't sure how to control it at will. Tom continued to watch curiously. She looked again at the silver sword beneath the bed. "That sword is silver, yes?"

"Yes it is. Why?"

"Take it in your hands and hold it close. I need to see something."

Tom shrugged, retrieving the blade from beneath the bed. The ship rocked unexpectedly and the blade tumbled from Tom's grip, falling across his thigh. "Whoa!" He jumped out of its reach.

Molly gasped as the ring emitted a brief but violent flash of light.

"Gah!" Tom stumbled backward, shielding his eyes from the light. The sword clanged, rattled, and slid across the floor into a chair.

Pleased, Molly grinned in surprise.

"Well, that's interesting," said Tom as he rubbed his eyes.

"It happens when you're in danger," she explained. "If that sword upset it, I wonder what it'll do in the presence of a few dozen demon-kin trying to bite your head off."

Tom rolled his eyes.

"I've also had time to learn quite a bit about my pistols, with the help of the spell books you so graciously lent me in London," Molly added, displaying the pearl pistols. Locking the hammers, she aimed them at Tom's chest.

"Hey!" Tom backed up one step and held up a hand.

"*Caeco et punire*," she enunciated clearly and confidently.

The chambers of the pistols blazed with white light, which traveled swiftly down the barrels as Molly pulled the triggers and the hammers clicked. Two bright balls of light blasted Tom in the chest, each evaporating in a brilliant display. Tom was pushed backward, but felt no painful physical impact. He chuckled and looked up at Molly.

"I imagine that is much more than a tickle to a vampire's skin," he said.

"Much more," Molly agreed, eager to punch a few holes in the Black Coats with her father's guns.

"Very well, I'll allow you to come along, but do try to stay near me, yeah?"

"Yes, Captain," she answered, folding her hands behind her back and cheerfully rocking up onto the balls of her feet.

"Accidents are unwelcome, you understand."

"Don't worry, I'll protect you," she chimed.

Tom smirked. "Oh, however will I repay you?"

"Just keep a better grip on that sword when you're actually using it."

Tom pinched the bridge of his nose and said nothing else.

Can our dreams truly tell us what is to come? More precisely, can they show us what is yet to happen, or do they only explain why something is to happen? Do the visions of our somnolent minds pour forth from a fountainhead of truths, desires, or something else?

After learning more about Thomas's past, I am now able to say he had an unusual trait. His mother Piroska was infatuated with magic, specifically clairvoyance and divination. She was an avid collector of sapphires for this reason. When Thomas was conceived, his mother was already practiced in the art of shaping and using seeing stones. Magic can be an imprecise art, and its collateral effects are numerous and often stranger than the intended results. I speculate that Thomas inherited a natural ability to "see" from his mother. To this day I do not think he was ever aware of the connection between his mother's hobby, her conceiving Thomas and Thomas's dreams.

Thomas's unusual trait reminds me that faltering precision has produced a great number of other curious things and specifically in the case of magical imprecision. In fact, it played a great role in the origin of werewolves.

Magical practices have been in existence since the earliest chapters of man's history. He used it to ward off foul spirits, to protect his home, to communicate with his gods and to aid him in the hunt. He also learned that magic could do much more than conjure and manipulate the basic elements. Magic, he discovered, could manipulate the body as well.

I said before that I do not expect to meet a lycanthrope, and for two reasons. One reason is that the term refers to ancient peoples who transformed into wolves by magical means, and such people do not exist any longer. The second reason, relating directly to the first, is that lupomorphs are the modern consequence of lycanthropic practices. Today, if one wishes to do what the lycanthropes did, all he or she must do is accept the werewolf curse. Lycanthropy is, in a word, archaic.

The first werewolf was born, as evidence strongly suggests, to lycanthrope parents, and what a shock it must have been, when the couple discovered their child transforming upon each full moon without magical aid. Like Thomas's acquisition of clairvoyance due to his exposure to sapphires while in the womb, the original, true werewolves were produced by the unexpected side-effects of lycanthropic practices. Pregnant mothers, whose mothers before them were lycanthropes and so on, began to conceive children by men whose lineages were touched by the same magic, and eventually gave birth to human beings who came ready to transform from the womb, and when they transformed, the product was not purely lupine, but something new and more powerful—a perfect cross between man and wolf. It was stronger than a four-legged beast, vastly more intelligent, and frightening to its fellow men. In the new creature's veins swam what was called a "sickness" and a "curse," communicable to human beings, which could turn the infected into a lupomorph within three months' time at most. The magical and biological had met one another halfway.

Werewolves inevitably identified themselves as being separate and distinct from mortals, but they developed their societies in a fashion similar to humans', living away from mortal kind, but never too far away. Hundreds of years passed, then thousands. Today werewolves have a history and a heritage as unique as any mortal culture on this earth. Most of their worldly influence has been made in the magical studies, including the development of the only known martial art based upon the strict laws of magic, called Manus Magia, or "magic hands." Lupomorph survival is difficult, and there is no doubt that one of the key factors threatening the species is, and has always been, the existence of the vampire.

The tale of the vampire's origin is strikingly similar to the werewolf's, but differs in ways that, though subtle, determined the greatest differences between the two species, such as the rules dictating the passing of vampire characteristics and the permanence of the vampire "curse." I'll begin with the origin.

Before the appearances of the first true werewolves or vampires, there existed creatures called hemonyxes. These beings were humanoid, and their intelligence matched that of human beings, but they were not human in many respects. Their origins are unknown, but my guess is that they were a nocturnally adapted, close relative of man. Their skin was pale, their eyes dark, their bodies sturdy. Their skin held an elastic quality, their backs were winged, but featherless, of course, and they were hematophages. However, they were not repulsive, as one might assume. Rather, they were said to have been as beautiful as any human being, sometimes called "night angels" because of their wings. However, they had no notable telepathic ability, as is found in vampires, which plays a key role in the process of seducing or controlling human beings. It is relevant to note that this feature of the vampire is unique. Werewolves, in contrast, are able to attract humans using a certain natural magnetism, which seems to strengthen when the lupomorph hormone is active in the werewolf's body. Coincidentally, Molly always described her attraction to Tom as being something she felt as though she "breathed in" when near him.

It was an unspoken law that human beings and hemonyxes never associated in close commune with one another. Neither species had ever offended the other, but neither trusted the other entirely, simply because it was clear that the species were evenly matched on the early food chain, and despite good relations, competition was unavoidable.

During a time of great expansion, somewhere in a land I can only identify as having existed near what would eventually be ancient Jerusalem, a small tribe of humans and a greater tribe of hemonyxes began to interact, as their hunting territories overlapped.

Sometime during this period a young woman referred to in vampiric texts as Liryne (Leer – in – ee) met a young hemonyx named Jas (Joss), a prince of sorts, who was the son of the eldest and most respected hemonyx of his tribe. The two developed a keen interest in each other. Liryne was dazzled at the sight of the handsome Jas; he, at the beautiful human features abundant in her. When the hemonyxes ultimately left the lands in search of less contested territory, Jas brought Liryne along with him.

The people of Liryne's village were not quick enough to notice her absence, and after a while it was thought that she had wandered too far from her father's home and been attacked by animals or lost her way in the forests and starved. Her loved ones mourned, and they never suspected she was still alive and pregnant by her new husband.

Liryne and Jas disappear in the folds of history, but what is interesting is that several generations after Liryne's death, coincidentally a short time after the first werewolves appeared, hemonyxes again appeared near human settlements in the Fertile Crescent, and a young girl wandered into Liryne's home village. Vampiric texts name her Corvessa, and she was unlike anything mortals had ever seen. She appeared to be human, being quite the sharp little girl, with fiery red hair, noticeably pale complexion, striking emerald eyes, and a very childish carelessness about her—a beautiful girl in every sense. She was taken in by a childless family, who raised her as their daughter.

Years passed and, as the legend goes, on a dark night, nomadic thieves came to the village, looking for vulnerable women to steal. Corvessa, a stunning girl of nearly seventeen, was startled when one of the thieves snuck into her bed and quickly bound her hands, dragging her from her parents' home and out past the village boundaries. Corvessa kicked and screamed for help. The thief, an able and very strong man, had great difficulty restraining her. She fought like a grown bear. Taking out a blade, he tried to jab her into silence, accidentally cutting the hand he held over her mouth. Upon seeing the blood, Corvessa became mad. Her eyes became tinged with pink and her jaw contracted, producing two sets of long fangs that slid over top of her human teeth and drove themselves into the thief's palm. Terrified and paralyzed, the thief could not escape as Corvessa drained him of his blood, afterward ejecting her own in a nauseous fit.

When Corvessa's parents woke that morning and saw that she was not asleep on her straw mat, they immediately ran outside, only to find their daughter standing a few paces from the door, shaking in fear. Her mouth was stained red, and her fangs still jutted out from behind her lips. Her parents, horrified at the inhuman girl before them, but still caring for their daughter, quickly sent her away from the village before anyone else awoke, afraid that Corvessa's condition could cost her dearly if the others did not feel safe around her.

Like her ancestors Jas and Liryne, Corvessa vanished from history, but only temporarily. She was the first of her kind—a pure blend that granted her agelessness that surpassed any other vampire to this day. She and the first vampires after her—born of human and hemonyx parents—are the most powerful of their kind. Modern vampire traits have been recombined again and again, much like the traits of mortals, and the same is true for werewolves, which produced a less monstrous individual over time.

Corvessa's appearance heralded the growth of the vampire population, which, in time, replaced the now extinct race of hemonyxes. It is widely held that Corvessa is the root of all modern vampire cults—a universal patron goddess of the undead. Her name leaps in and out of timelines, vanishes and reemerges here and there, leading most lorists to assume she died long ago, and her name is mere legend. But I know Corvessa did not succumb to death. Oh no, and this will not be the last time I speak of her or her legacy.

Geoffrey Mylus,

May 21, 1833

❧❧

Tom gazed hard at the cabin wall opposite him. Dozens of carefully balanced throwing knives jutted out from it haphazardly. He'd scratched a number of concentric rings into the planks like a target board. The knives fought for space, all having found their mark directly in the center of the target. Tom shouted, hurling another. The blade whipped across the cabin and planted its tip into the bull's-eye, knocking out three others in a shower of sparks. Hands on his hips, Tom examined his practice throws and grinned viciously. Walking over to the target, he jerked the knives out from the wooden planks and placed them in their respective leather sleeves inside his shirt.

It had been two months since the incident with the Leviathan. The crew had been given much time to prepare. The ship cruised silently and speedily toward Deep Water Harbour. Tom leaned over his desk where several loaded pistols lay in neat rows. One by one, he pocketed them in his gun belt (fastened loosely around his black trousers in anticipation of a transformation), leaving a few unbuckled for easy retrieval and securing others tightly. He then lay on the floor, placing one ear against the planks. He knocked against the floor, finding a hollow board. Smiling to himself, he sat up and lifted the board out of place. From within the hidden space he picked up a blunderbuss, loading it and dropping it into the sling strapped around his back and shoulders. From the small space he also retrieved a few glass vials of blood—his own, which he'd drawn, with much hesitance, and collected from his arm ahead of time—and two raw jades, placing all the small items in a safe pouch hanging from his gun belt. Last he took Brother from beneath his bed and, after sheathing it, wrapped a large black waistcoat around himself and Brother and placed his tricorn hat on his head.

Stepping out onto the main deck, Tom was illuminated in orange torchlight. The crew had assembled on deck, weapons at the ready, awaiting orders.

"Good evening, gentlemen!" Tom greeted them with a smile. "You all look as though you've congregated here for some special occasion!" Several men snickered. "Mr. Shaw, are you positive you know how to properly handle that device?" he asked, pointing at the pistol at Shaw's side.

Shaw shook his wild brown hair from his face and grinned. "I've held one or two of 'em, Captain." The men laughed again.

"Well, gentlemen, I figured after so long at sea and surely exhausted from your tedious duties, many of you would like some leisure time, yeah?"

The crew cheered.

"Well what do you say to a little hunt, eh?"

They cheered louder.

"And I'll tell you what! The man who bags the most of those filthy bats gets my cabin for the night!"

"Never mind the cabin, sir, give us a drink!" one of the men called out, laughing with half a mouth of teeth. The crew cheered at the suggestion.

"A drink it is, then! Winner's choice! Helmsman! Take us in, if you please, sir!"

"Aye, sir!"

Tom went across the deck, strolling toward Molly's cabin.

Molly sat on her bed, waiting anxiously. She was restless, her ring glowing in anticipation of the events to come. There was a knock on the door.

"Come in," she called.

Tom opened and shut the door, taking a seat on a small stool. "We'll be in port within the half hour. Now I must explain to you how we will go about this."

"There's a method this time, Captain?"

"I normally make my plans with a clear head, but I've been into the wine and I'm thinking much more creatively." He tried not to smirk. "Tonight the Society will be assembled for a special occasion, you understand that much. You and I will be attending. And ... you'll need to change. Your attire will be your ticket in, if you understand what I mean. You have only to give the impression I've brought you for entertainment and comfort's sake. I myself will be dressed like them—just an unimportant member of the Society."

"I suppose you can supply me with such attire," Molly said, irritated by the idea.

Tom revealed some folded clothes and handed them to her. She took them reluctantly. "The neckline was much lower, so I had it tailored. I thought you might appreciate that."

"You thought of this ahead of time?" She raised an eyebrow.

"I had the outfit made in London."

"There's no way you knew you'd need this that long ago, Thomas."

"When I bought it, it was just something of a little project, for a future gift, or..." Tom tried to explain.

"Hush." Molly didn't make him squirm anymore and grinned as she fiddled with the outfit.

Unfolding the garments, Molly saw that they were just as provocative as the captain had implied. The top of the crimson blouse was indeed very low, and split ever so subtly at its lowest point. The black bodice was surely going to boost anything Molly had to display, and for once in her life, she regretted how much she had. Molly stared at the garments in obvious distaste; Tom, not so much. But he hid his mounting interest. "I understand this isn't comfortable by any means, but it will ensure you do not arouse any suspicions."

"Don't mention arousal right now, Thomas."

"I'll make it up to you. You will need your rings of course, and your pistols. Do you still have the silver bullet I gave you when we first met?

"Yes."

"Load it into La Flor, but do *not* use it unless I tell you it is necessary. Do you understand?"

She nodded.

"That—above all else—is the most important thing I have to tell you." He gave her a hard look.

"I understand."

"Everything else will be relatively simple. I will lead you in. Stay close, and it's preferable you keep a good grip on my arm. They may be transformed due to the time of day. If they offer you drinks or anything of the sort, smile and accept them but do *not* drink. Rather, make it 'magically' disappear, yeah?"

"Being in their company takes the utmost caution in itself. I don't have an appetite right now, anyway."

"Well, I assume you are well aware of their tricks, but I'm taking an extra precaution."

"All right." She released her hair from it's tie and sighed heavily. "Where does your plan lead from there?"

"I will be waiting for their successor to show his face. At that time I will act. Once he is dead you are welcome to dispose of the others as you please, because I'll be looking for Harlan. Does that suit you?" He grinned.

"Just fine, thanks." She turned, removing the belt from around her waist and picking up the tight-fitting, black skirt Tom had given her. "If you'll excuse me, Captain, I must prepare for the party."

"I'll see you outside then, Miss." He politely bowed, smiled and exited the cabin.

Molly dressed quickly, letting her hair down, being sure to allow a few curly strands to drape carelessly in front of her cheeks. She hid her pistols within what little she was wearing and walked out the door, making her way to the main deck. Fiddling with her top and feeling extremely awkward in such risqué attire, she wondered how low the front had been before Tom had it altered, considering it wasn't as concealing as she would like even then. She hoped it wouldn't be a long night.

Tom paced before his crew, dragging the tip of his silver blade against the deck. It left scratches and notches in the planks as he walked. "You all know what to do. No man makes a move unless instructed by Mr. Shaw! Do not act carelessly! Do not draw attention to yourselves! Mr. Shaw, in my absence or death you are to protect the lady of the ship, do you understand?"

"With my life, sir." This notion made Shaw antsy for a few reasons. For one, disappointing Thomas, whom he'd served faithfully for so long, was not an option. Further, acting in Tom's stead might prod him to rely on more than just a sense of duty to his captain and long-time friend ...

Tom nodded.

Molly stood to the side, silently thanking Shaw, who quickly averted his gaze from her attire and nodded respectfully.

"When we reach port, anchor and disperse to your posts!" Tom ordered.

"Aye!" The crewmen loaded pistols and sheathed daggers and swords. One man tied a cross around his neck, hiding it beneath his shirt.

"Prepare to anchor!" Tom called.

The ship approached the docks, slipping past the sleeping merchant ships, fishing boats and smaller schooners. The blackness of the early morning shrouded the vessel as it crept into Deep Water Harbour. Tom motioned for several men to stay behind and for the rest to depart the ship quickly, in small groups so as not to create a disturbance. He found Molly behind the crowd. "Are you sure you want to come?"

"As sure as I was the last time you asked."

He smirked, trying to lighten the mood. "You look very nice this evening."

"I'm flattered, Captain." Despite her objections to her uncharacteristic role, it did lend her a great deal of courage and made her feel more like Thomas— uninhibited and unafraid. Still, as she spoke to Tom, she tried to maintain a demeanor of decency, and was embarrassed when his blue eyes told her he knew she was enjoying herself.

"Do you have everything you need?" He turned to head toward the gangway.

"Yes." Molly stared down at her rings for a moment. "I'm ready."

"Stay close."

She looped her arm around his. "Aye, sir."

Tom headed down the gangway, stepping lightly onto the dock with Molly. Bridgetown was dark except for an occasional glow cast through an inn window or a light burning on a street corner. The sea breeze strolled the streets with them and moved the clouds clear of the crescent moon above their heads. Mama Dlo was asleep, and Papa Bois must have been, too. The silence was unusual. A few crew moved ahead of them, cutting into alleyways and disappearing into the dark, hiding behind barrels and crates. "It's just ahead. Of course, you already knew that," Tom whispered, pointing to a large house positioned inconspicuously between a larger building and a gunsmith's—Christopher's, he was sure.

"Unfortunately." The jaw muscles beneath Molly's ears contracted.

Tom climbed the stairs to the front door and knocked lightly only once. He looked at Molly for a moment and tried to smile. A dim light grew from underneath the doorway. A panel slid open; it was black within. A hiss came from behind the door. "What is your business?"

Molly maintained a calm composure, one hand on her hip and the other around Tom, occasionally faking a sultry smile as Tom replied. "I seek a dark place to rest."

There was a pause and then the voice answered. "Very good. And *her?*"

"I think you know what her business is here." He put on his best lecher's smile.

"Good, come in quickly. Make no noise."

Tom entered and kept Molly close. Molly trained her eyes on the dark ahead of her. Tom led, although the room was nearly pitch black. Occasionally he paused to make sure Molly still had a grip on his arm. The sound of a doorknob turning broke the silence. A dim light filtered through the doorway, piercing the pervading darkness. As Tom stepped through, the source of the voice was revealed. It came from a lanky, pale fellow standing in the doorway in front of Tom. He allowed Tom to enter first. His eyes held a pale red shine. As Molly passed he flashed his white needle teeth at her, chuckling to himself. Another voice was speaking as they entered the room. A taller figure sat at the head of a long table. Along its side were gathered several members of the Society. The cloaked figures breathed as if they were stricken with fever. Hungry red eyes followed Molly and greeted Tom readily. In the corners and extremities of the room lounged a multitude of male inductees and their inductresses—fair, young women with pristine skin, red lips and all varieties of long, unruly hair, wearing much less than Molly, who clung to their fellows and spoke in soft whispers as their lips and tongues hovered next to their guests' cheeks and necks, fangs lingering over their skin. An overwhelming presence of perfume thickened the air. It mingled with older odors of blood and alcohol.

Tom recognized the tall figure at the end of the table—the recently appointed head of the Society and the one who would later present and hail in Mikael Sehović's successor. Tom took a seat, pulling a chair out for Molly as well and politely offering it to her. Molly nodded and sat down. Tom—his face hidden in a hood beneath his hat—turned and leaned into Molly. He whispered carefully to her. "Simon Deschamps, head of the Society. I didn't expect him."

Deschamps glared at Tom. "I'm sorry, did someone have something to say?" Tom kept his head low and shook it. Molly moved her gaze to the floor.

"As we were, then. Our late patriarch and noble leader Mikael Sehović would have looked forward to this evening. This night his successor will be sworn in. I know you are all as excited as I am. Mikael told me in his last breaths how happy he was ..." Deschamps rambled on, his wrinkled face smiling.

Tom whispered to Molly again. "He was there..." *That bastard!* He recalled the night quietly to himself. *I thought I saw someone else that night. I didn't kill them all in London, I knew it! That's why Harlan sent Christopher*

Barnes to Barcelona in the first place. How else would he know to even look for me?

Deschamps stopped again. Molly offered Tom a warning look. Tom quieted himself.

"If you will all excuse me," Deschamps said, "I shall leave you here while I go to meet the successor. I expect him to arrive soon." The vampire stood to leave. He was much taller than any of the others—a tree of a man. He bowed, stringy brown hair falling like spider webs on his aged forehead, and exited the dim, candle-lit room. The Society members relaxed in their seats and talked in hushed voices to one another.

Tom spoke, still quietly, but very emphatically. "He was *there*, Molly! Deschamps worked under Mikael!" There was much regret in his voice. "He escaped me. Who knows what he has been up to?"

"Now is not the time to worry yourself with that. He won't escape tonight," Molly assured him, grabbing his hand from under the table and giving it a soft squeeze.

The lanky, pale man who had greeted them before approached Molly and Tom. His eyes examined Molly invasively. She quickly removed her hand. "Ah, pardon me, brother, but you did say you brought the uh ...

entertainment tonight, yes?" A menacing smile cracked his pallid face as if it were made of dried clay.

Tom glanced up and nodded, playing along.

"And how is the lady this night?" another, younger vampire butted in, pushing the lanky man away. He took Molly's hand and placed a light kiss on it, flashing his teeth. Tom fidgeted furiously in his seat. Molly gazed hard at the man, breathing deeply. She struggled to maintain her confident composure. The young vampire was up to something. Molly felt attracted to him despite being repulsed by his intentions.

Tom looked uneasy but acted his part anyway. "I beg your pardon, what is your name, *brother?*"

The man looked up and smiled hesitantly. "The name's Zachary Flannet. And you are?"

Tom feigned a smile. "Flannet. I'll *remember* it." He did not give the vampire his name in return.

Flannet smiled back, nodding and turning to Molly with a dark smile. "Come. Join me." He watched her like a hypnotist.

Tom clenched a fist but hid it under the table. Flannet invited her to sit with him at the other end of the table.

Two other figures sat with him, very close to Molly, who struggled to avert her eyes from Flannet's handsome face.

Her posture was tense and stiff. Trying to play her part, she relaxed just barely and crossed her legs, socializing carefully with her audience. Tom surveyed their surroundings. The room was much larger than his first impression had given him. It appeared to be a banquet hall. The lanky man must have taken them to a lower level in the house. Most likely this was where the Society had been meeting since crossing the Atlantic— since the time he and Molly were still strangers.

"Tell me. Are you very shy?" Flannet asked, reaching to touch her leg.

Molly pulled back ever so slightly. "What do you prefer? I can be just about anything." She was careful to avoid his eyes, fearing that he would be able to read the terror in her own.

Tom kept careful watch over both of them, sitting low in his chair whenever a figure passed behind him and scanning the room again once they passed.

"What do I prefer? I prefer you to just stay still and quiet," said Flannet, leaning very close to her, eyes glowing brighter, opening his jaws to reveal his long needle teeth again.

Tom began to stand but decided to intervene from his seat. "Brother! I ought to tell you she works for *The Bonny Orchid*." Tom named a local brothel known to keep its comfort women saturated in a special gin redistilled with "nyxbane", an herb which, though not harmful to vampires, creates a flavor in the blood most vampires liken to mulled goat sweat.

Flannet paused, shrinking back in his chair while several other hopefuls groaned all around him. Molly breathed deeply, trying to settle her nerves. Flannet spoke quietly in her ear. "I'm sorry, my dear. Perhaps later, yes?" he hissed. Molly didn't respond. "Humph! A *proud* one are we? That's very brave of you, girl. You're something special."

Tom's hand reached slowly into his coat. Molly couldn't help but shudder in her seat. Flannet leaned in again, opening his mouth. A metallic shine flashed before Molly's eyes and Flannet shrieked. A single, flat knife pinned his collar to the back of his chair. Tom waved a finger of disapproval. "I paid her double for a whole night, brother," Tom quickly lied. "I get her first."

"How *dare* you?" Flannet fumed, wrestling with the knife. The hooded figures around him snickered. Others became restless.

Molly stood quickly.

"What is *this?*" Flannet hissed, unable to believe any woman would or *could* turn him down.

Tom beckoned Molly to hurry and took her by the waist, pulling her to him and setting her in his lap while flashing a smart grin at Flannet. Flannet raged, standing up from his seat. A figure behind him snatched his shoulder, forcing him back into his chair.

"Mr. Flannet, are you having trouble acting civilized? We are not animals." Deschamps reprimanded him as he walked in.

Flannet immediately calmed down, eyes wide. "I apologize, sir," he said meekly, shooting a death gaze at Tom and a wicked smile at Molly. Molly looked away quickly, her heart pounding. Tom held her steady, patting her thigh in reassurance.

Deschamps spoke to the attendees. "Brothers, Mikael's successor—our new patriarch—has arrived!" The cloaked members clapped quietly and calmly. The pale women looked around the hall greedily for the successor, each hoping to be his object of affection. "This brother of ours served Mikael faithfully and loyally for many years. He is a promising successor and leader of the Society. And as you all know, he is the first member of the Society to be gifted with both our ancestral powers and those of the clans in Eastern Europe." There was mixed a reaction. "Now, now, brothers, I know the clans have not always been in our good graces. Those who are cursed by the moon have long held a vendetta against us, and we against them. However this faithful member of ours has proven his loyalty by accepting the bite and serving the Society truly and selflessly. His initiation marks the beginning of a new, stronger species."

Tom began to pay very close attention.

"This intertwining of inheritances has made him very special. I have never seen one such as him, exhibiting both the traits of the wolf and our own. It is truly amazing!"

Tom fidgeted uneasily in his seat, a cold sweat breaking out on his skin. Molly quickly covered her ring with one hand as its glow suddenly brightened. The blue in Tom's eyes faded. His grip tightened on the arms of the chair. One of them splintered and broke.

"Brothers! I introduce to you our new leader!" Deschamps proclaimed.

Tom's eyes changed to a pale yellow. The glow of Molly's ring intensified, and she struggled to keep it unseen. Deschamps threw both arms high into the air in exclamation. "Harlan Crowe!"

Tom's eyes opened wide as he tried in vain to muffle what sounded like a gasping, choked growl of pain. He lowered his head, arms gripping the table and shaking uncontrollably. The Society members stood and applauded. Tom couldn't believe it.

Molly clenched her fist, turning the jewel of the ring into her palm. "Thomas," she whispered urgently.

Harlan stepped into the hall beneath the large iron candelabra hanging overhead, hands raised to hush the cheering. His smile was just like Tom's, inch for inch. His hair, however, was jet black, very straight, and his eyes a chilled ash-gray. He favored their mother in looks. Tom's face was longer; Harlan's was rounder. His nose was shorter than Tom's, and his jaw less defined, making him look many more years younger than Tom than he was. He did share the ferocity in his brow and eyes that Tom so often did. Though of mixed curses, he, like, Tom, had the demeanor and eyes of the wolf. "Good evening, everyone."

Tom flinched, his claws protruding from his fingers, digging into and mangling the polished table. Molly made a desperate attempt to calm him. "Thomas!" she whispered harshly. With her free hand, she grabbed his clawed one tightly.

Tom's eyes glowed golden.

"Now, my friends," Harlan said, "to celebrate the rebirth of the Society, shall we commence the ceremonies?"

Deschamps called out. "Stand!"

The members cheered.

"Tonight we mourn the passing of Mikael Sehović, noble Christopher Barnes, and those lost in the senseless murders in London," Deschamps continued. The pale women's eyes latched onto him as he spoke. "In *their* honor, we collect the debt owed to us by our neighbors for their inhospitality here in Barbados!"

Harlan's newly acquired vampire's fangs made him look like a wolf with rattlesnake mouth. His wolf's teeth emerged from his gums like saw blades, his fur thickened around the chest and stood up in tufts and he sprouted black, veiny wings from his back that opened two ragged holes in the rear of his vest and pushed his waistcoat away. His fingertips sprouted short, thick claws and his fingers elongated. His lupine snout turned up ever so slightly and his nose became a flat, stubby spade. He looked like nothing Tom had ever seen. The other members changed as well, growing lean, muscular and batlike while maintaining their humanoid posture and stature. "For Mikael!" Harlan declared. Tom had never heard a transformed werewolf speak, and it made his skin crawl.

The members cheered again, many moving upstairs to swarm the unsuspecting city outside. Allowing Deschamps to go ahead, Harlan started toward the staircase. He paused and looked at Tom writhing in his chair, with Molly sitting in his lap attempting to stop his fit. "What's the matter, brother? Are you not eager?" He smiled wickedly, with Tom's smile.

Tom roared, standing to his feet as his body mutated. Springing from the floor, he leapt at Harlan with jaws open, claws ready to kill. Molly fell to the ground, and her ring flashed violently. Tom caught Harlan in the ribs with two claws and Harlan shoved him away.

"What a wonderful occasion it is! My own brother! Here to wish me all the best, I'm sure." Harlan mocked him and ignored the injuries.

Tom spun around, poised to attack again.

"Hello, Thomas. Did you think I did not know you were coming?" His voice changed—a mixture of a high pitched screech and a deep drone. "It is in your best interest to leave. I will not warn you twice!" Both his arms grew to unusual length. His eyes were black instead of gold. The ring on his left index finger—the sister ring to Molly's—glowed a deep purple.

Zachary Flannet reappeared, weaseling his way past Harlan and grabbing at Molly while Tom was distracted. Molly gasped and ran. Flannet—pale and winged—seized Molly and rushed to the next room, tossing her to the floor. Molly yelped as she hit the solid stone, desperately digging a pistol out of its holster.

"My dear, I'm afraid you're going to have to overcome that terrible pride if you wish to last the night," Flannet warned, approaching with teeth bared as he shed his jacket and vest. "Do as I ask, and I may let you live forever!" He licked the sharp teeth and picked Molly up to face him. "Besides, what is it worth to you to die, hm?"

Harlan and Tom continued their battle in the banquet hall. Harlan batted Tom away with a swift punch, sending him back across the table, spilling glasses and overturning plates and chairs. Tom yelped in pain. At that moment, the ring on Molly's finger began to blaze in response to Tom's escalating peril.

"Ah! A pretty ring you have there," Flannet said, chuckling darkly. "Maybe I'll spare just that finger?" He laughed wickedly.

Molly glared at him. "I'm glad you like it. It'll be the last pretty thing you ever see."

Flannet's smile faded to a sneer. "I'll take that wager." He opened his jaws wide. Molly's ring flashed a blinding light that filled the room. Flannet's mouth turned from a vengeful gaping bite to a gasp of horror. He shrank back and shrieked. His skin burned and corroded away like paper over a match. In a final rage, he struggled forward, bony fingers reaching out toward Molly as they were stripped of skin and flesh.

"*Spuere ignis!*" Molly shouted, pointing her ruby ring at the vampire and following up with a blast of flames.

Flannet screamed as the stream of fire swallowed him and drove him back into the dark. Molly fell to her knees and trembled on the floor, breathing deeply for a moment. Flannet's ashes sizzled and smoldered until a last puff of smoke signaled his end. A burnt coat lay on the ground, along with a gold chain and pendant bearing the Society's mark. Molly gaped at the remants for a moment before rushing out of the room to find Tom, but not before snatching up the gold chain and looping it around her neck.

The grand banquet hall was vacant. Dishes and glasses were shattered, and smothered candles lay broken on the floor. Several chairs were overturned. Claw marks crossed the table, and red stains marred the stone floor. Following the aligned points of light projected from her ring, Molly sprinted through the darkness to find her way out of the house.

"Thomas! Did you come here to die?" Harlan asked, nearly completely transformed. His voice was warped and diabolical.

Tom was now fully transformed, having shed all but his trousers and belt. The tattoo around his mark could not combat his curse any longer and melted away, leaving only remnants of ink where it had been. Tom slashed at

Harlan, who swiftly dodged the attack. Harlan took flight and perched like a falcon on the roof of the highest watchtower in Deep Water Harbour. Tom circled below, huffing and panting.

Molly ran into the street, her twin pistols at the ready. She kept herself close to the buildings lining the street as she followed the bright path of stars dancing around her fingertips. Outside, Tom's crew fired into the air. The Black Coats above shrieked and darted in all directions. Shouts rang out in the city, and several forms lay motionless in the street. A nearby shop was burning. One of the Coats hopped from roof to roof, setting fire to each with a glowing torch.

"*Caeco et punire!*" shouted Molly, firing from her pearl-handled pistols. Two blazing orbs of light struck the torchbearer mercilessly in the right leg and ribs. The creature cried out, dropping the torch into the open market and plummeting to the cobblestone, struggling to return to flight. Molly continued on, desperate to end it all. Her stomach became weak each time she stepped over a body in the street.

A window within the gunsmith's burst outward, coughing glass and dark smoke into the air. Shaw stepped from a doorway, two compact pistols in hand, warding off a pair of vampires. Confused people spilled into the streets, yelling nonsensically. Molly turned abruptly, catching sight of Shaw and firing her pistols at the Coats attacking him. One of the shades fell into a heap, while the other slashed wildly at Shaw. He fired off a shot, tearing its wing. The creature retreated. Molly ran over to Shaw, observing his wounds. "Are you all right?"

"What a hunt, eh?" he answered shakily, checking himself for injury. "A few scratches. We should find Captain Crowe." He began to turn but paused. "You're all right?" he asked. His hazel eyes revealed a personal concern.

"Yes, of course." Molly continued along the path that her ring drew for her. Running as fast as her body would allow, she fought to ignore the burning, cursed mark on her shoulder. It played with her mind, making her vision intensely sharp and her hearing acute. Focusing on one object or sound was difficult. Looking beautiful and large, the moon above felt as though it were pulling at her chest. She thought she could hear a woman singing...

Tom had made his way to the top of the watchtower, but Harlan had gotten the better of him and now dangled Tom over the edge by his neck.

"Thomas, you and I both know what will happen if this keeps up. I will let you live if you leave this place and never come back."

Tom, squinting in pain, slashed at Harlan, who avoided the swipe.

"You are not listening!" Harlan shouted, tightening his grip.

Tom spoke through being choked. He was no longer fully transformed, and felt himself weakening. "You did...this...to me. Won't...end...until...you die." His speech was crude and barely human.

"You've cursed *yourself*, Thomas!" Harlan yelled furiously, shaking Tom. "You cannot possibly kill me now, Thomas! I never needed Father's ring to find you or kill you because I knew you'd be doing the same thing—trying to find me. All I had to do was wait for you to come knocking. Here you are now, just as I expected! You're here to be rid of your curse, aren't you? In truth, there is no getting rid of it, Thomas. Not for people like us!"

Harlan released Tom, who fell from the tower, crashing through a lower roof. Harlan followed him down. A pillar of dust and debris rose from the gaping hole in the building. Tom stood awkwardly, pushing his way out of the mess. "Leave!" Harlan commanded him, swinging a fist at Tom from behind. Tom reacted with excessive speed. He bent just out of reach, catching Harlan's wrist as it passed his face, throwing Harlan off balance. In the few seconds Harlan was stumbling, Tom reached into the pouch hanging at his hip and took a jade in each hand.

"*Manus magia*," he muttered, relaxing his breathing as his palms began to emit dark green aurae. His muscles swelled and flexed. With a roar, Tom attacked, thrusting a palm at Harlan's chest. Harlan deflected the thrust, and Tom caught his wrist instead, squeezing and snapping the bones. Harlan shrieked loudly. Tom caught Harlan under the arm, biting into his shoulder, then spun him around, released him and sent him staggering backward. Putting his left foot forward, Tom leaned and hammered both glowing palms into Harlan's ribs, blasting him through the front door and out into the street. Tom pounced again, fangs bared and claws spread wide.

Molly witnessed the destruction from farther down the street and saw Harlan sprawled on the ground. Her map ring glowed brighter as she approached the scene. Several more shots sounded out and numerous shrieks filled the air. Shaw approached, out of breath.

"Miss Bishop! You should not be here!" He seized her arm, tugging her in the other direction.

Harlan rolled out of Tom's reach. Tom landed solidly where Harlan once lay, cracking the stones underfoot with another thundering thrust of his palm. Little green sparks flew up from crevices in the ground several yards from the impact. "I did not kill Father! Is that what you think?" Harlan huffed. Tom rushed forward, tearing into Harlan with a fistful of claws. Harlan latched onto Tom's chest, and then kicked him backward. Tom tumbled into a wooden wheelbarrow.

"Even if I had tried, Father would have killed me just as quickly as he would any other Black Coat!"

"And for good reason!" Tom leapt to his feet, taking a vial of blood from his hip pouch.

"Thomas, do not force me to kill you!" Harlan delivered a hard blow to Tom's stomach. Tom shrank back, roaring through shaky breaths, nearly dropping the vial.

"Father abandoned Mother and me," Harlan said, breathing heavily between words, "but I have never wished him ill."

"*Accire canes!*" Tom threw the vial to the ground at his feet, smashing it open. From the small puddle sprang three living, breathing hounds, each large and muscular, with hollow, hellish eyes. They surrounded Harlan, working as a pack, attacking him in turns.

One of Tom's eyes was swollen shut, his legs and sides bloodied. "Father didn't abandon you. You abandoned us—your family."

"Liar!" Harlan cried, beating back the hounds. "*Occisus a corvis!*" he cried, puncturing his arm with his pointed teeth and then swinging the arm to shed his blood to the air. A thick flock of black birds burst from the droplets, swarming his body like bees. The mass of whirling bodies and feathers rose, carrying Harlan with them, then suddenly the flock formed a chattering, squawking stream, launching itself at Tom with full force.

"*A muro manus!*" Tom shouted, thrusting his palms out in front of him, using the jades to produce a protective, deep green magical barrier that received the onslaught of the dark flock and dispelled them outward. When the flock vanished, so, too, had Harlan.

Tom spun around, his lupine senses directing his attention to every minor disturbance of the air or its smell. His eyes flashed quickly from shadow to shadow, searching the most untrustworthy nearby areas for movement.

Whap! Harlan's fist struck Tom directly in the face as he turned to look over one shoulder, and sent him to the ground, dizzy and disoriented.

Roaring hideously, Harlan carried himself with black wings high up above the street. The crescent moon was eclipsed by his dark figure. Tom watched two, spinning images of Harlan hovering above, trying to determine which was the threat. Harlan opened his mouth with the shrillest cry. His teeth shone sickly white. His fingers extended, his body stretched and changed into its most grotesque form. Long claws like nails protruded from his fingertips. Wings folded back, he plummeted into a dive, with claws thrust forward like many daggers, aimed at Tom's chest. His black form tore toward the earth. Tom looked on quietly. Was he dreaming now? Harlan soared straight into Tom, the impact of his weight echoing like a

Chad T. Douglas

boulder down a mountainside as he struck the ground. The street beneath him, all the way to Molly and Shaw, cracked and tremored. Molly broke free of Shaw's grip and ran foward, screaming out to Tom. Shaw called out after her, fearful that he'd actually have to consider initiating Tom's final orders and take Molly back to the ship.

Harlan, hunching over Tom's body, breathed heavily and slowly, staring down at Tom with a desperate, angry scowl. His hands were planted on either side of Tom's body—he'd feigned the strike, and hadn't aimed his claws for Thomas at all.

His breathing slowed. He saw Tom's hands wrapped around something. A shiny blade stretched up from Tom's hands, plunged into Harlan's stomach. From a distance one could clearly see its silver tip standing tall and jutting from Harlan's exposed back. At the last second, Tom had drawn Brother from his side and raised it as Harlan came plummeting to his own undoing.

Harlan gasped very quietly, eyes wide. He rolled over and collapsed next to Tom. Some recently unloaded cargo stacked neatly behind Tom split and fell to pieces—rocked to ruin from the quake moments before. Small white flowers, moonbloom, packed neatly in bouquets, spilled out into the street. The flowers wrinkled and mashed under weight of the boards. Several pale petals floated gently down in front of Tom's face. He watched them touch the stone street and rest easily before being picked up by the breeze and carried away.

"What are you doing?" Tom said. He couldn't believe Harlan had missed—hadn't crushed Tom like a bug when he'd had the chance.

"Do you feel any different?" Harlan whispered.

"What?" Tom watched as Brother stripped Harlan of his life. A white stream flowed outward from Harlan's body and into the silver blade. Following it was an aura of black tar—the curse. Yet, nothing was being taken from Tom. "What's happening?" Tom demanded.

"A vampire by the name of Bijoux Darbonne once wrote a song, to be played on piano, called *Blackheart Reprise*," Harlan said, lying very still, face down, as if he hadn't heard Tom at all.

"Who was it? Who cursed me! You must know! I know you do! If it wasn't you it had to have been one of the werewolves at the camp that night!" Tom raged, bewildered by the discovery that his brother had been telling the truth.

"The piece," Harlan whispered, "ended with the words, 'refrain, *ad infinitum*', just after the last notes. The song was written to be played forever, to no end."

Tom shook uncontrollably as tears of anger and remorse wet his eyes.

"You and I and every other immortal has tried to play it, some longer than others, but the song isn't really meant to be played forever. It's an instructional piece."

Tom held his head in his hands, shut his eyes, and hoped it was all a bad dream.

"It's meant to teach you how to know when to stop," Harlan sputtered. "Look. I've taken my fingers off of the keys." Weakly, he raised his hands.

Tom was horribly dizzy, and not because of injury. It was something more disorienting that disturbed him—the realization that he'd killed Harlan with no satisfying end. Why had his dreams compelled him to Barbados then? What purpose had he just served, if not to release himself from a curse he'd never asked to bear? Where and who was his true infector?

"Jack Darcy will know," whispered Harlan, as if he'd read Tom's mind.

"Jack Darcy?" Tom repeated. The name wasn't awfully familiar.

"If you ever see our father again," Harlan said, ignoring Tom again and speaking quietly through troubled breaths, "tell him I was not an evil man."

Thomas stared silently down at his brother. "He's alive?" His hands shook and his soul felt empty.

Harlan blinked slowly, his eyes looking around at a broken and burning world that was quickly slipping away from him.

Tom paced around the street, wrenching his hands through his hair.

Harlan's eyes last fell on a bright light—Molly—as she stepped into view, but he did not recognize her or what she was.

"Do you see, Thomas?" he asked, "An angel comes for me." Harlan's eyes stopped moving. As his body became ash, a burst of light was drawn into Tom's silver blade. The ring he'd worn—John Crowe's second ring—bounced against the ground and was covered by white flowers and ashes before either Thomas or Molly noticed. The deep purple glow of the ring subsided.

Tom stood for scant minutes, but they passed like wet sand in an hourglass. Molly resisted speaking to him. Just as she opened her mouth, he spoke to her first. "Did you bring it as I asked?"

Molly gazed at him questioningly. "The silver bullet? Yes, I have it," she answered, her brow furrowing. "I loaded it into La Flor, as you asked me to do."

Tom studied her, his face soft and thoughtful despite his bruises. Taking one or two steps backward, he turned to face her directly and held both arms out at his sides. "Okay."

Molly gazed at him blankly, her eyes hurt, confused, and worried.

"Go on."

"W-what?"

"It's all we have left to do."

"What are you talking about?"

"I may not be freed of the curse, but you are still under its control. Rid yourself of it now, before it's even begun. Let's at least one of us be mortal again." He stood tall, keeping his arms at his sides.

"No, Thomas. I c-can't ..."

"Molly."

Tears poured from her eyes as Molly shook her head in defiance. "I won't!" she cried angrily.

"Unless you want to carry the curse with you for the rest of your life, you will pull the trigger."

"Then I will carry it!" she shouted, shutting her eyes.

"Shoot me." His one uninjured eye remained fixed on hers. Tom removed his coat, tossing it aside. "Now, make it count." The small golden locket hung loosely from his neck, swinging slightly with every fumble of his weak, wounded legs.

"I can't do this. I'll live a thousand accursed years before I shoot you."

"Shoot now and live without it. You can't kill me. I never died in the dream." Tom closed his eyes momentarily, remembering the sequence of events. He'd seen Harlan die, the white flowers, but not the light, and he wanted to know what it meant, so he lied. "I can't die, Molly."

"No," she said, refusing to obey.

Tom picked up one of his own pistols, cocked the hammer, and pointed it at Molly. His voice darkened. "Do it or I'll kill you." His eye showed frustration and insanity.

Molly opened her eyes in shock, afraid of the severity in his tone. She raised La Flor instinctively, and her finger touched the trigger. "You're lying. You won't do it! I know you won't shoot!"

"Molly!" he barked, spit flying from his lips.

"No! You won't do it!" She shut her eyes hard and shook her head, sobbing.

"Won't I?" Thomas asked, finger on the trigger. His good eye was wild.

The instant Molly heard the boom of Tom's pistol she screamed, and her finger pulled back the trigger of La Flor, failing to notice that Tom had dropped his wrist to shoot just to the left of her.

Tom's feet went numb, then his legs. Slowly he looked down at the hole in his chest. The silver began spreading its cure. As his torso lost feeling, the sky turned up on its side. The ground rushed to his head, where the cold stone beat against it.

Molly cried in anquish, sinking to her knees, sobbing furiously into her hands. The black crescent mark on her shoulder faded and ran off her skin like water, forming a stream and flowing into La Flor, lying on the ground next to her and exhaling a puff of smoke. The inky trail vanished, and La Flor began to draw the life from Tom. His curse followed the white stream from his body, winding around it gracefully and snaking toward the soul well by Molly's knees.

Tom felt weightless. The cold stone street was soft as a featherbed to his skin. He shut his eyes, feeling very sleepy and silent. The world pulled itself out from under him like a tablecloth, and then he was gone.

Shaw rushed toward Molly, gasping for breath, seeing Tom lying in the street, a small hole placed neatly in his chest. "Miss Bishop, we must go. The Coats just discovered our ship. We...must...go!" he persisted, tugging at her wrist.

"I'm staying," Molly declared, snatching her hand away.

Shaw looked at Tom again, then back to Molly. His captain would have ordered him to allow the young woman to do as she pleased. It was not his choice to force her to come with the crew, even though his personal feelings urged him to bring her along. "Miss Bishop, I can protect you," said Shaw, confidence in his eyes. Molly gave him a strange look, her attention snatched by some faint implication in his promise.

"I can't be sure, Morgan."

"But Thomas *himself* ordered me to act in his stead."

Molly's eyes searched his face for a moment before she turned her eyes away. "You should go, Morgan." She refused to speak with Shaw any further, already far too occupied with the emotional damage done by Thomas's death.

Unable to summon the gall to argue with her, Shaw conceded. "As you wish, Miss Bishop." He hurried away but turned back for a moment, raising a hand in a farewell gesture before limping down the street toward the port.

Molly sat still for a moment, waiting until Shaw was gone. She weakly crawled over to Tom's figure, her ring no longer glowing. She sobbed heavily, lying on the ground beside him and burying her face in his neck . *It isn't right. It isn't his time*, she thought. How she hated Barbados! How she wished for Tom's sake that he'd never met her! She felt as though her misfortune had ultimately caused things to happen the way they had, though it wasn't true. Still, she was the unforetold end to Tom's real curse that night. If she hadn't been so frail, he would never have made the costly decision to infect her just to keep her alive long enough to reach Barbados.

How guilty she felt, that Thomas had been unable to cure himself, and his last act alive was to willingly die for her sake. He'd searched for his brother for years just to destroy the monster he'd become and the abomination Harlan was becoming. He'd failed to free himself, yet in one night Molly was easily cured and had never even begun to taste the kind of pain the curse had dealt Thomas for so long. She loved him. Didn't she deserve to keep the man she had so dutifully cared for? Didn't he, tried and tested, beaten and forsaken as he was, deserve to live and be loved? This wasn't his time to leave her.

The small gold locket lay on his chest, bouncing gently with each of her sobs. It looked different. The surface shone in the dark in a way it did not normally shine. The seams glowed a hot orange like steel in a forge. Molly looked at it curiously through her tears. The locket's glow was the purest white. It begged to be opened and was struggling to do so. One by one, tiny letters appeared in the same hot color as the seal. They began to cover the outside of the locket, forming a spell. The words were in

Spanish and translated as: "Speak the name of the dead and surrender the life within."

Molly held the locket in both her hands, close to her face. "Thomas?" The locket began to shine brighter and brighter in her hands as she opened it. The light filled the street, and a white flash illuminated the world around Molly. The entire city was bathed in it. The streets were vibrant and beautiful, the buildings soft and towering. The figure of an older man stepped forward. He looked like Tom, but aged. In the next second, the vision burst into a white stream and took Tom's place in the soul well by Molly's feet. Tom's own life and curse were rejected and retreated back toward his dead body.

The light vanished. Tom felt as though the world had stretched its arms back to him, reached into him and pulled him back to life by his chest. He heard a faint voice. It was unfamiliar and eerie—the curse?

Tom smiled widely, lying face up in the street and gazing into the stunning dark eyes inches from his. With his old strength he threw his arms up and around Molly.

Her eyes teared up again in happiness, and she could find nothing to say that could express what she was feeling. Instead, she kissed Tom passionately. He returned her affection, holding her tightly and pressing his lips to hers, savoring their familiar, soft touch.

"I promised, didn't I?" he said.

"Yes, you did."

"After what's happened, I find it hard to believe you would expect me to forget a promise." He laughed. "It's a long trip, you know."

"To where?"

"London. Home." Tom's smile gradually flattened. Grateful as he was to have been saved, and to have saved Molly, too, in his own right, he hadn't so quickly forgotten his brother Harlan.

"We'd better get started then." Molly interrupted his thoughts. "Your crew is going to leave with the ship."

"What if we miss it?" asked Tom.

"Then we *borrow* a ship," suggested Molly.

"Good thinking." He got to his feet, lingering on his thoughts.

"Shall we?" Molly touched his face and looked into his eyes but did not press him with questions.

"Yes, let's go," he said at last.

"What shall we do about a crew if we don't catch up?" Molly asked.

"Borrow one," he answered without a second thought. "What's that?" Tom inquired, spying the golden Black Coat pendant hanging about Molly's neck.

"It's a trophy," Molly stated proudly, fishing it from between her breasts. It was exquisitely ornate. The gold crest depicted a dead tree circumscribed by a creeping vine of ivy and set against a hilly background. A capital "B" was etched into the trunk of the tree. "I thought I'd keep it."

As the Black Coats mourned their fallen patriarch and collected his clothes, one of the pale women who'd been haunting the banquet hall earlier that night discovered Harlan's ring. She grinned greedily and slipped it on for a try, amazed by the beautifully cut gem set in its floral band. It was shaped like a woman's face. Upon closer inspection, she noticed a swirling mist deep within the ring. It grew blacker and blacker. Disturbed by the apparent dark magic within the gem, the woman tried desperately to wrench it from her finger. She couldn't. It shrank when she tried to remove it. The other Black Coats around her were all staring, watching the screaming woman as she fought with her finger. She began to hear a voice. It introduced itself as Maria Vasquez and told the young vampire that she would make a wonderful vessel. The woman began to claw at her face, trying to tear the demonic voice from her head. Slowly her thoughts became clouded. She couldn't control her own actions. She felt as if she were being pushed from her own body, which rose and hovered about a foot off the ground.

The Black Coats backed away from the woman. A scream pierced the air as a black aura sprang from the woman's chest and was drawn into the gem in the ring. Immediately after, a deep purple aura burst back out of the ring and into the body. The woman's feet touched back down, and she looked upon the vampires around her with unnerving delight. She appeared to be the same as before, her wavy black hair having been tossed about a bit, but her eyes were different. The irises were a dull violet. The woman's expression changed, and she looked ill. Pulling the ring from her finger, she sneered, clenching it in her fist and crushing it to dust with inhuman strength. A black aura exploded from between her fingers like fine sand, and another scream broke the silence. It echoed long, uncontested by any other sound.

"I must eat," the woman muttered. When none replied, she shouted, "Now!"

The Black Coats backed away as she approached them. She seized one of the vampires by his arms and pulled him close.

"Your flesh is cold and dead!" she said in surprise. "I need a warm body! Bring me a mortal. No … bring as many as you can," she instructed the trembling vampires, her lips drawing back into a savage smile.

Thomas's smallest of trials at an end, he and Molly left Barbados, bound for London. For a time they would enjoy each other's company and the peace of a long, slow voyage home. But as Thomas put it, people die only when they have nothing left to live for—when they no longer have a purpose. As this story stands, Thomas Crowe and Molly Bishop are quite alive. Does the reader believe in fate? Does the reader believe in purpose? I wonder these things myself. Perhaps we will know what to believe by this tale's end, but we have much to attend to until then.

Geoffrey Mylus,
June 3, 1833

About the Author

Chad T. Douglas was born in Wilkesboro, North Carolina in 1989. As a sophomore attending the University of Florida, Douglas published A Pirate's Charm, the first novel of the Lore trilogy. One year later, he released his second novel, East and Eight, and in 2011 he completed his trilogy with the release of The Old World. Around that time, Douglas became a staff writer for the McGuire Center for Lepidoptera and Biodiversity at the Florida Museum of Natural History. When he wasn't working on his novels, Douglas traveled with and wrote for the McGuire Center. Since 2010, he has visited Honduras, Kenya, Ecuador, the Galapagos Islands and Mexico as a travel writer. Douglas's most recent novel, Earthshine, is the first installment of a science fiction series.

Made in the USA
Charleston, SC
03 November 2015